Praise for William X. Kienzle and his Father Koesler Mysteries

"William Kienzle is the Harry Kemelman of Catholicism.... Robert Koesler is the Detroit response to Rabbi Small."
—*Los Angeles Times*

"As Kienzle addresses serious modern issues, he stops to digress and tell his wonderful stories... providing a neat solution with a twist."
—*The Philadelphia Inquirer*

"There are few authors whose books a reader anticipates from the moment he finishes the last effort.... Add William X. Kienzle to that list."
—*Dallas Times Herald*

"As regular as the solstice, the former priest annually provides a new Catholic whodunit from Detroit, inviting readers to shut out the rest of the world and spend a few absorbing hours watching his venerable alter ego, Koesler, peel back the layers of a puzzle to plumb the tortured depths of the human soul and elegantly solve a mystery."
—*Chicago Tribune*

NO
GREATER
LOVE

William X. Kienzle

mys
c.1

FAWCETT BOOKS • NEW YORK

A Fawcett Book
Published by The Ballantine Publishing Group
Copyright © 1999 by William X. Kienzle

All rights reserved under International and Pan-American Copyright Conventions. Published in the United States by The Ballantine Publishing Group, a division of Random House, Inc., New York, and distributed in Canada by Random House of Canada Limited, Toronto.

Fawcett is a registered trademark and the Fawcett colophon is a trademark of Random House, Inc.

www.randomhouse.com/BB/

Library of Congress Catalog Card Number: 99-91475

ISBN: 0-345-42639-8

This edition published by arrangement with Andrews McMeel Publishing.

Manufactured in the United States of America

First Fawcett Edition: February 2000

10   9   8   7   6   5   4   3   2   1

For Javan,
my wife and collaborator

Acknowledgments

Gratitude for technical advice to:
Archdiocese of Detroit:
    Sister Bernadelle Grimm, R.S.M., Pastoral Care Department, Mercy Hospital (Retired)
    The Reverend Anthony Kosnik, S.T.D., J.C.B., Professor of Ethics, Marygrove College, Detroit
    Karen Mehaffey, Theological Library Service, Sacred Heart Major Seminary, Detroit
    Irma Macy, Religious Education Coordinator, Prince of Peace Parish, West Bloomfield, Michigan
Paul Connell, Vice President and Co-owner, A.J. Desmond & Sons Funeral Directors, Vasu Rodgers and Connell Chapel
George Lubienski, Attorney-at-Law
Lou Morand, Catholic Financial Development
Inspector Barbara Weide, Detroit Police Department

Any error is the author's.

In memory of Peter Bellanca and Marge Hershey, both of whom tried to make life less difficult for others and left a legacy of faith and laughter.

Epilogue

The Beginning

ONE BY ONE, *Father Robert Koesler lit the tall, unbleached candles. Three on either side of the open casket, then finally, the ornate Paschal candle that—as was customary—had been blessed during the previous Holy Saturday liturgy.*

Seven candles provided the only illumination in this dusky chapel.

Unaccountably the flames danced at their wicks' ends. Father Koesler could detect no breeze, no open door or window.

Perhaps some residual current of air . . . ?

As well, he would have said there was no sound in the chapel. Yet there was, indeed, sound.

The heat had been turned off for the night. The heating pipes groaned as they gave up the last of the furnace's comfort. Tiles shifted as they resettled. Hardwood floors rearranged themselves in terms of insignificant millimeters; supported statues followed suit.

There was sound, as there was movement of air. One had to be acutely attuned to one's surroundings to perceive all that was going on in this ghostly sacred place.

It was 3 A.M.

Over the years—and there had been so many of them now—he had come to realize that when he was this wide awake no way was he going to fall asleep.

Of course, seldom at such times had he a corpse with whom to commune.

1

Koesler was more than reasonably sure that he and the deceased were alone in the chapel. Indeed, he would have been as startled to hear another living voice as he would have been had the corpse sat up.

In his wakeful state, he had tried to read. But, oddly, every book on his reading stand seemed somehow depressing. That being the case, his attention had wandered toward the chapel. After a brief debate with himself, he had slipped a clerical collar atop his pajamas, pulled on a cassock, and stepped into his slippers.

He'd hesitated before deciding not to turn on the chapel lights. Candles seemed basic, more natural and fitting.

The flickering flames cast odd shadows. So different from just a few hours ago.

Then, a good-sized crowd had assembled. A reverential restraint pervaded as people conversed in barely audible whispers. Relatives and friends had read from Scripture. Hymns—or songs that seemed both relevant and meaningful— were sung.

Father Koesler had invited anyone who wished to share recollections to speak up. Fortunately, those who did kept it on the light side . . . humorous anecdotes and the like. That way it was easier on everyone.

Tomorrow—well, actually, later this morning—Koesler would deliver the eulogy.

That was another reason he had come to the chapel now. In peace and quiet and a modicum of light, he would ponder the life of the deceased. From this he would put together the personal details that had made this unique life distinct.

He pulled up a chair and sat at the opposite end of the casket from the Paschal candle.

Until now he had paid no mind to the coffin.

After the wake, things had gotten noisy and bustling, with friends greeting each other. Many of them met only on occasions such as this. Koesler had been swept up by the activity that bordered on tumult.

Now, with time seemingly suspended, he took notice of the coffin.

Koesler had officiated at so many funerals that he was familiar with, though not an authority on, the various coffins. This one was different from any he had seen before.

This definitely was not the Cadillac of the industry. That, unless he was mistaken, would be the "Marcellus"—premium with a polished Provincial finish and a "Roseton Allure" velvet interior—price: almost $17,000.

As for the coffin before him, only dully reflecting the candlelight, it was a wood wanna-be, with a gray doeskin finish and an ivory satin interior. The operative word for this casket was definitely "basic"—read, "cardboard." It ran a little over $300.

As far as Koesler was concerned, the "basic" made sense—for anyone. Particularly when the final disposition of the body would—as was the case here—be cremation.

Cremation was one more custom whereon Catholics had turned the corner. Father Koesler could easily recall a time when Christian burial (which to Catholics meant a funeral sanctioned by and conducted in a Catholic church, with interment in blessed ground) was not invariably granted.

One of the several reasons for denying Christian burial was the intention of having the body cremated—an action presumed to express a rejection of the resurrection.

That was no longer a factor; nowadays, one would have to have been extremely explicit in denying a resurrection before a priest would refuse a church funeral.

That is, Koesler amended himself, before some priests would refuse.

Shopping for an amenable priest had become a popular pastime for some in the post-Vatican II Church.

These musings were distractions. He had come to the chapel to gather inspiration for his eulogy. Now that he had begun his seventieth decade, he found himself more and more falling victim to stream-of-consciousness. Get down to business, he admonished himself.

But the stream rolled on.

* * *

Father Koesler heard a sort of hissing sound. It was not very loud, but, in the silence of the chapel, it attracted his attention.

He looked about, searching for the cause. He heard it again. This time, because he was looking for it, it was easy to pinpoint.

One of the unbleached candles either had been inserted crookedly, or had tipped a bit. The melting wax was dripping on the cold floor tiles.

Koesler straightened the candle and resumed his seat at the foot of the casket. He studied the body. He had read that there were some consolations in death, but very few, indeed, in dying.

For the figure that lay before him, death had not been a necessity. Death had not been from natural causes, such as disease, illness, or old age. It had been murder. A murder that might have been prevented if everyone involved had been more alert.

Koesler, bathed in candlelight, continued to gaze at the immobile body in the casket, but without really seeing it. What that he now knew might have prevented this murder?

He clearly recalled the moment, several months ago, when he had returned Pat McNiff's phone call. A phone call that had set off a series of events that could have—and should have—been avoided.

That, he assured himself, was hindsight, Monday-morning quarterbacking. In all probability nothing would have changed. Everything would still have led to this corpse in this coffin.

But Father Koesler would not have played a part in the events—or at least not such an integral part.

What was incontrovertible was that Bishop McNiff had called. And Father Koesler had responded.

That was the beginning of it all. After Koesler's initial plunge, the water just kept getting deeper and deeper. . . .

1 THE TIME OF pressure, stress, and tension was supposed to be past for Father Robert Koesler. After all, as of several weeks ago, he was officially in retirement. Or, as bureaucratic correctness preferred, he had achieved Senior Priest Status.

Whatever, he had stepped down and away from the day-to-day parochial duties that had filled the better part of half a century of priestly tenure. And no sooner had he become a Senior Priest than several of his former parishioners with impressive connections arranged a chaplaincy for him aboard a cruise ship.

Initially, he didn't see the point. Here he had just been relieved of official responsibility for the care of souls only to shift his workload to the high seas. With some reluctance he went along with the "gift" that was at least well intentioned.

But, as the two-week cruise progressed, island- and port-hopping around the Mediterranean, relaxation took on a whole new broader and deeper meaning.

His total responsibility aboard was to offer Mass at five each afternoon in the ship's auditorium. Beyond that there was sunning on the various decks; skeet; reading; dolphin watching; splashing about in the ship's pool, or off the beaches of the various ports of call; attending interesting lectures; enjoying evening entertainment in the lounge; and eating, eating, eating—each meal more delectable than the previous.

As for the care of souls, if any of the passengers experienced a problem, spiritual, psychological, or even physical, evidently such plight could wait until after the final docking.

5

All in all, it was the best vacation Father Koesler had ever experienced. He would for the rest of his life be grateful to those who had arranged this busman's holiday.

Too soon the ship arrived at home port, whence Father Koesler flew back to Detroit. His room awaited him at St. Joseph's parish—or Old St. Joe's downtown, as it was more familiarly known.

His residing there was on borrowed time as it were. He had for many years been St. Joseph's pastor and only priest. However, on becoming Senior Priest, at least in the Archdiocese of Detroit, one was expected to move on and out.

The bureaucracy had decided that a new pastor would have a better shot at a smoother, more successful takeover if he was not in competition with his predecessor. Also, absent the former pastor's presence, disgruntled parishioners would not be tempted to try the whipsaw ploy.

While Father Koesler had every intention of establishing himself elsewhere, there hadn't been time for this before the cruise.

Now he was "home." But happily his successor, Father Zachary Tully, seemed in no hurry to have Koesler gone. So, with no pressure to vacate, he determined first to come up to speed.

First he fingered through the phone messages. They fell into neat categories of priority. Mary O'Connor, longtime secretary to Father Koesler, had arranged them according to her perception of their importance.

Mary had intended to retire when Father Koesler did. But she took pity on Father Tully and offered to stay till a suitable replacement could be found. Both Koesler and Tully were grateful.

Atop the pile was a message from Bishop Patrick McNiff, rector of St. Joseph's Seminary. Although it had come in the day after Koesler had left for the cruise, and noted no urgency, only a request to return the call, Mary must have been impressed by the title of bishop, ergo the priority placement.

2 IF MARY O'CONNOR was impressed by bishops, it's a
   good thing she couldn't have seen this one.

Auxiliary Bishop Patrick R. E. McNiff stood in the doorway
of his living quarters in a first-floor corridor of Mooney Hall,
named after the late Cardinal Archbishop of Detroit. This was
St. Joseph Major Seminary, all that remained of what had been
an extensive training program for young Catholic males who
wanted to become priests.

In the sixties, two distinct facilities—this one in the heart of
Detroit and another newer one in Plymouth, Michigan—were
packed to the seams with aspirants.

Now, with St. John's closed, one could fire a cannon down
the hallways of St. Joseph's at most times, day or night, without hitting a soul. Most rooms were vacant; those in use served
the majority who were either priest candidates for dioceses
other than Detroit, or who were not headed for the priesthood.

For those who cared about and valued the priesthood and its
future, this seminary was a sad case.

Bishop McNiff seemed to personify, at least in this present
moment, the condition of the school he headed.

His ample white hair looked as if it had been subjected to an
eggbeater. His eyes were bloodshot. Salt-and-pepper stubble,
hobolike, shadowed the lower part of his face. His robe was
ratty. A large toe protruded through a hole in his right slipper,
which was scuffed to near disintegration. His smile was wry.
"Well, if it isn't Father Bob Koesler, Senior Priest!"

"Excellency!" Koesler bowed deeply from the waist.

7

McNiff snorted. He stepped back from the door. "Come on in."

Koesler didn't move. "I dunno . . . it looks as if you've got the bubonic plague. Are you quarantined?"

McNiff's smile didn't waver. "That would make you really happy, wouldn't it . . . if I had the plague."

"Not really. You're just dumb enough to go around confirming kids and spreading the disease. Then the kids'd give it to their hardworking pastors. And then where'd we be with no priests? Just bishops. Then we wouldn't get anything done."

McNiff's smile faded. "This is just the tail end of the common cold. Now, get in here!"

A casual onlooker might be surprised, if not downright scandalized, at such a colloquial exchange between a bishop and a mere priest. But Koesler and McNiff, seminary classmates and friends since their teen years, had always been close.

As he stepped forward, Koesler gestured toward McNiff's door. "What happened here?" he asked, in reference to the detritus splattered on the heavy oak door.

McNiff shook his head. "You should've been here a little while ago . . . matter of fact, if you'd been here, this might not have happened—"

"So . . . ?"

"The cook, in his heart of hearts, was worried that I wasn't getting anything to eat. So he sent up some soup and some spaghetti with meatballs. I heard her pushing the cart down the hall—that's where you would've come in handy."

"'Her'?"

"One of our young lady students—Patty Donnelly."

"And how might I have served Your Majesty?"

The episcopal grin reappeared briefly. "This cold has slowed me down. You could've gotten to the door faster than I.

"Anyway"—he shook his head—"she had a choice: She could have left the food on the cart on the landing"—he inclined his head—"and come down and knocked on the door. Or"—he winced—"she could have carried the tray down the steps and knocked on my door."

Koesler, getting the picture, chuckled. "She came with the food . . . right?"

"Right. She was balancing the tray against the door and—" He stopped and shook his head again. "If you'd been here, Bobby, you would've gotten to the door before she knocked."

"Maybe."

"Anyway, I didn't have any alternative: She knocked; I opened the door."

"All over?"

"Just so. As the door opened, the tray tipped and the food slid off all over the door."

Koesler looked at the mess. The damp streak that ran from midway down the door to the floor was—or had been—the soup. The blob still oozing toward the floor was the spaghetti. The small, dumpling-like heap at the bottom was the meatballs.

"What next?"

"She said, 'Are you hungry?' " McNiff grimaced. "She must've been in shock—"

"Obviously. And you said . . . ?"

"No."

"Typical."

"Typical?"

"Vintage McNiff."

"Well . . ." The bishop seemed to be regaining his spirit. ". . . are you coming in, or what?"

"I've come all this way. . . ." Koesler, closing the door carefully behind him, entered and dropped his hat and coat on a nearby chair.

McNiff, as not only an auxiliary bishop but also head of this institution, would be expected to have a large suite. And so he did. The quarters only gave the appearance of confinement. McNiff was, to mix a metaphor, a pack rat, squirreling away nearly everything he had ever acquired. This ample room was a jungle containing too much—and badly mixed at that— furniture, as well as books, papers, knickknacks, and statuettes everywhere.

"You're not as sloppy," Koesler observed wryly, "as you used to be before they made you a bishop."

McNiff did not respond to the heavyhanded irony. The two had exchanged barbs too often through the years to take them personally.

McNiff shuffled to his favored chair. En route, he picked up a box of Kleenex, which he placed on the arm of the chair as he settled in. "Sit, down, tall, dark, and tall." His deliberate decision never to use the word handsome in reference to Koesler was another of their playful insults.

Koesler tossed the paraphernalia from one chair to another, then eased himself into the spot he'd cleared.

As his host blew his nose, Koesler studied him with amusement. McNiff, at approximately five feet six, was a solid nine inches shorter than Koesler, who occasionally referred to him as Little Pat.

Although they had been classmates, McNiff was one year older—the result of his failing the English portion of the seminary's entrance exam, in the summer of '41.

After assiduously cramming for the English test, McNiff, the following summer, took the test for the tenth, rather than the ninth grade. He overlooked the fact that those who had entered in the ninth grade already had had a demanding year of Latin—a subject not taught in his public school—under their belts.

Since McNiff now qualified in English but not in Latin, he was accepted into the ninth grade—which is how he had become a classmate of Koesler's.

Vintage McNiff.

The bishop blew his nose again, then asked, "Can I get you something to drink?"

"Not really. I want to be clearheaded so I can pay close attention to whatever you've got in mind."

"Fine. I haven't got anything but good, refreshing water."

"Then I guessed right, didn't I?"

It was common knowledge—McNiff did not keep it a secret—that he was a recovering alcoholic. He'd been on the wagon for many years, and was rigidly faithful to the famous twelve-step program.

From his mid-twenties to his mid-sixties, McNiff had been

what he'd always wanted to be—a parish priest. Then, seemingly out of the blue, he was named a bishop. Endless clerical gossip followed, speculating as to why this should happen to him at his age, in his state of health and with his unexceptional background.

Had he remained a simple priest he would have been eligible for retirement in a few years. Without the glitches in his seminary entrance tests, he would have qualified for Senior Priest Status a year before Koesler. As bishop, he now took on another five years in the active ministry.

He had no "Roman connection." He had not spent a moment of study in any Vatican educational institution. And increasingly, the Roman connection carried ever more weight.

Perhaps most important there was his health—or lack thereof. He'd had several heart attacks. He'd had a quadruple bypass. And he had a stomach aneurysm that could pop at any time and conceivably end his life that quickly.

Priests and concerned laity could speculate to their hearts' content, but the fact remained: Father Patrick R. E. McNiff, sixty-five years old, a Roman orphan, with serious medical problems, had been consecrated a bishop. That was that.

Of course, Father Koesler had attended the ceremony—at one time referred to as consecration, more recently called simply ordination. Blessed Sacrament Cathedral was jammed with priests (mostly older ones), laity (mostly members of parishes McNiff had served over the years), and, of course, a few bishops.

Father McNiff became a bishop the way any priest becomes a bishop: in gradual crescendos. He was anointed, blessed, given symbolic implements, and attired in layered episcopal vestments. All the while, masters of ceremony, as well as other bishops, hovered about the fledgling. With all that going on, someone as vertically challenged as Pat McNiff from time to time disappeared from view.

Finally, with most of the prayers said and most of the vestments in place, the principal ordaining bishop positioned the miter on the new bishop's head and handed him the crosier—known irreverently as the walking stick—and Patrick R. E. McNiff was a bishop.

Then the masters of ceremony and the ordaining bishops stepped back from the newly outfitted bishop as if to say, "Look what we've created."

At that point, in this specific ceremony, Father Koesler, from his distant vantage point, was struck by the resemblance of Bishop McNiff to a small, ornate statue—perhaps the Infant of Prague.

The new bishop did not wait long for his assignment. He was named rector of St. Joseph's Seminary.

And then and there, at least as far as Father Koesler was concerned, the bishop fell out of circulation. McNiff was swept up in his new responsibilities. That and continual meetings prevented him from maintaining prior friendships. Since becoming a bishop and a rector over five years ago, McNiff had not—unlike the Good Old Days—shared a single meal, or palled around, or recreated with Father Koesler.

During infrequent phone conversations, as often as Koesler fished for the seemingly secretive reasons for McNiff's elevation to the episcopacy, the bishop firmly evaded any semblance of a relevant reply. Thus, Koesler, on his return from the cruise, had been surprised by the summons to meet at the seminary.

But he would not hurry McNiff. The ball was in the bishop's court; he would serve when he was ready.

"I suppose," McNiff said, "you're wondering why I asked you to come see me."

"You suppose correctly, Bish—uh, Excellency . . . uh, Pat . . . uh—what the hell do you want me to call you, anyway?"

"Pat will do just fine." McNiff looked at him in curious amusement. "I'm surprised you had any doubt. After what you used to tell me all the time . . ."

"What was that?"

"You don't remember?" McNiff chuckled, then made a

face. "You used to say that if you had a dog that looked like me, you'd shave his ass and teach him to walk backward."

"Oh, yeah . . ." With that youthful insult in mind, Koesler studied his friend more intently. The face squeezed into a map of Ireland, did, he thought, bear some resemblance to a Pekinese. "That's history." Koesler inclined his head in a semblance of a slight bow. "Your present dignity demands greater respect—at least face-to-face.

"But," he went on before McNiff could respond, "I'm much more interested in what's happened to you than what you want with me. Everybody in Detroit, Catholic or not—maybe everybody anywhere who knows about your appointment—wants to know—has been wanting to know for the past five years—why you were made a bishop at your age.

"So, ol' buddy, that's what I want to know—not what you want of me.

"After all, I'm retired—as you should be. It's not likely I'll do anything I don't want to. I mean, we didn't promise obedience to auxiliary bishops . . . just to the Ordinary."

McNiff blew his nose again. "It's not without precedent, you know," he said after a moment.

"Oh?"

"Fulton Sheen was in his seventies when he was given Rochester, his first diocese. And he quit after three years. Then there was Pope John Twenty-third, who was an old man when they elected him. And you can bet your bottom dollar *I*'m not going to get a diocese."

"And they're not going to elect you Pope."

McNiff winked.

"So, the question remains: Why? Why was little Father Pat McNiff made a bishop?"

"I intend to tell you, Bobby. The answers to why I asked you here and why I'm an auxiliary bishop are related."

"They *are*?" Koesler was incredulous. "Tell me about it." He could not help feeling elated that he was about to become privy to a tightly kept secret.

"What we're going to talk about now is just between us," McNiff stated firmly.

Koesler shrugged. "If that's the way you want it."

"That's the way it's got to be."

"Did you have to get someone's permission to tell me?"

McNiff grabbed for another Kleenex and quickly raised it to his nose. But the anticipated sneeze didn't come. He shook his head. "No, not exactly. I know I can trust you. . . .

"Besides," he said after a moment, "if you agree, you'll be involved in this thing."

3 PATTY DONNELLY HAD never been more embarrassed, and it showed. She was blushing profoundly.

She feared she was assuming some of the worst masculine traits. Balancing a loaded tray against a door that was most probably going to be opened! A typical male approach.

The result: the worst-case scenario. And then she'd been stupid enough to ask the bishop if he was hungry. For what—the food that was oozing down his door?

In time, she assured herself, she would be able to laugh at this.

But not now, and not soon.

How had she made such an obvious blunder? Did she want to be a priest so much that she was willing to betray her own sex and take on the shortcomings of the male sex?

Even worse, word of the incident had gotten out and was making the rounds. Probably someone from the kitchen. It was easy enough to piece it together. They had to know from the moment they saw her return with the messy tray, an empty bowl and a near-empty dish. No one, particularly an ill person, could have eaten a meal that quickly.

She promised to clean up the mess as soon as she finished her dinner. That was fine with the kitchen crew; as long as they weren't expected to clean it up, they didn't care how many meals she dumped.

But they hadn't lost any time in passing the story on. As she entered the cafeteria, the conversational hum came to a momentary halt, then slowly resumed. She proceeded to fill her tray, acutely aware—it was all too obvious—that the

15

clerically cassocked clique, seated together as always, were talking about—snickering about—her.

Four young men sat at a table set for six. Should she join them and deal with the situation head-on? Or should she sit with some of her fellow non-priest-candidate classmates, and wait for the incident to blow over?

No, it was not realistic to think it would blow over, given the characters—and they were just that, characters—sitting there so insolently, watching her amid barely stifled laughter. No, this bunch would not let her embarrassment fade away; these guys would spread the word like an arsonist's fire. She would have to confront them and get it over with.

She stepped toward the table.

Immediately, the two empty chairs were tipped inward against the table, barring her access. "Sorry, Patty; these are reserved." The seminarian who had tipped the chairs grinned cockily.

Wordlessly, she veered from the table. She had not thought it possible, but she was even more humiliated.

Banned from that company, she had few choices. She headed for a vacant table for two. No sooner had she seated herself than the young man who had tipped the chairs straightened them.

The point was made; the lesson clear: The seats were not reserved; simply, her presence was not desired at their table.

Once certain that the lesson had been absorbed, two of the four seminarians stood and headed for the door, thus leaving two at a table for six.

Patty Donnelly definitely was not wanted.

The two remaining seminarians now dawdling at the table—they had finished their meal several minutes ago—were deacons, one step removed from ordination to the priesthood.

Deacon Bill Page rose from his chair. "How 'bout some more coffee?" he proposed to his tablemate.

"Sure. Why not?" Deacon Al Cody responded.

Page brought the carafe to the table and filled both their cups. En route back to the hot plate, he stopped for a moment, and held the carafe out to Patty as if to offer her some.

Without looking up, Patty, face still red, shook her head.

Page returned to his seat, careful to pull the pleats flat beneath him as he sat down so he would not wrinkle his cassock. He smiled broadly. "A double whammy!" he gloated. "First she dumps McNiff's tray, then she tries to sit with us. Sometimes life is sweet."

Cody did not respond. He looked up to and was in awe of Page, who was older and far more experienced than the others.

Page was what used to be called a delayed vocation, although the term had virtually faded from usage.

When seminaries and convents were filled to overflowing before the onslaught of the conciliar era, the norm was for girls and boys to begin preparation for their vocations in high school, or shortly thereafter.

Now, in a desperate search for tomorrow's priests and nuns, people who were in the midst of, or even completing, their secular careers were being recruited.

Bill Page, in his mid-forties, would definitely have qualified as a super-delayed vocation in the earlier Church. Now he was one of the boys—perhaps one of the Good Old Boys.

Fresh out of Notre Dame and armed with that university's mystique, he had won a berth at a prestigious Chicago ad agency.

However, failing to make the most of his promising beginning, he found himself in a downward slide.

The inverse of his failures in advertising was his success at the dating game: He wooed and discarded many fine women.

As luck would have it—for those women at least—he had never married. His celibate state left the door open to the priesthood.

As a boy, Page had felt a slight, quiet call to the priesthood. Lots of little Catholic boys, particularly those who attended parochial schools, did. It was the mid-sixties, and Page was an altar boy mouthing unintelligible Latin prayer responses (so unintelligible that he might as well have been speaking in tongues as far as his comprehension of what he was saying went).

To this lad, priests were like God, above everybody and in

command of everything. And, in fact, he was taught that a priest was "another Christ." And Christ was God. So . . . there you were.

What really influenced young Page to at least profess an interest in the priesthood was the attitude of the teaching nuns. Almost as much as most Catholic mothers wanted a priest son, so did most nuns want a priest pupil.

No harm then in creating the impression that he favored this vocation. It won him special status at home, as well as in school.

However, high school, the earliest opportunity to enter a seminary, came and went. Notre Dame followed, and the concept of his priesthood was allowed to fade.

And then one day, he took stock.

He had to admit that he wasn't making it in the world. Realistically, he could look forward to nothing more than a series of failures that would terminate, if he lived long enough, in poverty and abandonment.

What to do?

He might marry well. He knew that in the twinkling of an eye he could marry more money than he could earn in a lifetime.

Clearly, he had nothing against women; he'd had his share and more. Quite frankly, he was good at women. He'd left many satisfied, although in the end, sadder and wiser.

But the very thought of marriage made him claustrophobic.

And then the Archdiocese of Detroit launched an ad campaign to recruit single Catholic males—of any age or background—into the seminary. The ads—featuring three extremely attractive clerically garbed young men—trumpeted, "We want to collar a few good men."

They hadn't pinched pennies in this campaign. The ads utilized print media, radio and TV, even billboards.

Page thought the copy was better than average. He liked the pun with "collar." But he wondered how effective the campaign could be. After all, this was not a pitch for a brand of cigarettes, a make of car, a detergent. This was an invitation to a lifelong commitment . . . more; once a priest, always a priest, the nuns had taught. Ordination imprinted an indelible, and fortunately invisible, mark on the soul. So no matter what, a priest was a priest forever, into eternity.

Could an ad campaign be enticing enough, compelling enough, to induce one to enter into such a commitment?

Then he paused. Something must have happened between his fling as altar boy and the present.

Seminaries, back then, were notorious for dumping students. Page recalled that the vast majority of the guys who had entered the seminary during high school eventually returned to finish high school in the parish. Standards must have been tough, he reasoned; advertising for priest candidates back then would have been a foolish redundancy.

Yes, something must have happened. That the Church needed—perhaps as never before—seminarians and priests was the only possible conclusion. In that case . . .

Bill Page decided it was very much worth a look.

As a boy, Page had been willing to grant the mystical near-divinity of priests—other Christs. He had been willing to convey the impression that he too might become one.

That superficial quasi-commitment was as far as he would go toward the priesthood.

Then came the realization that he was going nowhere in the secular world. Could he find success in a religious setting? Or would the priesthood be, like marriage, claustrophobic?

In the course of his deliberations, he stumbled upon the diaconate.

The diaconate ordinarily was a final step toward the priesthood. Or—and this marked the recent return of an ancient custom—it could be a permanent state. Deacons could do everything priests do, except say Mass and hear confessions.

At first blush, the permanent diaconate seemed attractive. Celibacy was optional, though oddly, that meant little to Page. The diaconate was not as confining as the priesthood; not being allowed to offer Mass or absolve also meant one needn't set aside time to perform these sacraments.

However, one feature of the permanent diaconate made it,

as far as Page was concerned, definitely and completely unfeasible. *Permanent deacons received no salary.* In addition to volunteering one's services baptizing, marrying, burying, distributing Communion, preaching, and counseling, one was expected to hold down a job to support oneself—and one's family.

That, Page concluded, would seriously complicate his already dismal future.

The priesthood promised more—much more.

Page knew that priests came in different sizes; they weren't cut out of a mold. He had not been aware that they came in different attitudes, outlooks, philosophies, and theologies. They ranged from the selflessly dedicated to those who did nothing exquisitely, to those who manipulated and abused the souls they had been sent to serve.

Once he made this discovery, it wasn't difficult for Page to select the personal model after which he would fashion his clerical self.

Particularly now with the priest shortage, it was child's play to pass the entrance tests. The studies were well within his grasp. After all, he had a degree from Notre Dame. He was a Catholic male who'd never married. He was sure he could bluff his way through growth in holiness.

Once he became a priest, his future would be secure. Never again need he worry about food, clothing, shelter, or, for that matter, the finer things in life.

Page would be happy to occupy the middle approach to priestly life. Metaphorically, he would turn over on his back and float through to comfortable retirement.

Perhaps the most momentous discovery he made shortly after being accepted at St. Joseph's Seminary was the importance of being T.C.—theologically correct.

The theology that was correct at St. Joe's was decidedly conservative. Well, Page could say Amen to that. Actually, Page could have said Amen to just about any theological approach.

In this he was not being eclectic—selecting what appeared to be best in various doctrines; all but a very few of the faculty of St. Joe's, as well as the vast majority of the entire student population, were staunchly conservative.

He had no quarrel with that. He just resolved to go with the flow.

This approach had served him well; in a few more months he would be ordained a priest. Nothing could stand in his way now. He was sure of that.

4 FATHER KOESLER AND Bishop McNiff inched their chairs nearer to each other. Their knees were not touching, but they were close.

"Have you paid much attention to the current crop of seminarians here?" McNiff asked.

Koesler thought for a moment. "Not really. Not for some time. What with the drought in the priesthood, I didn't think I was in line for an assistant fresh from the seminary. And, as it turns out, I was correct. Even the classic big parishes are down in priest count. I was pretty sure that St. Anselm's and especially Old St. Joe's would be one-priest parishes for the foreseeable future."

"Okay, so you're not up on the state of things. But do you even have a vague impression?"

Koesler didn't have to ponder this question. "A bit conservative, no?"

"Yes! And not just a bit. Very! Some off the wall on the right wing."

Koesler smiled. "You know, Pat, you've never been known as a crashing liberal yourself."

"That's a part of the point . . . my reputation. Here"—McNiff inched his chair even closer, as if proximity would provide greater secrecy—"let me give you some background."

Koesler's reaction was to lean farther back. He was not at all convinced that McNiff was on the down side of his cold.

"Bob . . ." McNiff's voice was taking on a hoarse quality. ". . . you remember as well as I how things were in the Church when we were ordained in fifty-four."

22

While it was true that Koesler remembered the way it had been as well as or better than McNiff, the bishop nonetheless proceeded to conduct a brief, nostalgic tour of the past forty-some years and the cataclysm those decades had brought to Catholicism. Some called the 1950s the last decade of American innocence. It was a marvelous time if you weren't a black in the ghetto, or fighting in Korea.

It was the beginning of the end of the Catholic priest as icon.

The Second Vatican Council took place in the sixties, when Catholic seminaries were still packed. It was an era of militancy.

Liberal theology sprang up and flourished like unplanned vegetation. Virtually all of the immutables were challenged, and some discarded.

Much of the seventies was spent questioning the sixties. The priest drain was gushing. Seminaries were precariously holding their own.

The battlefield was quieting in the eighties and nineties. The number of priests leaving the active ministry had slowed to a trickle—because most of those who hadn't retired had already left or were nearing life's final glide path.

But few young men were entering the seminaries. With the significant number of priests leaving and the virtual absence of seminarian replacements, the priest shortage was real, critical, and discouraging.

Something had to be done. But what? Prayer seemed the only answer.

"That," McNiff concluded, "pretty much brings us up to date."

Koesler, sitting motionless, had half-hoped to learn something new—like ultimately why McNiff had been made a bishop. He stood, grasped his lower back, and stretched his torso as far as he could. "Good for the arthritis," he explained.

"You too? Old age isn't for sissies."

Koesler looked down at the bishop in irritation. "I know that used to be a joke, but it's losing its humor as the years go on."

"Tell me about it." McNiff shook his head. "That aneurysm could call my number any moment."

"Which," said Koesler as he resumed his seat, "brings us back to the beginning: Why did they—"

McNiff convulsively grabbed for a Kleenex, missed it, and sneezed in Koesler's general direction.

Koesler dug out a handkerchief and mopped his face. He pushed his chair back a few inches.

"Sorry," McNiff apologized.

"Why don't you pull out a few sheets so you're ready for the next one?"

McNiff did just that. "See," he said, "you're helping already."

"Little Pat, cut to the chase: Why are you a bishop, and why are you here—and what I can do to help . . . that is, before your sneezes challenge the defenses of my immune system?"

"Okay, okay." McNiff shifted in his chair in an unsuccessful attempt to get comfortable. "So you're not very familiar with the current situation with St. Joseph's and our present seminarians."

Koesler shook his head.

"But what we've got here," McNiff explained, "is a kind of counterrevolution—or reformation, depending on your mind-set.

"Where we are in history is in a backlash of the liberal-conservative struggle. In the sixties and seventies, as a result of the Council, this archdiocese went wildly liberal—"

Koesler smiled. "You sure this isn't your conservative perception of how things were?"

But McNiff was deadly serious. "I'm positive this is the way it was.

"Anyway, we know what happened when a significant number of priests, seminarians, and laity caught the spirit of the Council—or what they thought was the spirit—and ran with it. All the while the institutional Church was digging in its heels.

"It wasn't too long ago that liberal thought controlled this seminary—"

"And now?"

"Now . . ." McNiff looked glum. "Now it's just turned around.

There are three—count them: three—outspoken liberal faculty members. It's possible there are one or two more, but if so, they're still in the closet."

"How about the seminarians?"

"On the surface, as far as the seminarians are concerned, they're *all* right wing—and pretty far out at that. By the way, we refer to the seminarians here as M.Divs."

"M.Divs?"

"Master of Divinity. That's the academic degree they need to be ordained."

Koesler scratched his head. "What about the others—the ones who aren't studying for the priesthood?"

"They can earn any other degree we offer."

"But . . . not the Master of Divinity?"

"The M.Div is reserved for seminarians exclusively."

"I hesitate to ask the logical question, because I'm afraid I know the answer. But anyway: What if one of the nonseminarians wants to take one of the M.Div courses?"

"Impossible. All M.Div courses are reserved for seminarians."

"I assume," Koesler said, "that one of the M.Div courses would be Homiletics."

"Uh-huh."

"And all of your students want a position of some sort in a parish—and all of them want at least instruction in preaching . . . right?"

"Uh-huh."

"So such a student isn't taught how to preach."

"You've got to remember, Bob: Only a deacon or a priest can preach. There's no point in teaching someone a skill she will never practice."

"She?"

McNiff was giving every indication that Koesler's line of questioning was making him ill at ease. "Well, yes, *she.* You know that no woman can be a priest. So, no woman can be a seminarian. So, no woman will be allowed to preach. So, there's no reason for women to learn how to preach."

Koesler, clearly taken aback, sat bolt upright. "Is that the way it is everywhere? In all seminaries?"

"No. It's actually about fifty-fifty. But it doesn't really matter. Whether a woman can go for a Master of Divinity degree or not, the bottom line is, women can't be priests. No matter how good or bad a preacher a woman would be, she is not going to preach. In a way, not offering women the opportunity to earn an M.Div degree is maybe more . . . more honest."

"More honest!"

"Yes! It tells her right up front how it's going to be in her ministry. It doesn't give her any reason to expect that things will change. The Pope said it: Women can't be priests. So why teach them how to do something they're never going to do?"

Koesler shook his head. "With policies like this, there can't be many women here as students."

"You're wrong, Bob. Want me to give you a breakdown?"

Koesler sat back and nodded.

McNiff wondered why the space between them seemed to be widening. He hadn't adverted to Koesler's gradually distancing himself.

"See, there are approximately three hundred and twenty students in St. Joe's Seminary. That's for four years of college and four years of theology. Of that number about seventy are seminarians. Which leaves about two hundred and fifty non-M.Divs—roughly a hundred men and a hundred and fifty women. The only way you can come up with more men than women is if you add the M.Div males to the nonseminarian men. That way, you get one hundred and seventy men and one hundred and fifty women."

"Frankly, Pat, I don't get it. Why would so many women sign up—freely—at an institution that discriminates against them?"

"Discrimination is a powerful word, Bob. We could argue about that—and we probably will before the evening's over. But there's a likely reason for their being here—all these women, I mean. I had a problem understanding this at first. But now it makes sense."

"Help me."

"As far as we're able to tell, not all the women who enroll here want to be priests—not by a long shot. The aim for many of them is to become catechists or directors of religious education . . . or some of the other degree positions we offer."

"But by your own admission, Pat, some of these women students do want to be priests."

McNiff nodded.

Koesler raised his hands in a gesture of incomprehension. "Why?"

McNiff shrugged. "Hope against hope. Hoping the Church will change its position."

Koesler thought for a few moments. "You have how many studying for the priesthood?"

"Seventy."

"Any idea how many seminarians we had here in this place's heyday?"

It didn't require any research on McNiff's part. Those figures haunted him and anyone else who was concerned with the seminary's future. "That'd be in the mid-sixties. There were seven hundred in high school. Of course we don't have a high school anymore. Then there were about two hundred and forty in college and approximately another two hundred and fifty at St. John's."

"So," Koesler summed up, "there were almost eleven hundred seminarians then to our seventy now. That right—counting the high schoolers of that time, I mean?"

McNiff nodded slowly.

Koesler turned his gaze to the window. But his focus was inward, not on the nondescript view of another brick wall. After a few minutes, without returning his gaze to McNiff, Koesler said, "I guess I'd have to put my money on the women who are looking for ordination. The Catholic population is increasing, while the supply of priests to serve them is bottoming out."

McNiff ran his hand over his facial stubble. "I don't know. I don't know," he repeated. "A lot of things have been tried. Nothing has worked. Oh, every once in a while there's a slight gain. But nothing that could match what we had back then . . . back in the sixties.

"Of course there's constant demand for an optionally celibate clergy, and for women priests. But the institutional

Church—mainly in the person of the Pope—keeps slamming the door.

"Will it happen?" he mused after a moment. "It looks like there's no alternative. If we're going to field a team, we'll have to fill it with women and men—married or not."

Their conversation had, to this point, been reflective and pessimistic. It continued in much the same mode. There seemed no escape from the autumnal state of today's Catholic seminary.

"However," McNiff said, "at this point, I think we can consider one of your first questions."

"Why they made you a bishop?"

McNiff nodded. "Why, at my age, and with my fragile state of health, they made me a bishop."

Koesler could not help believing that this—the explanation of why McNiff had been ordained a bishop—was at the root of why they were meeting this evening.

McNiff again shifted in his chair, still searching for that elusive comfortable position.

"It was a beautiful day in June a few years back," he began. "I was more than aware that retirement was only a few years off. The Cardinal's secretary phoned. The boss wanted to see me—that afternoon."

McNiff had reason to remember that meeting very clearly.

5

AFTER THE CALL summoning him to a command performance that afternoon, McNiff rummaged through his closet until he found a black suit just back from the cleaner's. Then a new, never-worn clerical vest. Finally, a freshly laundered clerical collar. It was good to have clean new apparel for special occasions. A meeting with Detroit's Cardinal archbishop more than qualified.

McNiff, splendidly—for him—attired, early for his meeting, waited fifteen minutes in the Cardinal's foyer.

He was one of the relatively few local priests the Cardinal knew well. From time to time during his nearly forty years as archbishop of Detroit, Cardinal Mark Boyle had called on McNiff to handle some delicate matters—usually troublesome parochial flare-ups that needed a firm, decisive touch.

Thinking about today's meeting, which had consumed his attention since the secretary's call, McNiff could not surmise what the Cardinal needed done. Particularly since the priest was so close to retirement age, whatever task Boyle might have in mind would have to be a short-term duty. But what could it be?

Exactly at two, Boyle appeared in the foyer to escort McNiff into the inner office.

That was out of the ordinary. Always previously he had been ushered in by the Cardinal's secretary.

The furniture in the rectangular office was configured for two distinctly different types of circumstances. At the far end, everything seemed "official," with a high-back office chair behind an oversize but extremely organized desk, before which

29

stood several straight-back chairs. The "business end" of the Cardinal's office.

The windows on the south wall overlooked a stretch of a once affluent, now nearly deserted, Washington Boulevard.

At the near end of the office, closest to the door, comfortably upholstered chairs encircled a low, round coffee table. Boyle's gesture invited McNiff to be seated in this more informal setting.

There was no small talk. Boyle was not one to waste time, and it was not McNiff's place to steer the conversation.

Boyle was tall, ramrod-straight, distinguished-looking, with thinning close-trimmed white hair. When stressed, he fingered the chain of his pectoral cross or twisted his episcopal ring. In an age when many priests and even an occasional bishop dressed down, Mark Boyle might conceivably have worn his clericals to bed.

"Father," Boyle began, "I am very concerned over St. Joseph's Seminary."

McNiff had been a student at, indeed had graduated from St. Joe's, as it was almost universally known among Detroit Catholics. At this stage of his life, he could not imagine why the Cardinal wanted to discuss this institution with him.

Without benefit of notes, the Cardinal proceeded to catalogue the statistics that composed the current state of the seminary. These accurate statistics Father McNiff would later cite to Father Koesler.

The admittedly lackluster figures depicted an institution a mere shadow of its former self when the clear need was for a major improvement of its present condition.

The St. Joe's numbers were truly depressing. McNiff knew the enrollment was low; he hadn't known how low.

Nonetheless, his attention began to wander. This was mostly because he had nothing to do with the problem as it existed at St. Joe's. He could, and did, pray for vocations. He tried to live so as to give an example that might attract young men to the priesthood. What more could he do? In other words, why had *he* been called in for this meeting?

On top of everything else, he had already begun to plan his retirement, which was just around the corner.

For that matter, why was the seminary situation bugging Cardinal Boyle? He himself was *past* retirement age. If the Pope were to accept Boyle's offer to retire—which he had made annually for the past several years—the state of St. Joe's would no longer be Boyle's concern. He could pass that and the other burdens on to his successor.

All of which brought up the matter of why the Pope hadn't accepted Boyle's offer.

On many occasions, McNiff had heard Boyle proclaim that labels were inaccurate . . . that no one was liberal or conservative all the time.

Even so, Boyle could not himself avoid being labeled.

Those who knew him well realized that the Cardinal was a loyal churchman to his core. What made his enemies hate him and his disciples love him was his simple ability to coexist with those whose opinion he did not share. For that, this loyal churchman, who had not a crashing liberal bone in his body, was tarred with the liberal brush.

Some held that the liberal label was the reason the Pope would not accept the Cardinal's resignation.

McNiff had heard, but did not understand this reasoning, until an explanation was offered by none other than Bob Koesler.

According to Koesler, the whole thing was vindictive.

According to Koesler, the generally accepted scenario was that the Pope, with a couple of exceptions, kept selecting very conservative priests as Boyle's auxiliary bishops. And of course, according to this explanation, these auxiliaries were imposing their conservative stamp on everything in the diocese they could touch.

In the midst of this, Boyle stood alone as the symbol of his reputedly liberal diocese, while the infrastructure kept growing in conservatism.

McNiff considered this theory deliberately Machiavellian, and he dismissed it because he could not believe that the Pope and his appointees could be that vindictive. It was unchristian and unworthy of those holy men.

But now Cardinal Boyle was wrapping up his statistical report; perhaps finally he would get down to McNiff's concern.

"So, that is a rundown of the numbers at our seminary. They are, admittedly, discouraging. The problem of the priest and seminarian shortage is, of course, for all intents and purposes, worldwide. It must be addressed on a global scale.

"But there is another problem that needs to be met on our diocesan level."

The Cardinal leaned forward, elbows almost touching his knees. It was a posture McNiff had never before seen Boyle take.

"The problem is philosophical—an attitude, if you will. Those who favor labels would call it conservatism. As you may know, I do not believe in across-the-board categorizing.

"It does not greatly trouble me that a number of teachers and students follow a conservative trend. The trouble is that this approach to their training is shared by the vast majority in the seminary. *And,*" Boyle emphasized, "that no other view is tolerated!"

He leaned back. "That is the sore point, Father: the intolerance. Respecting the opinion of someone whose opinion one does not share is a lesson we in this diocese learned only after much give-and-take. It pains me to see this hard-achieved openness and courtesy undone.

"This half-formed philosophy will close this diocese to forward movement. It will close our minds to the direction of the Holy Spirit. Do you not agree, Father?"

McNiff's vigorous nod evidenced wholehearted agreement. "I was aware that the seminary had drifted into a fairly conservative position, Eminence. And, frankly, I didn't think that was such a bad idea; I just thought it was merely a reaction to the previous liberal stand. But, if they won't admit any other approach, well . . ." McNiff hesitated. "Tell me, Eminence, how did it happen? How did they manage to pull it off?"

Boyle pronated his hands several times, a gesture that indicated that it had been done without his awareness or consent. "Appointments were made to the faculty over the years by a certain few members of the Curia. These appointments gradually changed the complexion of the seminary staff. My only contribution was to ratify the appointment of the new—now recently departed—rector. I knew little about the man. But my advisers assured me of his excellent qualifications."

Boyle shook his head. McNiff didn't know whether Boyle thought the Curia had betrayed him or if his consulters had been duped.

"Now," Boyle continued, "as you well know, the former rector has been named a bishop—an auxiliary, in Pittsburgh. In a couple of weeks, I will be attending his ordination there. That means that our seminary—St. Joseph's—will need a new rector." He looking meaningfully at Father McNiff.

McNiff raised an eyebrow. He couldn't help it. He'd been following the Cardinal's narration carefully. It wasn't what Boyle had just said; it was that significant look.

There were several moments of silence. McNiff was waiting for clarification. Boyle was waiting for his drift to wash through McNiff's mind.

"A new rector . . ." McNiff mused aloud. "I knew the monsignor was headed for Pittsburgh. And I knew he was going to become a bishop. And I knew he must be replaced at St. Joe's. But . . . what? You want me to be on some committee to nominate candidates? I can understand now why you told me about the present status of the seminary. And if you want me on a committee, I can assure you I would keep in mind everything you've told me . . . your concerns about how single-minded everything is. . . .

"But . . . can a committee do this? It doesn't have to go to Rome—?" McNiff was babbling. He feared he knew what was coming. But it couldn't break through as long as he kept talking.

Cardinal Boyle understood. A smile played at his lips. "Father," Boyle interrupted, "members of our Curia have already met and have nominated five candidates—each and every one of whom would assuredly maintain the status quo . . . of that I am certain.

"The committee is supposed to act in an advisory

capacity—to make recommendations: recommendations for me to take under consideration. I have not yet revealed to this committee that I intend to become more involved than on previous similar occasions. Nor have I even hinted that I have already selected the next rector—that is, if he will accept the post."

McNiff slumped slightly. "It's me, isn't it?"

Boyle nodded. The smile faded. McNiff's was a serious, difficult, and fraught decision. An affirmative response would run in the opposite direction from the retirement the priest had planned.

The silence continued.

"I'm no Jeremiah," McNiff protested after a lengthy silence. "But I feel like him when the Lord called him to be a prophet to the nations."

"At least you can't complain of being too young."

"No. But what if I point out that I may be too old?"

"A consideration," Boyle admitted. "But who among us can say how much time he has?"

McNiff considered the caliber of the man who was asking this favor—if it could be called that. How once each year for the past several years, Mark Boyle had submitted his resignation to the Pope. How each time it had been rejected.

How seriously did Boyle want retirement? McNiff had no way of knowing. Probably as much as most people who longed to rid themselves of the weight of authority, responsibility, and accountability. But the Cardinal continued to shoulder the burden at the command of his superior.

McNiff himself would desire to follow such a loyal example.

Still . . . there were practical considerations that needed to be resolved.

"Em—Eminence . . ." McNiff was stammering, something he'd never done . . . well, hardly ever. "Eminence," he repeated firmly, "I'm just on the verge of retirement. I have plans—"

"Tell me about it." This from a man who'd had to repeatedly postpone retirement plans.

"There's my health . . ." McNiff was reaching.

"Has your physician set any time limit on your active life?"

"Well . . . no." McNiff was crestfallen. Then, more firmly: "But it could happen any time. That aneurysm—"

"In the end, Father, you are no different from me or practically anyone else our age. None of us knows when the end may come. We try to stay healthy. We carry our crosses at this stage of life. We use the time we are given in God's providence. We try to do God's will."

"Eminence, are you telling me that my accepting the assignment as rector of the seminary is God's will?"

The Cardinal hesitated. His fingers formed a steeple and rested on his lips. "Let me ask you a couple of questions. Do you think—all other considerations aside for the moment—do you think yourself capable of managing the seminary on a day-to-day basis? Keeping in mind that there are very capable people working in the various administrative offices? Part of your responsibility would be to supervise them."

McNiff did not hesitate. "After all the varied jobs you've given me over the years, yes, I think I could."

"Then, Father, do you think you could try at least to instill a spirit of openness and tolerance as we have just discussed?"

McNiff bowed his head in thought, or prayer, or both.

"To be as honest as I can, I don't think so, Eminence. For openers, I doubt I'd be welcomed . . . particularly since my name evidently was not on the nominating committee's list. And I wouldn't have much, if any, clout. I am a simple priest. There are even a couple of monsignors on the faculty who outrank me."

Boyle smiled. "I think we can resolve that problem."

"How?" McNiff hadn't a clue.

"By making you a bishop."

McNiff's jaw dropped. He could not think of a single response.

"A bishop!" he said at length.

"A bishop," the Cardinal affirmed.

"At my age?"

"You would not be the first to become a bishop in later years."

"With my health problems?"

"You would not be the first bishop in a delicate state of health."

"B . . . but how could this happen?" As the words left his lips, McNiff realized they were the words spoken by Mary when the angel announced her divine maternity. To McNiff, they somehow seemed just as appropriate now. "A bishop!" he mused. "I can't imagine myself a bishop. I never in my life imagined myself a bishop."

"Yes." Boyle allowed time for the concept to sink in.

It had been no surprise when Mark Boyle began to climb the ecclesial ladder. A native of Cleveland, he spent little time in parish work—the service for which he had been trained. Always obedient to his bishop, Boyle filled one administrative post after another . . . including, oddly, that of rector of the local seminary.

Then, as would be expected, he was named an auxiliary bishop in Cleveland. Then Bishop of Pittsburgh, then Archbishop of Detroit. Finally, following in the footsteps of his predecessor, Edward Mooney, he became a Cardinal.

All as if it were foreordained.

Not so with Patrick McNiff.

While it was true that he had performed some special jobs on the parochial level, no one, including himself, could ever have suspected that he would be named even a monsignor, let alone a bishop.

"Is this tentative?" McNiff asked. "I want to be clear about this whole thing. You are offering me the position of rector of St. Joseph's Seminary."

Boyle nodded.

"I am free to accept or refuse your offer."

Again Boyle nodded.

"If I accept, I can forget about retiring in a couple of years."

Boyle shrugged slightly, but nodded . . . as if to say this was true—unfortunately true, but true nonetheless.

"This appointment," McNiff rattled on, "doesn't have to be ratified by anyone . . . I mean, it doesn't have to be cleared through Rome?"

"No. Not your appointment as rector. But we will have to get the approval of our Holy Father to ordain you a bishop."

"That was my final question. And I guess there is no guarantee that the Holy Father will consent. I mean, excuse me, Eminence, but scuttlebutt has it that your track record is not all that certain when it comes to naming auxiliaries. I mean, rumor has it that you generally get an auxiliary when you want one—and not many Ordinaries can say that—but—and I know this is hearsay—you don't always get the man you ask for.

"Wouldn't this be a concern if you asked for my appointment—especially to a job as sensitive as that of seminary rector?"

Boyle fingered the chain of his pectoral cross. "That, Father, is where your rather conservative reputation comes into play. I feel confident my request will be granted, not only to have a bishop as rector of the seminary for the first time in our local history but also that that bishop be you."

Then it was true! At least it seemed true. Boyle had not been getting the priests he'd been requesting. The Vatican must be extremely cautious, perhaps even fearful, in the face of Boyle's reputed liberal bent. Boyle had just admitted that the Vatican screened his nominees, substituting conservatives for supposed liberal candidates. The Roman hierarchy must feel exceptionally defensive to treat a Cardinal like this.

Maybe the entire scuttlebutt *is* true, starting with the Pope's refusal to accept Boyle's resignation.

Mark Boyle was at least perceived to be that rare creature, a liberal Cardinal. The Pope, as well as his administration, was staunchly conservative. With that as a premise, it would be logical to assume that when the liberal Cardinal submitted his resignation, the conservative Pope would accept it with pleasure.

Yet over and over again, the Pope had rejected the resignation.

Instead, the Vatican Curia, doubtless at the Pope's direction, continued to select as assisting bishops to Cardinal Boyle the most conservative of nominees.

McNiff conjured up the image of a prizefighter, a boxer, carrying his opponent. Rather than allowing the opponent to fall and thus ending the match, he keeps the adversary standing while continuing to punish him.

Is this what had been going on over the past few years?

McNiff did not want to believe it, but at this moment, it seemed the best explanation.

"If you wish, Father," Boyle broke into McNiff's mental musings, "you may think and pray over your decision for a few days. Take a week, if you find that necessary. Then come see me again."

"Thank you, Eminence. I'll get back to you as soon as I can. Surely within a week."

6 "IF I HADN'T quit smoking years ago, I might just light up now." Father Koesler spoke only half in jest.

"Isn't it nice"—McNiff paused to blow his nose—"isn't it nice," he repeated, "to know that you have some corroboration for your theory about the conservative auxiliaries? Not to mention the reason the Pope keeps rejecting the Cardinal's resignation?"

"Yeah, that's nice. . . ." Koesler paused. "How many people have you told?"

McNiff shook his head and gestured: "You're it."

"I can see why."

McNiff nodded. "It would have been counterproductive. We felt that the longer the faculty—and the students, for that matter—were in the dark about the real reason I'm here, the more chance of success I'd have."

"You couldn't even let the minority liberals in on it?"

"Uh-uh. They might have reacted with some wink-and-nod body language that would have tipped the whole thing off. This transformation had to be imperceptible, not apparent . . . you know, just a gradual kind of thing, for it to work."

"Well, I'll give you that. . . ." Koesler leaned back in his chair. "It's going so gradually that no one in the diocese seems to be detecting it. You've been here over five years and I haven't heard anyone comment on any kind of change going on here whatsoever."

"There have been changes." McNiff sounded a whit defensive. "I admit they're subtle. A couple of the priest faculty are gone—one to a pastorate, the other to Senior Priesthood.

39

Three of the lay staff have left. And I've replaced them all. No . . ." McNiff shook his head and waved his hand in a negative gesture in response to Koesler's obvious heightened interest. ". . . not with crashing liberals, but with conservatives who have that needed touch of tolerance."

McNiff began to cough, blessedly not in the direction of Father Koesler, who felt he would be fortunate to escape this bug-filled space without contracting pneumonia.

"So," Koesler said finally, "as far as you know, there are two, and only two, who are in on your secret mission: you and the Cardinal."

"Until this moment, yes."

"Okay, you've told me. Now, isn't it possible that the Cardinal has let someone else in on it?"

"The understanding is that we would share this knowledge with no one without informing each other. And the agreement affects me mainly. I'm the one on the firing line. I need more mobility in handling this policy."

"So you've told Boyle about our meeting tonight?"

"I'll tell him tomorrow."

Koesler paused, giving himself time to assimilate all this. "Okay," he said, finally, "I guess that brings us logically to the ultimate question: Why me?"

"Exactly."

Koesler noticed that McNiff's eyes were bloodshot and his face was puffy. He wondered whether this cold, or flu—whatever—had been at least partially brought on by the stress of this assignment. He was beginning to feel sorry for his classmate. Boyle had given McNiff a rugged row to hoe. Considering his age and physical condition, McNiff might well be flirting with death.

"I need help, Bob. And I need it bad."

Koesler could tell, both from this plea and from his long-time familiarity with his classmate, that the situation was taking a lot out of the man. McNiff was not one to ask for help. Knowing this, Koesler was motivated to supply whatever help he could. "In what way? How can I help you?"

McNiff shook his head. This was draining him. "I need

someone to confide in. I need to bounce ideas off someone I can trust. I need someone I can relax with. I need a friend—preferably someone who knows and understands my assignment here. And, to top everything off, someone who agrees with the need for this mission.

"Also," he added parenthetically, "someone who's got the time to do all this. Someone"—he winked one bloodshot eye—"maybe who is retired."

Koesler chuckled. "Did you gerrymander these criteria to fit perfectly my present lifestyle, or do I just happen to fit the bill?"

"Would I do anything underhanded to you?"

"Yes."

McNiff barely smiled.

"But," Koesler said, "I'm still not clear on what you expect of me. Do you see this as-yet-anonymous 'helper' as someone who responds to your decisions on a full-time basis?"

"No, not at all. Let's say for sake of argument that you were this as-yet-anonymous helper. I envision it this way. You'd have a suite here in the seminary. It would be yours to use as you will: complete freedom to come and go as you wish.

"It would be nice if you would attend—concelebrate—our daily liturgies. If you wished, you could also help out at the parish of your choice on a daily basis or on weekends.

"If you wanted, you could teach a class here. You'd get to know some of the students better. And you'd be sitting in on the faculty meetings, since you would be, in effect, an adjunct professor—"

"Of what?"

"I've given that some thought—"

"You've given some thought to everything."

McNiff was undeterred. "You spent some years at the diocesan paper. You could teach a course in journalism . . . or maybe creative writing."

"My career in journalism was at a small weekly paper that specialized in Catholic news and opinion. That's not a lot of background for a course. As to 'creative writing,' what's the opposite—'destructive writing'?

"I don't mean to put you down, Little Pat; I just don't think I'm qualified to teach one of your standard subjects."

McNiff sighed impatiently. "Look, Bob, within limitations, we can do pretty much what we want in creating and staffing classes. You could float a bit. Drop into the Homiletics class occasionally. You're a good speaker; for the love of Pete, I asked you to give the eulogy for both my parents. I didn't ask for you at that important time in my life because you were chopped liver!

"Hey, you've been a parish priest for forty-five years. For a dozen of those years you were also editor of the *Detroit Catholic*. Bob"—McNiff was both pleading and exhorting—"give the kids the benefit of your experience."

Koesler looked out the window in deep thought. "If I give them the benefit of my experience," he said, finally, "won't they begin to tumble to what you're doing? I mean, I am not now, nor have I been for a very long time, a member of the conservative wing of the Church. Nor do I even fit in with those conservatives that you're looking for now—the ones with a high degree of tolerance. I'm a liberal who tolerates conservatives—at least the ones who tolerate back."

"I don't see the problem, Bobby. You're retired. You're not on the firing line anymore. That's the image you've got. They—the faculty and the students—don't know that by joining me you've gone back to that front line.

"You'll see: You'll be venerated; you'll be a figure who's been through the battles. You'll be like the old professors here when we were students: a Father Klenner, a Father Leo Ward, a Father Stitt—"

"Wait a minute, Pat. I'm not a relic these kids will reverence after breakfast."

Their laughter was cut short by McNiff's coughing spell. Koesler rose, crossed over, and pounded McNiff's back. "Lay off," McNiff managed to gasp through his coughs. "You're gonna kill me!"

Koesler backed away and seated himself again.

McNiff grabbed some Kleenex and dabbed at his eyes. Finally, back in control, the bishop spoke. "Listen, Bob, we can work this out. I've given it a lot of thought. And you've had only a few minutes to let it sink in."

Koesler nodded. "You're right, Pat. What was the time limit the Cardinal gave you originally? A week or so, no? How 'bout I give you my answer before this week is out?"

"Great!"

Koesler rose, got his coat and hat, and insisted that he could see himself out. "Take care of yourself," he admonished. "You don't want to celebrate your victory at St. Joe's by dying."

"Don't worry about me, Bob. Oh, and by the way, if you should come across anyone in the hallway, would you ask them to clean up that door? And Bob: About tonight—"

"It's our secret."

After closing the door, Koesler took one more look at it.

Disgusting.

As he turned the corner at the staircase, he almost literally bumped into a young woman carrying a bucket of water with soapsuds popping on the surface, and a sponge.

She gave a startled little squeal. Koesler thought it a cute sound. "Let me guess: You must be Patty Donnelly."

She shook her head. "A friend."

"Are you about to clean the bishop's door?"

"Yes, Father." Although she didn't recognize him, she gave the title to his clerical collar.

"Then you are a friend in deed and indeed."

As Koesler drove to Old St. Joseph's, he reflected on how the parish and the seminary shared the same name. He wondered whether this was an omen. He also reflected on the conversation he'd just had with Pat McNiff.

Koesler felt privileged and gratified to have been let in on easily the most analyzed and most baffling puzzle in Catholic Detroit. Certainly the hot stove topic among Detroit's clergy.

He had put McNiff on hold as far as his participatory role in the St. Joe's mission. Now, in the shelter of his car, Koesler knew that he would go along with the bishop's proposition. But Koesler would wait until the weekend to make his acceptance official.

Meanwhile, he would work things out with Father Zachary Tully, the pastor of St. Joe's.

Koesler would have lodging—he was reluctant to call it a suite, even though it would be a couple of rooms and a bath—in the seminary. But if Zack wanted his presence in his former parish, Koesler would not refuse. The same would apply to weekend liturgies.

Any priest—in the world, practically—who could play free safety, to borrow a football metaphor, was welcome as the first flowers of spring to fill in on weekends. So if, for any reason, Zack did not need Koesler's help, there were plenty of other pastors who would grab him up thinking they had gone to heaven without benefit of dying.

In talking this over with Zack Tully, Koesler would have to be careful not to leak in any way the confidence he had agreed to keep. He knew that he need only indicate that certain questions were out of bounds and Zack would respect that.

It wasn't a long drive home. Both the parish and the seminary were not far from the heart of downtown Detroit, the parish being the nearer of the two. If he chose to live at the parish it would be only a short drive to the seminary. And, of course, vice versa.

He continued to mull over his meeting with McNiff.

Good Lord, it was tough to think of Pat McNiff as a bishop!

In their youth, Koesler and McNiff had been counselors together at a Catholic boys' camp. That, as well as being classmates for twelve years, had bonded them tightly. About the only thing they'd never tried was sharing the same assignment as priests. Now they would turn that page by working together at the seminary.

Koesler smiled, recalling the image of Pat McNiff at the door of his room, disheveled in Salvation Army pajamas and robe . . . not to mention slippers with a toe hole.

Koesler was reminded of the old story about a prodigal son–type priest. Having spent all of his pittance on wine, women, and song, the priest, who now looks and acts like a down-and-out bum, calls at a rectory and says to the priest

who answers the door, "*Sum sacerdos* [I am a priest]"—
to which the dapper, clean-shaven priest responds, "Some
sacerdos!"

In the case of Pat McNiff: some bishop!

However, giving credit where it was due, McNiff, in accepting this assignment, had exhibited a significant measure of clerical obedience if not downright bravery.

Which reminded Koesler to guard against any move to make him some sort of coadjutor to McNiff with right of succession. He could admire McNiff while having no intention of following in his footsteps.

McNiff had an extremely narrow line to walk. He had to move an ostensibly immovable culture several delicate degrees to the left. All the while the immovable object must remain unaware that it is sideslipping.

The purpose: to transform a faculty that had become largely closed-minded to one that was open-minded.

Koesler felt that Bishop McNiff was going about the task in the only possible way: gradually replacing the personnel. It was Koesler's experience that once a person either closed or opened his or her mind, it was likely to remain in that position forever and ever. Amen.

He did worry about McNiff's health. Those heart attacks, the quadruple bypass, and, most of all, the time bomb aneurysm—each and every one was a realistic cause for concern.

Koesler resolved that, insofar as he was able, he would try to be a buffer, protecting his friend from the powder keg of stress and hazard. If he could help it, Bishop McNiff would not die on Koesler's watch.

7

PATTY DONNELLY HAD forced down a simple dinner. She knew exactly when her appetite had vanished.

It wasn't the slopping of Bishop McNiff's food all over his door. That was boneheaded, not like her at all.

It was one of those embarrassing moments that would return periodically to memory, each time causing her to wince. Everyone has such uncomfortable memories that haunt and scar. Patty could have laughed the incident away had it not been for the seminarians—Reverend Mr. Horses' Asses—who made a laughingstock of her and turned her away from their august table.

That's when appetite had deserted her.

Page and Cody hadn't yet left, even though they had finished eating and were draining the coffeepot to the dregs. She could hear Page's distinctive tone. He was doing most of the talking in his sotto voce delivery, which was just loud enough to be heard but not loud enough for the words to be made out.

Patty was startled when, seemingly out of nowhere, another young woman sat down opposite her. "Andrea! Where did you come from?"

"Just doing a few chores." Andrea Zawalich set a cup of steaming coffee on the table. She took a cautious sip, then shuddered. "Ugh! Strong and hot and right out of the bottom of the pot."

"I think the mad deacons drained it. It's good you're holding the cup. If I had it, I'd probably pour it over their heads."

"Something particular tonight?"

Patty studied the tabletop. "Oh, I did something stupid.

Those jerks got wind of it and found it infectiously funny. Then they put on a public show of not letting me sit at their table."

"How'd they do that?"

"They pretended they were saving two unoccupied places."

"The old tip-up-the-chair routine?"

"Yup. What with one thing and another, I could kill them."

"I can think of one redeeming value in this incident."

"What's that?"

"I heard them talking about the bishop's door and what had happened to it—"

"What *I* did to it."

"Okay, what you did to it. The thing is, I just got done cleaning it up."

Patty reached across and affectionately touched Andrea's arm. "You're an angel."

"Oh, it wasn't so bad. At least the slop was fresh. A while longer and it would've congealed. And then you know what would've happened?"

Patty shook her head. Already she was emerging from her blue mood under the guidance of the almost always ebullient Andrea.

"Somebody would've looked at that mess that had become part of the door and seen the image of Jesus or His mother, or a favorite saint. Then they would've sealed Bishop McNiff in his room and declared the place a shrine.

"Then the next time you wanted to help the bishop, you'd have to climb outside on a ladder and spill the soup and spaghetti all over his window."

They both dissolved in laughter.

That irritated the Reverend Mr. Bill Page. If Donnelly could laugh after what she had done and the embarrassment he'd inflicted upon her, his lead was definitely narrowing.

"Why'd you do it?" Patty asked.

"Do what?"

"Clean up for me. I would've taken care of it. I just didn't feel like it at that moment."

"Listen, it's easier to clean up someone else's mess than your own."

"I'll have to think about that."

"While you're thinking about it . . ." Andrea tried the coffee again. It was cooler, but perhaps more bitter. "I've been thinking about a priest I almost literally bumped into on my way to cleaning up the bishop's door."

"A priest? What's so odd about that? This is a seminary."

"This was a strange priest—"

"He was wearing a false nose and a bushy mustache?"

"You didn't let me finish. I said strange because I'm pretty sure I never met him before. And yet I almost recognized him. Like I'd seen his picture in the paper, or maybe on TV . . ."

"Old? Young?"

"Old."

"That figures!" Patty sighed. "Probably a new faculty member. Probably the same age as the Pope. Probably agrees with everything the Pope says. Just like everybody else here."

"He had a kind face . . . and he smiled at me."

"Be careful then. Maybe he takes after Pope John Paul the First. He smiled a lot. But he didn't last very long."

"You know what?" Andrea pushed away from the table. "I'm going to make some fresh coffee."

"And let those two freeloaders have some?!" Patty was indignant.

"Maybe we'll win them over to decency." Andrea smiled as she went off to make the coffee.

When it was done, she poured some for both deacons. Al Cody seemed genuinely grateful and thanked her. Page groused.

Next she poured a cup for Patty and one for herself.

Patty sipped. It *was* good. "How can you be what you are? You're always cheerful and low-key. I wish I could be more like you."

Andrea caught the cheerless tone. "If you don't mind my saying it, you *could* lighten up a little. For one thing, I think you've wanted to be a priest for too long."

* * *

Andrea was correct, Patty mused. She had wanted to be a priest as far back as she could remember.

Her parents took her with them to Sunday Mass. Not all churches had "cry rooms"; the ones that didn't expected parents to keep their children at home until the young ones could behave.

But not Patty. As soon as she was free from the pacifier, she spent her time in church looking and listening.

Taking Patty to church was like putting a fish in water. If at that early age, she could've phrased anything, she would have paraphrased Paul's description of heaven. Except that for her, heaven was a church. So Patty's version would have read: "Eye has not seen, nor has the ear heard, nor has it entered the mind of anyone the joy that God delivers to people in church."

She was fortunate in being taken to a church where the priests were dedicated—serious about presenting a participation liturgy and providing a choir that sounded angelic.

Because Patty became so absorbed in the Church, as the years went by, she read extensively about that subject.

In one of her research projects, she came across a woman who would become her patron saint—even though nobody ever canonized her.

Her name was Jeannette Piccard. She was married to Dr. Jean Piccard, a famous scientist and, in his hot air balloon, a space traveler.

Sharing her husband's life as totally as possible, Jeannette Piccard learned how to pilot the balloon, and accompanied her husband on his voyages. She felt it wasn't right for him to be "up there alone."

In addition, Dr. Piccard needed someone he could rely on, someone who would not learn the secrets of space flight and then desert him. Of course, he knew he could rely on his wife.

In a historic 1934 flight over Dearborn, Michigan, Jeannette Piccard set a record when the couple's balloon rose to an altitude of 57,559 feet. But the record was unofficial; in 1934 there was no category for women. And when that category was established, it wasn't made retroactive.

They'd hoped to go to 100,000 feet, but couldn't get any sponsors for the flight. Nobody wanted to be held responsible for the danger or the possible death of a woman and mother.

"Danger?" Mrs. Piccard snorted. "Once I took our son up for a lovely flight in our balloon. Two weeks later I walked through a doorway and broke my hip. And doors are supposed to be safe."

In 1964 Jeannette Piccard was appointed a consultant to the NASA Manned Spacecraft Center in Houston. In 1970 she was cut from the program, a victim of the Nixon administration's austerity agenda.

Clearly, this was a woman who was all too familiar with the fabled glass ceiling.

But what most endeared her to Patty Donnelly was Jeannette Piccard's dogged pursuit of the priesthood.

In 1916, as a sophomore at Bryn Mawr, she wrote a paper on the ordination of women. Nearly sixty years later, in 1974, she received a phone call. Four retired Episcopal bishops were going to ordain women to the priesthood: Did she want in? Indeed she did.

When she was ordained, the NASA space staff sent her a congratulatory letter.

And so, after a lifetime of persevering in the face of discrimination, this dedicated woman achieved her "impossible dream." Asked when Catholic women might expect ordination to the priesthood, she replied, "When they get another Pope like John."

Patty Donnelly couldn't see another Pope John XXIII anywhere on the horizon.

However, even without a John as Pope, there was another crack in the dike.

It was by no means probable, but faintly possible, that what had served Jeannette could work for Patty.

Somewhere, somehow, there might be a Catholic bishop, perhaps retired—as were the four Episcopal bishops who had ordained the original eleven women priests—who would do the same for Catholic women.

But even should that happen, Patty knew the fight would

by no means be over. Even if a validly ordained—not under the pressure of an oppressive Communist regime—Catholic bishop were to ordain women who had no impediment to ordination except their femininity, the Vatican Church would fight it with everything in its power. Of this she was certain.

Patty had entertained these thoughts so often that now they passed through her mind in just a few moments.

Andrea could not have known the stream of consciousness her observation had triggered. To her it seemed Patty responded immediately.

"I've wanted to be a priest too long? Andy, isn't that like telling an astronaut she spends too much time thinking about flying? Or a writer that he's reading too many books? What's wrong with wanting to be a priest?"

"Nothing—on the face of it. But let me offer you a couple of analogies. Your wanting to be a priest is like a kid who wants to be an Olympic runner but she's paraplegic. Or she wants to sing for the Met, but she's tone deaf.

"Bottom line for all of you: It's not going to happen."

"Maybe it could. Maybe it will. What if we find a bishop who's willing to ordain us? What about Bishop McNiff?"

"Whoever it is, it's got to be someone who's willing to spend his remaining days picking buckshot out of his hide. And even in the unlikely event—as they say on planes—you do find such a dauntless martyr, Rome would not sit still for it. My guess is the Vatican would simply declare the ordination invalid, have some vino, and call it a day."

"Even then," Patty pressed on, "we would just carry the battle to a higher level.

"Those of us who were ordained would push on ahead to exercise our priesthood. We'd preside at the eucharistic liturgy. We'd absolve. We'd bless. We'd do everything the other priests do.

"The struggle would go on, as it does now."

"Now? Here?"

"Certainly. Here and now we want to be admitted to the M.Div courses."

"Again, why? Even if you're admitted and you pass them all, where does that get you? You're all dressed up with a degree and you've got no place to go."

"Not so. When we find our bishop we'll be ready to go. We won't be forced to say, 'Thanks very much for the call to orders, Bishop, but we'll have to take a few courses'—so a lack of preparation won't be thrown in our faces along with everything else."

"But, Pat, you can take these courses just a few miles from here at Orchard Lake Seminary. Why bang your head against the wall here?"

Patty nodded. "Cyril and Methodius does offer the M.Div courses to women—as do many other seminaries in this country. But that's like, before the civil rights movement, telling an African-American that there's a water fountain down the street so she doesn't have to try to get a drink at this fountain here that's reserved for whites.

"The point is, Andy: All the water fountains should be available to everyone, no matter what their skin color. And all the seminaries should have to offer M.Div courses to everyone, male and female alike."

Andrea, lost in thought, did not respond. Patty was content to let her argument sink in.

"I've got to admit you make a convincing case," Andrea said after a time. "And I can see parallels with the civil rights struggles—at least as far as I've read about them and watched the TV documentaries. But the civil rights struggle has one very important advantage over women's ordination . . ." She did not pursue the thought.

"So?" Patty said. "And that is?"

"They—the African-Americans—had friends in high places."

"Meaning?"

"Granted, in the beginning all they had was truth as a weapon. They didn't have law court victories. They didn't have the backing of leaders in Congress, business, or industry. With the exception of the best of the best—like Jackie

Robinson or Bill Russell—they were forced to play in their own sports leagues."

Patty looked puzzled. "Jackie Robinson? Bill Russell?"

"You could look it up. Anyway, it wasn't till Martin Luther King and his nonviolent crusade that black Americans began to get doors opened to schools, jobs, and all sports. Court decisions began to go in their direction. They got recognition and help from two Kennedys—one President, the other, Attorney General. Then Lyndon Johnson—a good ol' boy from Texas—pushed civil rights bills through a mostly cooperative Congress. That's what I mean by getting friends in high places. See?"

"Okay," Patty admitted, "suppose I agree with everything you've said. They had to have friends in high places. What's the point?"

"You haven't!"

"Haven't what?"

"You haven't got friends in high places."

Patty shrugged. "The Pope?"

"Him and all his buddies. Like Cardinals and bishops and priests—and just about every M.Div student in this place."

Patty made an expansive, palms-up gesture. "Haven't you heard? *We* are the Church. And there's a lot more of Us than there are of Them. So what do we need with friends in high places?"

"Pat, it's not just that you don't have friends in high places: The people in high places are your *enemies*. The possibility of ordaining women priests now is like the predicament of the blacks before Martin Luther King, Johnson, the courts, and the civil rights movement: Southerners didn't mind how close blacks got as long as they didn't get uppity. Northerners didn't mind how uppity blacks got as long as they didn't get close."

"Andy, you just don't understand. *We are the Church!* We don't need friends in high places."

"I know, I know. I read the documents of Vatican II. I know it says in there that The People of God are the Church. But

I've got eyes and I've kept them open. Not only do all directives come from Rome, the Pope has done a splendid job of stacking the College of Cardinals, as well as filling most of the bishoprics with men after his own mind.

"The Pope has taken on the clout of Infallibility. Even if he hasn't really used it, it's there as the ultimate threat. One Pope says women can't be priests because they don't look like Jesus—which, by the way, would disqualify most of the bishops and priests we've got. A Pope says women can't be priests because Jesus didn't make any women Apostles. And, finally, a Pope said that women never were, are not, never will be priests. End of discussion! There will be no more talk of it. Period!" The very words seemed to leave a bad taste in Andrea's mouth.

"But, don't you see, Andy: The talk goes on. That's part of my argument. Sure the Pope wants to run everything. He wants to be 'The Church.' And he certainly said there could be no more talk of women as priests. But—and here's the point—the debate goes on as if the Pope had never issued that edict. We *will* overcome, Andy."

"I'd give you a very weak 'maybe' on that."

"Your problem, Andy, is that you've never wanted something you should but can't have. You haven't walked in my moccasins."

Oh, yeah? thought Andrea.

8 ANDREA ZAWALICH AND Patty Donnelly were both a couple of inches over five feet. Each was of slender build yet amply endowed—one might say curvy. Their posture was straight, their oval faces attractive; both had blue eyes spaced widely apart. Each was in her early twenties.

About the only marked difference was their hair. Andrea's Cleopatra-style bangs were brunette; Patty's no-nonsense short bob was blond.

Except for that, they could easily have passed for sisters.

But it was not always so.

Andrea's father was Polish, her mother Irish.

Andrea was an only child, though her parents had hoped for many more children.

Her early life could best be described as ordinary. Much treasured by her parents, she tried to compensate for having no siblings by making and keeping friends easily. She was, in short, a happy, well-adjusted little girl.

She attended St. Hedwig school in the parish where her family lived. All was well—until sometime during the third grade.

Andrea began to gain weight—a noticeable amount. The gain necessitated fairly frequent wardrobe changes as the girl progressed through one size after another. Clearly, there was a problem.

The doctor found nothing physically wrong. He suggested that it was a phase some children go through, that in time it would take care of itself.

Bolstered by this diagnosis, the Zawalichs went home determined to weather the storm. It was all a matter of time. But time passed so very slowly. Day after day they approached their daughter apprehensively, expectantly. Still, Andrea grew heavier. Not as rapidly as in the beginning, but, heavier, nonetheless.

Andrea was consuming a lot of food. Perhaps, thought her parents, it was as simple as that: She was just overeating.

They restricted her menu. That slowed her gain, but didn't halt it.

They accused her of snacking when she was away from home. She denied it. It was a comforting defense for the parents. It wasn't their fault; it was *her* fault. *She* was responsible for her condition. The parents absolved themselves.

Both teachers and parents noted a pattern of indolence setting in. Never had Andrea had any problem with either schoolwork or chores at home. Now she was shirking both.

It was as if she were some sort of engine slowing down, running on fumes. Home was becoming a hell on earth.

Andrea's life was changing most depressingly in her relationships with her classmates and friends. In the school of hard knocks she was learning the truth of that old maxim: Laugh and the world laughs with you, cry and you cry alone.

Andrea cried—alone—frequently.

Her schoolmates were of the age when children can be brutally cruel. With Andrea they had plenty of opportunity.

She grew too large to share the double school desk. She more waddled than ran. Races were over before she had taken ten steps. Even after her weight gain slowed, her face continued to bloat.

Her former friends invented names to call her. She was Kong—for King Kong. She was Moby—for Moby Dick. She was Ellie—for elephant, Dino—for dinosaur.

In the playground during recess, somebody would take something of hers—a scarf, a hat—and play keep-away. She could barely turn, let alone run after her tormentors to try to regain the swiped item.

Over and above all, Andrea was terrified. She knew she wasn't overeating. If anything, she was eating less than she

ever had. Something was going on inside her body that was
blowing her up like a balloon.

She had no one to whom she could turn.

The doctor had dismissed her symptoms as something time
would take care of. Her parents eventually became convinced
that she wasn't overeating or snacking behind their back. Desperate, they debated sending her off to some sort of sanitorium
or fat farm for the duration. But would that be in perpetuity?

Meanwhile, the harassment by her peers continued unrelentingly.

One evening her mother bundled her up and carted her off to
St. Hedwig's rectory. She told the young priest who answered
the door all about Andrea and her hitherto normal, now af-
flicted young life.

She asked the priest to exorcise her daughter. Mrs. Zawalich
could come to no other conclusion than that the girl was possessed by the devil.

The mother had just read *The Exorcist*. She saw in that book
a young girl not unlike Andrea. The child in the novel had a
very normal life until, out of the blue, strange things began to
happen.

Granted, Andrea was not projectile vomiting. Her head did
not turn 360 degrees. Indeed, none of the preternatural events
that plagued the fictional girl had been evidenced in Andrea.
But, Mrs. Zawalich reasoned, theirs was a very religious
home; it seemed only natural that Andrea's torment was the
devil's work.

The doctor had found no physical cause. The condition had
not resolved itself as he had suggested it would. To the mother
there was no answer other than the supernatural. And it wasn't
the sort of supernatural manifestation that could be laid at
God's door.

What else? The devil!

And the cure? Exorcism!

The young priest was tempted to laugh. Fortunately he
could detect the terror in the little girl's demeanor.

How would I react, the priest reflected, if my mother or father presented me as a child to a parish priest to have Satan

knocked out of me? I would be terror-stricken—just as Andrea was.

The priest asked Mrs. Zawalich to tell him in the greatest possible detail just how this phenomenon had developed. He listened carefully.

The priest was not a physician, nor had he any medical training. But he couldn't help returning to some sort of physical cause for Andrea's distress—this despite the family doctor's diagnosis.

The priest had a friend, a young doctor in whom he had a lot of confidence. With great difficulty, he finally persuaded Mrs. Zawalich to take Andrea to this doctor, if for no other reason than to get a second opinion. A second opinion before they could consider an exorcism. The priest himself phoned the doctor and set up the appointment.

The new physician examined Andrea. He was sure of his diagnosis, but in view of the circumstances, he referred Andrea to an endocrinologist for corroboration.

The endocrinologist confirmed the GP's finding: hypothyroidism—an underactive thyroid gland.

Treatment was relatively simple. Andrea would take a replacement thyroid hormone, probably for the rest of her life.

After all that misery, anxiety, fear, confusion, depression, apprehension, self-rejection—not to mention the harassment from her peer group and her parents' unhappiness with her—the resolution of Andrea's problem was almost anticlimactic: a textbook case.

Their family physician had made an error that was rectified by another family practitioner and confirmed by a specialist.

From that time on, Andrea tried to make her thyroid imbalance relevant to her life as well as to the lives of others who needed her understanding.

The family doctor took the news of his misdiagnosis in stride. Mr. and Mrs. Zawalich returned to him with renewed if unearned confidence.

Andrea became again that pretty little girl she had been before her thyroid gland had betrayed her.

But the scars were there. She now knew what it was to be a

leper, an outcast, an object of scorn. She had tasted both worlds, the accepted and the rejected, and she would never forget.

Unlike Patty Donnelly, Andrea had never wished to be a priest. Partly that was because of her experience in trying to become an altar minister (in the days when—as far back as anyone could remember—they were known as altar boys). When her parish priest refused her request to be an altar boy— or altar girl—she asked why. The response was: "You are unworthy."

Patty Donnelly had reacted differently to a similar experience; in her case it simply added fuel to her desire to fight on to the priesthood.

Andrea Zawalich knew, from the school of hard knocks, that there were worse things in life than not being permitted to be a priest, or even an altar boy.

Andrea knew what it was to want something she couldn't have. She knew what it was to want her entire personality returned after it had been buried under layers of unwelcome and undeserved fatty tissue. She knew what it was to want her tormentors to be her friends again. She knew what it was to have her respected and revered parents believe she was possessed by the devil. She knew what it was to prefer death to life in an alien body.

Andrea was quite sure Patty Donnelly did not know what she knew. It wasn't that Andrea had not walked in Patty's moccasins; it was vice versa. But, true to their friendship, Andrea would do her utmost to see that Patty would never have to walk in those moccasins.

ANDREA BLEW ACROSS the surface of her coffee, then sipped. She had done well in brewing this batch and she was pleased. "You're right, Patty: I haven't walked in your moccasins." She looked across the room in thought. "I wonder if *any*one can do that. None of our experiences can be totally identical.

"But I think I know where you're coming from. I think I might have wanted to be ordained almost as much as you do if it hadn't been for that crazy priest."

"Which crazy priest?"

"Oh, I know I've told you about when I tried to become an altar server and the dear Father told me that, as a girl, I was 'unworthy.' Unworthy! He didn't know me well enough to pronounce me—specifically—unworthy. But it's really something when your entire sex is unworthy."

"You know what they say," Patty reminded. "If a priest is a jackass, there isn't a Roman collar in the world big enough to hide his ears."

"I've heard that—from you . . . frequently."

"It deserves repetition." Patty paused for a moment, enjoying her coffee. "But you know, Andy, I've thought of that experience you had . . . being called 'unworthy.' Isn't that a classic incident? I mean somebody has dealings with a clerical weirdo and he or she takes this to mean that the whole Catholic Church is reflected in this guy's behavior. And it isn't, you know."

Andrea grinned. "Pat! Are you trying to entice me to get behind you in a line that's going nowhere?"

Patty returned the smile, though not as enthusiastically. "Why not? The only way you're gonna know that this line is moving is if you join it. I mean, forget the silly priest who claimed you're unworthy. If he hadn't said that, wouldn't you want to be a priest . . . or, at least, be thinking about it seriously?"

Andrea warmed her hands by rotating the coffee mug between them. "I think, maybe, some years ago I might have. But it's too late now."

"Even if nobody's standing in your way?"

Andrea was sensitive to Patty's tone. Patty seemed to be seeking encouragement to continue her so-far discouraging pursuit of the priesthood. Andrea could understand Pat's need for reassurance. Pat needed Andrea's backing, reinforcement, moral support—something that testified to the worthiness of her goal and the possibility of attaining it, be that possibility ever so remote.

"Yes," Andrea replied. "If the M.C.P. priest hadn't thrown me out of the altar servers well before I could even get in. And if no one were able to block my equal opportunity . . . yes, I think I'd be with you."

Patty looked relieved.

"But, as it is," Andrea concluded, "I'm going to be in pastoral ministry in a parish where you're the pastor."

Both laughed equally heartily.

Their gaiety disgruntled Deacon Bill Page. "Damn! Damn! Damn! That Polack broad has spoiled everything. Here we had Donnelly on the verge of tears and now Mary Poppins comes along delivering sweetness and light."

Deacon Al Cody said nothing. He said nothing because he didn't know what to say. His relationship with Page was as a lackey.

Cody considered Page a man of the world. Page had had a life, a career, out there. Cody admired Page's sacrifice in giving up all that to dedicate himself to God's service.

Cody had no way of knowing that Page was using the priesthood as a flotation device. Page had been slowly sinking, financially, socially, and almost every other way. He had been about to go under before a burst of inspiration suddenly led him to the seminary.

But Cody had no way of knowing that Page was not what he affected to be.

Among other things, Page was capable of sexual, ethnic, and every other sort of slur. Never in the presence of faculty members or seminary authorities, of course, but freely among his fellow students.

So Cody was not unduly surprised when Page referred to Andrea Zawalich as a Polack. Cody wished his idol wouldn't do that. But he was willing to make allowances for one who was sacrificing so much to serve as a priest.

Thus, although Cody was somewhat offended by much of what Page said, as well as by his general attitude, the younger man attributed it to Page's worldly years; he forgave and somehow managed to keep his idol on the pedestal.

"Still and all," Page said with a lecherous grin, "you've got to admire their bods."

"What?"

"C'mon, Al baby, you want me to believe you haven't noticed? They may be harpies, but they're *built*. They're stacked. Just look at those"—his elbow delivered a jab to Cody's ribs—"tits and asses."

Cody was embarrassed and he showed it. He simply did not know how to deal with such remarks, so he chuckled.

Page saw through it. "C'mon, Al, let yourself go, won't you? Those"—he made a gesture toward the women—"are two very sexy fillies. Not gorgeous, mind you; not to die for . . . but sexy. And I'll bet they don't even know it."

"They don't?" Cody, of course, was well aware that the two young women were good-looking. It would never occur to him that they might be unaware of their attractiveness. Among the talks seminarians were obliged to listen to were periodic lectures on women. As a matter of course, the bottom line was: Look, but don't touch.

"You don't think they'd be holed up in here if they knew what they could get if they just put out a little," Page harped.

"But they'd have a hard time making it in here . . . shacked up with a bunch of celibates.

"This place protects itself pretty well. We get lectures on leaving everybody the hell alone. And on top of that, there's 'fraternal correction' "—he grimaced—"a greased-up way of urging us to rat on each other. Out in the world, squealing is cowardly. In here, it's"—the words were articulated mincingly—" 'fraternal correction.' But those gals don't know they've got something to put on the plate. And, oh, baby, I'd love to be the one who presides at their awakening! How 'bout you, buddy?" Page smirked.

"Yeah," Cody halfheartedly agreed.

Page winked. "Don't worry, old buddy; Bill Page is going to take care of it. I guarantee you will not go into the celibate life wanting for experience. You've got to know what you're giving up—because you're the kind of guy who actually will be giving it up."

What could he have meant by that? Cody wondered.

Did Page really plan on introducing him to the sexually active life? Cody couldn't speak for Page's past. But Cody was a virgin, and had every intention of remaining such for life.

He knew—or thought he knew—what that entailed. Not only would he remain unmarried, he would also be, for all practical purposes, asexual. He knew the rules. They had been explained clearly, decisively, and unmistakably—and more than once. Sexual activity was reserved exclusively for marriage, where no artificial means could be used to avoid pregnancy. Where every sexual action had to be open to possible conception.

Since sexual activity was reserved to the marriage state, all other sexual expression, with oneself or another, was a mortal sin. Cody knew this morality and he intended to live by it.

What, then, to do about Page?

Page dominated Cody, Cody knew that. What Page had just said—vowing to compromise Cody's virginity—was no idle promise. In all probability, Page was going to try. Would Cody have sufficient moral strength to fend off not only Page's attempt but Cody's natural attraction to the power of sex?

And what did Page mean when he said that Cody was "the type of guy who actually will be giving it up"? What was Page saying about himself? Was he referring to his past? Before the seminary? Before receiving the diaconate? He couldn't be referring to his future life as a priest . . . could he? Did he have no intention of leading—or at least trying to lead—a chaste life?

What would any or all of this have to do with fraternal correction? And who should correct whom?

Bill Page had many more years than Al Cody, and those years had been vastly different from Cody's.

Cody did not know all the particulars of his mentor's life. But what he did know would have constituted a fairly successful made-for-TV movie—to say the least.

He, on the other hand, had grown up in a family frozen in time. They seemed to mirror the old Robert Young TV series, *Father Knows Best*. The principal differences were that Al Cody was an only child and Mrs. Cody was not nearly as submissive as Jane Wyatt, who portrayed the TV mother. Otherwise, in the Cody household, Father did know best. Or so he thought.

William F. Cody was more or less named after William F. "Buffalo Bill" Cody. However, they were not related. And their middle names were different.

William Francis, Al's father, was born in 1952. William Frederick, the scout and abominable showman, was born in 1846.

Both of them were known as Buffalo Bill—William Frederick because he killed buffalo, William Francis because he was named partially after William Frederick.

William Francis Cody attended St. Ambrose school in the Chicago parish that would later be a workplace of noted sociologist and author Father Andrew M. Greeley.

Cody tried the Quigley Preparatory Seminary-South. Reluctantly, he came to realize that he was not cut out for the priestly life.

As good luck would have it, he finished college without being drafted. With the Vietnam War escalating at an alarming pace, he decided to enlist. But he would make no long-term deal with the army; he chose to do his two-year hitch and get on with his life.

Again as good luck would have it, he got through his stint without serious injury. And he was actually in Saigon on April 29, 1975, the day that war ended. He was among the last to be evacuated, carrying with him a trunkful of memories. He had seen death in all its forms, from those who died of old age to those torn from their mothers' bodies. Friends and enemies alike had been killed with age-old as well as modern weapons.

His parents had moved to a suburb of Detroit. Bill Cody enrolled in the University of Detroit Law School. Three years later he graduated from that Jesuit institution.

Shortly before graduation, at a campus Christmas party, Bill met Eileen Regan, who was studying dental hygiene at U-D. They courted and were married before either of them started a career.

Two months later, Eileen was pregnant. It was a difficult pregnancy leading to a cesarean section. Then her doctor discovered a cancer affecting her uterus. Consultation with an oncologist was followed by a hysterectomy.

Bill and Eileen had a healthy boy they named Albert, thus precluding any more Buffalo Bill jokes. They would have no other children. The couple grieved; they had planned for at least three, if not more, children.

The good news was that Eileen's cancer had been discovered in time; she could look forward to a normal life span.

Had it not been for the hysterectomy, future circumstances might well have called for a sexual hiatus. "Female trouble" perhaps, possible financial problems—anything, in effect, that would make having another child inadvisable. Bill was far too faithful a Catholic to resort to any form of outlawed contraception. Now he had no worry along those lines. Eileen's condition was a green light for all future sexual activity without fear of unwanted consequences.

Eileen's outlook was less rosy. She worried: Had the surgeons gotten it all? Or would it be the once and future cancer?

The other silver lining for Bill was that his one and only child was a boy. Bill had plans for this lad.

Albert would develop as a macho man. They would hunt and fish together. Togetherness would be the primary goal. Although fishing and hunting had their place: Bill would teach his son how to bait and cast and, mostly, how to kill and prepare his food.

It was, however, the hunt that offered the greatest opportunity for manhood.

It began with knowing your weapon. Being able to field strip and reassemble it. How to make it an extension of yourself. How to bait and stalk your prey. How to bring down the victim. How, in instances when the prey is merely wounded, to track it and deliver the coup de grâce.

In the face of growing controversy, Bill would indoctrinate Albert in the precept that said animals have no rights. Bill remembered his training in Catholicism; man's role in the earliest moments of creation was spelled out in Genesis:

"Then God said, 'Let us make man in our image, after our likeness. Let him have dominion over the fish of the sea, the birds of the air, and the cattle, and over all the wild animals and all the creatures that crawl on the ground.'

"God created man in his image;

"In the divine image he created him;

"Male and female he created them.

"God blessed them, saying: 'Be fertile and multiply; fill the earth and subdue it. Have dominion over the fish of the sea, the birds of the air, and all the moving things that move on the earth.' And God also said: 'See, I give you every seed-bearing plant all over the earth and every tree that has seed-bearing fruit on it to be your food, and to all the animals of the land, all the birds of the air, and all the living creatures that crawl on the ground, I give all the green plants for food.' And so it happened."

At first blush it would seem that God was giving mankind carte blanche over the rest of creation. Words such as "dominion" and "subdue" are powerful incentives to be lord and master of all creation and to treat animal life in cavalier fashion.

Those prone to take the first couple of chapters of Genesis literally also should conclude that God intended all animal life—including mankind, fish, birds, cattle and creepy crawlies—to be vegetarian.

Mankind's food is "every seed-bearing plant all over the earth and every tree that has seed-bearing fruit on it." And God gives all green plants as food for all the animals of the earth, and the birds, as well as the creatures that crawl on the ground.

So much for Wendy's, Big Boy, Arby's, Burger King, etc.

Latter-day Scripture scholars have placed more emphasis on mankind's obligation to conserve rather than dominate or subdue creation.

But a macho mankind with the mandate to treat earth and its inhabitants as it wished was the image inculcated in young Al Cody's psyche as he passed from one parochial grade to another.

And things once planted in the senior Cody's mind, particularly religious concepts that were drummed in, were there for life. "As the Church has always taught . . ." was a phrase often used in the Church in which he grew up.

Thus it was no surprise that Bill Cody never bought in on Church changes effected by the Second Vatican Council. Postconciliar teaching hardly ever used the cautionary, "As the Church has always taught . . ." Because, over the centuries, there was very little the Church had "always" taught.

And now he had a son to indoctrinate in the *vera doctrina*—the True Doctrine.

The end product Bill Cody wished to form was a priest.

Bill had attended the Chicago seminary, where he had reluctantly concluded that the clerical life was not for him. He regretted his decision to this day, yet did not repent of it; he had no doubt that he had made the correct decision.

It would be different with Al. Bill would make certain that his son would have no doubts about being a priest.

Al would not be the type of hippy-dippy priest that you

found in so many parishes. Bill would see to it that his son was familiar with the Latin Tridentine Mass, frequent confession, baptism as soon after birth as possible. Black and white in doctrine: God was He, Jesus was He, as was the Holy Ghost. Black and white in morality; none of that situation ethics garbage.

Granted there were exceptions that simply could not be avoided. The vernacular Mass was inescapable. An abomination compared with the old Latin, it now was the least common denominator.

As Bill coaxed the infant to wrap his tiny fingers around his father's thumb, he pictured his son the priest. Like the macho men of the past who weren't embarrassed to wear the clerical outfit. Who hung out together. Who hunted and fished on vacation together. Who displayed the pelts, the skins, the heads on their rectory walls. Who were portrayed in movies by the likes of Spencer Tracy, Gregory Peck, Humphrey Bogart, Barry Fitzgerald, and Bing Crosby. Men's men.

That was Bill's mission—to turn out a priest in this mold.

He did not stop to consider that he was only one of two parents.

Eileen had dropped out of college when she became pregnant, happy to be a full-time mother. But her plans for her son did not mirror her husband's.

When little Al wantonly killed a small bird, his mother gave him a lecture on the sacredness of all life.

Albert was confused.

When Al played in neighborhood games, he objected to letting girls join in. He got a firm lesson from his mother on the equality of the sexes.

He was confused.

When a black family moved in, Albert refused to play with the neighbors' son, though they were the same age. He got a talking to from his mother on the equality of the races.

He was confused.

Bill gave Albert, now approaching his teens, an air rifle—over Eileen's most strenuous objections. One day he grew tired of the stationary target mounted on the garage. He began shooting at rabbits and squirrels. His mother scolded him, and confiscated the gun.

That led to the worst argument between his parents that Albert had witnessed to that point in his life. He was frightened by it. He would never forget it.

And he was further confused.

Albert's father never wavered in his determination to lead the boy into the priesthood—Bill's kind of priesthood.

Albert's mother steadfastly opposed this career choice.

It was a strange turnabout from the traditional Catholic family, in which, if there was any impetus to a boy's entering a seminary, almost without fail it was the mother who encouraged the child, while the father sought to discourage him.

Eileen, however, felt that entering a seminary at the present time was like booking passage on *Titanic*. This whole system of a cultic priesthood was going down the drain; anyone could see that. The priest shortage was nearly worldwide. It was reaching drastic proportions in America and was becoming critical even in Ireland, one of the most Catholic of nations.

Eileen could not begin to guess how it all would end. She wouldn't even have been concerned except that her husband was brainwashing her son to climb aboard what she considered a dead-end vocation.

In subtle ways Eileen tried to tip the scales away from the seminary. Meanwhile, Bill continued to take for granted Al's eventual ordination.

Albert was confused.

10 BY THE TIME Albert was ready for high school, his father had become a well-heeled attorney in one of the area's top law firms. The family now lived in the pricey suburb of Bloomfield Hills.

Albert was accepted by St. Mary's Preparatory at Orchard Lake.

There was method in the elder Cody's choice for his son. The complex of Lake schools included, in addition to the high school, St. Mary's College and Sts. Cyril and Methodius Seminary.

The religious atmosphere was almost palpable.

Though Bloomfield Hills was not far from the Lake, Al needed transportation. His mother became the designated driver. She was free to be such while Bill took on the rush-hour commute to and from downtown Detroit.

When the elder Cody had attended the Chicago seminary high school, there was not a girl to be seen. Now, Detroit's St. Joseph's Seminary did not even have a high school.

But St. Mary's covered both counts: It was all male and had a thoroughly religious atmosphere. Thus at a time when a youth's testosterone is raging, temptation is not at hand.

Now and again there might be a bit of masturbation. But masturbation didn't carry the threat of pregnancy. Fathering a child was definitely a no-no for a priest candidate. One more potential impediment to holy orders forestalled.

Eileen rather enjoyed her chauffeuring duties. Al didn't ordinarily run off at the mouth, but he did confide in his mother on their daily drives.

Later, the Codys moved to a high-rise in downtown Detroit. It was a move conveniently close to Bill's practice. But not at all convenient to Al's school at Orchard Lake. No matter. Bill insisted his son complete his high school education at St. Mary's Preparatory. In effect, all that changed was the length of Eileen's drive.

Actually, she treasured the extra time spent with her son. Eileen tried to sway her son away from his father's conservatism-bordering-on-fundamentalism. She endeavored to accomplish this without undermining the bond between father and son.

For they had bonded and it was a beautiful relationship qua relationship. But without his mother's strong humanizing influence, Al would have been merely a younger Bill: careless of life values, blind to the threat of racism and/or sexism.

Eileen had a difficult time identifying what it was about her husband she tried to shield Al from. In many ways Bill was a decent, even admirable man. Surely he was deeply committed to Catholicism, even if his faith was outdated. Indeed, that may have been at the root of the problem. His early training taught, for instance, that man was the head of the home and woman its heart. His interpretation of that gave a husband complete control over his wife. The husband made all important decisions autocratically. And the wife was supposed to love him for it.

According to Bill's determinate creed, God had placed the animal kingdom on earth for mankind's use or abuse. Animals were at the complete disposition of humans.

Bill's war experience further had eroded his respect for life. This was reflected in his attitude toward wrongdoers. Was someone guilty of homicide? "Fry him!" Convicted of a lesser crime? "Lock him up and throw away the key!"

Precisely because he so loved the Church of his youth, he was intolerant of most of the changes that had affected it since the despised Council. He would accept the English Mass only because there was no viable alternative.

That which he could not accept he derided.

He was easy to understand, but difficult to live with.

Mr. and Mrs. Cody were the odd couple who packaged their son.

Albert Cody tried to please his father and his mother. It was like hitching two horses to opposite ends of a chariot and expecting someone to drive it.

If Albert came home from a hunting trip with no game, his father was disappointed in him. His mother was thankful that her son had not killed.

On the rare occasion that Albert had a date, his mother encouraged him to have a good time, hoping that this might be the girl who would turn his head from the celibate state. Meanwhile his father took him aside to impress upon him, in vague generalities, the trouble he could get into if he didn't keep his distance.

All this repeated conflicting guidance took its toll.

Albert was a sorely confused boy. And his confusion led to his being in a constant state of anxiety and fear—fear that he would offend someone by making the wrong guess as to the right decision.

Albert was a prime candidate for psychotherapy. But it would never happen. His mother would probably understand—possibly even approve. His father would not hear of it. Men did not get analyzed. Women were the sole subjects for therapy, since women, by definition (from the Greek *hystera* [womb]), were the only ones who became hysterical. Men who sought or received therapy were "as weak as women."

So, for example, when Albert went out on the rare date, he was gentlemanly and respectful (for Mother) and distant (for Dad). Girls found Albert safe and boring.

There certainly was nothing wrong with Albert physically. At approximately five feet eight and likely to add another couple of inches as he matured, he was slender but well built. He avoided contact sports, competing against himself. He excelled at track and swimming. That way, he could be alone with himself while setting his pace and making the turns.

And, like Dad, Al wore his hair in an almost military brush cut. It was a statement.

Before graduating from high school, he completed driver's training and got his license. His father gave him a new Volvo. It was an expensive gift. But Dad firmly believed that, as long as the priest was "good"—loyal to the Pope and *vera doctrina*—nothing was too good for Father. That byword included his son, who, without question, would be a good seminarian and priest.

With satisfactory academic marks, very little maturation, and his virginity intact, Albert went on to college and the seminary.

Had he lived back in the fifties, at this stage of his life he would have been one of some nine hundred and fifty seminarians, almost all of whom would have been of minimum age for their grade years.

As it was, he was one of seventy-some seminarians of widely varying ages. Of the nonseminarian student body, the vast majority were women, mostly women of Al's age.

Albert had not had female classmates since grade school. He quickly concluded that college women were a very different consideration from elementary school girls.

Albert was confused.

He needed someone older and wiser to guide him through this traumatic time.

Enter William Page.

Someplace along the line of accommodating the shrinking number of seminarians, a rule was made that candidates must spend at least six years preparing for priesthood. This law allowed for few exceptions. If Latin had not been reduced to an elective course, preparation time might well have been longer.

William Page had a degree from Notre Dame, a university with a stellar reputation for scholarship, even with regard to its athletes. He also had many years' experience in advertising. Here at the seminary neither mattered.

Page and Cody were juniors in seminary college when they first met at St. Joseph's. Now, five-plus years later, they had spent a goodly amount of time together. Class size, in any subject offered, was small enough that the students got to know each other well.

From the very beginning of their relationship, Cody had deferred to Page in a dependent sort of way.

Page didn't mind. Cody's dependence was not of an

annoying nature. Besides, Page enjoyed Cody's gradual metamorphosis into gofer, researcher, ghostwriter, surrogate son—in sum, a creature only a few steps up from a flunky.

Cody was glad to perform small services. He had so much to learn. As the years rolled by and ordination neared, he grew more and more aware of his arrested adolescence. It seemed to him the seminary system was designed to slow his development.

In only a few more months, I will be a priest, he thought.

He compared himself with his mentor, Bill Page, who was old enough to be his father.

When the two talked, as they frequently did, it was clear that Page was ready on all counts to assume the new clerical role. He was of an age that he could realistically be called "Father"—if parishioners wished to so address him. Sure, a lot of them would be older than he . . . old enough even to be *his* father. Still, the span of the mid-forties was, objectively, an age of maturity.

Page also was ready for ordination theologically. Though he had no independent conviction about such matters, he had learned to rely on the theological bent of the majority of his seminary professors. Thus he was in complete conformity with the magisterium, i.e., the Pope.

It was a safe, comfortable path. The magisterium instructed you what to believe and what laws to obey. Believe this and do that and heaven is guaranteed you.

Page was ready.

Cody was not.

At his ordination, Cody would be all of twenty-five. Not a child by any means. Yet nowhere near as mature as contemporaries in the big, bad world. He had so little experience. Out there, men his age had begun a distinctively adult life. They had to hold down demanding jobs, into which they had to grow.

They were starting families, undoubtedly their primary responsibility. They had to budget their incomes—and they knew how. They knew the rules and regulations that governed their lives in the workplace as well as in the home.

Some belonged to Catholic parishes and attended Mass on Sunday. These—the Faithful—could be divided roughly into three groups: the main body of middle-of-the-roaders, the liberals, and the conservatives. Both of the latter were deeply—sometimes intensely—committed and involved in the Church structure on the diocesan and parochial levels.

Meanwhile, Albert Cody was still a student. He attended school—much the same sort of school he had attended on the elementary, high school, and college levels. He and his fellow students seldom questioned what they were taught. They learned basically from the magisterium. There was enough of this to tide them over from year to year.

Far from starting a family, Al Cody barely knew where babies came from. No matter how long he preached and taught, he would never completely grasp the responsibility of raising a family or holding down a job in order to provide that family stability and security.

All in all, unlike his mentor, Albert Cody felt childlike in relating to his coming parishioners. To them he would be "Father"—the way things were going in parochial life, probably "Father Al."

He would, of course, have to deal with the right, the center, and the left. But how? He had no convictions of his own, nothing he could depend upon. He was pretty sure he would be conservative to the right, liberal to the left, and at relative ease with the uncommitted.

He was confused. And he was afraid.

His only hope, as he saw it, was to depend on and learn from Bill Page.

They were an odd couple, in more than one respect. Page at approximately six feet was some inches taller than Cody. His oval face usually wore a bland expression. His seasoned eyes seemed older than the rest of him. They had seen a lot.

His dark brown hair was combed straight back. He was a tad overweight, soft from a life that had involved little physical exertion. He smiled effortlessly and often—like someone bent on selling you advertising space or time.

He made few friends. Which is why he had so much time for Albert Cody.

Page and Cody had overlingered in the dining room; it was time for evening study. Donnelly and Zawalich had long since departed and were in their respective rooms preparing for tomorrow's classes.

The two deacons rose. Page made a great show of the sign of the cross and a loud recitation of the grace after meals. Cody could not bring himself to follow suit. Even though he was preparing to lead prayer as a professional, he could not pray that ostentatiously. He finished his silent, almost surreptitious grace, and waited patiently for his companion to grind to a halt in his pretentious prayer.

As they left the dining room, Page said, "Hey, before we split for our rooms, let's go take a look at McNiff's door—the one that Donnelly mucked up."

Laughing conspiratorially, they made their way to the bishop's quarters.

Thanks to Andrea Zawalich's compulsive cleanliness, they were, of course, sadly disappointed.

11 THREE WEEKS PASSED. Things were settling
down into the sort of routine Father Koesler found
comforting.

When Koesler told Father Tully about the conversation he'd
had with Bishop McNiff and the bishop's invitation to help at
the seminary, Tully seemed relieved. This reaction surprised
Koesler.

Though Koesler was fully in accord with the school of thought
that said a retired pastor did not hang around his former parish,
still, he had been ready to make himself available to St. Joe's
parish as well as the seminary. It would have made for a busy
ministry, but he was sure he could handle it—he would even
welcome it. Especially in retirement, it was nice to be wanted.

He had not planned to remain in residence at the parish, but,
at Tully's invitation, had stayed on temporarily till he found another residence.

Tully, upon learning of McNiff's invitation, made it clear
that Koesler would be welcome anytime for any reason to bunk
at St. Joe's. And it would be great if Koesler would cover at
times when Tully was away on vacation or any other absence.

What Father Koesler found odd was that he would not be
needed for regular weekend fill-in.

Detroit pastors who successfully recruited or lucked into
such a commitment from outside counted their blessings.

But Father Tully was the pastor now, and could do what he
wished with this unexpected offer. If the new pastor handled
all the Masses, daily and weekends, the parishioners would be

getting the Gospel According to Tully. More and more these days one was apt to receive a personalized message from the pulpit. Homolists, in this postconciliar age, differed not only in their public speaking talent but also in their interpretation of the particulars of Church, State, and Scripture.

So, while Koesler did leave a few items of clothing behind at St. Joe's rectory, he had taken up residence more or less permanently in the seminary.

His responsibilities there were left ambiguous. He made himself available to the students, both M.Divs and nonseminarians. The students, for their part, approached him tentatively. He was an unknown factor. And until they discovered whether he represented the center, the left, or the right, a good bit of testing would take place.

Early on in his residence, he had volunteered to coach in the Homiletics program. Regretfully, that cut him off from the non-M.Divs, who were excluded from any course directly aimed at preparation for the priesthood.

However, Father Koesler was convinced that homilies, whether given for just a few minutes daily, or slightly longer on weekends, were among the most rewarding and important opportunities of priestly services. He wanted to give the students the benefit of his many years' experience along these lines.

Increasingly immersed in the students' lives, in this short three-week period, he had almost forgotten good old St. Joe's. Thus he was surprised when he got a call from Bill Cody. So surprised that at first, Koesler drew a blank. Cody? Who was Cody? As memory slowly widened, Koesler recalled first the brush cut; gradually a more detailed mental image of Bill Cody followed.

After meaningless pleasantries, Cody got down to business briskly: Could he meet with Koesler?

"Well, yes, of course. Is it urgent?"

"I think it is!"

"Care to tell me what it's about?"

Hesitation. Then, "Better to do this in person."

"Okay. When and where? I've got some time tomorrow afternoon. Or Wednesday morning. Breakfast? Lunch? Dinner?"

"How about tonight? Your room at the seminary. Say, seven-thirty?"

There's no such thing as a free lunch, thought Koesler. "Okay. You know how to get here?"

"Yes, yes, of course."

"I'll give your name to the guard, Bill. Security is pretty tight here."

"See you then. And thanks."

Koesler hung up and leaned back in his chair, lost in thought.

The wisdom of having a retired priest move out of his parish was being brought home to him for the first time.

Bill Cody was president of St. Joseph's parish council. He'd held the post for—what—about two years now?

The parish council was one of the first offspring of Vatican II. Its purpose, patently, was to give the laity a voice in running the parish.

But how large a voice? How much clout?

From the beginning, in many parishes, pastors and councils were at loggerheads. At times, open clashes left the pastor furious and the council frustrated. Now, after some thirty years of coexistence, there generally was a better rapport. Still, things could get dicey. This was especially true when a Bill Cody was on the parish council or, *a fortiori,* president of it.

Although it could be said that there never was much friction between pastor Koesler, and council president Cody, that was due largely to the liturgies Koesler conducted.

Everything was on the "A" list. The Scripture readings, the Mass prayers, the hymns—all were approved by the proper authorities.

Once a month—again locally approved after Vatican permission was granted—there was even a Latin Mass—and a choir trained and able to render both plainchant and polyphony. Bill Cody could have asked for little more.

Koesler, in the privacy of his room, chuckled. It was a good thing Mr. Cody had been unaware of what went on in the rectory where Church law was benignly interpreted to shield and free troubled souls.

Oh yes, Bill Cody would not have found Koesler's implementation of law intended for the preservation of the institution amusing.

As to the reason for Cody's rapidly approaching visit, Koesler could only guess. Bill's tone sounded barely controlled. This would not be a pleasant encounter. But then it was not Koesler's experience that people rang his doorbell to bring unqualified good news.

Whatever burr was under Cody's saddle, it probably had something to do with the parish.

It couldn't be anything that had taken place on Koesler's watch; Cody would have complained much earlier than this. So, what could it be?

Koesler checked his watch, something over the years that he did regularly and frequently. Time enough to find out at seven-thirty what was troubling Bill Cody. Meanwhile, Koesler donned cassock and collar—a custom resurrected by the present faculty and one with which he had no quarrel—and betook himself to the faculty lounge for an appetizer and a drink.

By and large the faculty might be a conservative lot, but Koesler enjoyed them and their spirited conversations. Although occasionally he wondered what they thought of him.

Face-to-face, at least, they were polite and courteous. They couldn't have agreed less with his opinions on the Church magisterium. And the teaching authority of the Church was the highest priority of their lives.

Perhaps their outward acceptance was a reaction to his friendship with the boss, Bishop McNiff.

As time ran on, Koesler was certain he would learn what was more important in this setting: *what* he knew or *who* he knew.

Although Father Koesler had been in residence for several weeks now, he had not yet dined with the faculty. He thought it wise to climb aboard gradually, so he'd eaten at restaurants or with friends. Tonight, he decided, he would mingle.

In the faculty parlor before dinner he joined a group discussing the pedophile charges that persisted against priests. The discussion had started before his arrival, so he merely listened.

One priest discounted the claims in general as being no more than a means of making a quick buck; so many of the dioceses affected tended to settle out of court. Kids now grown could accuse priests of long-ago molestation and, rather than go to trial, the diocese would pay serious amounts of dollars.

Most of the others in this group tended to agree, but with reservations. According to them, the out-of-court settlements were not a knee-jerk reaction to bad publicity, but an unpleasant matter of fact.

Another present wondered why any priest would commit such a serious sin, let alone crime.

The consensus seemed to focus on deficiency in prayer life. What did Jesus have to say about it? "This kind of devil does not leave but by prayer and fasting."

There followed a roundtable discussion.

"It's all a matter of money."

"Isn't everything?"

"Be serious. It started almost twenty years ago. That's when bishops petitioned the Holy See to allow laicization of priests under forty."

Koesler remembered the time during the present Pope's reign when the Vatican would not consider laicizing any priest—for any reason—before the priest reached age forty. Why forty? Koesler had never completely figured that out.

The discussion continued.

"Well, then the Roman congregation asked the Holy Father to consider 'exceptional reasons' for the dispensation. And you know what those exceptional reasons were?"

"I think so. But you seem to have researched this recently. Go ahead."

"Well, you needn't be so brusque. Anyway, the congregation wanted to get rid of any priest who had some form of defect that would invalidate his ordination."

"Just like in marriage."

"Exactly. Just as in a marriage that is annulled. There has to be a defect before and at the time of the marriage that makes the marriage invalid."

"I see. Say two people want to get married, but one of them has been married before. And the previous marriage is presumed valid. Then the second marriage cannot be valid because of the previous and present impediment."

"So, the burden of proof lies with the priest who alleges that his ordination is invalid because of some defect. Like he says he was forced into ordination."

"Mother won't talk to him if he doesn't get ordained?"

"That's one reason. But, a couple of years ago, the bishops asked for and got a further warrant for laicization. Under this category, they want Rome to rush through the laicization process for any priest involved in sexual misconduct or abuse. And you know why?"

"To get rid of him, I imagine."

"Exactly. Charges are being brought against a priest—and his diocese. And the diocese"—breaking into laughter—"is claiming, 'He isn't one of ours!' "

General laughter. Koesler looked troubled.

"You're not laughing, Bob," in a stern tone. "What's the matter? I think it's rather obvious—even ingenious. The diocese is served papers of intent to sue and, instead of being dragged into court or forced to settle out of court, the diocese goes on the attack. Isn't that better than giving up without a fight? Don't you consider that"—intensely argumentative—"a wise and long overdue course of action?"

Koesler cleared his throat. "I was just thinking about your comparison of a marriage annulment to a priest's laicization."

"And?"

"And, I was wondering . . . Church law never initiates an annulment procedure, does it? I mean, the process of securing an annulment always begins with the person who wants one."

"So you're saying . . . ?"

Koesler began to wonder how he'd gotten involved to this

degree. But he couldn't put on the brakes at this point. "What I'm saying is, Canon Law . . . nowhere in Canon Law does a marriage court, a tribunal, move to invalidate a marriage. The challenge to the validity of a marriage always comes from one or the other of the parties to the marriage.

"On the other hand, you were talking about a priest who is accused of child abuse—molestation. He doesn't question the validity of his ordination. But his bishop does. And his bishop wants the Church not only to judge that this priest's ordination was invalid, he wants Rome to be quick about it.

"I mean," Koesler continued, "it's possible for a marriage case to trickle on for months . . . years. All depending on whether the matter is being processed by a friendly diocese or one that is stonewalling—being deliberately slow. If the case has to go to Rome, then you're talking major league delay.

"But with a priest charged with sexual misconduct, his case goes to Rome—normally the most time-consuming and sluggish agency in a marriage case. And the Roman decision, unlike its procedure in an annulment"—Koesler had worked himself into an indignant mood—"is expected to be granted yesterday."

Koesler was gazing into five sets of unfriendly eyes.

After a brief, studied silence, one of the group said, "I suppose, Bob, you'd prefer that we join forces, circle the wagons, and deny all accusations."

"Well, no, of course not. Part of our problem now is the result of just such a reaction. We all know that some of our number have actually been guilty of this crime. And, far from facing up to the problem, the diocese just sends the priest to another parish, maybe another diocese . . . where the same thing happens all over again. Here's a case of both the priest and the victim or victims needing help.

"But it seems to me that throwing the guy out of the priesthood—retroactively—is not a constructive, loving, or Christian way of dealing with the problem."

Koesler's statement was followed by a couple of harumphs and several barely audible grumpings from his listeners.

It was time for dinner.

Koesler noted that no one was exactly walking with him down the corridor toward the refectory. Maybe, he thought, he ought to keep his comments in the yes-and-no category—at least until he got a better appreciation of who was to the right or left of whom.

Dinner, as usual, was cafeteria-style. After Koesler had filled his plate, he looked around for a place to sit. He turned just in time to see the five faculty members he'd been talking to in the parlor. They were in the process of inviting another faculty member to join them. That filled that table of six.

Was it his imagination, or was he being shunned?

He scanned the room and found a table just forming. He would be the sixth—that is, if they let him join them.

They did.

One of his tablemates was a permanent deacon. He was not a full member of the faculty. He was in charge not only of the diaconate program but also of the required classes for deacon candidates.

Evidently the deacon and the others were continuing a conversation begun in the parlor. It concerned one Henry Sawyer, another deacon who had recently become a widower.

"Poor Henry," the deacon said. "I think his age did him in."

Koesler looked up from his plate, a forkful of potatoes poised in midair. He was confused. Was it the death of the husband that had created a widow? Or the wife's passing that made the deacon a widower? In either case, Koesler was not going to question this odd statement.

But it did bring to mind one of the more glaring blunders made in many parishes when praying at Mass for special intentions. The error concerned burying the wrong person—as in, "Let us pray for Andrew Brown, the father of Edward Brown who was buried from this church last week." If that prayer were correct, poor Eddie Brown had been buried alive.

However, Koesler remained determinedly silent, hoping that the question of who had died would be resolved in the succeeding conversation.

Light was cast on the subject by another faculty member's

question: "Well, why in the world would he want to get married again anyway?"

That sparked some less than pious repartee.

"To find relief from concupiscence."

"Henry? Why, Henry must be in his—what?—eighties?"

"Eighty-seven!"

"That's why I said that his age did him in," the deacon asserted. "He doesn't fit into any of the three categories for a dispensation."

"Will someone tell me what you're talking about?" This from an elderly priest who, till now, had not spoken.

The deacon attempted an explanation. "It's about remarriage, Father. Married men can be ordained to the permanent diaconate. But if such a man becomes a widower—or if he's divorced, for that matter—he can't get married again."

"That's silly!" said the elderly priest.

The comment shocked Koesler. Not because the priest's statement seemed inappropriate; Koesler just was not used to this faculty's making common sense. Then he recalled: The elderly priest was one of the three reputedly liberal members of the faculty.

The deacon grew defensive. "I wouldn't call it silly, Father. It's a law of our holy Church. And we permanent deacons understand this very well before we're ordained. Any deacon who is married at the time of ordination, and who then loses his wife, cannot marry again. The diaconate becomes an impediment to remarriage."

"Then," asked the elderly priest, "why would you say Henry's age did him in? What's his age got to do with it?"

"Because . . ." The deacon gave every indication that his food was cooling and he would rather eat than talk. ". . . our Holy Father, about a year ago, ruled that there were three conditions for the remarriage of deacons. He said that a dispensation is possible if any one of the three is present."

"Pray tell, what might these three compelling reasons be?" The elderly priest was smiling, enjoying something. Either the absurdity of the argument or forcing the deacon to delay his supper.

The deacon managed a bite and answered while still chewing. "The first condition: 'the great and proven usefulness of the ministry of the deacon to the diocese to which he belongs'; the second, 'that he has children of such a tender age as to be in need of motherly care'; and third, 'that he has parents or parents-in-law who are elderly and in need of care.' "

"That's silly," the elderly priest repeated himself.

"What's so silly about it, Father?" The deacon was growing testy. But the question might well have been his way of borrowing time to eat before his dinner got stone cold.

"Well, take the second condition, for instance: The kids are so young they need a mother."

"So?"

"So kids need a mother their whole life long. There are a whole bunch of guys whose wives die and they need a wife and their kids need a mother. There are a whole bunch of guys who aren't deacons or priests who lose their wives and they never find another mate. So, they muddle through. It's silly to make remarriage be dependent on kids needing a mother."

The deacon forgot there was food in his mouth. "It's our Holy Father you're talking about!"

"I guess there was a time in his life when *he* needed a mother. Only he wouldn't have had to wait for his father to get a dispensation to go looking for a wife."

"Well!"

"And take the third condition. Same as the second. The deacon's wife dies and his parents or her parents are old and need care."

"What's wrong with that?"

"His wife dies and he goes looking not for a wife or a mother for his kids, but for somebody who will marry him and take care of the old folks. He's not looking for a wife; he wants somebody who works in a nursing home."

"But—"

"And as for the first condition—the usefulness of his ministry has been great and proven—I know what they're going to ask downtown. 'How many hospitals did he build?' 'How much money did he give to the diocese?' Something along that line."

"But—"

"And on top of all that, you said that a dispensation from the impediment to marriage was 'possible,' didn't you?"

"Well . . . yes, that's true, but—"

"That means a guy could meet one of those cockamamie conditions and still not get permission. So, I go back to my original statement: This is silly."

The deacon stood abruptly, and threw his napkin on the table. "I've lost my appetite." He stormed out of the dining room.

Several moments of silence followed at his table as well as at adjoining ones. The elderly priest did not seem particularly contrite. Finally, he looked across the table. "You're Bob Koesler, aren't you?"

"Yes."

"It's been so long since we last got together that I nearly forgot you." He extended his hand. "I'm Paul Burke. What do you think of all this, Bob?"

"Interesting." Koesler was wary of falling into another trap. "But I don't understand why poor Henry, whoever he is—or was—was done in by his age."

"Oh," a nearby priest said, "even—maybe especially—a man Sawyer's age would appreciate a wife who would care for him. If she was elderly too, they could care for each other.

"The point is, the choice is taken away from a guy like Sawyer.

"Sawyer certainly isn't indispensable to the diocese. He's not likely to have young children who need a mother. And"— he grinned—"if Sawyer's parents are still living—well, they don't need him; they could make a mint appearing on talk shows, or on the lecture circuit."

His listeners chuckled.

"So," the priest concluded, "Henry sort of slipped between the cracks." He offered Koesler his hand. "Cliff Rogers. You don't remember me. I was several years behind you in the seminary."

"And you teach . . . ?"

"Homiletics."

"Oh yes." Koesler recognized the name as that of another liberal member of the faculty. What were the odds of having two thirds of the faculty liberals at the same table? Then again, why not; they probably huddled together to stay warm.

"So," said Burke, "Henry slipped through the cracks?"

"Isn't it sort of obvious?" Rogers said. "Especially after you put flesh and blood on the three conditions. Henry was way too old to have either dependent children or dependent parents. And Henry lived almost hand-to-mouth, so he wasn't likely to build any hospitals or bail out the archdiocese."

"I still say it's silly!" Burke emphasized.

"I couldn't argue that," Rogers agreed.

"It's this preoccupation the Vatican has with marriage," Burke stated. "Why in the world would a widower not be allowed to remarry just because he's a widower? It makes no sense. A guy gets married. Then he becomes a deacon. Then his wife dies. Everybody else—except another deacon, apparently—would be free to marry again. But not this deacon."

"You know," Koesler said, "it's the same with these married Anglican priests and other Protestant ministers who convert to Catholicism. If their wives die, they can't remarry."

"Actually," Rogers said, "that this Roman congregation gives the deacon widowers *any* escape clauses is a big break for them."

"If that's a break," Burke said, "I'd hate to think what they'd have to do without the three conditions!"

"Quite simply," Rogers explained, "if they wanted to remarry, they'd have to try to get through the laicization process. Just like a priest would. And the chances in either petition of getting 'reduced to the lay state' are mighty slim.

"As a matter of fact," Rogers continued, "about the same time last year as the Vatican gave the deacons a break, they also gave one to ex-priests—at least, in both cases, the Vatican considers it a gift."

"Doesn't ring a bell," Burke said. "That one must've gotten by me."

"I thought it was weird at the time," Rogers said, "and I haven't any reason to doubt my original reaction." He turned to Koesler, then back to Burke. "See if this makes any sense to either of you.

"A guy leaves the priesthood. He doesn't get laicized— either he doesn't apply for it, or, more likely, they refuse him. Then he gets married. Since he's not laicized, the marriage is invalid and he's excommunicated. Then he falls ill; now he's in danger of death.

"Next, they throw this condition into the procedure: His marriage has to be capable of being convalidated. Which nine times out of ten means the wife has to be free to marry—no previous marriage or anything like that. Then the bishop has to send the request for a dispensation to Rome. And, mind you, it's a *request*, a petition—so it's still possible that even though the guy is dying, the Congregation won't bail him out."

"And if he doesn't go through this process, or if it's too late, or if it's turned down . . ." Burke asked, "what then?"

Rogers shrugged. "I suppose they'd deny him Christian burial. What more could they do to him at that point?"

"I remember hearing about that set of circumstances," Koesler said. "It didn't seem fair."

"What's fair and what's foul," said Rogers, "depends on the umpire's call."

"In baseball as in theology, it seems," commented Burke.

"Besides," Rogers said, "the ultimate explanation, if we care for the solution given by the recently departed deacon, is that we knew what we were getting into before we got ordained."

"Maybe, maybe not," said Koesler. "Those of us who were ordained before the Council had no way of knowing what was coming . . . how much things would change."

Burke nodded. "That's true."

"Virtually no one was retiring," Koesler said. "I've just recently retired—something I thought I'd never do. Another big change was priests resigning. I'll bet they never thought it would be so tough to get released from the obligations of the priesthood."

"So," Burke said, "unlike the permanent deacons who had everything spelled out clearly for them before they were ordained, the priests who've left maybe didn't know what they were getting into."

Burke shook his head slowly. "Silly rules!" he said, barely audibly.

12

HITHERTO, FATHER KOESLER had kept a comparatively low profile.

Coming fresh from retirement and being a classmate and friend of the rector, he did not want to give the impression that he was at the seminary as some sinister force. For, indeed, such was not the case.

So, other than periodic chats with McNiff, an occasional student consultation, and helping out in Homiletics, when Koesler wasn't catching up on visitations or taking in a few movies and plays, he pretty much stayed in his room, answering correspondence and indulging in the luxury of reading.

But now he was in the water.

As for the seminary faculty, most of the members were too young for him to know. Priests, especially, knew their older confrères at least by name. Younger priests were a vast unknown. Those priests on the faculty who were Koesler's age or older, such as Father Burke, had been immersed in this subculture so long they scarcely remembered priests in the outside world. And vice versa. As for the deacons and lay faculty, men and women, Koesler had never had occasion to know or even meet them.

All that would change now. He would mingle. He would try to inject a measure of tolerance and moderation into these rock-ribbed people.

Koesler had just gotten a taste of the two camps. It was not encouraging.

After a postprandial cordial, Koesler meandered back to his

room. He thought over the conversations he had heard and the ones in which he had, at least partially, participated.

If one could trust this evening's samplings to reflect the conservative majority's opinion, there was a long way to go before everyone could be open-minded, let alone indulgent and merciful.

If a priest was in trouble and that trouble was likely to cost the diocese large sums of money, dump the man! Thus not only washing one's hands of him but denying that he was ever a validly ordained priest.

In the case of deacons who lost their wives—surely a crushing blow—those who wished to remarry had to fit into at least one foreordained condition before they could even petition for permission. And there was no guarantee that permission would be granted. This seemingly arbitrary rule was justified by the cold explanation: He knew what he was getting into.

Finally, the case of an excommunicated priest in a canonically invalid marriage. If he is in danger of death he can apply for a laicization decree and a convalidation of his marriage. All of that to qualify for Christian burial, with no guarantee that permission will be granted or that he will live long enough for the procedure to be completed.

So much for the conservative majority.

As for the liberal minority: Once they got the head deacon on the defensive, they pursued the matter unrelentingly.

Not a lot of tolerance. And certainly not any mercy.

Koesler wondered where this might end.

He was about to pass the rector's office when he hesitated, then decided to knock.

"Come in." Loud voice, bored tone.

Koesler entered. "I was concerned about you. You weren't at dinner."

"But *you* were." McNiff smiled mischievously. "I have my spies."

Koesler shook his head in mock despair. "Okay, so you

knew I wasn't going to join you, as is our occasional custom. How come you played hermit?"

McNiff, his desk covered with books and papers, sat back in his chair. "Two things. I had some work to do. Plus I wanted you to mingle with the faculty without my being around."

Koesler nodded.

"How'd it go?"

"Pretty well, I guess. But it's going to be hard to stay neutral."

"Sit down, why don't you?" McNiff indicated a chair near the desk.

"Can't. There's a guy coming to see me . . . from the old parish—St. Joe's."

"Anything I can do to help?"

Koesler shook his head. "I don't think so. Actually, I don't know yet what he wants. But I'll keep in mind that you offered . . . just in case.

"And you . . . you're feeling okay?"

"Yeah. Like I said, paperwork, and leaving you to get acquainted. I've got a microwave; I'll heat something up in a little while. If you get done, come on down later on. We can chat, and split a cool one."

Koesler inclined his head to one side. "I thought you were off the sauce."

"I am. But I've got some pop in the fridge. And the makings for just about anything you want."

"Okay . . . if it's not too late." Koesler turned to leave.

"By the way," McNiff said, "did you notice my door?"

Koesler studied the door, then turned the knob, opened it, and stepped out in the hall, where he stood examining the outside of the bishop's door as if he'd never seen it before. "Okay. So?"

"It's clean."

Koesler looked at McNiff quizzically.

"It's been clean ever since it was scrubbed after Donnelly dumped supper all over it," McNiff clarified.

"What did you expect?" Koesler said. "Somebody had to clean it."

"Not so. It was just as likely to remain in status quo until the whole mess became part of the wood."

"Well, in that case"—Koesler bowed his head in acknowledgment—"congratulations."

"I know Donnelly didn't clean it up . . . though she should've. Somebody from the kitchen told me she dumped the empty dishes off and ate her own supper. Somebody else cleaned it up before it congealed. I haven't been able to find Donnelly to ask her. If you come across her, find out, will you? Such attention to a job that needs doing should not go unrewarded."

"Okay. I'll find out for you."

Why hadn't McNiff found out for himself? It couldn't be that difficult.

But it was a minor request, and Koesler would look into it.

He continued down the hall to his own room and let himself in.

Technically it was a suite. But to his mind that term connoted something a whit more elegant than this hodgepodge. His quarters consisted of a bedroom, something that might be called a den or a sitting room, and a bathroom with shower, toilet, and sink.

It seemed comfier than it actually was because most of the furniture was his own.

No sooner had he settled in than the security guard rang to announce the arrival of his guest. Having ascertained that Cody knew the way, the guard sent him on up to Koesler's room.

Koesler was experiencing bad vibes over this appointment. No specific reason, just a hunch.

From the first parish council meeting after Bill Cody's election as president, he had given notice that his would be a hands-on presidency. And so it had been.

As far as Koesler's pastoral role went, there was little if any friction between pastor and president. Indeed, Cody had been extremely helpful in offering advice and guidance in several legal matters.

This suited Koesler perfectly. He had no legal skills and he appreciated Cody's help and guidance.

The parish liturgies were well planned and effectively presented. They were about as traditional as they could be, given the prevalence of the vernacular and the increased participation of the congregation.

There were no Folk Masses to speak of. So few children or young people attended Mass that there was no groundswell of support and thus no call for them.

Koesler had the feeling that anything even faintly resembling a Pentecostal Folk Mass would have ignited a strong, relentless, hostile reaction from Bill Cody, and—under his leadership—from several other council members as well.

Koesler considered himself fortunate that Cody's interest in St. Joseph's parish was limited to the liturgies and to any financial or legal questions that affected the parish.

Conceivably, it was Cody's legal training that kept him at a good arm's length as far as the counseling and sacramental services Koesler offered. These, Cody believed, constituted information even more privileged than lawyer-client confidentiality.

In the end, what with the satisfactory liturgies and respect for inviolability, the relationship between Koesler and Cody was practically trouble free.

Then why these vibes?

This was not going to be a cordial meeting between old friends. Something was amiss.

There was a knock at the door. Koesler invited Cody into his parlor.

They settled in, facing each other across Koesler's desk, and exchanged pleasantries after Cody had declined a drink. "Have you seen Al yet?" Cody asked.

Koesler hesitated for a fraction of a second. In his preoccupation with trying to figure out the purpose of Cody's visit, it had slipped his mind that Cody's son, Al, was a student in this seminary.

"No, I haven't. I meant to, but I'm still getting settled here. Of course Al is tops on my agenda, but also, I have to make it clear to the students generally that I'm here for them. They can come to talk or whatever. It'll just take a little time."

Cody pursed his lips. "Why did you do it, Father?" Cody would never call him Bob; he too respected the office. "I mean, why did you accept this assignment? You're retired. And you worked hard . . . I can testify to that."

" 'Why?' " Koesler searched for a way to explain. "I did it for a friend."

Cody looked wonderingly at the priest. "You gave up retirement for a friend? That's hard for me to understand."

Koesler smiled broadly. "Don't get the wrong impression, Bill. I don't know how much more time God will give me. I hope it'll be a lot. But I don't really expect to do this until I drop. The help I may be able to contribute here will either take effect or not within the next several months."

Cody stared at the floor briefly, then looked up. "Well, let me ask you this. You've been a priest for . . ."

"Almost forty-five years."

"A long time. You can look back now on a lot of service. Was it happy? Were you happy?"

Koesler paused to reflect on the question. It had been thoughtfully proposed; it deserved a thoughtful response. "Everybody's life is a mixed bag, I think," he said finally. "There've been times when I've been extremely discouraged. Times of loneliness. But I guess the conclusion is: If I had to do it over again, I'd do it just the way I have done it. So, in a nutshell, I think I can say yes. It's been a happy life."

Cody silently considered the statement.

Koesler wondered at the question—a question a lot more personal than any that Bill Cody had ever asked him. Was this the urgency, Koesler wondered, that Cody had advanced when he proposed this meeting?

Koesler thought he knew the answer. "Is your concern about Al?"

Cody nodded. "He's got just a few more months till ordination." He gazed fixedly at Koesler. "I know all about the priests who defected. But I consider the priesthood something that goes beyond the grave. That's the way I've raised my son. It's certainly no secret to Al that I would be the happiest guy in the world if he became a priest.

"I've prepared him for this from the beginning. By the time he got to college, he was ready. I knew he could make it academically. I knew he had the self-discipline. I saw that he dated during high school. But I warned him that women and the priesthood don't mix.

"He is the most important thing in my life."

Koesler had long been aware of, and disturbed by, Cody's monopolization of Al's upbringing and training. Not once had Bill mentioned his wife, Eileen, and the powerful influence she must have had on the boy.

But Koesler quickly decided to let Bill set the direction for this meeting.

"The point I'm making, Father, is that Al is ready for the call." His expression was grim. "I do not intend for anyone to block his path or turn him aside."

Koesler had never heard any comparable statement from a parent of any seminarian. Was it a threat? A challenge?

Koesler returned to a prior point. "Are you concerned whether Al will be happy in the priesthood?"

"To a degree, yes. In my opinion, you're a good priest."

Koesler almost blushed. "Thank you."

"You do your job as a priest and you do it pretty well," Cody said. "Considering that—well, coming from the pre-Council Church and living through this plastic age of the Church, as far as I can see, you're a good priest.

"And you just confirmed my opinion that you're happy being the kind of priest you are.

"That's what I want for Al. I want him to be a good and a happy priest. That's what I've formed in him. And I will not appreciate it if anyone gets in the way of Al's being a good and happy priest."

Koesler leaned forward in obvious concern. "You speak as if you know of someone who might do that."

Cody's brow knitted. "This rector!" His tone was that of a physician identifying the location of a cancer. "I've had my eye on him for five years—since the day he became a bishop.

And from some of the things Al tells me he's said . . . well, I'm telling you, Father: Bishop McNiff is *suspect*!"

Koesler was unsure how to respond. He decided to take Cody seriously. "Bill, don't worry about Bishop McNiff. He's a classmate of mine, and he's very conscientious."

"I wish I could be as convinced as you are. But I've heard that McNiff is soft on things like liberation theology and easy divorce and annulments . . . a whole shopping list of things condemned by the Pope—"

"Wait, Bill. I doubt the Pope has a more faithful follower than Pat McNiff. I know him well, and I can assure you that the last thing on Pat McNiff's mind and agenda is a return to the days following the Council—when it didn't seem possible for things to change any faster than they were."

Cody nodded once acceptingly. "I'll take your word on that, Father. But I should tell you that if it were completely up to me, Al would be joining the Jesuits."

"Really!" Koesler thought he could make an educated guess as to why the Jesuits.

"I wasn't so interested in them as teachers or missionaries, but—"

"That special vow of fealty they make to the Pope . . . right?"

"Yes. That's it. Although lately, it seems even *they* are cutting corners on their obedience to the Holy Father. So I suppose Al is just as well off here in this diocesan seminary. Over the years I've checked things out. And there are only a few teachers here that are at all suspect. Which is not a bad average. Then this Bishop McNiff comes from out of nowhere. And I'm just not sure . . ."

"For one thing, Bill, the rector is only one person."

"I know. I know. But a rector has a lot of clout."

Koesler had no reason to argue over the role McNiff continued to play in the orderly transformation of this seminary. Bill Cody feared that the rector was a crashing liberal. But whatever Bishop McNiff was, he was *not* that. "Has Al said anything to you about this?"

Cody shook his head. "No. Neither of us has broached the matter."

"How about Eileen? Is it possible he's talked to her about it?"

Cody's jaw clenched, then just as quickly relaxed. "No. He's not as close to his mother as he is with me."

"But, Bill, you just said neither you nor Al have talked about the new rector. How would you know whether he and Eileen did or didn't discuss it?"

"I'd know!" The matter was closed.

"I accept your evaluation of this matter, Father," Cody said after a moment. "There's just one more thing that troubles me about this place."

"What would that be?"

"There's another deacon here who I think exercises quite a bit of influence over Al."

"Oh?"

"A William Page. He's an older man."

"So many in this seminary are."

"This guy is a graduate of Notre Dame University. He had a career in advertising. Now he's about to become a priest."

"There's a lot of that going around, Bill. Some of the better sources for vocations are older men. Call it a mid-career change. Whatever. There are quite a few who are bankers, architects, technicians, lawyers like yourself, even travel agents. You never know where they'll be coming from. If it hasn't already happened, I think it will happen soon that people Al's age—which used to be the norm for seminarians—are going to be in the vast minority."

"Do you mind if I walk around a bit?" Cody anticipated no problem; he was already standing.

"Sure. Go ahead. I'm just sorry I can't provide more room for pacing."

"It's all right." Cody was not long on the light touch. "I understand about the delayed vocations. And I think the jury's still out on that one. But I was interested in Page particularly . . . only because Al seemed so taken with him."

"Did you come up with anything?"

"I think so. I have some friends in various agencies. I asked around."

"And?"

"And, it turns out that William Page started strong—as most Notre Dame graduates do. Then things got tough. He was losing more accounts than he was selling. In short, he was headed for bankruptcy.

"Then he started talking about how he'd always wanted to go to the seminary and become a priest. Bottom line: He talked a great seminary but never went to one.

"So, he joined this seminary for a six-year course—the minimum training required for a delayed vocation. Six years! Hell, when I was a kid it was twelve years—through high school, college, and the theologate."

"Me too, Bill. But even in my day, when young men were ordained ordinarily at about twenty-five, give or take a year or two, there were still delayed vocations, some of whom made it every bit as well as the rest of us."

Cody nodded throughout Koesler's statement. There was something more to be said, and Cody was going to say it.

"My point, Father, is that I believe this Page fellow is looking for a life preserver in rough waters. He wants to be a priest for the only reason that will motivate him—financial security. And he thinks he'll find it in the priesthood. That spells out the kind of priest he'll be . . . mark my word."

"That's quite a charge, Bill."

"I know. And I know that it's hearsay. And I know that hearsay is not allowed in a court of law. But we're not in a court of law. This is your room and I trust you with what's said in here."

Koesler nodded. "There's nothing I could do about what you've said. Precisely because it *is* hearsay . . . whose, by the way?"

"Some of these agents I mentioned. Seems Page likes to talk. He also likes to brag. They opened up to me because I asked them directly . . . and because they are my friends."

Koesler's fingers built a pyramid. "What, if anything, do you expect me to do about this?"

"Just be aware of it. Didn't you say you'd soon be talking with Al?"

"Yes."

"See if you can find out how much influence this Page has with my boy. I'm not asking that any sort of charges be brought against Page. What this faculty does about Page— whom I consider to be a featherbedder and a fraud—well, that's their business. I just want to protect my boy." Cody ceased pacing and stood, almost menacingly, over Koesler. "And, by damn, I will!"

Koesler was somewhat taken aback by Cody's vehemence. But before he could say anything, Cody, still standing, continued. "There's one more thing I found out about Page. And I'm telling you this because I don't want you wasting your time questioning it."

Koesler nodded, and listened intently.

"Whatever screening procedure you have for candidates to the seminary, I'm sure you didn't go into Page's background as thoroughly and carefully as I have."

"I'm not sure what the procedure is now, but it's got to be more thorough than we went through," Koesler pointed out. "In our day, we took a standard test. Brought in some documentation—a copy of our parents' Church wedding certificate, our baptism and confirmation records. We had a brief interview with one of the faculty members. That was about it. On the strength of the test and the interview we were accepted or rejected.

"I'm sure we go into the candidate's life a lot more deeply than that nowadays."

Cody started pacing again. "Yeah, the interview is more thorough, I'll give you that. But you don't go checking to get an actual report on the guy's lifestyle."

"What—?"

"My antenna went up several degrees when I found out that Page was in his forties when he applied here. And he'd never married. He's willing to live a celibate life among men."

"You thought he might be gay? That's a condition they look into in the screening—that I know."

"But they don't go out and check into it. I *did*! It's true he's never married. It's also true he's had something like the girl-of-the-month. He's not gay. He might be trying to become the father of our country."

"Even if this is true—"

"It's true!"

"Okay, it's true. But that's not to say a person can't change or mature."

"Oh, I'll admit change can happen. But for Page to give up his seduction of women would be like Larry King becoming a Trappist monk."

Koesler was about to respond when, uncharacteristically, Cody held up a silencing hand. "Don't get me wrong, Father. I'm not entirely concerned that Page is a womanizer. At least he's not trying to enter into a gay relationship with my son. If there was a chance in hell of that happening, well . . ."

Koesler, of course, understood the uncompleted ultimate threat, but shuddered to contemplate it.

"But I would be concerned if Page were to infect Al with the physical side of sex—even if it was heterosexual.

"My boy, Father, is right where I want him to be. The only threat I can see to Al's becoming a happy and fulfilled priest for a lifetime of service comes at this moment from William Page.

"Your paths may cross, Father. I mean you and Page. If you sense there is any trouble that he is making for Al . . . I want you to threaten his ordination."

"But—"

"No." Cody would not be contradicted. "Trust me, Father. Page wants one thing above everything else—including women—and that's to float through life, free of worry, as a priest. Trust me on this one: He will do anything to get ordained. After that . . . ?" Cody shrugged. "After that . . . well, once he's a priest, all bets are off.

"The big thing for me, anyway, is that whatever Page does *after* he's ordained likely will not influence Al. But for now till their ordination day, if Page wants to get there in one piece, he'd better stay the hell away from my son.

"And that's about all I want to say about that!"

On that unequivocal note, Koesler felt sure this matter was concluded. Cody could scarcely have been more explicit. Koesler would make contact with Al Cody, befriend him if he seemed to feel in need of a friend.

As for Bill Page, the water was murkier. At this juncture, Koesler quite possibly knew more about the Reverend Mr. Page than did any faculty member. Whether or not the senior Cody's appraisal would prove accurate only time would tell. Meanwhile, Koesler would keep a weather eye out for developments.

In any case, for the moment it seemed that all of Bill Cody's concerns had been addressed. "Okay," Koesler said. "I would have seen Al in the course of events anyway. After all, he is a former parishioner. I'll just make our visit sooner rather than later. Thanks for coming in and telling me about all this." He was getting to his feet when Cody motioned him back down. "Please bear with me some more. I wanted to tell you about Al, but that's not the main reason I'm here."

13

FATHER KOESLER WAS reminded of a story told by a priest-professor from his seminary days.

That priest had related that there were times when one or another seminarian would request an appointment, during which the student would go on and on, rambling from topic to topic: war to sports to politics and the like.

Then, after the first hour or so, the priest-professor, unable to pinpoint what in this unholy mess was bothering the student, would be on the verge of concluding the tête-à-tête. At which point, the student would announce, "By the way, I'm quitting." Presenting a topic worth several more hours of study and counseling.

He wanted to talk to me about Al, Koesler reflected, and only now he gets to the main point.

Even Cody's body language was eloquent. While talking about his son, he had first sat quietly in his chair, then gotten up and paced, which showed disquiet.

But now he had arrived at the main item on his agenda. Which was . . . ?

It could have been his relationship with his wife, always volatile. Or maybe it had to do with his practice of law. Or perhaps something about St. Joseph's parish. If Father Koesler had to bet, it would be on the last of those possibilities.

Cody actually pulled his chair adjacent to the desk and rested his elbow on the desktop. His head was only inches from Koesler's.

The priest's instinctive reaction was to lean back, away from

Cody's intensity. But he quickly decided to go along with Cody's choreography. "So, what is it, Bill?"

"It's our parish!"

Bingo!

"Have you been back to our parish since your vacation?" Cody pressed.

"Yes. But it's not 'our' parish. It may be yours, the pastor's, and the other parishioners', but it's no longer mine. I'm retired, remember?"

"Of course. But not so long ago you were the pastor. You gave us a lot of yourself. You can't tell me you've lost all interest in Old St. Joe's."

Koesler hesitated. This was leading to something. And he wanted to avoid entrapment. "Of course I haven't forgotten St. Joe's. But I'm no longer responsible for it. If you've got a problem, Bill, you should go to the pastor."

"The pastor *is* the problem."

Now Koesler did lean back. And he fell silent. Right around the next bend in this conversation lurked a dilemma. He could see it coming.

"You said that you've been back at St. Joe's since your vacation."

"That's right."

"Well, I'd wager you haven't attended a weekend Mass since you got back."

Koesler made no reply.

"Well, have you?"

"I'm sorry; I didn't realize there was a question there. You just said you'd bet I haven't been at a weekend liturgy since my return. I couldn't bet with you since I know the outcome: No, I haven't been there on a weekend.

"In fact I only just returned when I received a message that Bishop McNiff wanted to see me. That's when he invited me to live here, teach a little here, and—as one fuddyduddy to another—keep him company. By swapping stories of the good old days, presumably.

"I didn't want to commit to the bishop's invitation until I had cleared things with Father Tully.

"I don't know whether you're aware of this, Bill, but the Detroit archdiocese has a rule that discourages retired priests from remaining in their former parish. And, to be perfectly frank, I agree with that policy.

"But I offered to help Father Tully until he felt perfectly comfortable in my old parish—his new parish. I didn't think staying there temporarily would violate the spirit of the rule.

"I must say I was a bit surprised when Father Tully—graciously—declined my offer. I'm sure you know—probably better than anyone else, with your son about to be ordained—priests are hard to come by these days. During my years as a pastor, I've had a couple of priests volunteer to help out. And I can assure you, in each case, I accepted practically before the offer left the priest's mouth.

"As I say, Father Tully was very gracious about it. But he did send me on my way.

"And just in case he ever did need me to help—and if I should be available—he suggested that I leave some of my stuff in my old room in the rectory. And so I have.

"And that, William, is the state of the parish as far as my being a part of it. I'm not punching a time clock here at the seminary, but this is as close to a full-time ministry as I have right now.

"As for St. Joe's, it's a great old place. I enjoyed my years as pastor. But they're over now. I've got a toothbrush and some stuff in the rectory. But, as they say, I'm outta there. Father Tully's running the show."

"Right into the ground," Cody said, with some bite.

"What?"

"You say that you were surprised when Father Tully turned down your offer of help. I think you should've been more than surprised; you should have looked into what would motivate Father Tully to decline your offer."

"It didn't occur to me for an instant—"

"Can you think of any other priest-pastor doing that? Rejecting out of hand this kind of proposition? In this day and age?"

Koesler gave it a moment's thought. "I can think of a priest or two whose offer I could and would turn down."

"Because . . . ?"

"Because they're wacko."

"But that's not the case between you and Father Tully."

"No. We respect each other. You'll recall that when I was on vacation I entrusted the parish to Father Tully. I assure you I would not have done so without having a great trust in him."

A momentary smile. "I remember that vacation. It was the first time in anyone's memory that you took any time off. I don't know if anyone ever told you, but your parishioners were well aware of your dedication.

"The more involved parishioners still joke about how you phoned the rectory every day—sometimes more than once a day—from Canada . . . just to make sure everything was copacetic."

Koesler grinned. "I couldn't help myself."

"So you trusted and respected Father Tully, but you checked on him the whole time you were away."

For an instant Koesler had forgotten that Bill Cody was a very successful attorney. He was building an argument here, and Koesler had been walking into a trap. "Bill"—Koesler spoke with great sincerity— "I would have done that no matter who had spelled me while I was away."

"I'm sure that's true. But does Father Tully have a similar trust and respect for you?"

"I'm sure—I'm certain—he does."

"Then why would he refuse your offer?"

"Because he didn't need my help, I suppose." Koesler raised his hands and shrugged. "We have three Masses on the weekend—one late Saturday afternoon, two Sunday morning. That isn't a backbreaking schedule—especially for one as young as Father Tully. For heaven's sake, I did it for years, and quite obviously it didn't kill me.

"Besides, speaking at all the Masses gives a sense of continuity and constant direction to the congregations. I assume that's why Father Tully didn't need me: He should be able to preside over three masses in two days with no ill effects whatever."

"You haven't been back, Father," Cody reminded him. "Father Tully isn't presiding over three Masses in two days." Cody paused and drew closer to Koesler. "He is presiding over *four* Masses!"

Koesler's mouth dropped open, something that frequently happened when he was startled or surprised. "He added a Mass?"

"Yes."

"Well, now, that does give one pause. The three Masses we had seemed adequate."

"I can remember when you first came here, Father, the congregations at both daily and weekend Masses were very slim. You built them to a respectable size."

Koesler dismissed the compliment with a wave of his hand. "The priest who preceded me was busy about lots of worthwhile enterprises. He didn't have time to give a lot of attention to the parish. It wasn't his fault that attendance was down."

"Yes, but you went around the town houses and high-rises and rang doorbells." He smiled. "You even rang mine—figuratively."

Koesler well remembered. He remembered with mixed emotions. Bill and Eileen and Al. Living in a high-rise in the shadow of the Renaissance Center, with breathtaking views of the swiftly moving Detroit River.

Koesler, working from a diocesan list of Catholics, had phoned. Eileen, the homemaker, who had given up a possible career as a dental hygienist, happened to be home when Koesler rang. She invited him to drop by.

Bill was home irregularly. His law practice was extremely demanding. Then there was Albert, attending St. Mary's Prepatory High School. Wonder of wonders, he was thinking of entering the seminary. So few young men today give the slightest thought to the priesthood that having one in the parish was like finding an endangered species.

Once, not that long ago, the Codys had lived within the territorial boundaries of St. Waldo's in Bloomfield Hills. Even though they had moved to downtown Detroit—many miles and cultures from that affluent northern parish—they still attended and contributed to their former parish.

But Father Koesler had called, had blessed their penthouse, had shown an interest in them. It was time for a change. The Codys became active, involved parishioners of St. Joe's.

All went well, except . . .

The chemistry between Bill and Eileen just didn't seem to make it. The signs of conflict were quiet and subtle. But they were present to the careful observer. And Father Koesler was nothing if not that.

Bill seemed affable enough. But that was a surface virtue. Down deep he strove mightily to keep an aggressive personality in check. This emotional muscle served him well in court. He had just never learned to leave it at work.

Koesler quickly became aware of Bill Cody's rigid and judgmental nature. During homilies, Koesler frequently was drawn to making eye contact with Cody. And Cody would return the contact through tense eyes that seemed never to blink. At such times, Koesler was reminded of a feral animal stalking prey.

The parish council of St. Joe's, after some experimentation, had settled on a body of six members with four as a quorum. Add Koesler as pastor and Mary O'Connor as secretary and the council was complete.

A couple of years ago, Bill Cody had run for a seat on the council.

Koesler was concerned. It was one thing to be scrutinized and patently evaluated during Mass when the priest had a captive audience. Quite another when the predator wielded some ill-defined clout as president of the parish council. Which is what Bill Cody became by popular vote.

Seriously complicating this situation was the coincident election to the parish council of Eileen Cody.

Under the best of circumstances, Koesler was dubious about having a husband and wife as members of a body such as a parish council. Particularly since he knew, or at least sensed, the complex relationship of Bill and Eileen, he considered inserting into the council's constitution language that would prohibit spouses serving on the same council.

But, in any case, such legislation could not be made retroactive.

As it happened, there was little conflict in the business and parochial doings of St. Joseph's parish. And while tension between the Codys was manifest to Koesler, who was painfully aware of it, no words were spoken that would evidence any conflict between the couple.

Now, Koesler clearly perceived, something had happened in the parish that had caused Bill Cody to abandon his stalking mode and pounce. Something to do with that additional weekend Mass.

Koesler was being drawn into a conflict he loathed to enter. He felt the vortex.

With more caution, he returned to his conversation with Cody. "I guess I'll never forget the census calls, the doorbell ringing. It struck me as terribly sad that that beautiful old church was serving so few people. Little by little, we did turn it around until we gathered a pretty respectable number. But a fourth Mass on the weekend..." His brow furrowed. "It's been a little while since I was there, weekend *or* daily. But it seems inconceivable that Zack could have attracted enough new parishioners to need another Mass. I must say, I'm at a loss—"

"The extra Mass, Father, is a Folk Mass!"

There was no denying that Folk Masses were common now. And there were a variety of them. Almost any form of liturgy, except those legislated and found in the Roman Missal, fell into the general category of "Folk."

It started with a guitar instead of an organ or even a piano, and it went from there in every conceivable direction.

Clearly, a Folk Mass at staid St. Joseph's was a radical departure from what had come to be expected there.

"Was this okayed by the parish council?" Koesler asked.

"It wasn't presented to the parish council!"

Short of hearing Father Tully's reasons for this, Koesler tended to think that was a mistake. "You've attended this Mass?"

"A few times." Cody's tone left no doubt that he was disgusted by what he had seen and heard.

"Would you describe it?"

"Sure. It's an outrageous blend of Baptist and Catholic. The only Catholics that service—I won't call it a Mass—the only Catholics who could relate to this are blacks and hippie whites." It was evident that Cody found this Folk Mass, if not the entire genre, an abomination that scandalized him.

It was quite obvious to Koesler that his intercession was going to be sought. This was what Bill Cody had been aiming at from the outset. Could he head off this ambush at the pass? Koesler wondered. The best way he could conceive was to get this ball into another court. "I imagine that this Folk Mass began after the most recent council meeting . . . otherwise you surely would have debated it then and there."

Cody nodded.

"And the next scheduled meeting?"

"Tomorrow night."

"Have you tried to talk to Father Tully?"

"Of course. I haven't been able to pin him down. He never returns my phone calls. Whenever he says Mass he always has to leave immediately. 'Pressing pastoral duties,' is the word. I've tried time and time again."

"Well, he will undoubtedly be at the council meeting tomorrow evening."

"Yes, and I'd like you to—"

Koesler began shaking his head before Cody completed the invitation. "Out of the question. As I said, my duties . . . my sphere of influence at St. Joe's is over. I have no entrée to a council meeting. It would be as if a stranger were to barge in. The council would sic the dog on him—or, at very least, call the cops."

"It's not as bad as all that," Cody said soothingly. "We all know what you've done with St. Joe's. You can't feel nothing for the welfare of your parish—"

"It's not my parish!"

"We know that. We also know that besides caring about the

parish, you are a good friend of Father Tully. As the president of the parish council, I'm inviting you to attend this meeting."

Koesler seemed as wrung out as a washcloth. Much of what Cody said was true: The old parish, as well as its present pastor, were dear to Koesler. Yet he could not, in any way, shape, or form, barge into that meeting, which had every promise of being a knockdown-dragout confrontation.

"I'll tell you what I'll do . . ." Koesler's demeanor showed that this was his final word on the subject. "I'll get in touch with Father Tully tomorrow. Or, judging from your luck, I'll try to get in touch. I'll talk to him. I can't predict which direction we'll take as a result of our talk. But I'll see what, if anything, can be done."

Cody hesitated. He wanted a commitment from Koesler. His legal experience told him he wasn't going to get it. "Fair enough." Smiling, he stood, signaling that, as far as he was concerned, this meeting was over. "All right if I phone you late tomorrow afternoon and see how we stand with Father Tully?"

"If you must. I should be here about five. But I doubt I'll be able to do more than tell you that I touched base with Father Tully—especially since the council meeting is tomorrow evening. I doubt we can reach any sense of agreement in this time frame—not on a subject as volatile as this."

"I know you'll do your best. That's why I came to you." Cody turned to leave, then turned back. "And you won't forget Al and that Page fellow."

"No. I won't forget."

Koesler sighed. This—being at the heart of conflicts in the seminary and the parish—was not what he had planned for his retirement.

14

GETTING AN APPOINTMENT with Father Zachary Tully was every bit as difficult as Bill Cody promised. Especially if the get-together needed to be held on the same day as the request, and before the evening council meeting.

But because it was Koesler, Father Tully extended an invitation to lunch. It seemed to Tully the very least he could do for his predecessor and, in some regards, mentor.

It would be a working lunch, but not a lengthy one.

Father Tully's schedule for this afternoon called for hospital visits. This was among the many customs carried over from the Koesler regime. Complicating this task was the multicultural makeup of St. Joseph's parish. Parishioners ranged from the indigent to the affluent. So they could be hospitalized in any institution from Receiving Hospital to the University of Michigan.

Thus, Koesler, and now Tully, had regularly set aside at least three afternoons each week for ministering to ill parishioners.

Koesler of course understood the necessity for a brief luncheon. The parish's part-time cook served sandwiches and coffee. Mary O'Connor, still hanging in there while the search for a parish secretary continued, brown-bagged it in her office.

Father Tully took a bite of an egg salad sandwich. A small bite, so he could chew and talk simultaneously without seeming a slob. "So, Bob, what's so important that we have to get together before tonight's council meeting?"

Koesler worked on a cheese sandwich. "I had a visitor last night. Ordinarily I don't play this stupid game, but in this instance I think you might guess who it was."

113

"Hmmm. Ordinarily I wouldn't be able to. But your time frame—before the meeting—leads me to figure that it was one of the council people. And since there are only six, I'd guess it was the president."

"You'd be right."

"By the way . . ." Tully laid the sandwich down and tried the coffee. Very hot, but oh, so much better than when Koesler used to brew his own incredibly bad potion. ". . . I never thanked you for holding the council membership to six. Most of the parishes I've checked with have twelve."

"Save your gratitude. The number was set by my predecessor. But it does make things less troublesome."

"So . . . Bill Cody. I guess I've been a thorn in his side from the start . . . although I don't really mean to be. I think we just don't see eye to eye. Probably never will. What's his problem now?"

"You don't know?"

Tully put both hands on the table, palms down. He sat back, brow wrinkled in reflection. "There are so many things. For me, what's wrong—or what Cody perceives to be wrong—could be a multiple choice."

"It's the Folk Mass."

"Really!"

"I'm pretty sure Old St. Joe's never had a Folk Mass before."

"Sort of overdue, don't you think?"

"I don't know." Koesler put what was left of his sandwich aside. "Bill sounded pretty convincing last night. But I know you had your reasons. I just didn't know what they were. Thus"—his gesture encompassed everything that had been thus far said—"this meeting. Do you mind telling me where this—if Bill's description is accurate—this Folk Mass came from?"

"No, I don't mind. Of course not. I just can't figure what the big deal is here.

"Some of our black parishioners—you know them, Bob—asked to meet with me. I agreed. At that meeting they brought along a pretty healthy contingent of blacks who live in our parish but don't attend church anywhere. What these people wanted was their own Mass."

"But, Zack, there are already nearby parishes that offer just that. Sacred Heart, Rosary, some others. Their liturgies are really quite good, and definitely centered in the black experience. These parishes host a good group of people, but they've all got room for a few more. Why not suggest to your contingent that they go to one of the parishes that already have what they want?"

Tully sighed. "Because, Bob, they are *ours*. Even the ones who are unchurched live in our parish. They—both groups, our active black parishioners and the others—want their own experience in their own parish. I don't think that's too much to want.

"Besides," Tully continued, "these other parishes you mentioned, almost all of them have white pastors. Now, don't get me wrong, these are great guys . . . some of the best priests in the diocese. But"—and he emphasized each word—"*I am black.*"

The look that appeared on Koesler's face clearly said, *But you could pass.*

"Yeah," Tully said, "I know: I could pass for white. But I'm *not* white. I'm mulatto—and that, in our culture, is black.

"Lemme put it this way, Bob: One school of thought has it that to be Jewish, a person needs to have a Jewish mother; it's no good if the father is Jewish and the mother is not.

"Another school of thought puts it more broadly and I think more realistically: If a person was sent to Hitler's ovens for being Jewish, that person was Jewish—Momma or not.

"Bob, I grew up in a racially mixed neighborhood. There was a sharp distinction between black and white. Both sides considered me black—even though I had a white mother. And even though my black father died early in my life.

"Or, take my black half-brother. We shared a father. Zoo's mother was black, mine was white. I am accepted by Zoo and his wife, Anne Marie, as a black man.

"Now, a bunch of black Catholics—some practicing, some not—came to me and asked for a liturgy in their parish that spoke and sang to their culture. They recognized me as a black priest who finds the African-American experience personal and natural."

It rang a bell. Koesler recalled someone—who was it?—saying, "Guys my age aren't uptight about adapting the liturgy to the occasion." After a moment's thought, he remembered: It was Father Zachary Tully who had given Koesler that explanation just about one year ago when Koesler had entrusted his dear old parish to Tully while he, the pastor, went on vacation.

But there were two more questions.

Koesler sipped his cooling coffee. He did not judge it; it was brown and warm; that was enough for him.

"Zack, a couple of things puzzle me. First, when I offered to help you with the weekend liturgies, you declined the offer. Bill Cody thinks you didn't want me around to witness the Folk Mass. Is it possible he's right?"

Tully laughed heartily. "Lord, no! You're welcome as the flowers in spring, man. Come see our Afro Mass. Hell, join us. I declined your offer of help because . . . well, you were a real popular guy around here for quite a few years. I wanted to avoid exactly what happened when Cody went to you instead of coming to me. If you had hung around here on a regular basis, you would've been Pastor A and I would've been Pastor B. That would never have worked. But"—he grinned—"you're *always* welcome here.

"Besides," he added, "I didn't think this Folk Mass was all that big a thing." He stood, preparatory to leaving for his sick calls. "So what was the other thing on your mind?"

"It wasn't on my mind as much as it was on Mr. Cody's. Although I must admit, after he told me about the Mass, I did wonder why you added it to the schedule—and you just answered that. The second question is about the role of the council. According to Bill, you didn't mention the Folk Mass at any council meeeting. And there has been a meeting since I returned from vacation.

"Given the fact that these parishioners came to you just as I was moving into the seminary, you had an opportunity to consult the council. But you didn't. So my question is: Why not?"

Tully's jaw clenched a couple of times before responding. "It was a liturgical decision. I think I'm qualified to make that decision."

Obviously being taxed with this had reached him. In Koesler's experience, this was the first time Tully had reacted sharply to anything. "Whoa," Koesler said, "I'm on *your* side. Maybe you don't see this added liturgy as something well out of the ordinary for this parish. If that's your opinion, we disagree."

"This is not your parish."

"Admitted. I'll even add to that: I can't think of another priest in our diocese who is better qualified to be pastor here than you."

Tully was standing now. He pushed his chair tight to the table. He looked down at the chair for several moments. When he finally spoke, his tone was apologetic. "Hey, I'm sorry. I haven't forgotten that you went to bat for me to get me this parish. You went well beyond just putting in a good word; you really went out on a limb for me. And I'm grateful . . . always will be."

Koesler was embarrassed. All that Tully had said—and more—was true. But Koesler never expected any return or reward for services he performed. "You owe me nothing. You *are* the perfect pastor for this parish. My concern is not so much how the long-term parishioners will adapt to the Folk Mass. My guess is that the vast majority of them will simply go on attending their regular Mass. They couldn't care less what happens during any Mass as long as it doesn't happen during *their* Mass.

"What I'm concerned about is how the council will react during their meeting tonight. I'm concerned mostly about Bill Cody. I've got a hunch he'll be furious . . . and he won't be hiding his anger underneath a basket."

Tully winced. "I know. I agree. If you want to know the real reason I didn't bring it up at the last meeting, it's because I didn't want to go through this twice."

"Twice?"

"Twice. If I had announced the Folk Mass, I would've had to fight off Cody. And then, after he attended the Mass, I'd have to deal with him again. This way I'll only have to do this once. Tonight."

Koesler rose and eased his chair beneath the table's edge.

Both men were standing; in a short while they would be about their business. "I cleared my calendar. If you like, I'll attend tonight's meeting. Matter of fact, I've already been invited."

"By Cody?"

"Uh-huh."

Tully chuckled.

"Only trouble," Koesler said, "is that Bill doesn't know which side I'm on."

"Just as well he doesn't." Tully, smiling slightly, shook his head. "No, Bob. Thanks for your offer—but no use having both of us in his gunsight." He chuckled. "Anyway, if Cody gets any place close to ballistic, I know I'll get some help from Mrs. Cody."

Koesler nodded gravely. "You're right there."

"Talk about canceling out votes," Tully commented. "I wonder how they do it? I mean, who goes first? Does Bill somehow discover that Eileen is voting Democrat so he votes Republican? Or is it vice versa?"

"I don't think that principle applies when it comes to religion," Koesler said. "Especially not when the subject is a Folk Mass."

"And most especially when it comes to an Afro Folk Mass."

"I can imagine."

"Can you?" Tully said lightly. "You should've been at the one P.M. Sunday Mass the past few weeks."

"They were both there?"

Tully nodded. "But not in the same mode. She really got into the spirit of things. I mean really. *He* was the furtive presence—sometimes lurking in the rear of the church; occasionally he even opted for a better view in the choir loft."

They had walked through the rectory, bade good-bye to Mary O'Connor, and were standing on the porch about to go their separate ways.

"Well," Koesler said, "it all comes out in the wash tonight."

Tully sliced his index finger across his throat. "Pray for me."

15 IT WAS 5:30 P.M. Happy hour in some bars and restaurants. Preprandial time at the seminary—at least for the faculty.

Father Koesler had decided to skip this ritual in favor of spending some time with Bishop McNiff. Both hoped it would be that sort of time called "quality."

Both priests wore the cassock and clerical collar. Koesler's vestment was a plain black garment that covered from his shoulders to his black shoes.

Bishop McNiff had abandoned the simple black cassock in favor of his usual episcopal raiment. He might not have become so formalistic but for his position as rector of this very traditional seminary.

As he accepted a glass of wine from McNiff, Koesler, an amused smile on his face, looked down at his vertically challenged friend.

Crowning McNiff's abundant white hair was a red beanie, more properly called a zucchetto. Red piping set off the black cassock and cape. A string of red buttons ran the short distance from neck to pants cuffs. A wide red sash served as a belt. A silver cross suspended from a long silver chain completed the uniform.

McNiff's nonsensical grin mirrored a like expression from Koesler. "So," McNiff said, "what's your problem, tall, dark, and tall?"

"Nothing, really. It's just that every time I see you all dressed up, I can't help thinking of the Infant of Prague."

"Listen," McNiff said as if giving a command, "if I wore

119

plain black like you, let alone what I'd rather wear—just pants and a T-shirt—they'd run me outta here in tar and feathers."

"Come on," Koesler chided, "this crowd wouldn't treat a bishop like that."

"Like hell they wouldn't. Haven't you gotten to know them better than that by now?"

"Yeah, I have. And I suppose you're right." Koesler apparently found something arresting about McNiff's footwear. "You're wearing white socks!"

"My feet have some kind of skin disorder. The doctor told me to wear white socks."

"With a black outfit?"

"The doctor said."

"Haven't you ever heard of socks that are white on the bottom half and black on the top?"

"What's wrong with what I'm wearing?" McNiff's tone was argumentative.

Koesler studied the white on black several long moments. "Nothing!" he said at length.

McNiff did not sit behind his desk. They took facing chairs. As they sipped their drinks, each was lost in his own thoughts.

At long last McNiff broke the silence. "Do you ever think about it? We go back a long way."

Koesler did some mental arithmetic. "Almost sixty years!"

"That long!"

"We met for the first time in our freshman year in the seminary—1942," Koesler said.

"How different everything is now. Today's kids can't even comprehend how things were back then."

"The Church has changed several times over . . . and the seminary with it."

McNiff gazed at his glass of Diet Coke. It didn't even resemble wine. "Any contacts with our students yet?"

"Bumped into a few. But nothing in depth . . . yet. I did, however, have a long chat with Mr. William Cody last night."

"Oh, yeah: Albert's father . . . that the one?"

"Indeed." Koesler went on to give the bishop the substance

of what they'd discussed. Cody's fear that a student named Page might be a questionable influence on Al. And, second, Cody's distress over the newly introduced Folk Mass.

"Have you met Page?" McNiff asked.

"No. Not yet. But I plan on doing so . . . soon."

"After you do, I'd like to know how he impresses you. He's a big question mark to me. I may be seriously mistaken about the young man. When I think of him, the image I get is a chameleon. He would've made his way safely through England with Henry VIII and his successors. For Henry, Page would belong to the schismatic Church of England. And for Bloody Mary, he'd be staunchly Catholic. Then back to Henry's Church under Elizabeth. As I say, I may be mistaken. . . .

"But, tell me: What was the other thing?"

"With Cody last night? The Folk Mass. I didn't mention it, but it's an Afro Folk Mass."

"Oh, boy! The red flag and the bull. How did they ever get that past Cody? He's a vigilante. I picture him up on the ramparts guarding the Church from any breach in the wall around the fortress."

Koesler chuckled. "A mighty fortress is our Church."

"Who's the pastor there now? Your successor . . ."

"Zachary Tully."

"Uh-huh. Came up from Texas?"

"Dallas."

"Was a Josephite?"

"Is."

"His brother's a cop?"

"Half-brother."

"Oh, yeah, that's right: The priest is mulatto."

"Zack says his Mass is kosher. He invited me to come see. I think I will this Sunday."

"Kosher or not"—McNiff set his now empty glass on the desk— "he's going to have one hell of a time selling the concept to Cody. I don't think it's possible."

"I agree." Koesler emptied his wineglass in a swallow. He glanced at his watch. "As a matter of fact, Father Tully is scheduled to meet with his parish council in about an hour.

And the Folk Mass certainly is going to be the first order of business."

McNiff shook his head. "Poor guy! He must be sweating bullets about now.

"Well . . ." He stood. "It's beyond our power to help at this point. Let's eat."

As the two left McNiff's suite, Koesler said, "I offered to be with him at tonight's council meeting. But he wanted to take them on himself."

"That was good of you—to offer, I mean. The guy is either pretty brave or pretty stupid."

"One thing I can attest to: He's not stupid."

Father Tully shook the bottle. A small, white pill dropped to accompany the other two in his palm.

Ordinarily he could get by with just two aspirins. But this was no ordinary headache.

Father Tully was nervous—very nervous. And that disturbed him. He was not one to scare easily.

Everything had been fine until today's earlier visit with Bob Koesler.

Tully was well aware that the post–Folk Mass council meeting would probably be acrimonious. He was prepared to face the music.

Then came Koesler, whose foreboding about the meeting had proved contagious. As a result of Koesler's apprehensiveness, Tully now had misgivings.

He tried to settle himself but, like many qualms, this one would not yield to rationalization. He tried first a book, then the newspaper, but found himself rereading the same paragraph over and over without comprehension.

Finally, at seven twenty-five, the doorbell rang. That would be Hans Kruger, typically just a bit early.

Tully opened the door. Kruger entered with his usual ebullience, which was dampened not a whit by Tully's consternated attitude. The priest let the council member find his way to the basement meeting room.

Tully's stomach was churning. He would not try another

aspirin; it was too soon since he'd swallowed the previous three. He stood at his office window and stared into the gathering darkness.

The bell rang again. Tully checked his watch. Exactly seven-thirty. That would be the Codys. They always came on time and they always came together. As far as Tully could ascertain, that was the only thing they did together.

Tully admitted them.

Eileen was distracted when she greeted Tully. It appeared that husband and wife had been discussing something. Perhaps angrily—Bill's countenance was frozen. He gave no greeting.

The couple headed for the basement. Tully waited for more council people. Fervently, he hoped no more would show up.

The bylaws of the parish council called for six elected positions, with four members constituting a quorum.

As of this moment, there were three in the basement. Not enough for an official meeting.

Of course there was Mary O'Connor. But she was not an elected member. Her presence was as parish secretary and, as such, secretary to the council. She was waiting in the housekeeper's quarters. Waiting for word that the council was ready to start. Or that the meeting had been canceled.

Father Tully checked his watch again. He did not do this habitually as did Father Koesler. But this was not an ordinary evening.

Seven-forty. Five minutes to go. According to the bylaws, a quorum was needed and if a quorum wasn't achieved within fifteen minutes of scheduled starting time, the meeting could be postponed.

Seven-forty-three. Seven-forty-four.

The doorbell rang.

Tully exhaled, then realized he had been unconsciously holding his breath.

It was Molly Cronin. She was usually a few minutes late— a big family to care for. Tonight she was—for her—a bit early. Wouldn't you know! Otherwise Tully could have had a cold beer in his hand and his feet up on an ottoman.

But Molly was here and one couldn't even complain about the time; she had a minute to spare.

Tully gathered in Molly and Mary O'Connor and the three descended to the netherworld.

Hans Kruger greeted them cheerfully. Bill Cody still wore no appreciable expression. Eileen Cody seemed disappointed . . . as if she, like Tully, had hoped that the meeting would be postponed.

Once everyone was seated, Tully led them in a generic prayer.

Next, it was up to the president, Bill Cody, to set the agenda.

To just about everyone's surprise, the first item of business was not the Folk Mass. He must, thought Tully, be saving that for a fireworks conclusion.

Cody called on Kruger for a report on the repair of the rectory roof.

Kruger quoted figures and estimates and concluded that the main body of work would be completed on time and on budget. But a small section would have to wait for a special order of material that simply wasn't on hand.

Normally Cody would not have let such a foul-up go by without caustic comment. Tonight he seemed preoccupied.

Next he asked Molly Cronin how the church cleaning project was progressing.

She replied that a generous number of women *and* men had scheduled a floor cleaning a week from this Saturday. Little by little, they were getting the job done.

Cody thanked her.

He noted that since two members were missing, there would be no report from the Christian Service committee or the hospitality group.

He shifted in his seat to lean forward. He asked his wife for a report on the liturgy committee.

If it was going to happen, it probably would happen now.

Eileen shuffled a few papers, cleared her throat, and reported. "The new missalettes have arrived. They will be placed in the pews before the next weekend." She paused.

"The new extraordinary ministers of the eucharist and the new readers will be installed this weekend at the ten A.M. Sunday Mass."

Unexpectedly, Hans Kruger objected. "I've been watching this for a long time. And since I'm now a member of the parish council, I want to say something about it."

Cody nodded, silently giving Kruger the floor.

"Why? That's my question," Kruger began. "Why do we have just ordinary people distributing Communion. And why do we have ordinary people doing the readings? That's what we've got priests for . . . isn't that right?"

No one replied. No one wanted to get involved in what was obviously a rhetorical matter.

"Well," Kruger pressed, "isn't it?"

The others looked to Eileen. After all, the liturgy was her slice of the parish pie.

"Hans," Eileen said, "the Council . . . the Vatican Council had a lot to say about the laity and the part they're supposed to play in the liturgy—the Mass. And it's because of what the Council said that we do more than we used to do. And a couple of those things are helping distribute Communion and doing the readings before the Gospel."

Kruger's jovial demeanor had utterly disappeared. The burr had been under his saddle for roughly thirty years. This was his first opportunity to void his displeasure in an official—or quasi-official—capacity. He had a chance to say his piece, and by God he was going to say it.

"I don't know much about that Council. It seems to me that a bunch of Catholic mavericks just go around doing anything they want and blame it all on that damn Council—you'll pardon my French!"

Just about everyone else around the table seemed to appreciate, to some degree, this lone voice expressing his deep-seated objection to decisions that were very much a fait accompli. Tully, however, wondered: If this group was going to object to even the smallest changes that everyone else pretty much took for granted now, what would be the reaction of these people to an Afro Folk Mass?

The ball appeared to once again be in Eileen Cody's court. "Hans," she said, "the questions you raise have been answered long ago. There's no argument left. The laity are not only permitted to read from the Bible as part of the Mass; they are encouraged to do it."

"What about Communion?" Kruger grumbled. "That's certainly the priest's job. Why, shoot, I can remember when nobody could touch the host except the priest. Now every Tom, Dick, and Harry can handle the host!"

"There's a priest shortage, Hans," Molly Cronin contributed. "If no one but a priest could touch the consecrated host, we'd be at Communion forever and ever, amen."

More muttering and grousing from Kruger. "I don' know. I don' know. Okay, so there's not enough priests to go 'round. We've got one right here: Father Tully.

"Father Tully"—he directly addressed the pastor—"you're a priest. How come when you haven't got the Mass, when some other priest is the celebrant, how come you don't come over to the church to help him out with Communion? How come you leave that up to the ordinary people?"

Cody stared resolutely at Tully, awaiting a response to Kruger's question, or rather, Kruger's challenge. "Father?"

Tully had not anticipated being called up on so inconsequential a matter. He was taken aback.

"Hans," he said, faintly, "it doesn't really matter whether I help with Communion or not. We're still going to have extraordinary ministers giving Communion. We always have at least three people distributing. If another priest has the Mass, and if I come over to help, we still need an extraordinary minister to help.

"Besides," he continued, "that won't be a problem for you any longer. I'm not going to be asking for help from another priest. I'm going to take all the Masses—both weekends and daily."

"Isn't that a bit much, Father?" Mrs. Cronin knew what work was. "We need you. We don't want you getting sick."

Tully smiled. "Not to worry, Mrs. Cronin. I'm healthy and still fairly young. Besides, I have Father Koesler's assurance that if and when we need him, he will come unless something makes that impossible."

Silence for several moments. Evidently, the pause was to allow Kruger to pursue the subject if he so chose.

"If you are satisfied," Cody said to Kruger finally, "we'll move on."

Another short silence.

"Eileen," Cody addressed his wife, "you may resume."

She hesitated briefly. "Well, there's the Folk Mass that's been added to the schedule—"

"Yeah," Kruger dove in, "I was meaning to ask about that. What in tarnation is that? I sort of figured it was going to be some kind of group Mass. Like the Veterans of Foreign Wars, or the Knights of Columbus, or the Daughters of Isabella, or something like that. I figured it didn't involve me. So I just kept going to the ten o'clock.

"But some of the people have asked me what's going on. So . . . what's going on?"

"Father?" Once again Cody called on Tully to respond to a Hans Kruger question. This time, there was no sense of respect in the president's tone.

Tully felt like standing and pacing. He didn't think that would be appropriate. So he forced himself to stay seated.

"We have," Tully said, "begun a Mass at five in the afternoon on Sundays. I intend it to be part of our regular weekend schedule—"

"Excuse me," Kruger interrupted, "but they tell me that there isn't a single one of the three Masses we already have that is crowded. I know that's true of the ten o'clock one that I attend. So, my question is: What do we need another Mass for?"

Before replying, Tully looked around the table. All eyes were on him. But each face had a different expression.

Father Tully had been well briefed before he'd ever attended a council meeting, on the personalities of the members. Cody, of course, was a staunch conservative, bordering on the fundamentalist viewpoint. His wife, Eileen, might be liberal—or maybe just opposed to whatever her husband favored.

Hans Kruger was conservative, but could be swayed by sufficient argument. Although, at least at the outset of any matter brought before the council, he tended to agree with Bill Cody.

Molly Cronin leaned slightly left on most issues, but could be convinced otherwise.

Of the missing council members, John Falahee leaned right and Harvey Wilds favored the left.

If all members were in attendance, Tully could count on the probability of an even split: two following Bill and two responding to Eileen. The priest was able to break any tie vote.

This evening, even with two absentees, the same configuration applied. Except that now, one would be on Bill's team and one on Eileen's. The deciding vote was still Father Tully's.

Which, Tully knew, didn't make all that much difference. But thus far in his relationship with the parish council, he hadn't had to use all of his power as pastor.

Tully returned to Kruger's question. "That's true, Hans: We don't come close to an SRO crowd at any of our Masses."

"Excuse me, Father," said Mrs. Cronin, "what do you mean by an SRO crowd?"

"Sorry, Molly. That's a standing-room-only crowd."

"The kind we get at Christmas and Easter?"

"That's the kind." Tully smiled. "We're not doing badly, particularly for a core city parish. And for that, I'll tip my hat to Father Koesler. He gathered in a lot of those town house and high-rise people."

He paused and glanced at Bill Cody. Cody was one of the high-rise people. His jaw was clenched and his eyes were not kind. His brush cut, in this context, created the image of a soldier. An angry soldier.

"So why the Folk Mass?" Mrs. Cronin asked.

"What is a Folk Mass?" Kruger dug for the root of the matter.

"Okay . . ." Tully took a deep breath. "I understand St. Joe's parish has never had a Folk Mass before. But I can tell you, it's a very popular liturgy. Almost all parishes have them regularly or from time to time.

"It's called a Folk Mass because it is not as formal as a regular Mass. And it usually has a specific theme. Maybe the most popular Folk Mass is one for children. The idea is to take the structure of the Mass and make each part relevant to the age and interest of the children. The hymns, the songs, the prayers will be ones that the kids can relate to. The children will take a much more active role in the liturgy. There's room for a lot of creativity in a Folk Mass."

"You make it sound very sweet and attractive for the children," Mrs. Cronin said. "It makes me wonder why we haven't had this kind of Mass before."

"You mean the new Mass on Sundays is going to be for children?" Kruger asked.

"Why don't you tell them the purpose of this Folk Mass, Father?" There was something almost sadistic about Bill Cody's smile.

"It's not for children?" Kruger seemed perplexed.

"Then why did you tell us about a children's Mass?" Mrs. Cronin demanded.

Tully sighed inwardly. "It's not for children," he said. "There aren't enough Catholic kids in our parish to warrant that kind of program . . . at least we haven't been able to find enough as yet.

"Look," he continued, "a substantial number of African-Americans came to me. They are Catholic, though some had not been practicing for some time. They wanted a liturgy that spoke to them and their families. They made a good case for it.

"So, after a lot of thought and prayer I said okay. At least we'll try it for a while and see what happens."

"The Mass is for Negroes?" It was not an insulting designation to Kruger.

"It's for African-Americans," Tully corrected, "and for anyone else who finds meaning in that liturgy. It's about the same thing as whether anybody besides African-Americans can appreciate Aretha Franklin, Bill Cosby, Sidney Poitier, Harry Belafonte, Paul Robeson, and so on.

"It started out being for and by African-Americans. But the clear idea at the outset was that anybody who wanted to participate would be welcome. As of now, quite a few white people have joined in. And, I should point out, we've gained quite a few new members for this parish."

Kruger and Cronin seemed impressed.

"Maybe you could clarify some considerations," Cody said.

"Yes?" Tully focused complete attention on Cody.

"Are there any other churches around here that offer this kind of thing?"

"Well, yes."

"How many would you say?"

"I don't know."

"There are four or five practically surrounding us. In fact," Cody pressed, "just about every inner-city parish has got a program like this."

There was a significant pause. Why, thought Tully, had Cody asked when he obviously knew the answer.

Cody pressed on. "You mentioned that Father Koesler offered to help. Is that offer effective right now?"

"Yes, I believe it is."

"As a matter of fact, it is. I talked to Father yesterday. He would have come to this meeting if he had been able. Isn't it a fact"—Cody might have been in a courtroom—"isn't it a fact," he repeated, "that you practically pushed Father out of the parish so he would not see this travesty for himself?"

"Of course not! And it is not a travesty. It's a legitimate form of Folk Mass."

"We'll see about that. Father Koesler will observe that thing next Sunday. And I'm going to get the director of worship to come too."

"You been at this Mass, Bill?" Kruger asked.

"I've been there," Cody answered. "I've seen it with my own eyes! Hans, earlier tonight you brought up some things about the Mass that troubled you. Specifically, lay people doing the readings and distributing Communion. You were correct in saying that these functions used to be performed by priests. Priests did read from Scripture. Priests did distribute Communion. Then came the *Council*. . . ."

He managed to make the Council's very name sound evil.

"Then came the Council," Cody repeated. "John Twenty-third was described as opening a window to let in the fresh winds of change. They called the process *aggiornamento,* an Italian word.

"But once the window was opened, a lot of things flew out. The venerable Latin, the impeccable staging of the Mass, the time-honored reverence for the priest—another Christ—who always wore an impressive uniform that identified him, solid theology based on centuries of development. Now it's priests leaving by the carload, vocations to the priesthood bottoming out—"

"Bill," Eileen said shortly, "what does any of this have to do with an innocent Folk Mass that's just being tried? Get hold of yourself!"

"What does this have to do with an *innocent* Folk Mass?" Cody's fierce eyes skewered his wife. "I'll tell you what!

"It was the mid-sixties. We had a Pope who looked and acted like Santa Claus. The bishops of the world gathered in Rome. Except that the bishops didn't do their homework. They didn't know what was going on.

"They brought so-called experts with them. The experts had done their homework. The bishops were like dummies sitting on the experts' laps. The bishops by and large did what the experts advised them to. That's when we got our bastard Mass language and plastic prayers. That's when we got the seeds of liberation theology. That's when we got this whole stinking mess we call the liberal Church.

"The Council ended and we got all this crap foisted on us. On you, Hans. And on you, Molly. We thought all these changes must be good; after all, the Holy Spirit guides His Church . . . doesn't He?" Cody's voice rose to a crescendo. "He does," Cody answered his own question, "unless some-one seemingly in authority betrays the Spirit.

"And that's what happened. We gradually accepted all

those early changes, new rituals for our beloved Mass. Now it's too late.

"Hans . . . Molly . . . you remember how it was. It seemed one week we attended a Mass that had been celebrated the same way in the same language for a hundred years and more. And the next week we had this bastard ceremony with poorly constructed English texts.

"Well, we learned to accept that. We didn't realize that the changes were going to keep coming . . . that they would never stop.

"So, Hans, you can bellyache all you want about priests not carrying out their roles in the Mass. You can even go back to the earliest changes and argue against them. But it won't do you any good . . . not any good at all.

"It's too late . . . it's too late. It's a done deal.

"Now, along comes the Folk Mass. It's not exactly brand new. It's been around.

"But it's not been around St. Joseph's before. Not ever. Not until some weeks ago when our pastor, all on his own, with no one else's input, with not a nod to the parish council, starts having a Folk Mass, on Sundays, in an extra Mass we don't need.

"Well, Hans, Molly, it's not too late for this one! This one we can—and must—nip in the bud. Either we stop this Folk Mass nonsense right now, or we lose another battle for good and all.

"I motion"—Cody emphasized every word of his motion—"that the Folk Mass recently inaugurated in our parish schedule for Sundays be discontinued and never be revived."

"I second that motion," Kruger echoed.

"I feel," Cody said, silencing what Tully was about to say, "that there has been enough discussion on this topic. I call for an immediate vote. Those in favor of the motion?"

Kruger and Cronin raised their hands along with Cody.

"Those opposed?"

Eileen raised her hand. Slowly, Tully raised his, then turned. "Molly!" Tully said the name softly. He seemed stunned. It was as if he'd said, "Judas."

Molly blushed and stammered. "I . . . I'm sorry, Father. But if they have their own Mass in all these neighboring parishes . . ."

"That's not the point, Molly. This is their parish too," Tully insisted. "This Folk Mass is geared for their needs, their lifestyles—"

"It's a little late to continue the argument, Father," Cody said. "The vote's been taken. Sometimes you win, sometimes you lose. This time you lost."

"What do you mean?" Tully addressed Cody.

"The vote, of course. This is the end of your Folk Mass."

"You mean you don't know?"

"Don't know what?" Cody's voice had lost the edge of victory.

"Why," Tully replied, "the role of a parish council."

"It's an administrative body. It makes law for its parish," Cody responded.

Tully shook his head slowly. "It's not an administrative body; it's consultative. I thought you knew that."

"That can't be!"

"That is what it is."

"This has never come up before," Cody protested.

"Very probably in the pastorship of Father Koesler, there had never been an issue where the council and the pastor were on a collision course.

"Think about it for a minute," Tully said. "Father Koesler was settled in here before you people were elected. You didn't stand in the way of all those changes that had become commonplace in all the parishes. Like the vernacular, the priest facing the people at Mass, communal penance services, and the like.

"For his part, Father Koesler didn't hit you with a Folk Mass—a legitimate form of liturgy. But a major step away from the more traditional Mass.

"So," Tully continued, "the waters remained calm. Evidently, Father never brought up the status of the council—what sort of role it plays in the parish. During his watch the need never arose to clarify the relationship between the council and the pastor.

"When parish councils began, I was in Texas in a parish so poor that a parish council was near the bottom of their concerns. But I was aware of what most of my priest colleagues were going through. At that time, there was a good deal of sparring going on as to who was going to run the parish. Just because of that, a lot of priests stepped down as pastors and became assistants; some retired, some even had breakdowns.

"So, eventually, the matter was settled: The pastor had complete responsibility for the parish. The parish council advised. Following or ignoring that advice was the pastor's prerogative.

"Evidently, you simply didn't know," Tully concluded, "what the limits are to your role. But, Bill, you above everyone here would be well aware that ignorance of the law does not excuse—"

"This is ridiculous!" Cody was almost shouting. "There is no point to this council. It's toothless. We've been led down another blind alley."

"It's not that bad." Tully tried to be conciliatory. "You have given your advice, and I would be foolish not to consider it carefully. I also noted that the vote was not a landslide.

"But Mary O'Connor will type up the notes of this meeting and they will be published in the parish bulletin this weekend.

"For now, the Folk Mass will continue. However, I will consider your concern, after which a definite decision will be reached whether to retain it or lay it to rest. I can't tell you now just when that decision will be made, but certainly it will be within the next couple of months.

"Meanwhile, you are cordially invited to attend if you wish. Just remember, it will be a bit different than the liturgy you're used to. But then, that's one of the purposes of a Folk Mass."

"I don't understand this at all, Father," Molly said. "If the council can't make policy in the parish, why weren't we told about that?"

Tully shrugged. "I have no idea. I assumed you knew. All I can think of is that there was a lack of communication here. Let's see . . . this decision, this clarification, was handed down when Father Koesler's predecessor, whoever that was, was pastor. He undoubtedly decided, for whatever reason, not to advise the parishioners. Or if he did, that council is long since gone, and perhaps none of you were involved at the time.

"When Father Koesler became pastor, he probably assumed our people knew. And, as I explained before, the problem didn't come up at any time during his pastorate.

"On the one hand," he concluded, "I'm happy that we—pastor and council—have not had a serious disagreement until now. On the other hand, I'm sorry this ever happened."

A quiet that was more bemused than acquiescent.

Mary O'Connor, the silent guest, tapped her pen against the pad. A nonverbal question as to further business.

Was there any other business, Cody asked somewhat distractedly.

There was none. But, before closing the meeting, Cody shot his final arrow. "One more point. Supposing we get the head of the Liturgy in the archdiocese, and what if he finds the Folk Mass inappropriate and orders it abolished. What then?"

Tully smiled. "That would be a whole new ball game."

16

THE COUNCIL MEMBERS had left the rectory, presumably headed home. Mary O'Connor remained long enough to check with Tully on the format for publishing the notes of the meeting in the parish bulletin.

Now the rectory was otherwise vacant. Tully took a beer from the fridge. He thought he deserved a reward for his stand in this evening's miniwar.

After he got comfortable, he phoned Father Koesler at the seminary.

"How'd it go?" Koesler asked without preamble.

"I don't really know. Maybe it's too soon to tell."

"Did Bill Cody challenge you?"

"Oh yes. Yes, indeed."

"I can't quite figure out why. The decision is yours, not his."

"The trouble is . . ." Tully noted there were a lot of words on a Budweiser label. ". . . Cody—in fact everyone who showed up tonight—wasn't aware of the limited role of the council. They didn't know its restrictions."

Koesler was silent for a few moments. "Now that's strange. Of course the clarification came long before your present council was elected . . . even before I came to St. Joe's. I guess we just never went toe to toe on any issue. Short of having any radical difference on parish policy—and I can't recall any—we never needed that definition of roles.

"Holy crow!" Koesler reflected. "When I offered to come to this meeting, I didn't realize how much flak you were going to take. If I had anticipated this, I would have made my offer much more insistent."

136

"Well, as it turned out, they voted the Folk Mass out three to two. Then it became clear that they thought they had ended this experiment. When I told them their job was to advise me, not set policy, the wind sort of went out of their sails. Then I told them the Mass would go on for the foreseeable future on an experimental basis."

"And that's where you left it?"

"Pretty much. Cody wants to play one more card. He vows to bring the archdiocese's head honcho of Liturgy to the next Folk Mass. Apparently, he doesn't know that's Monsignor Rooney. But he'll find out; obviously he's ready to go to the mat on this."

"I think you handled this about as well as anyone could," Koesler commented.

"Thanks. Coming from you that means something."

"I can recall—*very* clearly—a council I had at another parish. Before they got straightened out, it was a knockdown battle to see who was going to run things. On the one hand, I had the pulpit—and a bully pulpit it was. On the other hand, frequently it was twelve to one.

"So I was happy to discover that St. Joe's bylaws set the council membership at only six. For that and a few other reasons I was grateful to my predecessor, God rest him. But I wish he hadn't kept that clarification of roles confidential."

"Maybe," Tully said, "if they'd known their limitations, they wouldn't even have run for council."

"Oh, I don't know. Other councils have functioned very well with that knowledge. By the way, is Mary going to publish the minutes of tonight's meeting in the bulletin? Maybe you could send me a copy."

"Better than that, Bob: Why not pick up a copy when you attend next Sunday's Folk Mass?"

"Did I miss something? Am I expected to attend? Are you inviting me?"

"As far as I'm concerned, you can come anytime you want. But I'm not the one extending the invitation. In fact, I wouldn't be surprised if Bill Cody's been dialing your number all the while we've been talking."

"Bill wants me to come?"

"You and Monsignor Rooney."

Koesler chuckled. "That's what's important about having a program. You can't tell which team the players are playing for without a program."

"Then we can expect you Sunday?"

"Only if Bill Cody issues a command performance invitation."

"See you Sunday."

It was only 9:30 P.M.

Father Tully's adrenaline was still high after his conversation with Father Koesler. Back in his Texas parish in a situation like this, he would ordinarily watch TV until its mindlessness lulled him to sleep.

Now he had his recently discovered family to turn to. Alonzo Tully, a half-brother, and his wife, Anne Marie, lived only minutes away in a Lafayette Park town house. They usually didn't retire until at least after the eleven o'clock news.

Father Tully phoned. Lieutenant Tully answered. Of course they would be happy to have a visitor.

After hugs and handshakes, the three settled around the kitchen table. Anne Marie put on the coffee. It was late in the evening, but it was decaffeinated.

Zachary, still pumped, began rattling off the day's events, culminating in the acrimonious council meeting.

"This Cody fellow," Zoo said, "he a rabble-rouser type?"

"Not in real life," Zachary said. "From what I read about him in the papers, he is a calm, self-possessed, efficient, and very well-paid lawyer."

"Lawyer!" Zoo exclaimed. "*That*'s where I've heard of him. Interesting. He could live just about anywhere and practice law. But he must live around here if he belongs to this parish."

"In a downtown high-rise."

"And he got all worked up about a . . . what?"

"A Folk Mass." Zachary had to keep in mind that Zoo belonged to no church and that, basically, he had little or no interest in religion. What involvement he had in things religious was the result of having a priest brother.

"A Folk Mass . . ." Zoo mused. "That the new service you started a while back?"

Zachary nodded.

"You've been goin' to that, haven't you, honey?"

"From the beginning," Anne Marie said. "It's by far not the first one I've ever attended. But it's good." Her enthusiasm, she knew, was at least partly the result of this being the handiwork of her brother-in-law.

Anne Marie was Catholic, born and raised. She, like Zoo, had been dumbfounded to learn of Zachary's existence, and was perhaps even more astonished to learn of his vocation.

But in the couple of years since their first meeting, they had completely bonded, and now were as tight-knit as any interdependent extended family.

"I don't see the problem," Anne Marie said. "It's a very meaningful ceremony. Everyone is reverent in a relaxed sort of way. The hymns are great, and just about everyone participates. On top of all that, we aren't doing anything that would disturb the other ceremonies. We aren't even close to them in the schedule. So why is the parish council so uptight?"

"Well . . ." Zack sipped his coffee. ". . . most of the members see the changes in the Church since the Vatican Council as one gigantic mistake. They'd like to go back to the fifties or better yet a hundred or so years before that. But no matter how hard they try, it just won't work.

"As for our council, they tried to draw a line just this side of the Folk Mass. That's what all the ruckus was about tonight. Add to that, tonight they discovered how limited their power really is."

"I still don't get it," Zoo said. "From Annie's description, it doesn't sound as if this new group is standing on anybody's toes. Whatever happened to peaceful coexistence?"

Zachary searched for a way to explain this situation. "Let's put this in the perspective of your job," he said to his brother. "You are really, totally absorbed in your work . . . right?"

"Uh-huh."

Zachary realized he was treading on dangerous ground here. He knew that Zoo's dedication to his work had, thus far, cost him a wife and family as well as a lover. So far, his present marriage was surviving quite well, due almost entirely to Anne Marie's ability to more than compromise.

In comparing St. Joe's parish to Zoo's work, Zachary wanted to be careful not to undermine a loving relationship by holding it up to unwelcome scrutiny. "Okay," Zachary said, "just supposing that Walt Koznicki, your friend and head of Homicide, were to retire. And suppose you considered his replacement inadequate for the job.

"And suppose this new inspector started changing everything; all your tried-and-true processes went by the board. Every new procedure this guy came up with was poorly conceived. It was getting laughable. Pretty soon the elite Homicide Division got to be a joke among the other departments in the Force.

"Supposing your back is about ready for the last straw. And then the inspector installs one more stupid requirement. But this time, you figure you can finally block him. You're sure you've got the right to check him. You're anticipating and savoring your victory that is all but sealed and delivered.

"Except at the last minute, you find you've lost again.

"What really hurts is the disintegrating image of the Homicide squads. The work you're so proud of. The work you do so well. The work you love."

"What really hurts," Zoo said thoughtfully, "is that your scenario could take place."

"My point," Zachary said, "is that this is about the way a lot of Catholic conservatives see their Church now. Everything seemed to be running so smoothly. Then the leadership changed. The new Pope set the mechanism of change in operation.

"People who were very satisfied with the status quo were bombarded with one change after another. These people were reeling. And, in the case of my parish council, led by Mr. William Cody, they saw a chance to for once turn things around. It was only a small step—the outlawing of a Folk

Mass—but as far as they were concerned, it was a step in the right direction. It would be a victory after so many consecutive defeats.

"And it all fell down around their ears tonight. From anybody's standpoint—even mine—it was kind of sad."

They were silent for a brief time during which Anne Marie refilled the coffee cups.

"I didn't know," Zoo said. "I had no idea they felt that strong about it. It's just how and where you go to church."

"Right," Zachary agreed. "But their religion is as important to them as your homicide investigations are—"

"I know: as important to them as my investigations are to me. It makes more sense now. And the reason they don't just get in their cars and drive a few blocks to get a service more to their liking?"

"Some do. This thing works both ways. Territory used to be a dominant consideration. There were parish boundaries. And Catholics were expected to attend and support their parish—the parish they lived in. Lots of them still do that—especially older Catholics. But if you want a by-the-book Mass and your parish provides a polka-and-pizza celebration—or vice versa—you get in your car and go elsewhere.

"So, what motivates people like the ones tonight who tried to kill the Folk Mass? Different things. They're tired of being pushed around, going from church to church shopping for their kind of Mass. Or, like Rosa Parks, they're just not going to give their place up to anyone else. Or, they want to save the Church from itself.

"And, by the way, Zoo: My analogy broke down when I compared Pope John with a crackpot inspector in the Homicide Division. And the changes in the Church to crazy procedures in your division. John Twenty-third, in reality, might have been literally a godsend. And most of the changes were needed and overdue—"

"I know. I know."

"I just wanted to be sure you knew."

"One thing that's becoming clear to me," Zoo said, "is the leader of your council—Cody. He comes across as a really zealous guy. He's the one who was affected most when you pulled the carpet out from under them . . . no?"

"Yes."

"Is he a violent guy?"

"Violent? I've no way to know that."

"Think," Zoo commanded. "Think about it. Does he ever talk about hostile action? Is there anything about him that would make you think there's a violent streak in there someplace?"

Zachary took seriously Zoo's directive. He thought. His expression changed as something came to mind. "One thing, I think," he said slowly. "He is out there beating the bushes every hunting season. He always takes his son with him.

"And that's another thing: His son is a seminarian. There aren't that many nowadays. Al Cody is a kind of endangered species."

"Does he talk about the hunting expeditions?" Zoo probed. "Does he come back with a deer strapped to his car? Does he dwell on the kill?"

"I'm just not that close to him, Zoo. I was at his apartment once for dinner just after I was named pastor of St. Joe's. I can tell you that at least on that occasion he didn't have any trophies on his walls . . . no deer heads or anything like that.

"And I've never heard him bragging about the hunt. But, a-hunting he does go—faithfully."

"What about the son?"

"Albert? He's in his final year in the seminary. He'll be ordained in a few months."

"How does he take to hunting? Like father, like son?"

"I don't think so. You know in a lot of hunting parties there are a few who go along just for the ride. Maybe one who cooks for the gang . . .

"That reminds me, if you'll pardon my going off on a tangent: Did you hear about the foursome who go off into the woods? One of them nominates another as cook. The vote carries three to one. But the designated cook says, 'Okay, but the first one of you who complains about the food takes over as cook.'

"The next day the cook finds some deer dung on the trail.

He takes it back to camp and cooks it up for dinner. The first guy to take a bite spits it out and shouts, 'This stuff tastes like deer dung!' and then immediately, in a softer tone, '. . . but good.' "

His listeners laughed, knowing that their brother had cleaned up the story slightly—undoubtedly for Anne Marie's benefit. Anne Marie was grateful.

"To get back to my point," Zachary said, "Al always played the role of cook on these hunting jaunts. I'm not sure his dad is happy with this; I think he'd be delighted if Al bagged a deer. But I also think that Al would get physically sick if he actually harmed a living creature."

Everyone seemed lost in thought for a while.

"What are you fishing for, honey?" Anne Marie asked finally.

"This guy, Cody," Zoo responded, "he sounds to me like a bomb waiting to go off."

"You think that Zachary is in some kind of danger?"

"Maybe, yes," Zoo replied after a moment. "Probably, no. But," he added, "we see it all the time. Somebody goes berserk and shoots somebody. Afterward, we interview relatives, friends, neighbors. Was the guy violent? How did he relate to others? Was there any provocation? Did he seem calm, deliberate? Was he irrational? Questions like that."

"Is there a pattern? Is there a common denominator?" Zack asked.

"If there is one, it's that the perp had an angry, violent streak. He had reason—or thought he had reason—to direct his pent-up hatred at the victim."

"What you're getting at," Zack suggested, "is that after such an incident, people generally were not surprised."

"Yeah! Call it Monday-morning quarterbacking. But, yeah. Say the guy is maybe a postal worker. One morning he comes in to start his shift. Then, in the middle of things, he leaves his station, seeks out his supervisor, and shoots him point-blank. Maybe he shoots some more—mainly his superiors. Then he turns the gun on himself.

"It happens. Again and again."

Silence.

"Then . . ." Zack hesitated. ". . . then you think this could happen to me. You think Bill Cody could do this . . . to me."

"In a word, yes. It's possible, anyway."

"Oh, sweetheart, no!" Anne Marie exclaimed. "You can't mean that someone might shoot Zachary!"

Zoo hung his head. "I don't want to suggest anything. Particularly something as bad as that. But it happens. It can happen . . . and," he said firmly, "it does happen."

"But William Cody is a civilized man," Anne Marie protested. "He's a lawyer. He knows what would happen to him if he were to do anything like that. Shoot a priest!"

"All these guys, all these shooters, are law-abiding citizens—until they go off the deep end. They're not professionals," Zoo said. "They're not habitual criminals. They're not hit men. They are lawyers, office workers, truck drivers, you name it. But they have an obsession, a fixation about something—or somebody. The target may or may not even be aware of how the perp feels.

"Maybe the target is aware of the underlying problem. Maybe he has fired or demoted the perp. Maybe he's hounding the guy. But no matter what sort of pressure the target is applying, he usually doesn't expect what can happen.

"Then, all of a sudden, the perp has busted into the guy's office. He's flushed. His eyes have a wild look. The perp usually doesn't say a word. He doesn't have to. In just this one last second, the victim knows the whole story. One, because the guy has no reason to burst into the office; two, because the guy's got a gun and it's pointed right at the victim's head or heart. It's gonna be a fatal shot nine and a half times out of ten."

Anne Marie was silent, but there were tears on her cheeks.

"So," Zachary said, "the police and the news people would be asking Mary O'Connor, the other council members, Bob Koesler, *you* . . .

"Was there any indication of bad feelings between Father Tully and Mr. Cody? Yes, there was. Did Mr. Cody make any threatening remarks? Not that we can recall, but there were some pretty harsh words.

"Things like that, eh?"

Anne Marie wiped her eyes with a lacy handkerchief. "You can't let this happen, honey," she said to her husband. "You can't let him get killed. How can you even sit here and anticipate these awful things? You've got to protect him!"

Zoo shifted in his chair and turned sideways toward them. "He hasn't done anything yet."

"Who?" Anne Marie asked.

"Cody."

"The object is to stop him from doing anything . . . isn't it?"

"You know the drill, honey," Zoo replied. "We've been through this before. The police are powerless to take any action in a situation like this. We can't operate unless there's been a crime."

"When we talked about this before, we weren't talking about a brother . . . a brother we love."

"Sweetheart, we were talking about everybody."

"You can't even protect Zack? You can't go to this Cody fellow and warn him away?"

"Not unless I want to lose my job. Just because Cody is a possible enemy of, well, anybody, doesn't give me the right to take any action. That sort of thing happens all the time. Nearly everybody's got somebody who hates him or her. But that's not a crime."

"Isn't there anything you can do to protect your own brother?" Anne Marie pleaded.

"The only way we can come close to that is to put Zachary in some setting that we can control. Put you," Zoo addressed his brother, "in, say, a hotel room with a cop. That sort of thing might happen in the case of a witness who's going to testify tomorrow and we want to see him live to do that. But there's no compelling reason to do it in this case. And you wouldn't want that."

Zachary waved away a refill of his cup. "No, I wouldn't. I didn't become the pastor of a parish so I can hole up in a room and hide from one of my parishioners.

"Anyway, don't you think we're getting carried away with this? What we're talking about is a tiff at a parish meeting between a council member and a pastor."

"The way you described this 'tiff,' " Zoo said, "it was considerably more than a mere disagreement. You impressed me, anyway, that this guy is desperately involved in his church. From all you've said, I'd have to conclude that there's a possibility that this could get physical. And, if it got to that point, I don't see it ending in a fistfight. He's got guns. I believe he might think about using one."

Zachary stood; the others followed his lead.

"We all have to work tomorrow," Zachary said. "We'd better call it a night. Thanks for the company . . . though I must say that I'm leaving somewhat more disturbed than I was coming over."

Zoo patted his brother on the back. "Sorry about that. As far as I'm concerned, what we said had to be said. I don't think there's much chance of anything extreme happening. It's just barely possible. Not likely.

"But I would appreciate it if you were extra careful. Particularly since you are determined to go on with the Folk Mass. Just watch yourself."

"I know, I know," Zachary replied. "As Cromwell said, 'Trust in God, but keep your powder dry.' "

"That's it," Zoo chuckled.

Amid handshakes and hugs, they parted.

17

"THAT WAS SOME show you put on tonight."

Bill Cody, who had just hung up the phone, paid no attention to his wife.

Eileen Cody, in nightgown and robe, stood in the middle of the living room. Her arms were folded across her chest; her slippered feet sank into the deep pile of the off-white carpet. "Did you finally get Father Koesler?"

"Yes, yes. He didn't say so, but I think Tully had reached him before I could call. He probably phoned right after we left the rectory."

"I don't blame Father Tully for getting his foot in the door with Father Koesler before you could pull off poor Tully's arm and beat him over the head with it."

He mumbled something in response. She didn't understand him, but cared too little to ask him to repeat it. "So, did you get him to attend the Mass this Sunday?"

"He'll be there. I knew I could count on him."

"Have you given any thought to whose team he'll be on?"

"Koesler? Of course not. In all the time I've—*we*'ve—been on the council, how many times have you seen us at loggerheads?"

"How many times has a Folk Mass been inserted in our schedule?"

"Look, Eileen, I don't need you on my back. I've got a big plagiarism hearing early tomorrow and I've got some last-minute case reading to do."

"Plagiarism! That should be duck soup for you."

147

"Not when the judge tells us in chambers that there's nothing new on the face of the earth."

"What?"

"Far as I can see, if there's nothing new on the face of the earth, there's no such thing as plagiarism."

"You sound like you're on a roll. The judge pulls the legal rug from under your feet and you count on a vote from the parish council only to find that it doesn't mean a damn.

"By the way," she added, "do you figure on taking Father Tully's word about the council being merely a consultative body?"

"I'll check it out tomorrow. But I doubt that he's leading us on. It'd be too easy to refute. He'd be up the creek without a paddle if he lied. Besides, I've got one small victory: You lost a vote."

"Molly Cronin?"

"She switched sides. She always votes with you. But not tonight."

"Who cares? As we learned, the vote means nothing."

He pushed off his loafers and let his feet luxuriate in the carpet. "Oh, the vote will mean something."

"Tell me."

"Mary O'Connor will publish the minutes of the meeting in the bulletin. The parishioners will read about the Folk Mass. They'll read about the vote. And for the first time for most of them, they'll know that their council is a paper tiger.

"I think when they see how close the vote was and that we won only to be vetoed by the pastor, their reaction will be interesting, to say the least."

"I think you're wrong, Bill."

He smiled mirthlessly. "Nothing strange about that, is there, darling? You always think I'm wrong."

"It's not so much that you're always wrong. It's more that you're so unbelievably bullheaded. Once you make up your mind on something, it's damn the torpedoes; full speed ahead."

"You exaggerate beyond all reality."

"Oh? How about our son, for instance?"

"Please!"

"Do you ever wonder if Al really wants to be a priest?"

"Don't be silly. Of course he does."

"How could anyone tell? You hardly give him room to breathe!"

"Eileen, we've been through this before. And I've got work to do."

"Sure, that's your out every time we get close to actual communication: You've got work to do. You've got a case to prepare. You're late for a meeting."

"For the love of God, Eileen, the kid has been in the seminary for nearly eight years. That's time for the candidate and the faculty to be sure that the vocation is real. I know: I've been through it."

"Then how come priests leave? When you were in there, there was more time—four years more. And after twelve years, some priests still left. According to you, the more time spent trying out the idea of being a priest, the more certain everyone is. But priests leave. To me, that means that even though Al's been in the seminary eight years, maybe he's not sure."

"That's nonsense!"

"Is it? It's not a case of *Al's* being sure. *You're* sure for him. You have been since he was an infant. If you had your way, you'd have had him ordained as soon as they cleaned him up after birth. You couldn't—or didn't—make it. But your son would."

He waved both arms, as if shooing flying insects. "You claim we don't communicate. That's because every time we talk we disagree. We reach an impasse. Like the one we're at now. I say Al's freely chosen to be a priest. The faculty agrees or he wouldn't be this close to ordination. And don't give me this stuff about priests leaving. Every profession has its failures.

"What's the matter with you, Eileen? You're on the verge of being the mother of a priest. A priest's mother. You're supposed to glory in that title. You're Irish. Irish women are famous for wanting a priest son. You act like it's a curse!"

"It's as simple as it possibly could be: I want my boy to do what he wants to do. I want him to be a success—but in the field *he* chooses."

"And"—he sighed deeply—"if that field is the priesthood . . . ?"

"How will he know?"

"If there's any doubt in Al's mind, *you* put it there. All you do is confuse him."

Eileen turned and walked toward the bedroom. Then she turned back toward her husband. She spoke as if it were a last-ditch effort. "Look, Bill, there's still a little time. He'll have Easter vacation. Why don't we send Al to a kind of retreat during Easter week?"

"A retreat! He doesn't get enough of that in the seminary?"

"I found this program—now, don't get your back up, Bill. It's a program run by a group of psychologists at a resort and clinic just outside Traverse City. It specializes in assisting people in resolving conflicts. It's got a great reputation for helping people who have a hard time making up their minds. We could send him up there. Give him this last opportunity to make up his mind. In solitude for a change."

He looked at his wife for a long moment. As if he were seeing her or something about her for the very first time. "What can I say that will finish this topic for the last time? Al has made up his mind. He's going to be a priest. That's it. Final. Bottom line. I'm certainly not going to send him off to where a bunch of quacks mess with his mind, hopelessly confusing him. He's going to be a priest. And anyone who stands in his way will answer to me. Is that clear enough?"

Eileen didn't respond. She turned and walked into the bedroom. She closed the door tightly. After a moment, there was a click as she turned the lock.

Bill shook his head.

This was not the first time that a locked door had stood between them. The first few times he had talked his way through the lock. Once he actually broke the door down—and badly hurt his shoulder in the process.

That was a long time ago. In recent years he had grown more stoic. Besides, a common bed no longer solved many disagreements or offered much pleasure. And the bed in the guest room was comfortable.

He took his briefcase to his desk in the den to finalize the material for tomorrow's trial.

He dropped a couple of ice cubes into a glass, poured two to three fingers of Dewar's scotch, and topped the glass with water.

He would nail that stupid son-of-a-bitch judge to the wall. But, he reminded himself, it all must be accomplished using the language of diplomacy.

He gave not another thought to Eileen—or to her assertions.

Al would be a priest. That was that. Al worshiped his father; Bill knew that. It was only natural that the son would be attracted to a calling, a vocation favored by the father. But that alone was not enough to motivate a boy to dedicate his entire life to that vocation. The priesthood would demand everything Al had to offer. His priesthood would be the very air he breathed throughout life and into eternity. Al knew that. Bill had made sure he did. It was just impossible for the young man to invest his entire life in a most demanding vocation simply to please his father.

Al wanted to be a priest. Al would be a priest. And let anyone who blocked his path beware.

Eileen put the book aside. She had read one page three times, and couldn't remember a word it said. She turned off the light and pulled up the quilt.

The night lights of the city played on the ceiling. She lay on her back and fought against thought. But she couldn't turn off her mind.

She was convinced this whole thing with Al was a horrible mistake. How could it be otherwise; her son majored in doubt.

She thought once again of her own life.

Her father, infinitely proud of his Irish ancestry, had considered himself God's gift to everyone—men and women alike. Her mother, also Irish, but in a lower key, might have settled for his being God's gift to her alone.

Dad's appearances at home were a matter of speculation at best. Work was over at five-thirty weekday afternoons. His earliest arrival home was never before eight in the evening.

The hours between were spent in the pub, where he and his chums would drink much, if not all, that had been earned that day.

These absences should not be confused with the midnight homecomings. Not to mention the nights when there was no arrival at all.

In any of these scenarios, there inevitably followed seemingly endless recriminations, loud and angry, frequently leading to violence.

Each morning, if he had indeed come home at any time the previous night, Dad would wake bleary-eyed and unsure of what had happened the evening before. He would shave and shower, put on his most charming Irish smile, and expect to begin the day with a clean slate.

Hardly ever was that to happen. Mother would greet him with last night's evidence. Lipstick of varying shades, suggesting more than one participant in the night's revels. Or semen stains. Or blood. Or torn clothing. Or condoms in his wallet.

Little Eileen, watching her mother in action, gained almost all the knowledge she might have needed for a career as a private eye. Hers was not a nurturing home.

Before the ink on her high school diploma was dry, she was out of the house and engaged in a series of barely gainful employment.

Finally, after scrimping and occasionally going hungry, she saved enough to enroll in the University of Detroit dental hygiene course. It was not beyond imagination that she might meet a dental student and that they might hit it off.

While dental hygienists did fairly well as far as income, dentists for the most part did fabulously. And what could be wrong with that? She had tried it poor; it was her turn to try it rich.

However, as it happened, she met a lawyer. Another student, who studied law in a neighboring building affiliated with U-D.

They courted. They married.

Her private vow as she entered their life together was to give however many children they would produce a secure home. A home free of loud, undisguised rancor.

In this she was helped along by her husband.

It simply was not in his disposition to try any of the tricks her father had. Eileen didn't have to microscopically investigate him or his clothing. He saw to it that she could depend on his being where he was supposed to be.

His income was more than adequate for their needs. Eileen continued her courses at U-D. Then she became pregnant.

Bill could not have been more solicitous. He encouraged her to drop her classes, at least for the foreseeable future.

She had gone from one of the world's most dysfunctional families into the hope of a career. Then into a marriage happier than she could have anticipated. And now, she was fulfilled: She would be a mother.

Eileen had her baby.

Then things began going downhill. There was the terrible and frightening word *cancer.* And major surgery. Followed by uncertainty: Had they found and removed every bit of the cancer?

Relief. The prognosis was only slightly guarded. She would lead a normal life, with one drawback: She would be barren.

This would not have been so crushing, but for two developments.

Bill began treating her as a "thing," an object of his pleasure. The previous tenderness was gone. Their sexual relations bordered on the mechanical. There was no genuine sense of love. No play to the foreplay. Sex now had little meaning for her. Kisses, hugs were memories. She sensed it clearly: Theirs was a relationship that was traveling in one direction only—toward a crash. All because she was no longer a baby machine, merely a pleasure outlet.

The other occurrence was even more subtle, since it developed over a much longer period of time.

It began with Bill's insistence that their child, Albert, be baptized at the earliest opportunity.

Eileen considered herself a practicing Catholic, though somewhat eclectically picking and choosing and practicing what she considered the best to come out of the Vatican Council. One of whose teachings had relaxed the necessity for speed to the baptismal font. But their baby was healthy. There was no reason to fear the rite could be physically harmful. So the second Sunday after birth—ten days, actually—Albert was christened.

At first Eileen was fascinated by her husband's absorption with their son. There was nothing Bill would not do for the infant, including diaper changings and staying up through the night when Albert was colicky or teething.

As far as Eileen was concerned, all this was unalloyed good. Just the opposite of life with her father.

But something else was building. It was a metaphorical wall between her and Albert. As far as she could tell, there was nothing deliberately malicious about the wall. But her husband was definitely building it.

Call it a sort of breakdown in communication between husband and wife. Bill was taking Albert and running with him absent any explanation or consultation.

Eileen had by far the major share of time with Albert. Weekdays during Bill's working hours, Al existed in his mother's loving world. Even when Al started kindergarten, Eileen had him on his way to school and on his return. But evenings and weekends, when work did not interfere, it was father and son doing things together.

Eileen was not jealous. Far from it. She felt blessed compared with many of her friends who were golf, sailing, football, baseball, etc., widows.

However, there were hints of trouble.

Such as: when Bill took Al to the firing range and introduced him to guns and rifles of almost every make and kind. Or when he taught his son that while it was not a good idea to kill animals just because they happened to be inconvenient occasionally, still, they had no rights and were on earth solely for the use and benefit of mankind. Or when he suggested that people of color might better separate themselves from white people, even though all were fully human with equally immortal souls.

These and other highly controversial matters troubled Eileen to her core.

This led to many a heated reasoning session with her husband, to no conclusion. If anything, Eileen's protestations drove her husband into a sort of underground indoctrination of the boy. At best, Eileen could only attempt to counter the questionable teachings and principles of her husband.

The result: a very confused young lad. He loved his parents, both of them equally, but in different ways.

And then there was church.

Generally, regular church attendance is associated with women more than men. This pattern was broken decisively in the case of Bill Cody.

At one time, a young Bill Cody had been a faithful altar boy, serving Mass daily. He was a shoo-in for the seminary. Although he eventually dropped out, he was proud of having spent those years in training for the priesthood.

That's where Al was headed from the time his father took him to Mass, explained everything, and gently but firmly let him know that the father would consider himself the luckiest and proudest person on earth if his son became a priest.

The pressure was building.

The mother could see clearly the pitfalls. Cataclysms were about to rattle the present Church structure. The priesthood, once one of the world's most stable vocations, would be shaken to its foundation. The hierarchy was shoring up the floodgates.

But the day was coming, Eileen knew, when things would have to change sharply. And the traditional male priesthood would become obsolete.

Perhaps even worse than what might become of this sublime vocation was the fact that Al was being brainwashed.

That was a harsh term, but it accurately described what Eileen saw in what her husband was doing to their son.

Eileen Cody, the product of a miserable childhood, desired above all that her son, her only child, lead a happy and fulfilled life. But how could he? He was being given no choice in the form and function of that life. While she, his mother, was forced to sit by as her husband pushed the boy down a conceivably disastrous path.

Of course, "good" Catholic parents—especially mothers—wanted a priest son. But "good" Catholic parents usually had large families—sons and daughters to provide grandchildren, and comfort in one's old age. Less usually did an only child become a priest.

And how many young men who didn't really want to be priests served time as they guiltily waited for the deaths of their parents to free them from a priesthood that they had entered only to please those parents. Was that what Al faced? Would he suffer through years of priestly misery, only to finally leave, a shell of a human being, on his father's death?

Time, now, was perilously short. Everything she had tried had failed. Not one of the dozens of irons in the fire had worked.

The proposed Easter vacation retreat, she had to admit, was a last-ditch attempt. Bill had seen through it, as inevitably she had known he would. And he had just shot it down. There was no getting around him. She had tried every which way. He was the power who was driving this disaster forward to the rocks.

There was no doubt about it, her back was to the wall. If something drastic didn't happen soon, Al would make a lifelong commitment. He would be doomed.

If there was no way around Bill, there had to be a path through him.

She had to eliminate Bill. The question was how.

Eileen Cody would sleep very little this night.

18

PATTY DONNELLY WAS in the sacristy vesting.

In a gesture intended to mollify the conservatives, some of whom inevitably would be in attendance, she would wear a traditional set of vestments.

She kissed the amice before letting it lightly rest on the back of her head, then tucked it around the neck and tied it after wrapping the strip around her body and back again.

Next she donned the alb, the long white gown that covered all but her head, hands, and shoes. The cincture tied around her waist let her adjust the alb so it would hang evenly.

The maniple she draped across her left forearm and pinned to the alb.

The stole traditionally marked a person's stature in the Roman culture of the Caesars. Until relatively recently in the Church, deacons wore the stole draped over one shoulder. Priests wore it over both shoulders, but crossed in front. Bishops wore it over both shoulders but hanging straight down in front, indicating that bishops had the "fullness" of the priesthood.

Patty wore the stole over one shoulder. She was about to become a priest, but she was still, as they termed it now, a deacon in transition.

Lastly, she slipped over her head the chasuble. The outer garment in ancient Rome. The back of this vestment was pinned up.

It was time for the procession to begin. The organ thundered and the choir sang. It was most impressive.

157

As she entered, the congregation in the crowded cathedral stood and applauded. She had never been more happy.

The ordination Mass began. After the welcoming prayers, Bishop McNiff, as rector of the seminary, testified that she was worthy.

Cardinal Boyle, as ordaining bishop, in a loud voice asked if anyone knew of any reason why this candidate should not be ordained. It was meant ordinarily as a rhetorical question. In this company there was an anxious moment of silence, in which Patty's many friends hoped and prayed no one would speak.

But a voice rose from the rear of the cathedral.

Those close to the sanctuary thought they heard someone shouting, "I object! I object!" followed by confusing sounds of tumult. A contingent of police wrestled the protester out the narthex doors to the sidewalk of Woodward Avenue, where he was arrested and carted off.

Gradually the interruption was played out. Everyone wondered who the interloper was. Those who'd managed to get a brief look at him described him as rather tall, a bit heavy, with straight black hair. He could have been that deacon, Bill Page. He was dragged out so rapidly that it was difficult to make an identification.

In any case, the ordination ceremony settled down and proceeded.

Patty knelt at the top step of the altar. Cardinal Boyle put both hands on her head, pressed down lightly, and held that position for a few moments. "Thus," read the commentator, "in sacred silence is the sacred character of the priesthood conferred." Then, one by one, all the priests in attendance took turns placing their hands on her head, sharing their priesthood with hers.

One by one the powers of her calling were spelled out publicly.

The stole was crossed over her other shoulder.

The words attributed to Jesus, "Receive the Holy Spirit. Whose sins you shall forgive, they are forgiven. Whose sins you shall retain, they are retained," demonstrated her power to absolve.

She was invited to offer Mass, to offer sacrifice for the living as well as for the dead, in the name of the Lord.

Finally, the pin was removed that had held the back of her chasuble.

She was a priest forever, sang the choir, "according to the order of Melchizedek," the King of Salem, who, as priest, uniquely offers bread and wine in sacrifice. He moves in and out of the Bible in three verses.

Patty was completely fulfilled.

The ordination Mass continued. Now it had become concelebrated by Cardinal Boyle, Bishop McNiff, and all the priests gathered in the sanctuary—including the Reverend Donnelly.

The prayers moved the ceremony through the offertory into the Canon of the Mass when the new priest for the first time pronounced the words that Jesus had spoken at the Last Supper: "This is my body. This is my blood."

In a short while, everyone was urged to share a greeting of peace. And for the first time at a Mass, Patty was at peace, complete peace. Her life was no longer incomplete. She no longer yearned for something that everyone told her she could never have. She had it. And no one could take it from her.

After the Communion service, the ordination Mass would have come to a swift conclusion if not for a surprising development.

Another—and, as far as Patty was concerned unexpected— ceremony began.

Bishop McNiff climbed into the pulpit and read from an official-looking document. It came from Rome, the Vatican. It was the announcement that the Reverend Patricia Donnelly was named titular bishop of the Bronx, New York, and an auxiliary bishop of Detroit.

Once again Cardinal Boyle read a notice informing anyone who had an objection to this appointment, to speak up now or forever hold his or her peace.

This time several voices were raised in protest.

Once again the police whipped into activity and the objectors were carried from the cathedral and carted off in the paddy wagon.

Members of the second procession took their places surrounding Patty. Another ceremony had begun.

Patty was led back to the altar and told to kneel. She had to be coached at every turn, since she'd had no reason to anticipate this development.

Someone held a book of the Gospels and rested it on the back of her bowed head. Unintelligible words were spoken.

Someone else came with a vessel of oil. He emptied the oil on her head, later necessitating a shampoo to degrease her hair.

Quite obviously, it was time for something else to happen. But no one seemed to know what.

Cardinal Boyle looked around, his heavy eyebrows nearly meeting at the bridge of his nose. Clearly, he was angry. "The miter!" he demanded, in what for him was a loud voice. "Who has the miter?"

"I gave it to Mickey—the altar boy," one of the priests in attendance said. "I gave him strict instructions not to put it down under any circumstances. The only one he could give it to was you, Your Eminence. So that you could put the miter on Bishop Donnelly's head. I don't know where Mickey is, but I'm pretty sure he's still holding the miter."

There followed an unorganized search for the altar server, while the congregation buzzed about what was happening.

Then a nun shrieked. She had found Mickey, his cassock raised and his pants dropped. He was sitting on a toilet. He hadn't exactly put the miter down. He had put it on. He was wearing it.

"I'm sorry, Father," he apologized, "but I had to wipe."

Someone snatched up the miter. It was not the nun; she was frantically searching for a priest to hear her confession.

Miter returned, the ceremony continued with the congregation still in the dark as to what had happened.

Cardinal Boyle, now smiling broadly, placed the miter on Patty's head. Then he handed her the crosier. It had all happened so rapidly and unexpectedly that Patty was near breathless.

But there was no time to stop and put some order into

the proceedings. Tradition called for her to process through the cathedral, carrying the shepherd's crook and blessing the congregation.

She was about to begin, when Cardinal Boyle touched her arm and beckoned her to follow him out the back way.

In some futuristic manner, after the fashion of *Star Trek,* Boyle and Donnelly were beamed inside the Vatican, into the Sistine Chapel.

Well over a hundred Cardinals were seated in the chapel. Bishop Donnelly was, indeed, the only non-Cardinal there. There was no mistaking it, they were present at a conclave, a meeting to elect a new Pope.

There were two unoccupied chairs at the rear of the chapel. But they were tipped forward as if reserved for someone else. Just like the refectory and those rotten deacons. However, in this case, a gracious Cardinal, noticing them standing, invited them to be seated.

She turned to Boyle. "What am I doing here? This is restricted to Cardinals."

Without turning his head, Boyle replied, "You won't be permitted to vote."

Once again, an ecclesiastical figure was telling her what she couldn't do, what she couldn't be. Even though she had never wanted to be a Cardinal, she thought it discriminatory that she was blocked from that office.

The Cardinals had just taken a vote. No candidate had won a simple majority. This had been their forty-first ballot. Prayers were said to the Holy Spirit for guidance and direction.

Now another vote was begun. One by one, the Cardinals marched, wobbled, or waddled to the altar, where a silver chalice waited for their ballots. Again the ballots were counted. There was a majority for the first time in this conclave. The name of the nominee was . . .

The silence was almost palpable. The nominee was Patty Donnelly.

The Cardinals looked at one another. How could this be? Who here would dare vote for a mere bishop—an auxiliary bishop at that! Titular head of some presumably fictitious diocese—the *Bronx*! And a *woman*!

"But I'm a woman!" she said to Cardinal Boyle.

Boyle shrugged. "Anyone can be Pope, as long as the Cardinals vote for that person."

A Cardinal approached Patty, knelt before her, and asked if she would accept the office.

"What do I say?" she asked Boyle.

"*Nolo* means you refuse. *Volo* means you accept."

Patty gave it a brief moment's thought. Then she cried in a loud voice, *"Volo."* And she hugged herself.

One by one, the Cardinals approached and offered her obeisance.

She was ushered to an adjoining room and outfitted in white-on-white with scarlet trim. The Papal colors set off the highlights in her blond hair rather nicely, she thought.

All the while, white smoke billowed from the special vent on the roof of the chapel. Hundreds of thousands of people crowded into St. Peter's Square.

The new Pope—Popess?—stayed just out of view behind one corner of the balcony.

A Cardinal came out on the balcony and read from an impressive scroll: *'Annuntio vobis guadium magnum. Habemus Papam!'"*

The crowd went wild. Then it quieted to hear the most important part of that "great joy"—the name of the new Pope.

"Patriciam . . ." The crowd became hushed. Was the Cardinal looped? He couldn't be serious. It sounded for all the world as if he'd said Patriciam. Feminine for Patrick! *Patricia?* Impossible!

But the Cardinal went on. "Patriciam," he said again, as if even he didn't believe what had happened. Then he read the parenthetical identification. " *'Sanctae Romanae Ecclesiae . . .'* " Here he stumbled. He almost bowed to hundreds of years of tradition and said, *"Cardinalem."* But after the brief pause, he read, " *'Episcopum,* Donnelly.' "

So there they had it. "I announce to you a great joy. We have a Pope. Patricia, bishop of the Holy Roman Church, Donnelly."

It was perhaps not totally applicable to apply the age-old cliché to an arena as vast as St. Peter's Square with hundreds of thousands in attendance, but you could hear a pin drop.

The Cardinal went on to announce, in Latin, "She has selected the name Toots the First!"

Still there was silence. As if the crowd, comprising hundreds of thousands of mainly Italians with a few thousand visitors, held its collective breath.

Then Patty stepped onto the balcony all dressed up in her white and gold and crimson vestments. From the distance of the crowd to the balcony, she looked like a doll. A Pope doll— uh, a Popess doll. That would have to be worked on.

Then one man, who must have had lungs of iron, since he could be heard clearly throughout the square, shouted, *"Vive la Papa!"*

Suddenly the crowd realized that it was foolish to be dumbstruck by this event. This was a unique occasion. They would be able to boast of this, to tell their offspring that they had been present at a priceless moment of history. The shout was taken up by every throat. *"Vive la Papa!"* They were careful to use the correct article: *"la"* instead of *"il."*

Pope Toots I was unsure what should happen next. The shouts crescendoed, peaked, echoed, and reechoed.

She had seen scenes like this on television and in movies. As she recalled, in similar situations, the Pope usually gestured with both arms. The gesture that suggests, "Get off my lawn, you crazy people!" She tried the gesture. It must have been correct because no one left the square, and the shouts wishing long life to the Pope continued unabated.

She should say something. But what? She was, of course, totally unprepared. She prayed to the Holy Spirit for the exact words and thoughts that would be perfect for this unique opportunity. She had some time to commune with the Spirit as the chant continued.

Finally, out of sheer fatigue, the crowd quieted and the acclamations virtually ceased.

She began by noting the obvious: that her election to the Papacy was so completely out of the question that this could only be the result of divine intervention. So everyone should, in utter humility, consider this a primal act of God.

She told them—and the world, by satellite television—of her principal concerns.

The first of these was ecumenism. There would be no more pussyfooting with the challenge of religious unification of the peoples of the world.

As a gesture of sincerity on her part, at her earliest opportunity she would seat herself on the Papal throne and using the unmistakable language of infallibility she would proclaim that she was not infallible.

Let the theologians wrestle with that one!

Next, she would abrogate Church or Canon Law. She was certain that no one, with the possible exception of hierarchical bureaucrats, would miss it. Instead, Catholics would be urged and taught to observe the Law of Love, the Law of Christ.

It was, as G. K. Chesterton had observed, not that the Christian ideal had been tried and found wanting; rather it was that genuine Christianity had been found difficult and thus not tried.

Well, by God, she said, we are going to give it a whirl!

At this, there seemed a shouted groundswell of affirmation for what she proposed. However, some of the Cardinals standing on the balcony with her began to slink back into the building. Lip-readers in the television viewing audience were able to discern that some of the Cardinals were mouthing variations of "What in hell have we done!?"

Furthermore, Toots I added, to move this genuine effort toward ecumenism, she would forgo the grandiose titles that contributed to the stumbling blocks against unity. Such titles as Vicar of Christ on Earth. She would concede that she was successor of Peter. But everyone should know that Peter was not God, he was not Jesus, he was not lord of the other Apostles, he was not a dictator, and he most certainly was not infallible.

He was first among equals. And that is precisely what Pope Toots I wanted for herself. Something that most other Christians, of whatever persuasion, would be happy to acknowledge. She would be the unifying factor in a global effort to live Christ's one and only law. The Law of Love.

She would be first among equals. And that equality would extend to gender as well as to theological principles. No more mealymouthed policies that demanded dignity and equality for women all the while denying equality at the core—the priesthood.

Her support from the crowd wavered a bit at that.

She was conscious that she had lost a few thousand with her determination to extend equality where it was needed—to everyone.

Nevertheless, she went on to her final—at least for this beginning—statement. She wasn't altogether sure this one came from the Spirit. But it was something she wanted. And it wasn't all that great a demand.

She announced that, with all deliberate speed, the seat of Catholicism—and hopefully of all Christianity—would be moved from the Vatican to Hawaii, specifically to Maui.

She realized this would be a jolt to the lifestyle of Italy, and particularly to Rome. But the people must remember—and here she was grateful that she had paid attention in Ecclesiology class—that, *Ubi Petrus, ibi Ecclesia* (Where Peter—in this case, Petra—is, there is the Church).

Well, Petra, in the person of Toots I, was headed for those sunny beaches of Maui. And the Church would simply have to hurry and catch up.

At this, there was no applause whatsoever. The Italians in attendance knew that without the Pope, Italy, Rome, the Vatican especially, would be a second- or third-class tourist spot.

Well, thought Patty, *tough*.

To deafening silence, she left the balcony.

No sooner was she inside than the Cardinal who seemed to be running things approached her. "Holiness—"

"Toots will be okay," she corrected.

"Holiness . . ." he repeated. He could not bring himself to use the adopted name of the new pontiff. ". . . there is a room full of news media types. Will it please you to see them?"

"Why not? I am pleased."

He led her into a room that could only be called a hall, so large was it. As she entered, everyone stood. She waved them back into their seats. Hands were raised all over the room, begging for recognition. She pointed at a reporter in the first row. "Al Neuhause," he identified himself, "of *USA Today,* winner of a Pulitzer Prize paragraph. Your Holiness—"

"Toots will do."

"Fine. Toots, we journalists will be covering your pontificate on a day-to-day basis. It looks as if it's going to be an exciting ride. Have you anything to tell us right off the bat?"

"Sure. Kiss my ring!"

She woke gradually, chuckling.

She'd had similar dreams before—but never in such rich detail.

She groped around her nightstand for the clock. It wasn't even midnight. She'd been overly tired and had gone to bed much earlier than usual. That must have brought on such a detailed dream.

She lay on her back, hands beneath her head, thinking.

It was a crazy dream, a home for her subconscious to play in. And a playpen for her stream-of-subconscious thoughts. Toots I—really!

And yet, getting down to the manifest content of her dream, these were the directions she'd hoped and prayed the Church would take.

Moving the seat of the Church to Hawaii was, of course, patently ridiculous. But the rest . . . ?

So far, ecumenism had been largely talk. With rare exception, the Catholic approach to Church unity had been a demand that the Protestant, Orthodox, and other sectarian Churches unite themselves with the Catholic faith by agreeing with the principal tenets of Roman Catholicism—all couched in carefully formulated diplomatic language.

To many mostly traditional Catholics, compromise and concession were two impossible words when referring to the True Faith.

John XXIII, the patron saint of the progressive wing of the

Church, realized that he, his office, and all it stood for, constituted the major obstacle to reunion. But notwithstanding the wide range of Church changes for which he was responsible, he could not bring himself to modify his job description to "first among equals."

And John was as close to making this leap as the progressives had gotten. After him, the ship of Peter veered in the other direction.

So much of the reality behind her dream was utterly beyond her wide-awake power to do anything about.

She was not Toots I. She couldn't bring everyone of faith into one fold. She could not erase infallibility. She wasn't going to move the Vatican—literally or even figuratively—one inch.

But she could, just maybe, do something about the equality the Church liked to run on about.

She thought of her idol, Jeannette Piccard. If Patty were married and her husband wanted to accomplish an important experiment that was dangerous as well, she'd assist him, as had Jean Piccard's wife, piloting a hot air balloon and setting a world's record.

But this assistance had been rendered by an equal. Perhaps even more than equal, since piloting the balloon may well have required more skill than merely conducting experiments at a great altitude.

At any rate, neither husband nor wife had played an inferior role.

When Mrs. Piccard achieved her life's goal, she was not in a begging posture. She was invited to be among the first women ordained in either the Episcopal or Anglican sects. She set the standard for equality in her Church.

Because of her courage in embracing holy orders, other Episcopal women achieved their dreams God only knows how many years earlier than they might have had to wait.

Mrs. Piccard died less than ten years after her ordination. But she died in greater peace than she might have because of what she had accomplished in the cause of equality.

And that was a thought.

How dedicated was Patty to her own goal?

She realized fully that she was in much the same situation as Jeannette Piccard had been. Of course, no figure appeared who would invite Patty to ordination. She would have to break through that glass ceiling on her own. But once she did, other Catholic women would enjoy the promise of genuine equality.

And, if this might require her life—remembering that Mrs. Piccard had survived less than ten years after her triumph— Patty was certain she herself was willing and ready to die for her cause.

Realistically she could not foresee how her ordination might cost her her life. But if it did, so be it.

19

Andrea Zawalich propped the book against a statue of the Blessed Mother on her desk. At the base of the statue were the words *Sedes Sapientiae*—Seat of Wisdom.

She had been trying to study, but she was preoccupied.

She kept thinking of her friend, perhaps her best friend, Patty Donnelly. As far as Andrea could see, Patty was on a treadmill to oblivion.

It wasn't that Andrea could not understand, empathize, sympathize with her friend's desire and goal. At one time, many years ago as a small child, Andrea had dreamed of one day leading a congregation in prayer. Of preaching. What's more, she knew she could do better than most of the priests she'd seen and heard.

She had a natural love of the liturgy, the vestments, the pageantry. And, to be frank, she knew she would appreciate the deference and respect shown to the clergy. It would be nice to be treated with respect and called . . . what? Not Father. Not Mother. Reverend?

In any case, she wouldn't wait around for people to honor her. Her preference would be her given name. Just plain Andrea.

She would wear clerical clothing just about all the time. She could help people in so many ways. Get them jobs. Give them money. Soothe troubled consciences. And on and on. Life would be good.

Those had been her dreams when she was very young. Now they were not even daydreams.

If one is going to be a priest in the Catholic Church, one ought at least to be able to be an altar server.

That thought returned her to the moment she had been labeled "unworthy" to serve at the altar. Unworthy not because she had committed some heinous sin, not because of anything her parents had done. Unworthy simply because she was female.

Sometime after she had been unilaterally rejected, someone told her the story of Branch Rickey and how he had integrated professional baseball by signing the uniquely talented Jackie Robinson to play for the Brooklyn Dodgers. Robinson was baseball's version of Sydney Poitier in *Guess Who's Coming to Dinner.* It helps the cause if one integrates with the very best of any race, color, or creed.

Andrea was particularly impressed by the preamble to the story of Rickey and Robinson. How deeply moved Rickey had been one day when he observed an earlier black athlete, qualified in every way to play in the major leagues, sitting by himself, endlessly rubbing his hands. Trying to erase the dark color from his skin. The color that was the only thing that kept him from competing in the all-white majors. And there was nothing the athlete could do about it.

Not until Jackie Robinson came along and heroically broke the color line.

Andrea could not get over how similar the plight of women was to the prejudice against African-Americans.

No matter how long or how hard that young athlete rubbed his skin, he could not blot out the color. Black was the inescapable and incidental hue of his skin.

Color had nothing to do with his ability to do what he wanted to accomplish. Yet color alone prevented him from accomplishing it.

So it was with Andrea. And Patty. And so many others whom Andrea would one day meet.

Their sex was what clothed their souls, their personalities, their bones. Their sex was what kept them from becoming what they wanted to be. And there was nothing they could do about it.

The athlete could not become white. Andrea could not become male.

There was, however, a difference that proved to be decisive. No one could sanely or reasonably argue that black men could not play at least as well as, if not far better than white men. Barring black men from baseball, football, basketball, whatever, was sheer, naked prejudice, flat-out racism.

Without question, black men were not allowed to play big league baseball due solely to their color. It was not due to lack of ability; it had nothing to do with ability. There was nothing even remotely associated with a single rational argument.

There was a slight, but again decisive, difference between the color barrier that had blocked black athletes from baseball and the sexual classification that barred women from the priesthood. And that difference was the reason for the prejudice.

The ostensible reason advanced by the Catholic Church for the "impossibility" of ordaining women is: Jesus did not select any women to be Apostles.

That's it. That is the rationalization for the argument against ordaining females.

It is hardly a substantial enough argument to bother with a serious refutation. But, unlike the erstwhile barring of blacks from baseball, at least the Church law blocking women from ordination *does* have a reason—no matter how spurious—behind it.

Where baseball had a heroic martyr to break through the artificial barrier, Andrea could not envision a Jackie Robinson-type female who could accomplish the same sort of breakthrough in the Church.

Secular courts of law would not dare to touch a case of gender discrimination perpetuated by a major, mainline religion.

No Catholic bishop—active or retired—has dared to simply ordain some women, as did the Episcopal bishops of the seventies. And if one or another were to do so, the Vatican surely would simply declare the ordination illicit and invalid. And the priesthood would still be a dream for Catholic women.

All Andrea needed to experience was that one word—"unworthy"—to know that she was jousting against windmills.

Once that priest had passed sentence on her, she never again seriously aspired to the priesthood.

She firmly believed that Patty, as determined as she was, would not breach the barrier. Not a hundred, not a thousand Pattys.

While Patty tried to figuratively knock down the door, Andrea planned to squeeze through a window. All she had to do was find an appropriate pastor and parish. The rest would be pretty much a downhill glide all the way.

She had been quite certain she had found the missing link. Last summer she had staged a full court press, attending a different church each weekend, even, in some parishes that seemed very close to the ideal, attending daily Mass.

Her exhaustive research appeared to pay off in late August when she chanced upon St. George's parish in Southfield, whose pastor was Father Benedict Manor.

Southfield, a northern suburb of Detroit, was a rapidly developing, still evolving suburban metropolis. It almost had a downtown, but had to settle for an extensive civic center with courts, police department, municipal offices, and an extensive library. Many doctors had offices throughout the suburb, which also boasted a major Catholic hospital and a good mix of black and white residents, many of them professionals.

It was the sort of mobile metropolis in which Andrea felt comfortable.

St. George was a large parish of 3,000 families, a grade school, and a pastor who should have been quintuplets, all of them priests. Instead, Father Manor was the lone inhabitant of the sprawling rectory originally designed to house four or five priests. And, indeed, before the priest shortage hit, St. George did support a pastor and two associates. The then pastor actually expected a third associate, who, as fate would have it, never arrived.

Instead said pastor, Leo Andover, lost one, then the other associate. Left to his own devices, he developed an arrhythmia. He gathered together his medical records and brought them to the chancery. The head of the archdiocesan curia granted Father Andover an early retirement, and he became a snowbird.

He helped at various Detroit-area parishes, supplying a weekend ministry through spring, summer, and fall. Then he wintered in California with his sister and brother-in-law.

That was five years ago. In the succeeding years, Father Manor had made few waves.

The principal of St. George's school was in her mid-forties. Forget teaching nuns. During her entire career to date she had filled educational and administrative duties in parochial schools exclusively.

A volunteer couple from the parish conducted an Adult Education venture, consisting mainly of guest speakers and film presentations. An active St. Vincent de Paul Society was the only apparent effort at Christian Service.

There were other activities going on in the parish. But the great lack was continuity, organization, and a spark of enthusiasm. Andrea saw herself as the mortar that would tie up all the loose ends and pull things together. She arranged an interview with Father Manor.

It was a desperately hot early Friday afternoon in late August. Andrea was kept waiting only a few minutes before the priest entered his office. She stood—it couldn't hurt—and shook hands. He motioned to her chair and she reseated herself.

He flopped into his heavily upholstered, leather-covered swivel chair. He wore black socks, black trousers, and a black shirt, the sort of shirt that takes a small, white plastic collar insert. The insert was missing and the top two buttons were open.

Father Manor was perspiring, even though the rectory was comfortably air-conditioned. The perspiration likely was caused by the priest's obesity. His hair looked windblown, rather than combed. "Just finished my swim," Father Manor wheezed. "Every Friday. Got to stay in condition. We've got three thousand families or more. If I go down"—he chuckled and everything moved—"the whole place grinds to a halt."

"I can well imagine." For a moment, Andrea harkened back to her youth and all her unwanted weight. However, she had been the victim of a thyroid condition. Father Manor probably was a host to food. She guessed the swimming might well be the extent of his exercise. Just think what would happen if he didn't get that swim!

"So . . ." Manor leafed through the documents that Andrea handed across the desk. He said nothing more than "So . . ." as he read them without apparent comprehension. Then, "Says here you're going to the seminary." He looked at her with heightened interest. "Something happen when I wasn't looking? You gonna be a priest?"

"No, Father—"

"Bennie. Call me Bennie. Everybody does."

"Uh . . . okay. No, Bennie, I'm a major in Pastoral Ministry."

"Pastoral Ministry," he repeated. "Hey, what's that? I'm the pastor. And what I do has got to be called 'Pastoral Ministry' . . . no?"

Andrea had the strong feeling that he was putting her on.

"Father—"

He raised a hand, stopping and reminding her.

"Bennie," she corrected herself, "I've got a sneaking hunch that you know very well that (a) the seminary is not advancing women to be ordained, and (b) Pastoral Ministry is a graduate degree that can be earned by the laity for service in the Church."

Manor smiled as a small child might when caught in a little mischief. "Yes, yes. You're right. Just a little funnin'." He leaned forward, placed her documents back on the desk and nudged them toward her.

She wished he had taken the documents more seriously. But, realistically, she had known this would be a hard sell.

She aligned her documents by tapping them together on the desk, then tucked them into her attaché case. "Bennie"— she was beginning to like the sound of it—"I think you hit the essence of this whole thing when you said, 'If I go down, the whole place grinds to a halt.'"

"You agree?" He seemed surprised.

"I couldn't agree more. Do you know how many priests it took to keep this parish from grinding to a halt? I mean, twenty or thirty years ago?"

"Yeah, sure. There was a pastor and two associates. And

that was hardly enough. Back then," he amended, "they were called assistants. Probably a better name for them. They 'assisted' the pastor; they didn't 'associate' with him." He smiled broadly.

"But," he went on, "you're right about the three priests not being enough. I've read some of the correspondence between old Father Andover and the chancery. He was flat-out begging for help. And," he said with conviction, "there weren't anywhere near as many families then as we have now!"

"Exactly," she agreed. "And the guys downtown expect you to do the work of three—or even four priests. But I ask you, Bennie, how long can they expect you to keep doing the hard job you're doing right now? And doing it so well?

"If you wear out—and who could blame you?—this fine parish grinds to a screeching halt."

He lowered his head in thought, thus forming four or five chins. A minute or so passed. He looked up, a bit of anguish showing. "But what can I do about it? It's not a case of withholding priests that they've got on tap. Sometimes they'd do that in the old days. They'd squirrel away some guys who were really available, waiting for the right spot or the right request for help. Those were the days when it paid to get mad as hell—and get some help in the bargain.

"But now"—his gesture denoted hopelessness—"what can we do? What can *I* do? The priest shortage is real. They can't send help. There isn't any help to send!"

"That, if I may be so bold as to say it, Bennie, is where I come in."

"You?"

"Little me. In June of next year, I will graduate from the seminary. I will be a pastoral minister."

He'd have known this if only he'd taken the trouble to actually read the documentation she'd presented. But, no mind; she'd just have to remember that Bennie didn't like to read. She was willing to spell it out for him.

"The people—your people—need you for the essential things nobody but you can give."

"They do." It was halfway between a question and a statement.

"Yes. Only you in St. George's parish can offer Mass."

"That's true."

"Of course that could be remedied. Other priests could be recruited to help on weekends and holy days."

"Well, really, I can handle things just fine on holy days."

"Well, that's brave of you. Let's concentrate on weekends then."

"We do get help."

"You do?" She knew he did.

"But I have to scrounge around. . . ."

"And that takes a lot of time from important things. Like preparing your homily each week." Actually, thought Andrea, give him his due: He did offer a fairly decent sermon.

"Well, yes," he said. "Now that I think of it, it does take a lot of time."

"Time that could be better spent."

"Absolutely."

"I could see to that. Notice I didn't say, I could *do* that."

"Hmmm." It was a distinction he hadn't considered until she called his attention to it.

"How about the liturgy commission of your parish council? Easy enough for some of them, say on a rotating basis, to arrange for sufficient weekend help. Could even develop into permanent assistance."

"That's an idea." Manor wondered why he hadn't thought of this. He'd just taken it for granted that the searching out of extra priests was solely the beleaguered pastor's job.

Andrea pressed on. "How about an evangelization program?" She knew they didn't have one. Actually, outside of Mass and a parochial school, there wasn't much going on in St. George's parish. It was open season for the enterprising young woman.

"Well . . ." Manor was growing defensive. ". . . there's been some talk of that."

"I don't mean for a minute, Bennie, that any of these services and activities should be *your* responsibility. Only that I'll bet the guys downtown wonder about them. I mean, a parish this size . . . and you just a short time from retirement. It's not unheard-of that sometimes pastors are made to delay their hard-earned retirement until a few of these services are in operation."

Really? he thought.

There had been talk over the clergy grapevine of retirements granted earlier than programmed. Usually with some medical urgency. In that sort of situation, the question was whether to grant full retirement income or prorate it. But Manor was not aware of any priest being forced to postpone his retirement. The very thought of it made him perspire in abundance and produced in him a strangely claustrophobic anxiety. As if he were trapped within St. George's parish, and the parish, in terms of the rectory and church, were shrinking and closing in on him.

He knew that St. George's was pretty much a run-of-the-mill parish. The sole feature that made it at all outstanding was its grade school. Yet the school's existence was much more the product of luck plus Father Andover's extraordinary labor.

Parochial schools began to live on borrowed time once the convents began to empty. Then the few remaining teaching sisters spread out to varying apostolates not remotely connected to schools and teaching.

Without the sisters' coolie labor—offering up their lives, chastity, obedience, and poverty—it is solidly doubtful that a Catholic parochial school system in this country even would have been attempted.

In recent years, a significant number of parochial schools had closed, victims of the need to pay a living wage to the laity who staffed the schools and who very definitely had not taken the vow of poverty.

But if a parish could weather the storm, hang on until the financial drain was plugged, there was a chance of survival. The solution: Charge a realistic tuition and count on enough families to pay it, even if these families did not reside within the boundaries of the parish.

Father Andover's heart condition was largely the product of his so-far successful efforts to keep his school open. If the

Church ever got around to passing out beatifications for giving up one's life for the parish school, Father Andover would be in the running.

All this Father Manor inherited when he took over the reins of St. George's parish from Father Andover.

Since then, Father Manor had presided over the status quo, doing nothing even vaguely innovative during his watch at St. George's.

Andrea knew this. That is why she was able to intimidate Bennie. He had been counting so on the joys and well-earned pleasure of retirement. Till then, all he really had to do was stick with the tried-and-true routine, and in a little while he would be all set for the rest of his hopefully long and well-deserved leisure.

He was delivering daily Mass. He scrounged up help for weekends. There was a parish council. It wasn't doing much, but it was there. The good old St. Vincent de Paul Society was doing its job taking care of emergency charity needs.

The precious school was . . . well . . . there.

Father Manor did little in or for the school. It functioned. He had made it quite clear to the principal that she should take complete responsibility for its operation.

She handled enrollment. People calling at the rectory hoping to get their children in school were referred to the principal. Parents protesting discipline problems in school were referred to the principal.

Father Manor had inherited the principal along with the school. He was completely uninformed as to the lady's qualifications, if any, for the position. As long as the school continued to function, he gave it no thought.

Now this young woman was disturbing him greatly. She was forcing him to question what he had been depending upon without question: the light at the end of the tunnel.

All the while he was mulling these thoughts, Andrea was interpreting his expression. She detected by turns anxiety, concern, qualms, self-doubt, and a pinch of panic.

She knew she had him on the ropes. "I don't want to suggest that there would be the least chance that the guys downtown would actually block your retirement. But, on the other hand, I don't think anybody wants to risk the slightest possibility that something might go wrong."

"Do you think so?" He pulled out a handkerchief and mopped his face and the back of his neck.

"All I'm saying is that it's not something you'd want to leave to chance . . . don't you think?"

He thought. "But the others . . ." he said in a tone of desperation. "So many of my buddies have retired. And some of them left their parishes no better off than mine!"

"Did many of them have a school?"

He thought. "Not many. But some did."

"In the same shape as St. George's?"

"What do you mean?"

"Well, for starters, the enrollment—it's been going down."

"It has?" He paused. Then, "How would you know a thing like that?"

"Father—Bennie—you don't think I just walked in here blind? Without doing a considerable amount of research?"

He felt guilty, very guilty. He should have known about the enrollment. Hell! Why hadn't the principal told him?

On the other hand, he'd been very strong about her not bugging him about school matters. She was supposed to solve whatever difficulty arose.

"The thing is, Bennie, you shouldn't have to be bothered except in extreme emergencies. And then you should have someone to inform you of all the facts, give you all the information so you can render a decision with no wasted time."

Manor shook his head. "There isn't anyone like that . . . I mean, anybody who could do that for me."

"I don't have to tell you how important your school is. Not only to this parish and to some of the families in your neighboring parishes. It's important to the diocese too. The education office downtown takes special interest in the few parochial schools that are left.

"I think it's important to make sure the school is operating as perfectly as possible. One of the things I'm pretty sure of is that the people in the education office downtown want to see enrollment going up. Not down."

"Well . . ."

"I don't want to even suggest this, but what if you reach retirement date and you find out they want you to straighten out the school before you go? I'd say that now is the time to make sure all the t's are crossed and the i's dotted.

"But let's not stop there. St. George's could be the envy of the diocese. I think we"—she slipped in the plural effortlessly—"should think of taking on some coordinators."

"Coordinators?" He was swept up in the flow of her suggestions.

"Yes. A coordinator for liturgy. Not just ensuring the weekend help you need, but planning—from week to week, season to season—themes that will involve the congregation.

"Then there's a Christian Service."

"We've got an active St. Vincent de Paul—"

"Marvelous! But the Vincentians should be a dynamic part of a larger vision that doesn't just react to problems, but is aggressive in shaping programs like visiting the sick, the jails, and so on.

"And there is so much more. Coordinators for the youth of the parish. There are wonderful programs for family life and adult education and religious education for the children.

"And to do all that we'd have to form and train catechists.

"And let's not forget music ministers. It's not enough anymore to just have somebody playing the organ without encouraging full participation—"

"Wait! Wait a minute!" She was bombarding him. He was aware of almost every program she was suggesting. But he'd never seriously thought of implementing any of them.

For the simple reason that, at best, it needed somebody young—young and energetic—to take on the challenge of these programs. Someone as young as . . . this young woman who had painted a picture so bright with promise that he almost considered passing up retirement and getting involved in a parish once again.

Almost. "Let me see those documents you put on my desk."

Smiling, she retrieved the documentation from her attaché case and passed the papers to him.

He riffled through them. She wished he wouldn't do that. They deserved to be kept and studied. They contained not only her résumé and transcription of grades, but also a blueprint of just about everything she had just presented.

He paused at one document. "Your graduation is in June of next year?"

"But I can begin building everything we've talked about right away. It's just a matter of interviewing and selecting the right people. And as far as the next scholastic year is concerned, I can pretty much come and go as I please."

Manor smiled. "You strike me as someone who knows what you're doing."

"I think so." She returned the smile.

"So what do you need with another year in the seminary?"

It was a good, thus difficult, question to answer in twenty-five words or less. "There are a few courses I want to take to upgrade my knowledge and experience. Plus there's the diploma that states I am a pastoral minister. That will satisfy the bureaucrats downtown, and it will make it lots easier to deal with our parishioners."

He seemed to still have some doubts.

"Look," she explained, "after Vatican II nearly everybody in the pews was overwhelmed with changes. It seemed as if anybody who wanted to could get up and initiate some program or other. And in a lot of instances that was true . . . sadly.

"It is extremely important that the person who heads a program as vast as the one we're talking about be well qualified. I dare say that without the diploma, this program would die aborning.

"The authorization that my graduation provides is crucial. So what I'm proposing is that you let me start now, before school begins in another month. I can meet the parishioners who really want to get involved and get them reading and studying. Then, as the school year progresses we can lay all the groundwork.

"And when I graduate, we can hit the ground running." She folded her hands on the desk. Her proposal was finished.

He swiveled his chair so that he was looking out a side window. "You present quite a package," he said, without turning back to her.

"I know that. But it will work. I know that too. By the time you're eligible to retire, you can hand the diocese a parish that is a smoothly running machine. Not that the machine is the end product we're working for. Our program has to be, at all times, Christocentric. It's just that everything in the parish will lead smoothly to that end."

He rocked back and forth for a few moments. "And what will all this cost?" As he asked the question, it occurred to him that as often as he had dealt with priests or religious, the subject of money, reimbursement, salary, seldom was raised.

But this was the age of the laity. Theirs was a far greater need for a decent wage than priests or religious whose maintenance and even a modicum of comfort were all but guaranteed.

She nodded. It was a decent question, one that needed to be explored. "Bennie, I am not going to be living the high life on any wage the diocese or parish pays me. I know that. There are guidelines sent out by the diocese suggesting a certain salary for employees. It will cost the parish something for me and for many of those coordinators. I will economize as much as possible. But the conclusion you must reach is that it will be money well spent.

"I know your present budget doesn't provide for these outlays. Your next budget will have to reflect these expenditures. But I can assure you, once your parishioners experience what we can provide, you won't get many complaints."

He deliberated. Slowly he swiveled back to face her. "*If* we do this, what assurance do we have that you will follow through? I mean, I don't have anything but your word and an attractive plan. Do you have any . . . what? Collateral?"

"Sure. How about this: In this beginning phase, as I get things ready to go, until June of next year when I graduate, you put my salary in escrow. We'll put it in the contract that I won't collect the salary unless and until everything is ready to go and I have my diploma."

"Sounds like something I could sell to the council and the parishioners. Are you sure you want to put that thing in about the diploma? That seems a bit chancy. I'm just thinking about you now."

"I know you are. And thanks. But it's not that chancy. It's the next best thing to a lead pipe cinch. Besides, as I said before, I'm nothing without that diploma. It's my badge. It's my license to practice. I want it in the contract. If not for you, for the parishioners."

"Andrea"—he rubbed his hands together—"I think we can do business."

"Bennie, I was counting on that."

"Call me in a couple of days—make it the first of next week. I'll do a little checking and we can haggle about some money."

That was last August. And since then both sides had honored the bargain.

Father Manor had sold it to both his parish council and the parishioners. The atmosphere was not unlike that of Vatican II. In a way, that might have been expected, since that Council had passed over St. George's parish without stirring up much enthusiasm. So there was plenty of bottled-up sentiment to spare.

Andrea quietly organized the various coordinators, some from St. George's, some from among her friends outside the parish.

All the while, Andrea kept a low profile. She would not actively begin the program until after her graduation from the seminary. That diploma would be her ticket to implement the programs without valid opposition.

She envisioned how her work would develop.

Only a small percentage of the parishioners would respond to her call and become active. The majority of the rest of them would be pleased that all these things were happening. Given good direction, they would participate more actively than they had—especially in the weekend liturgies.

And then there would be a vocal few whom the changes would hit hard. They would object that Andrea and her precious programs were going too far.

Andrea would treat them gently. But her trump card was the certificate naming her a pastoral minister. And if they didn't know what that was, Andrea would be happy to explain. Or, if push came to shove, they could look it up.

Now she was only a few months from her dream assignment.

Things were on course and on time.

Her future was pretty much assured.

She would, in effect, be the pastor of St. George's.

Father Manor would be pastor by the book. He would offer Mass. No one could take that from him. He would deliver the homilies, something he did quite well. But, through weekly conferences with him, she would have considerable influence on both topics and development.

The rest of the parish would be hers. She could never have hoped to do this so well had not Manor, in effect, already abdicated and become absorbed with his coming retirement.

Of course she had no idea who would follow Bennie as pastor. But it didn't seem to matter. Either she could continue as she was, controlling virtually everything, or she could carry her by-now impressive credentials to another parish of her choice.

She was about to arrive at her life's goal.

Some priest might have thought her "unworthy" to be ordained. But she clearly was not "unworthy" to be the pastoral minister, who was, not counting the deacon, the next best thing to a priest.

Now that her full potential was about to be realized, thoughts of her friend Patty flooded her mind more and more often.

Patty banging her head against an unyielding brick wall. Patty, ever the optimist, hoping against all odds to be ordained.

Patty doomed somehow equaled Andrea guilty.

There was no way Andrea could save Patty from herself. Earlier on, Andrea had tried to get Patty into the pastoral ministry program. But Patty's invariable response was to try to coax Andrea into participating in the protest against women being banned from the Master of Divinity courses.

Now that her own future was assured, Andrea focused on Patty. What could Andrea do for Pat?

She asked herself the question so often that it almost became a mantra.

Then something occurred to Andrea. A scheme that might accomplish much in the area of evening scores. It was a tricky, even dangerous plan. And it was just those adjectives—tricky and dangerous—that endeared themselves to the heart of this confident young woman.

She would need help carrying out this scheme, but with a little bit of luck, Patty Donnelly would end up a very satisfied camper.

20

IN THE SEMINARY'S basement was a small room lined with snack dispensing machines. A few small tables and chairs filled the remaining space.

It was midnight. A lone figure sat very still. On the table before him was a pack of cheese crackers and a small carton of milk. The young man had sampled neither. He was lost in thought. So much so that he jumped, startled, when another man entered the room.

The newcomer was also startled. He had not expected anyone else to be here at this time of night.

The only light in the room came from the vending machines. So it took a few moments for them to recognize each other.

"Al! Whatinhell are you doing here?"

"Couldn't sleep," the man at the table replied. "It was here or chapel to be alone and think. Chapel's so creepy at night. But come on in, Bill. On second thought, I could use some company."

"Yeah, sure." Page produced from beneath his bathrobe a pint bottle of Jack Daniel's. He placed the bottle on the table. "Want some?"

"No, thanks. I'll stay with milk." Cody opened the carton and took a sip. He marveled at Page's daredevil approach to seminary rules and regulations. For Page, rules were little more than a challenge, hardly anything to be observed as part of character formation.

Page fetched a bottle of Vernor's ginger ale. He took one of the Styrofoam cups and mixed the Vernor's with a heavy dose of whiskey, then tasted it. "Could use ice. But"—he smacked his lips—"it'll do for now."

Cody smiled. "Bill, don't you take anything seriously?"

"Sure." Page thought for a minute. "Let's see . . ." He smiled. "Good alcohol, good food, and good sex. None of which do we get in here."

Cody hardly ever could tell the difference between Page the epicure and Page the kidder. "Come on, Bill: All you have to do is stick to business, and in a few months you'll be able to have at least two of your requisites."

"Why settle for two when you can have all three?"

"Quit kidding."

"Who's kidding?"

Cody shook his head. "Do you realize the chance you're taking right now with that booze?"

"Chance! Al, do you think for a moment they're going to boot a deacon out over a little moonshine? Kid, I'm everything they want. The 'mature vocation' they're trying to sell. A nice, conservative theologian. And an all-but-up-there-on-the-altar ordinand." He snorted. "At this point in time, they need me more than I need them."

"Do you really believe that?"

"Okay, okay; so maybe I'm exaggerating a little. I'm not about to bring some booze into the refectory at mealtime. I'm not going to beg them to fire me. That would be idiotic—and I'm no idiot.

"But, Al! Baby! The *snack room*? At midnight? C'mon . . ." It was a combination of a grin and a sneer. "I can bluff any security guard who chances in here. And if it's a faculty member, he or she has got more explaining to do than we have. After all, they've got a suite of rooms. They've got a fridge in their rooms. They've got all the snacks, drinks, or whatever right there in the comfort and convenience of their own rooms. So whatinhell are they doing down here? At midnight.

"Meanwhile, I slip the bottle back under me robe as I ask, 'Excuse me, Father, is there anything I can get you that you don't already have in your room?'"

"I still think it's chancy."

"Lighten up, Al. Most rules can be bent a little, at least. The talent lies in knowing just how much you can get away with—how far you can go before the rule is fractured. And, if you're smart, you stop just in time."

Cody recalled something the rector, Bishop McNiff, had mentioned in one of his spiritual conferences. It fitted Page to a T.

McNiff was talking about the rule of life laid down for seminarians. He compared it to a fence around a yard. There'd always be at least one seminarian who kept kicking against the fence.

As the years progressed, and ordination drew closer, the fences expanded, allowing room for development and maturation. But the lad kept kicking against the ever-retreating fence.

At ordination, the rules that had guided the seminarian disappeared. Not that there were no more rules. But there was no reinforcement as there had been. The fences stood for reinforcement. The man who was kicking against them now had no more fences holding him back. Where he went from there was anyone's guess. To the moment of ordination he had exhibited little or no self-control. Now, it was possible the man's priesthood might self-destruct.

Could that apply to Bill Page? It certainly seemed so.

Page poured more whiskey in the cup. He neglected to add anything else. "Hey, Al, you sure you don't want some of this? There's plenty more where this came from."

Cody hesitated. Finally, he stood, emptied his milk into the sink, got a Styrofoam cup, and extended it to Page, who splashed some of the whiskey in. "Want some ginger ale?"

"No. This will help me forget things. Which is why I came down here in the first place. Maybe a drink or two will let me get some sleep."

Page extended the bottle and Cody let him fill the cup to half full.

"You wanna forget," Page said, "enough of this should do the trick. And don't worry, I'll be the designated walker. I'll see you to your room. I wasn't planning on getting blotto anyway.

"But, Al—forgive me, but this isn't like you. What's the matter?"

Cody sipped from the cup and let the warming liquor linger in his mouth before swallowing. He shuddered. This was powerful stuff. "You weren't at spiritual conference last night," he said.

"What else is new?" Attendance at these conferences was not a command performance, Page had learned. So he rarely attended.

"McNiff told this story about a Trappist abbey back in the days when the monks never talked." Cody tasted the whiskey again.

"Seems," he went on, "that a bishop was visiting the abbey. He was walking around the garden when he spotted this Brother working in the garden. The guy seemed very depressed.

"The bishop prided himself as a great if amateur psychologist. So he called the Brother over to him. Here you gotta remember," Cody explained, "that even in those days of perpetual grand silence, the monks were allowed to respond to a bishop.

"So the bishop says, 'Brother, you look ill at ease—downright depressed. I think I know what's troubling you: It's that perpetual silence. You really want to talk again—freely—if only for a short while . . . that it?'

"The Brother thinks about this and after a moment says, 'I don't think so, Bishop.'

"So the bishop ponders a bit. 'I think I've got it,' he says. 'It's the food. Never any meat, small portions, no snacks allowed—and all of this in silence, so you can't even complain . . . that it?'

"The Brother considers this, then says, 'It seems like you're coming close, Bishop. But no, it's not that.'

"Now the bishop is really puzzled. After some thought, he says, 'Probably it's your sleeping arrangements. I mean, trying to get a good night's rest while you're lying on a lumpy straw mattress while all around you in their own cubicles the other monks are snoring and making noises as they also toss and turn on these uncomfortable mattresses . . . that must be it!'

"The Brother mulls this over. 'Nope,' he says, finally, 'I don't think that's it.'

"The bishop throws up his arms in defeat. 'All right, Brother, I give up. What do you think your problem is?'

"And the Brother drops his hoe and says, 'Bishop, I think it's the whole damn thing.' "

Page chuckled and poured a little more whiskey in his cup, adding a bare dash of Vernor's—probably to keep his promise of being the designated walker. "And that's it with you, eh? It's the whole damn thing?"

Cody nodded and swallowed a generous mouthful.

"Well, take it apart a little, Al: What's one part of the whole damn thing?"

Cody gazed lingeringly at the little whiskey remaining in his cup. "My father," he murmured.

"Your dad?" Once again, Page was forced to appreciate that he was indeed old enough to be Al Cody's father. Just barely, but old enough nonetheless.

"Yeah. Earlier tonight he was going to go to the mat with his pastor over a folk liturgy they started in the parish. It's got to be over now. And I don't know how it came off."

"Pretty bad for your father, I'd guess," Page said. "He's in the parish council, right?"

Cody nodded. "The president."

"Even so, he's going up against a battleship . . . I mean, standing up to the pastor—who is he again?"

"Tully, Father Zachery Tully."

"Oh, yeah. He's the mulatto—the guy who came from Dallas. The Josephite guy."

Cody nodded again.

"And he took over St. Joe's from the guy who's here now— uh, Koesler . . . right?"

"Right again. On top of that, the pastor's got a brother in the Detroit police force—a homicide detective."

"No shit! I didn't know that."

"I tried to tell Dad that opposition was futile. But, typical of Dad, he wouldn't hear of it. Once he makes up his mind, that's all she wrote.

"But he can't win this one . . . I know it. And I just couldn't get through to him." He shook his head. "He must feel lousy now. And I can't help him. I feel rotten." He drained the cup and held it out for a refill.

Page too shook his head, but poured more whiskey in Cody's cup. "Okay, so your dad is part of the whole damn thing. And you can't do anything about it right now. But whatever happened tonight he'll get over in time. It ain't like a Folk Mass is gonna bring down the Roman Empire."

Cody nodded.

"So," Page said, "what's some more of 'the whole damn thing'?"

Cody tried to think of all the rest of the mess inside his head. It was, thanks to Jack Daniel's, getting muddled. "I dun— dunno, Bill," Al slurred. "I coulda sworn there was more. But it dunn't seem to matter." He knew a big part of what had robbed him of sleep was his pending ordination. He just couldn't get his mouth to cooperate.

"God, Al! I wish you would spit it out. You are so damn depressing. Maybe it would help if you hadn't gotten loaded so soon. It might have helped if you could have talked about it." Page screwed the top back on the bottle and slipped it into the pocket of his robe. He pressed Cody to lean against him as they wove their way out of the snack room and down the corridor toward the residence wing.

Page continued to talk, not at all sure that Cody was conscious or even semiconscious. Whether he could even hear, much less comprehend.

Actually Page was finding it a bit of a lark. At least Cody wasn't in any condition to interrupt.

"You wanta think about something that's really depressing?" Page stage-whispered. "My sex life. Like, it's a big zilch.

"If I could paraphrase Alfred P. Doolittle, I'm gettin' ordained in June. Ding-dong, the balls are gonna chime. There's girls all over the place, and I've got just three months to lay every one of 'em. Heh, heh, heh!" He laughed mirthlessly.

"Nothin' wrong with the Doolittle character. The problem

was Lerner and the way he wrote the role," Page mused. "Doolittle grieved because he was gettin' married in the morning. And then Lerner wants us to believe that he's gonna live faithful to his wife from that moment on.

"Now I ask you, Al: What was there in the character of that cockney bum that would lead anybody to imagine he'd be faithful? Nothing, I tell you. Nothing!" Page almost shouted his conviction.

Cody, through his drunken haze, shushed Page.

Page reverted to the stage whisper. "Sorry. But that's God's truth: Nothin'. Doolittle may get married in the morning, indeed. But how long do you think that'll last? Huh?"

Cody mumbled something totally unintelligible.

"That's right," Page affirmed the gobbledygook. "Probably on the way to the wedding reception he'll screw the bridesmaid—all of 'em if there's more than one."

For no good reason, Cody found a corner of sobriety for just a moment. "You mean that's what you're gonna do when you're priested?"

"Hey, good goin', good buddy. I didn't think you had any more language in your head.

"But, no, I don't plan on laying anybody for a long, long while. You've gotta be careful with a thing like that . . . although, now that I think of it, the chancery crowd would probably be relieved that I wasn't a pedophile.

"Still and all, I'm not *Father* Doolittle. There's a certain amount of discretion expected—Al . . . Al . . . wake up!"

Cody had, indeed, fallen asleep in a vertical position. For the past few steps, Page had been literally dragging Cody's limp form.

With great effort, Cody once again got both feet on the ground.

"That's more like it." Page was congratulatory. "Say, we're almost to your room."

Cody looked up for a moment and managed to keep his head straight.

"Al, since you told me the little morality tale about the

bishop and the Trappist monk, I've got one for you. And it speaks right to the subject I've been running on about."

"Unh . . ." Cody responded in a somewhat affirmative tone.

"This is about a guy who is playing his usual lousy round of golf. On the fifth hole he's off in the woods looking for his drive. All of a sudden the devil comes out of nowhere.

" 'How would you like to play scratch golf for a change?'

"The guy says he'd love it.

" 'Okay,' the devil says, 'you can have your great golf, but it's going to near ruin your sex life. Still want the golf gift?'

" 'Yeah,' the guy says, 'anything for that.'

"So the guy's game just takes off. He wins every match and tournament he plays. Then, one day, about a year later, he meets the same devil on the same course in the same rough.

"The devil asks him how his game is coming. The guy says it's terrific. He never thought he'd ever play this good. 'So,' the devil asks, 'how's your sex life?'

"The guy shrugs. 'Not so bad. I get it about once a month, maybe a little less.'

" 'Gee,' the devil says, 'I wouldn't think that was any good at all.'

" 'Oh,' says the guy, 'it's not so bad for a Catholic priest in a small town who doesn't own a car!' "

Once more, Page broke himself up with his wheezy laugh. "Get it?"

After a moment's thought, Cody half-nodded. "You're gonna get good at golf?"

"Well," Page said, "that's sort of it. I don't plan on scoring like I did when I was with the ad agency. But I figure quality will have to make up for quantity. It'll work out. Only . . ." There was a long pause.

"Only . . . what?"

"Only I just pray that no dame makes a play for me."

"How come?"

" 'Cause as horny as I am after this long period on the sexual wagon, I'd never be able to resist, no matter what she looked like."

21

THE KNOCK ON the door was almost apologetic. As if whoever was there had second thoughts.

Father Koesler glanced at his calendar. No appointment was noted. But any hesitation on his part and the bashful caller would probably run away. "Come in," Koesler called out, just loudly enough to be heard through the heavy door.

The door opened about halfway and an obviously embarrassed Deacon Al Cody slipped in. "I'm sorry, Father. I know I don't have an appointment. Is it okay to come in? Are you busy?"

"No, no. Come in. Make yourself at home."

Koesler, in black trousers and a white T-shirt, had been reading. He picked up a cassock from a nearby chair and quickly buttoned it on, interrupting only to motion Cody to a seat.

Both now formally cassocked, they sat facing each other across the desk.

"So, Al," Koesler broke the ice after a few moments, "what brings you here?"

"I need some help, Father."

"With what?"

"A homily. You volunteered to help any student who wanted it. I want it."

"Okay, we can give it a whirl."

Was a homily help the real reason for Cody's visit? From long experience, the priest knew that people often camouflaged a perplexing, perhaps threatening problem beneath a trivial, even fictive concern. Time would quickly tell in this visit.

Cody's presenting problem was, indeed, a homily he was supposed to prepare, compose, and commit to memory. It was natural for him to seek help from Koesler. He had long admired this priest. Father Koesler always seemed so confident in all he did. Characteristically, in any given circumstance he would gather all the information he could, then reach a decision and act on it.

Decisiveness, determination, incisiveness—qualities Cody most wanted and least possessed.

Ever since his family had moved into St. Joseph's parish and gotten to know their pastor, Cody had admired him. Father Koesler was a role model for Cody.

At those occasions when the young seminarian was able to concentrate on the way Father Koesler practiced his priesthood, his doubts would lessen as he would tell himself, I want to be a priest like him. But such occasions were few and far between; most of the time Cody was away from home and parish.

The seminary, his real home over the past several years, was filled with students who tried to conform to the conservative, traditional philosophy and theology that was at this school's core, while trying to discover what they truly wanted to do with the rest of their entire lives.

It was also filled with students who, like Pat Donnelly, wanted something from the seminary that they would never get.

Amid all this searching, praying, reflecting, meditating, contemplating, and indecision, Al Cody felt adrift.

He could look at someone like Father Koesler and say, I want to be like that. But then he would return to classes and be lost in doubt. Did he want to—could he—be a priest day in and day out for the entire long stretch of the rest of his lifetime?

Father Koesler pushed aside a pile of books he'd been using for reference and research. The middle of his desk was now clear and ready for action. "Well, Al, first thing we need to know is when this homily is going to be given."

Cody blushed. "This Sunday," he murmured.

"This Sunday! You're not giving yourself much time."

"I know. I know. But I did this on purpose."

"Oh? What purpose?"

"Well, see, Father, I figured that in the priesthood there'll be lots of times when I'll be busy with lots of things and I'll come up on a Thursday night—like this—when I've got only a couple of days to get things together for the weekend liturgy. And that includes, especially, the homily."

"So you're going to try the just-about-worst-case scenario—a homily whipped up at the last minute. You've got to do it now. But let me give you a bit of practical advice—at least it's been practical for me."

"Sure, Father . . . please."

"When you get done with the last of the Sunday Masses, give yourself the rest of the day off. You'll need it. But Monday morning, read the text of the three readings for next week and then develop a link between them. Pray over it. Then, for the next several days, keep thinking about that common theme. Most of all, try to find anecdotes and illustrations to bring out the point of that theme. Then you won't come up against what you've got here: Thursday night and . . . nothing."

Cody did not and would not confess having last night guzzled himself up to and including theological intoxication—to the point of being falling-down drunk. He would not reveal this to Koesler because of embarrassment. Cody had planned on starting the Homiletics assignment last night. Then he began drowning in doubts. Thence to the snack room, followed by the liquor supplied by Page—just now, a dubious friend.

"Next on the checklist: What's your congregation?" Koesler asked. "What parish will you be at?"

"No parish, Father. Here . . . the seminary, I mean."

Koesler pursed his lips. If he could have whistled convincingly, he would have. "The toughest audience in creation—your fellow students. The average parish congregation hopefully tries to get something from the homily that'll help them live as better Christians. Your crowd this Sunday will be critiquing *you*."

"I know. This is not the smartest thing I ever did—to let it go this long, I mean. That's one of the reasons I came to you; if anybody knows about preaching, you do. And I'm not trying to suck up!"

"I know you're not, Al. Well, let's get at it. Got any idea where to start?"

"Yeah . . . if it works out. I've been reading, for the second time, Charles Dickens's *A Tale of Two Cities*."

"Okay. That's a decent place to begin. And I've got a throw-away for you, if it works out. I say 'if' because you can go down the wrong path by forcing an anecdote into your homily.

"Anyway, this was a cartoon years ago in the *New Yorker* magazine. It showed a bearded author sitting on one side of a desk. On the other side is an editor fingering a manuscript. The editor is saying to the author, 'Really, Mr. Dickens, was it the best of times, or was it the worst of times. It could scarcely have been both.' "

They laughed.

"That's a good story, Father. Think anybody in the student body will have seen that?"

Koesler shook his head. "I shudder when I think your average student here was in pure potency when that cartoon was published.

"Now, is there something special you want to focus on from *A Tale of Two Cities*?"

"Yes, Father. The end. The very end of the book."

Koesler smiled. "Yes. I can see and hear Ronald Colman speaking those lines. A smile of satisfaction on his face and a tear in his eye."

"Ronald . . . ?"

Koesler shook his head. "You've never heard of Ronald Colman."

"The name's sort of familiar. He was . . . an actor?"

"A very good actor. And, among lots of other movies, he played the lead in *A Tale of Two Cities*. But I see you've got the book there. Read me the lines."

"Sure . . ." Cody opened the book and turned to the end. "Sydney Carton has taken Darnay's place to be executed," he said, setting the scene. "And Carton is now waiting his turn to be guillotined. As he moves up closer to the block, he says—and these are the last lines in the book—'It is a far, far better thing that I do, than I have ever done; it is a far, far better rest that I go to than I have ever known.'"

The two sat in silence for several moments.

Koesler wiped a tear from his cheek. "That's such beautiful writing. It was, indeed, the best of times and the worst of times. But, obviously, you've found some specific moral from the work. Otherwise you wouldn't be thinking of using it as the basis for your homily. Can you tell me exactly what has so impressed you?"

"I've been thinking about that a lot, Father. An awful lot."

"And . . . ?"

"Well, it's the decision he made . . . Carton, I mean. It was so . . . final. I thought it was so neat . . . no, that's not the word . . . so dramatic, so impressive when he's waiting for his plan to be set in motion."

Cody flipped a few pages back into the book, and read, " 'The hours went on as he walked to and fro, and the clocks struck the numbers he would never hear again. Nine gone forever, ten gone forever, eleven gone forever, twelve coming on to pass away.' I mean, saying good-bye to the time that will soon become eternity for him."

"Yes," Koesler agreed. "Now, how are you going to apply that?"

Cody smiled engagingly. "I'm not sure. I thought I'd open with the basic story of the book."

"Maybe you could start with the *New Yorker* cartoon."

"Yeah, that'd be good."

"A little humor in the beginning is one of the best ways of getting their attention. Then, after telling them about the cartoon, as you suggest, a sort of Cliffs Notes setting of the stage for that ending. But you want to center on what the book's ending signifies."

"Yes, Father, the decision. Once Carton decides to take Darnay's place and, as it turns out, to die for him, Carton grows more at peace with himself. I want to bring that out."

Koesler went to the bookcase and removed the lectionary

that held the Scripture readings, daily and Sunday. "Let's see what the Church is offering you for this Sunday."

Silently, Koesler scanned the three readings; first from the Old Testament, second from one of the Epistles, and third from a Gospel.

Having read the three, Koesler looked at Cody with a hint of disbelief. "Are you sure you didn't rig this, Al?"

"No, I didn't," in innocent protest.

"This Gospel, it comes made to order."

"How so, Father?" Cody felt exhilaration.

"It's from St. John. It's from that long discourse of Jesus that John chronologizes as being after the Last Supper. Get this— I'll just skip around a little so you can see what it has to do with Carton and Darnay:

" 'As the Father has loved me, so I have loved you. Live on in my love. You will live in my love if you keep my commandments, even as I have kept my Father's commandments, and live in His love. All this I tell you that my joy may be yours and your joy may be complete.

" 'This is my commandment: Love one another as I have loved you. There is no greater love than this: to lay down one's life for one's friends. You are my friends . . . I call you my friends.'

"Doesn't that fit, Al?" Koesler placed the book on his desk and looked intently at the seminarian.

Cody nodded enthusiastically.

"You saw," Koesler said, "how Sydney Carton would lay down his own life to save Darnay's. And how, once he took the decisive steps to pull that off, how calm he became.

"And then Jesus, using different words, says the same thing. He says, 'There is no greater love than this: to lay down one's life for one's friends.'

"Then Jesus becomes very calm. Maybe, aside from the terror he realistically felt in the Garden of Olives when he sees clearly the nightmare he will have to go through—aside from that, Jesus is about the only one who stays calm through the whole ordeal of His crucifixion and death."

Cody began to scribble notes on a legal pad he'd brought along.

"Now," Koesler said, "we have to figure where you're going with this."

Cody looked up and thoughtfully tapped his lips with the pencil. "The value of friendship . . . The importance of friendship . . . The demands made of friendship . . ."

Clearly, Cody was shopping for an idea, and stating whatever came to his mind. He paused, obviously searching for more ideas.

"Let's try it this way," Koesler suggested. "Let's concentrate on commitment. What we've got are two examples of what we might call the maximum commitment of friendship.

"Jesus states something that could be taken as an axiom. He talks of the highest measure, testing, of friendship. There is no greater test of love than one's willingness to die for his or her friend.

"Dickens puts this into a concrete example. Not only is Sydney Carton willing to die in Darnay's stead; he actually does so. Carton goes off to the guillotine and death.

"You could talk about the similarities and differences in the deaths of Jesus and Carton. They both gave themselves up to a death they could have escaped. All Carton had to do was not take Darnay's place. Jesus would have had to fudge His principles, recant some of His 'Good News.' Because of their commitments, they died prematurely. They were executed. Jesus proved His love for all who would be His friends. Carton died for the happiness of one man. Carton's death was horrible but quick. Jesus' death was torturous and lingering.

"But, Al, after pointing all this out, you've got to draw a practical lesson for your listeners. How many of us will ever face a predicament like this? How many of us get a chance to prove our love by dying for a friend? The only modern example that comes to mind immediately is Maximilian Kolbe, the Franciscan priest in . . . Auschwitz, I think. Some inmates escaped from that concentration camp. Nazi policy, in reprisal, was to select some prisoners at random and starve them to death. Father Kolbe stepped forward to take the place of one of the condemned, and he died for the man."

"I remember reading about that."

"Well, okay then. It's good to point out the selflessness of a sacrifice like that—the supreme sacrifice. But you're going to have to bring it down to something practical. And the practical lesson is *not* that we should go around looking for someone unjustly condemned to death and then volunteer to die in his or her stead—" Koesler stopped himself. He wanted Cody to find the application on his own.

Cody sensed that and searched his mind. "It's commitment, isn't it?" he said finally. "That's the lesson . . . the point. And it applies to everyone in this school."

Koesler smiled and nodded.

"Jesus was on a confrontation course with his country's elders," Cody said thoughtfully. "As soon as He began His public life, He made the choice to go forward. That was His commitment. His love for his friends—for all people—would carry Him on. This commitment would lead Him to the cross. And that would allow Him to say that no one could love more than someone who was willing to die for that love.

"And in Dickens's story, as soon as Carton decided to save Darnay, the commitment was made. And it gave him the strength to trade clothing with Darnay. And then his fate was sealed.

"It's all about commitment, isn't it?"

"I think so," Koesler affirmed.

"Everybody, every student in this seminary," Cody said, "whether they're preparing for priesthood or service to the Church, has to make a commitment to the Church. Every one of us, someplace along the line, has to say, 'This is it.' "

Koesler smiled. "I think you've got a really good homily in there."

Cody sat back in his chair, lost in thought.

"What is it, Al?"

"I think you're right, Father. There *is* a good homily in what we've talked about. But I've got to preach it to me."

"Come again?"

Cody hesitated. He was as embarrassed as anyone on the verge of admitting something he considers a shameful failing.

"Father . . ." Cody took a deep breath and slowly exhaled. ". . . in all the time I've considered becoming a priest—and that goes back to when I first crawled out of my crib—in all the time I've been in the seminary, I have never committed myself to the priesthood."

Koesler tried not to look shocked. He very definitely was not of the "You did *what*!?" school. But in his heart, he was astonished.

Undoubtedly what Cody had just said was true. It also was strange—very strange.

Koesler knew the Cody family pretty well. He knew Bill Cody was dedicated as no other parent Koesler had ever met to his son's ordination. More than dedicated; he was near consumed by it. That may have been a highly motivating force—but could it possibly have been the sole motivating factor in this crucial step Al was slated to take?

Hoping he had his emotions masked, Koesler said, "It seems silly to point out you've got only a few months before your ordination."

"I know."

"I know you know. You couldn't have picked a better audience for your Sunday homily than yourself. It's sort of like a woman marrying a man who has some serious flaws, confident that she can reform him. It hardly ever works.

"Married people make a lifelong commitment too. We priests are not unique in this commitment business."

"Do you mind if I stand, Father? I'm getting too nervous to sit still."

"Of course. Stand. Pace."

Cody did both. He stood and began pacing.

"I know married people make a commitment, Father. I also know that there are thousands of annulments every year. So much for commitment in marriage.

"On the other hand, it's next to impossible to get a laicization. A woman marries a man who has flaws. She has every intention to fix him up like new after the wedding. But the flaws ruin the marriage. They get a divorce. Then they get the marriage annulled.

"But a seminarian who has doubts about the priesthood gets ordained. He figures he'll work out his problems in his day-to-day life as a priest. But what if it doesn't work out? What if the problems begin to take over? He can apply for laicization. He can petition to return to the lay state. But there's not much chance that it'll be granted.

"And"—Cody stopped pacing, faced Koesler, and extended his arms in a gesture of helplessness—"even in the remote possibility that it's granted, he's a marked man. For Catholics particularly. It's one thing to have been married and divorced and have the whole thing wiped out with a declaration of nullity. But an ex-priest, as far as Catholics are concerned, carries this invisible, indelible mark on his soul that will identify him as a priest into eternity.

"With marriage, once there's an annulment, everything is over. Once a marriage is annulled, if that couple were to have sexual intercourse with each other they would be committing fornication—adultery if either had married again.

"However, if a priest has been laicized there are situations when he can or even must use his priesthood. If someone is in danger of death, the ex-priest can absolve. Even if an active priest is on the scene, if the dying person wants the ex-priest— the nonactive priest—he can function." Cody began pacing again.

Koesler felt frustrated. "Al, what do you want of me?"

There was no reply.

"Do you want me to tell you to quit?"

"No!" Cody said decisively. "Just your saying that . . . that you would be willing to tell me to quit . . . it makes me almost sick."

A long pause followed, during which Cody stood stockstill.

"Then what, Al? Did you come to see me to get help with your homily? Or did you really come to settle your doubts about your priesthood?"

Another long pause, during which Koesler was determined that he would not be the first to speak.

Cody slumped into a chair. "I came here for help. Help with the homily, I think. It developed into something else. I don't know exactly how we got into this. I do know one thing: I needed to talk. Would you believe it? This is the first time in my life I've had a serious venting of my doubts.

"You know what: I feel better. I still have some doubts . . . but I feel better."

Cody looked intently into Koesler's eyes. "Tell me this, Father, if you will. I am now the age you were when you were ordained. Was it at all like this? Did you have any doubts at all?"

Koesler smiled. He always smiled when contemplating his ordination and the events that surrounded it.

"Al, it was different back then. So very, very different. It was a different Church before the Council, of course. And the training was almost incomparable. I had twelve years of seminary life; you've had eight.

"There were so many of us the place was bulging at the doors. The faculty had the luxury of being extremely selective in judging who among us could stay or had to leave. Not that there aren't some high-class candidates now. But the numbers are not in the same ball park . . . Hey, wait a minute! These are just the ramblings of an old man—"

"You're not an old man!" Cody protested.

"Maybe you're right. Outside of a few aches and some stiffness, I don't feel so old. But I'm trying to get back to your question. About doubts: I must confess, I didn't have any. Not a one."

"Not one?" Cody sounded discouraged. How, he wondered, do you deal with someone who had not a single doubt—especially when so many were pounding in your own brain?

"Oh, I guess I shouldn't put it that way. Doubts came eventually."

"Can you remember any? Any one?"

"Yes. As a matter of fact, I can remember the first one. Clearly."

"When did it happen? When did you doubt?" Cody was eager.

"During my first assignment. Oh, maybe three or four

months into my priesthood. It was a warm, sunny Sunday afternoon. I had the baptisms that day. There were lots of babies, with twice as many godparents and close to twice as many parents—some of the wives stayed home to cook the meal.

"The babies were crying so loudly I had to almost shout to be heard. Now that I look back on it, my yelling probably made them cry with more vigor.

"Finally it was all done. And all the people and the babies went to their homes for the baptism parties.

"And I was alone.

"Here I was, young, your age. And I was all dressed up with no place to go.

"I was just . . . alone.

"My future played out in my mind. I would be alone for the rest of my life. I can tell you, Al, just between the two of us, I had doubts. What had I gotten myself into?

"What I didn't realize was that being alone didn't necessarily mean I had to be lonely."

"That's one of mine! That's one of mine!" Cody almost sprang from his chair in excitement. "That's one of my doubts! How did you handle it?"

"You pray and you wait. My closest friends were my classmates in the seminary. One of the reasons I didn't feel lonely in school was because I was surrounded by all these friends. Now that I was ordained, these friends were gone. Well, not up in smoke . . . but they were never again going to be as accessible as they once were.

"So you pray. And you wait.

"The prayer has to be there in the lives we lead. Of course everyone needs to pray. But a priest without wife and family needs prayer even more. You'd be surprised: Prayer can fill in the gaps.

"And you wait for new friends from among the wonderful people you meet over the years. New and different kinds of friends are waiting just around the corner—if you can hang in there.

"Now, in the relatively brief time you've got before being

ordained, you haven't a lot of time to wait, but there's plenty of time to pray. And I'll join you in prayer. If it's any help, I think you would make a fine priest. But it's a commitment that only you can make."

"Thanks, Father. One more thing . . ."

"Sure."

"I've been over this so many times, back and forth, how will I know? I mean, how will I know I've made the right choice?"

Koesler stood and extended his hand. "I'm not certain, but I think I can give you a clue. You should know the same way Sydney Carton and Jesus Himself knew. You should experience a deep and abiding peace. So," he said, as they shook hands, "peace I wish you."

"Thanks. Thanks very much." Cody's eyes were brimming. He turned and left the room before any tear could escape his eyes.

Father Koesler sank back into his chair. He was tired to the point of exhaustion. It had been a long day, capped by the drain of this evening's unexpected visit. An intensive counseling session always depleted his physical and emotional energy.

He didn't envy young Al Cody's upcoming bout with himself. In this corner was Al the seminarian. His goal, the priesthood. At this point the goal was eminently attainable. But was that his real calling?

In that corner was Al the bright young man whose father had so pressured his son toward the priesthood that no one, least of all Al, could tell where one's aspiration began and the other's ended.

Yet, let events take their course and Al would be a priest. A casual observer would find it incredible that the young man could at this stage harbor any doubt whatsoever about his future.

From his own experience, Koesler knew that life as a priest was unpredictable. To a greater or lesser degree the same could be said of any of life's vehicles.

But at this stage there should be no doubts.

If, in a few months he were going to be married, he might

well be tortured by doubt. There is no specific training for the role of husband or wife, father or mother. One marries, then wings it; there is ample room for serious doubt about one's qualifications.

However, Al had been contemplating the priesthood all his life. And for the past eight years he had been trained for that role almost exclusively.

That he could still wonder about his future was thanks to his father's overwhelmingly pervasive influence.

At least Al was on the right track now, Koesler felt. The lad must put his future to the test of intense prayer.

In prayer he would not be alone. Father Koesler would join him.

Al Cody slowly made his way to the chapel. He had a lot to ponder.

Earlier this evening he'd gone to visit Father Koesler in order to get help on his homily. There had been no ulterior motive—at least none that came to his conscious mind.

It was in the development of the sermon topic that the emphasis on commitment came. And then the thought turned in on him.

Doubt! It had become a way of life for him.

He entered the chapel. It was so dark and so peaceful, at least at first. He knelt and waited. Sure enough, once you were quiet you became aware of the sounds. Creaking, grating, squeaking—the sounds belonged to the chapel. You heard them only if you were alone and still.

There was no doubt about it, he felt better. And he had not even been aware that he was as deeply troubled as his conversation with Koesler had revealed. It had all come out in a stream of consciousness.

Psychology suggested the talking cure. To suppress threatening thoughts and feelings one had to exert pressure. And that pressure took its toll of psychic energy.

But if you could bring it out, the stress tended to release, and you felt better. It was thought by many that that was the miracle of confession—the sacrament of penance.

Most of the time, among Catholics, confession became a routine exercise, a pointless recitation of peccadilloes offered for the confessor's consideration.

But once in a while a conscience held the secret of something terribly embarrassing or, for one reason or another, troubling. Speaking of this matter, expressing it verbally, would reduce the painful secret's threat. It didn't hurt that the Catholic understanding of confession not only involved the talking cure but also the belief that the sin was forgiven.

Something like that had happened in Father Koesler's room just a few minutes ago. And even though Al understood that he still had a lot of thinking and praying to do, he felt better.

It was a gift to have someone like Father Koesler around. Undoubtedly there were other priests as approachable, experienced, charitable, and caring as he, but Al knew he personally would never experience another priest quite like Robert Koesler.

And what did that portend?

Father Koesler was seventy years old. Cody was twenty-five. A forty-five-year gap. It certainly seemed safe to predict that Al Cody would be alive a lot longer than this aging priest.

In other words, Cody could not count on Koesler's presence and help for as long as the young man might need it. Whatever resolution his prayer would reach, Cody realistically would have to learn to handle doubts on his own.

He was so confused that he had no idea how to pray, or for what to pray. He tried to compose an outline. An outline for God? Well, he had to start somewhere.

God . . . Jesus, I want to be a priest. I think. My father wants me to be a priest. Does he want this more than I? Does he want it so much that he has absorbed my willpower into his?

Maybe it would be better if I didn't consider my father at all. Just the two of us, Jesus. You know the good I could accomplish as a priest. You also know the harm I could do if I were not a good priest.

All right. I am on a different level. I've taken a major step.

Canceling my father's influence over my decision helps. It helps a lot. I can see a little bit of light at the end of this road.

This, plus what Father Koesler told me, gives me maybe my first decent chance at making a decision. Making a decision on my own.

Jesus, you knew you had made the right decision when you were at peace within yourself. Just as the fictional Carton knew he was doing the right thing when he was at peace with himself.

That's what Father Koesler told me. And it makes sense.

Except that if I must be at peace with myself, I've got a long way to go.

22 MARCH COMES IN like a lion and goes out like a lamb. Or it comes in like a lamb and goes out like a lion. Or any of the other variables. Michigan's March weather is unpredictable even by those whose job is to predict the weather.

This day, near the end of March, featured February-like weather. It was overcast, cold, and blustery, plunging the wind-chill factor to barely ten degrees above zero.

Nevertheless, Deacon Bill Page had been briskly walking around the fenced-in seminary grounds. On his final turn he picked up the pace. He could hardly wait to get back into the warmth of the building.

He pushed his way through the door and thanked whatever powers might be for heat.

He went directly to his room, where he turned his radiator on full and removed and hung up his outer clothing. He almost bonded with the iron pipes until he felt the chill start to depart from his bones.

He sat at his desk and pulled from the shelf the weighty Coriden, Green, and Heintschel edition of *The Code of Canon Law, A Text and Commentary.* He paged through the text until he came to the marriage laws, Canons 1055 to 1165. One hundred and ten laws to complicate the lives of those who wanted to get married, were married, or wanted to get out of marriage. All with or without benefit of Catholic clergy.

And that wasn't all. Later, in Canons 1671 to 1716, there were the procedures for granting or withholding decrees of nullity. Forty-five additional laws. And he had to know the content of all of them.

Why?

He wasn't going to use any of them. He was an unmarried deacon and soon-to-be priest. So he would never be allowed to marry. Or, rather, to be more precise, he could attempt marriage, but the Church had gotten there first and ruled all such attempts to be illicit and invalid.

Be that as it may. It mattered little. With the number of women he'd been involved with in the past, he could have married any number of times. And now he knew all the rules for marriage in the Church. As long as the prospective partner was free to marry and the happy couple exchanged consent in the presence of a duly authorized priest and the required witnesses, the two would be husband and wife—validly married. If the partner was—as was Page—baptized, it would be termed a sacramental marriage. Then, the easiest part, when they consummated the marriage, it would be about as unbreakable as the Rock of Gibraltar.

That would be that unless one or the other harbored some impediment such as serious and hopeless immaturity.

He shut the canonical textbook. He knew the stuff well enough. Besides, the final exam before priestly ordination would be oral. And Page considered himself one of the more suasive talkers of all time.

And don't bring up that business about not cutting it in the advertising game. He would have made it had not the other sales reps been jealous of his sexual successes. And well should they be—especially those with whose wives he had frolicked.

Just thinking these thoughts was warming him. But not enough. Some steaming coffee might help.

The snack room was otherwise unoccupied. But the coffee was steaming hot. He wrapped both hands around the Styrofoam cup and let the warmth penetrate his fingers.

To entertain himself while dispersing the chill, he called up a memory. There were so many to choose from but this had always been his favorite.

* * *

It happened during his junior year in high school. At his present age, with the wealth of experience he had built up over the years, it was hard for him to imagine how he had managed to remain a straight arrow all those early years.

He attributed it now, in a vague sense, to those hellfire and brimstone sermons with which the Catholic clergy had threatened him and everybody else. But everything has to begin sometime.

For him it began seriously on a chilly January evening after a sock hop.

Mary Lou.

He could not remember a time when he had not been fascinated by girls. Why did they wear dresses and he wear pants? Short pants, but pants.

Sometime during the first or second grade, a developing brazen hussy had lifted her skirt and dropped her panties. He was dumbfounded. She didn't have anything! He began to feel proud and superior at having a penis.

Still, there was something mysteriously attractive about girls. They smelled different. Their hair was different. Their eyes were different. Their voices were different. They played differently. They related to each other differently than they did to boys. They were *different.*

At that tender age he had not yet heard the French phrase *Vive la différence.* Later it would become his motto.

But back to Mary Lou and that sock hop.

She was the first girl about whom he was serious. He was seriously interested in scoring with Mary Lou. And then all those lies he kept telling his buddies would finally be true.

Trouble was, he had been pursuing the girl for a matter of months. He had nothing to show for it except periodic cramps in his groin. Mary Lou was a tease.

A typical get-together at this time consisted of a double date featuring a guy who had a license and the use of a car. The destination: a drive-in movie. The goal: as much groping as circumstances allowed.

Funny how many movies he attended and afterward had no

recollection of what they were about. His attention had not been on the big screen but on Mary Lou.

Years later, when one of those movies was on TV, it would be as if he'd never even heard of it.

One night, his buddy with the car drove to a lovers' lane. He told Bill and Mary Lou to get in the front seat, while he and his date used the backseat. Page felt awkward having the other two in back. It was as if he and Mary Lou were expected to perform for a couple of voyeurs who would be able to watch them fumble through a series of practiced but unsatisfactory maneuvers.

After some time, when Mary Lou turned her head to avoid another one of his kisses, Bill turned around to see what the couple in back were doing.

The couple in back were, for all intents and purposes, naked.

Bill gasped.

Attention attracted, Mary Lou followed Page's gaze. Quickly she turned his head back to her. She rewarded his renewed attention by kissing him passionately, voraciously. This impelled him to try diligently to remove at least some of her clothing, but to no avail. Somehow she managed to keep everything in place, if somewhat rumpled.

And he had missed the show in the back.

Gradually but eventually, Page realized he was doomed to repeated wrestling matches with Mary Lou, every one of which would end in a draw.

It was kismet. He would not and could not abandon this object of his desire. It was chemistry. It was fate. It was probably not God's will.

As time progressed, Page settled for the kisses that were his. He no longer groped into inevitable frustration.

Then came the sock hop.

Afterward he walked her home. She invited him in. That was not entirely out of the ordinary. Sometimes they would sit with her parents, watching TV and eating popcorn, which her mother made by the bucket.

One of the reasons her parents trusted Page so was his ease

at being with them. Their theory had it that any boy who is not ill at ease with the girl's parents is probably not out to deflower their little darling. Even as a lad, Page put up a good front.

However, this time the progression of events was definitely out of the ordinary.

There were no house lights visible. Perhaps her parents had gone to bed. Even the possibility of the old folks slumbering did not stir Page, so well conditioned had he become.

He followed her docilely into the darkened house. Oddly, she led him up the stairs. This definitely was not part of the drill.

They entered a room that was dimly lit by the beam of a streetlight. Mary Lou immediately pulled down the windowshade, leaving the room in total darkness.

Even when she turned on a small reading lamp on a night table, most of the room was still in shadow.

She took off her jacket and dropped it on the floor.

In a studied manner she unbuttoned the neck of her dress, pulled it up over her head, and tossed it on a nearby chair.

She kicked off her shoes.

"Wh . . . where are your parents?" Page stammered.

"Out of town. They left this afternoon. They won't be back until late tomorrow." Her voice took on a seductive huskiness. "Now, Billy, all you've got to do is call your folks and make up some excuse why you won't be home tonight."

"Wh . . . what?"

"Tell them anything. Ask one of your closest friends to cover for you if your parents check up."

She pushed her half-slip down over her full hips and let it fall to the floor, then nudged it away with her toe.

She now wore only a bra, panties, and knee stockings.

She sat on the bed and removed her stockings.

He had seen her on the beach clad only in a bikini, considerably less clothing than now covered her. But this was different. This really was different.

Once again, in that husky voice, she spoke. "Don't you feel a bit overdressed?"

He began to fumble with his trousers as she reached behind her to unhook her bra.

Rats!

Somebody had entered the snack room. Just when he was about to reach the heart of this, his favorite memory—albeit embellished with a few fanciful details!

Bill Page had learned more about women during that long, immortal night than he had—now, wait a minute. His education *had* continued over a span of time. Although it had ground to a screeching halt over the past few years in the seminary.

The rewarding thing about this memory that he'd just milked was that it had warmed him thoroughly.

The irritating thing, of course, was that he'd been interrupted just as he came to the story's climax—in more ways than one.

The intruder was Andrea Zawalich.

"Well," Andrea said, "if it isn't the Reverend Mr. Page. How's it going, William?"

"Hi, Zawalich," he murmured. Things had been going quite well until he was interrupted, he thought.

She slid a coin into the coffee machine as she studied Page. He had the most peculiar look on his face. Almost a pained expression. "Are you really all right?" she inquired.

"Yeah, yeah." He tossed off her solicitous question.

She took her coffee from the machine and gestured toward the chair across the table from him. "Do you mind?"

He merely shrugged.

She took the chair.

They were not more than a couple of feet apart.

A feeling of hostility was beginning to bubble inside Page. It was visceral much more than intellectual. And he wondered why. Especially in light of all he'd been preoccupied with just moments ago.

Why did the presence of this young woman upset him so?

He looked at her more closely.

She did have a certain measure of attractiveness. Indeed, one could make a case for her being stacked. She was friendly much of the time. Considering the sort of treatment she got from him, from most of the male students, particularly the seminarians, all in all she was more than affable.

She was a woman. He liked women. Had since he was in short pants—when of course he had pitied them for their lack—or so he had thought—of sex organs. Even so, he had enjoyed all the differences he could find between boys and girls.

He liked them boundlessly when he discovered that not only did they have sexual organs after all, but those organs were destined to blend perfectly with male counterparts. He had dedicated and devoted much of his energies to the exploration of pleasure between the sexes. To that end he had invested more effort than a combined Lewis and Clark.

He liked women.

So why this inner hostility now?

He looked at Andrea.

She smiled at him. The total picture she presented was what the English call comely and the Scots bonny.

Oval face; arching eyebrows neither heavy nor absent; bright, lively eyes under lush lashes. Her nose was perky, her chin small but determined. Her lips were full, but not overly so.

Elegant neck, delicate shoulders, graceful arms, shapely legs. While veiled by her clothing, the promise of ample breasts was evident above a narrow waist, curvaceous hips, and firm thighs that hinted at something more than merely connecting her knees to her pelvis.

In short, all the things Page most prized in life besides money.

So, why wasn't he attracted?

Was it a by-product of this chaste life he'd been living in the seminary? Was he ignoring the maxim, Use it or lose it? Did he feel threatened by intelligent women? Was he getting prematurely senile?

Was it all of the above? Part of the above?

He was in a near panic with the hint of that dreaded state called impotence.

Admittedly he could still be aroused by erotic thoughts. He had been just a few minutes ago.

Until—and here, a small light seemed to go on over his head—the fantasy was extinguished by the arrival of a real, live woman.

Was it possible he had lost it—his virility?

One thing seemed clear: He had better establish live communication. No reason he couldn't begin with this one. "So, Andrea, how are you?"

"Fine. If spring would get here for keeps, I'd be just about perfect."

"Well, you know what they say about Michigan weather . . ."

"If you don't like it," both chorused, "just wait a few minutes and it will change." They laughed.

There's no doubt about it, Page thought, with very little effort I can be charming. "You're going to graduate this June, aren't you?"

"Yes. And you'll be ordained."

"Right. Got anything lined up for gainful employment?"

"Bill," she said in a shocked tone, "you know as well as I that employment by the Roman Catholic Church can seldom be called gainful."

"Right!" He smiled disarmingly.

"Actually," she continued, "I've got something lined up and just waiting for me and my diploma." She looked at him for a moment, then said confidingly, "I'll be pastoral minister at St. George's."

Page thought that over. "George's in Southfield?"

"Uh-huh."

"Who's the pastor there . . . ?"

"Father Manor."

"Of course. Bennie." Page felt mildly embarrassed for a moment. He prided himself on knowing who was where in almost all the suburban parishes. He had no interest in the core city parishes.

"He does like to be called Bennie, doesn't he?" she said.

"Yeah. But . . . but isn't he scheduled to retire soon?"

"Uh-huh. But I put a little of the fear of the Curia in him."

"No kidding." Page found himself genuinely interested. "What did you do?"

She explained factually and in detail her surveying of likely parishes until she'd homed in on St. George's.

Page listened avidly. "What was that about putting the fear of the Curia in him?" He was soaking up useful information. One could never have too much preparation for a spot of blackmail—all in a good cause, of course.

"You see," Andrea explained, "Bennie was drifting. He had a big parish, a good percentage of whose members were ready for action. And that competed with his plan of floating into retirement. So I went about convincing him that I was capable of taking that ball and running with it."

"Even so," Page asked, "why would he bother with you?"

"That's where the fear of the Curia comes in."

"Yes." This was the part that most interested Page.

"I hinted that when it came time to assume Senior Priest Status . . ." They both snickered at the euphemistic phrase.

"When he was ready to retire"—she reverted to plain speech—"the Curia might well look at the parish he was leaving behind and think that he might have left it in better shape. They might think that he should get things moving before he was permitted to leave."

Page was dumbfounded. "They don't do that! At least not in Detroit. I mean, I've studied this business pretty carefully. I can't think of a single incident when they've refused a request for retirement. There are some who get an earlier medical leave. But not this!"

"Remember, Bill, I hinted. I suggested." She smiled conspiratorially. "I didn't imply they would . . . just that they might."

"And he bought it. I'll be damned."

"It was part of my investigation. He's not the type to gamble on long odds. Plus, he's *really* been counting on that retirement." She smiled again. "And, yes, he bought it. I've been working with some pretty dedicated people getting these leaders primed. They're in good shape now. So, once I graduate, I'll just hop over to St. George's and get the various programs going."

"And"—Page had been swept up in the mood—"Bennie will be able to relax. No nasty bogeyman will fool with his retirement." He chuckled.

"Some people," she observed, "like to wear a belt and suspenders."

At the mention of clothing, he was momentarily distracted. Mary Lou had been removing her bra and Page fumbling with his belt when Andrea had burst the bubble of his remembrance. He almost drifted back.

"How about you?" Andrea once more cut into his erotic fantasy. "After you're ordained, got any plans?"

The direct question pulled Page back to the present. "You bet. I did some internship at St. Waldo of the Hills. That's where I'm headed."

"Waldo's . . ." She whistled softly. "*Très* posh. Not a bad way to start."

He smiled. "No, not bad at all. Do you have any idea how many movers and shakers live in that parish?"

"I've never counted heads."

"You might run out of numbers. I'm banking on them to introduce me to the fast lane."

"You were never in it?" She seemed surprised.

He held up his hand, measuring barely half an inch between his thumb and forefinger. "About *this* close. When you're fresh out of Notre Dame a lot of things open up for you. But the door that opens can close pretty fast.

"Anyway, it looks like you and I have our immediate future pretty well set."

"Our *immediate* future?" She winked.

He was taken aback. Why the wink?

"Up till now," she said, "I thought we were talking several months ahead. After graduation . . . after ordination. That's not my idea of immediate."

For a lingering moment Page was back in junior high school. And Andrea was Mary Lou.

He'd been down this road before. He knew the path and he

was sure he knew the signs. "W-e-l-l"—he drew out the word—"if this isn't immediate, what is?"

"You're sort of the man of the world," she said winsomely. "I thought you'd know."

Whoosh! he said to himself. Remember Mary Lou.

And he did remember. Mary Lou had acted the innocent virgin. Page had been cast as the hormone-happy sex maniac. As long as both were faithful to their roles, nothing had changed.

It had been one of the most frustrating times of his life. She would tease and he would respond. Then when he would reach the point of total loss of control, she would apply the brakes.

The naked couple in the car's backseat: She hadn't wanted Page to see what they were doing. That sort of thing Mary Lou was saving for the indeterminate future—if ever.

So she'd managed to turn his head and smother him with kisses. With that he'd lost interest even in the torrid and unconventional adventure going on in back.

He'd thought for one brief, shining moment that she finally was actively involved. But his every effort to duplicate what the couple in back were enjoying was parried.

Gradually, Mary Lou trained Page to be a good boy. Somehow she kept up his interest even though he never got beyond French kisses and clumsy groping of a well-clothed maiden. By the time of that sock hop, he was a well-disciplined young man.

Once she had established control, it was time to get serious.

So he had learned. The first conquest was not his, it was hers. It didn't matter. In fact, with very few exceptions, it was better to be cool and let the lady lead.

If what was happening now had happened without a Mary Lou in his history, Page would've been all over Andrea. She would have fought him off. Or at least put up enough of a battle to leave him achingly frustrated and wildly unhappy.

"So," he said, "you believe the immediate future is, like, now?"

"Something like that."

"Somehow, the snack room doesn't seem to be the place to develop this idea to its fullest. Maybe we could adjourn this conversation to my place—such as it is."

"Sounds like a capital idea."

They dumped the remainder of their coffee and left the snack room.

Together they headed down the corridor, anticipating no problem. Unless there was a summons to classes or chapel or something of that nature, hardly ever was anyone in the hallways.

Besides, this institution bore little resemblance to the seminaries of the past within whose walls females had no place. Now there were nearly as many female students as males. And since many of the courses were coed, there was nothing untoward about a mixed couple walking together. Indeed, many of them studied together.

When they reached his room, he opened and held the door for her.

She sat in the only chair in the room. There was no other place for him to sit but the bed. So he did. The mere fact that he was occupying the bed in any manner kept the fires going.

"You're sure," Page checked, "this is where you want to be—I mean, I don't want you to think that I planned this—ending up here in my room, I mean."

"So far, you seem to have read the signals correctly. How, I wonder, do you see me? What do you think of me?"

"You're intelligent, competent, and beautiful." He listed the qualities he genuinely perceived, in the order, he felt, she would prefer. "And, fair is fair: What do you think of me?"

She regarded him thoughtfully, as if seeing him for the first time. "I'd say you are in control of your fate, very good-looking, and"—she smiled—"soon to be off the market."

So, he thought, she buys this bit about celibacy *and* chastity. All the better. She probably feels that coupling with me would be akin to throwing a life preserver to a drowning man. All the better, indeed.

He stretched out on the bed. She could tell he was aroused. "Not so fast," she said.

He sat up.

"What do you want to do?"

He shook his head. "I don't know. It seemed as though we were headed for bed. I just sort of thought that if eventually we found each other in the nude, somehow something would occur to us."

"That's all well and good. But I'm a virgin!"

She's a virgin! If he'd had to guess he would have been correct. There was something about virgins—like uncharted territory—that gave him double the pleasure. "So, you're a virgin. I'm not sure what that means to you."

"Among other things, I'm not sure what to expect. But I have my fantasies. I've read a romance or two."

"I don't mind being honest with you, Andrea. I'm definitely not a virgin. But I assure you I would be as concerned about your orgasm—or orgasms—as I would about my own."

This was ludicrous! She'd never thought she would be talking like this with a man who in a short while would be a priest. "I appreciate your concern for me, but . . ."

"But what?" He was so near to closing this deal. And he wanted a woman so badly. This on-again, off-again was driving him mad. He wanted more than anything to jump her bones. But the memory of Mary Lou kept intruding on his libido.

"You'll think I'm crazy!" she protested.

"No, I won't."

"Even *I* think it's silly. . . ."

"No, it's not."

"I can't even bring myself to tell you."

"Try!" He was about to forget Mary Lou.

"I want you to write it out. Tell me what you plan to do to . . . with me."

". . . what I . . . ?"

"Years ago, I read a story about a small town where there was a rapist who would send his intended victim a note telling her exactly what he planned on doing to her. The victim was alerted. But she couldn't be vigilant all the time. When she least expected it, he would strike—am I boring you?"

"Not hardly."

"Well, the sheriff of the town decided to use his new and beautiful wife as bait. By herself, she went to movies, restaurants, shopping, all over town. Sure enough, she received a note graphically spelling out what the rapist intended to do to her.

"So her husband set the trap. He didn't tell his wife, but he kept her under surveillance. Then, one night, about midnight, the rapist came and tried to enter the sheriff's house. But before he could get in, the sheriff, who had been waiting outside in the dark, grabbed him and, after a struggle, killed him.

"Then the sheriff entered his house. He was startled to find the back door unlocked. It was supposed to always be locked. He made his way through the darkened house to the bedroom. He cautiously opened the bedroom door, which squeaked. And in the darkness, from the direction of the bed came his wife's whispered voice: "Hurry!""

Page sat looking at her, his mouth hanging open. "That's your fantasy! You want me to write down exactly what I intend to do, from foreplay to orgasm?"

She blushed. "I told you you'd think I was crazy . . . let's just forget the whole sorry mess."

"Wait! Wait!"

In the silence that followed, bells were ringing furiously in Page's warning system. Aphorisms were drumming. *Do right and fear no man. Don't write and fear no woman.* And suchlike.

But he wanted her. Oh, how he wanted her!

He put the alternatives on a hypothetical scale. On one side, a naked and compliant Andrea. On the other, a vulnerable and seriously endangered Bill Page. The scale threatened to fluctuate toward the center, favoring neither side. Then he metaphorically pushed the weight to Andrea's side. So she wanted it in writing. If that's what would turn her on . . . well . . .

"Okay," he said at length, "I'll do it. We can't fool with this too long. You want it very explicit?"

"The more the better. I'm counting on your experience and

the gentle side of you to make my 'coming out' memorable. And"—she winked—"maybe even worthy of reprise."

A repeat performance, he thought. Worth every effort he could make. "Okay!"

"Put it in my mailbox just outside St. William's Hall tomorrow night at eight. And we'll go from there."

As she left his room she made sure her bottom wiggled fetchingly as she closed the door behind her.

He left the bed and began pacing the small room. What the hell, he'd never done anything like this before. And he'd thought he'd done just about everything.

He might just find this stimulating. Although God knows, he didn't need any help!

23

I**T WAS** 4:30 P.M., one half-hour before the Sunday Folk Mass at St. Joseph's.

Gathered in the rectory living room were Fathers Zack Tully and Robert Koesler and Monsignor Patrick Rooney. None of them was there willingly. Tully should have been readying the church for Mass. Koesler might have been enjoying good music in his room in the seminary. Rooney would be late for his sister and brother-in-law's wedding anniversary party.

They had been summoned by William Cody, who demanded a ruling on the legitimacy of the Folk Mass. He was scheduled to meet them here in just a few minutes. Cody was always prompt.

Tully's guests had passed on the offer of a drink. They wanted to be cold sober and out of here at the earliest possible moment.

"You might find this amusing," Tully said as he handed each of them a sheet of paper. "This," he continued, "contains the minutes of a meeting that never took place, by a committee that doesn't exist. After we finished planning this Sunday's Folk liturgy, the group put this together. I suppose it could be considered their response to the latest meeting of the parish council."

Rooney and Koesler began to read.

AGENDA
Opening Prayer
Minutes of the Last Meeting
Old Business

New Business
> Worship Commission
>> Discussion of a special service to honor the Pope
>> Preparations for the elevation to the episcopacy of Father Zachary Tully
>
> Administration Commission
>> Creation of required dress code for Folk Mass at St. Joe's
>> Presentation of plaque commemorating support given by William Cody
>> Plans for map to show children various routes to the church bathroom
>
> Education Commission
>> A class for parish youth: "Is there a traditional Church in your future?"
>> Swimming lessons for those to be baptized by immersion
>> Christian Service Commission
>> A party for those who benefited by the opening of two dozen casinos

Closing Prayer
> We will need more prayers than ever if this agenda continues any further.

Monsignor Rooney looked up. "They're not taking this very seriously, are they?"

"They're a laid-back group," Tully replied. "Besides, they're pretty confident about the outcome of this investigation."

"Please," Rooney said, "let's not characterize this procedure as an 'investigation.' It's like the scenario of *Wag the Dog*, which wasn't a war; it was a pageant. In this case, this isn't an investigation; it's a . . . a visitation."

Their laughter was cut short by the doorbell.

Father Tully admitted Bill Cody and introduced him to Monsignor Rooney. Cody nodded to Koesler, then glanced at his watch. "It's just about time," he announced.

"Before we go," Rooney said to Cody, "maybe you'd like to take a look at this." He held out the agenda. Tully moved to intercept the sheet but Rooney waved him off.

Rooney studied Cody as he scanned the document. At first he seemed bewildered. But as he read, his face took on a knowing look. At one point he even smiled. Rooney was now satisfied that Cody had a sense of humor. It was a better beginning than the liturgist had expected.

As they walked over to the church Cody explained to Rooney why this investigation had been requested. Rooney did not quibble over the word "investigation." He did, however, wonder why Cody was carrying a briefcase. Did he intend to tape-record the proceedings?

Cody, Koesler, and Rooney repaired to the choir loft while Tully began vesting for Mass.

The crowd was somewhat larger than usual. That, thought Cody, was to be increasingly expected as word of this Mass got around.

As was typical with a Folk Mass, people freely mingled in a babble of voices. Cody spotted Eileen in animated conversation with a good-looking, middle-aged woman he finally identified as Anne Marie Tully, sister-in-law of the priest. And presumably the wife of the man who stood with them but seemed to be taking no part in the socializing going on around him. That would be Tully's brother, the Detroit cop.

The music began. Piano, tambourines, and drums.

Cody removed a yellow legal pad from his briefcase and began taking notes. So, thought Rooney, it was going to be that way: chapter and verse. The monsignor knew that Cody would be quizzing him about the particulars in this Mass. He had better pay close attention. The musical trio gave him little choice.

Cody scribbled on his pad.

Rooney was probably the world's worst singer. But he was able to recognize "Shall We Gather at the River." He joined in the refrain. More scribbling by Cody.

The procession entered from the rear, the narthex of the church. Father Tully wore traditional vestments. No problem there. Those who entered with the priest wore an assortment of outfits of no recognizable group. The only familiar article of attire was the stole, worn in a rainbow of colors.

When all the costumed people had settled themselves in the sanctuary, the musicians began another spiritual, "Rock My Soul in the Bosom of Abraham." And from the narthex, a shapely young woman in a snug black leotard began an interpretive dance, writhing down the center aisle in time to the music. Except that at each repeated "Rock my soul," her movement could better be described as more of a bump than a writhe.

By this time, Bill Cody was looking up only intermittently. The rest of the time, he was writing furiously.

Rooney leaned over to speak to Koesler. Due to the decibel level coming from below, the monsignor, head turned to Koesler's ear, was able to speak without being overheard by Cody.

"Did you hear the one about the bishop who hated everything about liturgical reform?"

"I don't think so," Koesler said.

"Well, more than anything, he hated, abhorred, loathed, detested, and despised liturgical dance."

"Like what's going on now."

"Exactly. Everybody in this guy's diocese knew this. Still, one pastor invited the bishop to come for confirmations. So the bishop and the pastor process into the church. Once they're seated in the sanctuary, this young woman in a leotard comes dancing in."

"Like this one."

"Exactly. So the bishop sits there frowning and fuming. When she starts dancing up the side aisle, the bishop leans over to the pastor and says, 'If she wants your head on a platter, she can have it.' "

Koesler grinned. "Did that really happen?"

"I don't think so."

"But it could have."

"Absolutely."

The Folk Mass at St. Joe's continued, as did Cody's notations.

The hymns and spirituals, most of them seldom if ever heard in traditional Catholic services, were not only sung, but sung with enthusiasm and deep-felt emotion. The term "belted out" came to Koesler's mind. If each spiritual had not been identified when announced, the trio in the loft would not universally have recognized "Get on Board, Li'l Children," "Jacob's Ladder," and "Everytime I Feel the Spirit." "Make a joyful noise unto the Lord," thought Koesler, recalling one of David's most beautiful Psalms.

The congregation's syncopation on "Roll, Jordan, Roll" gave it a true spiritual sound. The refrain was split between the female voices—"Oh, brother, you ought to be there . . ."—and the male voices—"Oh, sister, you ought to be there. . . ." And for the final "Oh, Preacher," the voices of the entire congregation emphasized the admonition, "you'd *better* be there." The concluding "I want to go to heaven when I die," was sung softly, yet firmly, slowing up on the grace-noted "die." By the time the female voices soared to the high F for the final "roll," there was hardly an uninvolved bone in nearly everyone present. Always, of course, excepting Bill Cody, whose pen from time to time almost pierced the paper on which he was feverishly entering God alone knew what.

Two of the costumed ministers gave the first two readings from Scripture. Nothing much wrong with that, according to Bill Cody—except, of course, for their unwarranted costumes.

Father Tully preached an interesting and thought-provoking homily. Subdued, to fit the somber nature of the Lenten season.

At the offertory, all the "ministers" took part in the offertory prayers. That caught Cody's attention.

During the preface and into the Canon, or body, of the Mass, the entire congregation left the pews and gathered close in around the altar. Definitely not kosher.

Then came the greeting of peace.

In the traditional Mass in traditional settings, after "The

Lord's Prayer," the priest bids the congregation offer to neighbors "some sign of peace." Which, in the traditional setting, usually is a perfunctory handshake and the uttering of the single word, "peace." In this Folk Mass—as in most others—this is a signal to really mingle.

Everyone went everywhere. Hugging, shaking hands, asking after the health of a loved one who had been identified as ill, talking, laughing, moving about. This continued for approximately fifteen minutes, ending only when Father Tully invited everyone back to prepare for Communion.

The Communion hymn was "Beulah Land." "I'm living on the mountain underneath a cloudless sky—Praise God! I'm drinking from the fountain that never will run dry. . . ."

What particularly galled Cody was the way his wife blended in with the extended inappropriate behavior of this . . . this "congregation."

Mass wound down quickly after Communion.

The recessional hymn—during which no one left the church—was a rollicking version of "When the Roll Is Called up Yonder." The refrain, repetitious enough to be a modern rock tune, got everyone, with the exception of Lieutenant Tully, and the small group in the choir loft, holding hands and swaying to and fro.

Zoo Tully was present, presumably, either to swell the numbers in the congregation or to protect his brother, should anything amiss occur. Or both.

Once the recessional and spiritual were complete, the mingling continued, giving no indication that it would ever end. But, clearly, the liturgy—which had taken almost two hours (as against a normal time of approximately forty-five minutes to an hour)—was over.

Immediately, Cody turned to Rooney. "Look at this!" Cody had filled four legal-size pages with notations on the Folk Mass.

Rooney did not take the proffered documentation. "Before we get into a bill of particulars," the liturgist said, "let me just say one thing for the record: That was a legitimate folk liturgy. They stayed well within the guidelines."

"What are you saying!?" Cody felt he had put together an open-and-shut case. He looked incredulously at all the notes he had made. How could anyone not see all the excesses in this travesty of a Mass?

"What I'm saying, Mr. Cody," explained the monsignor, "is that a Folk Mass isn't anything like the Masses you and I grew up with. I know how you feel. I remember well the Latin, the chant, the whispered prayers. That was my Mass for quite a long time after I was ordained. We still have—what?—a traditional Mass, which, despite being offered in English, is not *that* different from the ancient Tridentine liturgy.

"This is merely another step. It's mostly joyous, as you can see." Rooney gestured toward the congregation below. Their facial expressions were open, reflecting everything from happiness to concern.

"What this definitely is *not*," Rooney continued, "is the ordinary parishioners who go to church regularly, and passively absorb what is going on. And this exodus is a lot better. You and I can remember when the end of Mass on Sunday started a mad stampede—the race to the car and the free-for-all leaving the parking lot as quickly as possible, with safety not a high priority. We're doing better with that now. But still we don't hang around with real interest in each other like these people are doing."

Bill Cody heard almost nothing of what Father Rooney was saying. The council president was aware only that he was losing the battle. "But," he protested, "didn't you see that dancer? The way that leotard fit her, she might as well have been nude! They've got an excellent organ—the king of instruments—but they use a rinky-dink piano, and drums—and tambourines! What is this, a church or the jungle? And all this noise! Isn't there a place for silence?"

Rooney realized that he and Cody could continue this conversation forever and never reach agreement. He felt sorry for Cody, but there was nothing he could do about it.

"I saw the dance," Rooney said patiently. "I heard the

music. I saw the vestments. I witnessed the spirit of acceptance and camaraderie. It's all quite legitimate . . . even restrained. You should see what some of your neighboring parishes are doing with Folk Masses—"

"I don't give a damn what my neighboring parishes are doing! This is St. Joseph's. This is *my* parish. And they're making a mockery of the Mass . . . here in *my* parish. . . ." Cody was close to tears.

"Mr. Cody"—this was intended to be Rooney's final word on the subject—"you're a lawyer. Look at it this way: You could bring the matter of this Folk Mass before the diocesan tribunal. But I can tell you, as sure as we're standing here, the verdict would be in favor of Father Tully and the people who have put together this Mass.

"And consider this: I would be the 'expert witness.' In all honesty, in the archdiocese there is no one more expert in liturgical matters than I.

"The only advice I can give you, Mr. Cody, is to save yourself from a heart attack: Just go to the regular Masses and don't ever attend a Folk Mass again."

With that, Monsignor Rooney left the choir loft, and the church. He would have bade good-bye to Zack Tully, but he was already late for his sister's wedding anniversary party.

Koesler, silent bystander to the foregoing, stepped toward Cody. "Bill, would you like to grab a bite to eat with me? We could talk about this."

Cody raised his head and looked over the railing at the people milling about below. As far as he was concerned, he was Jesus sighting the moneychangers in the temple—the difference being that he could do nothing to stop it.

He did not look at Koesler as he said, "Thanks, Father. It's kind of you. But I don't feel like being with anybody now." There were tears in his eyes.

There was nothing he could do but to offer up his son as a messenger of sanity to a Church gone mad.

Father Koesler patted him on the back as Bill Cody turned, then walked slowly, almost blindly, away.

24

THE SEMINARY HAD two separate and distinct sets of student mailboxes.

One set was at the entrance of St. Thomas Hall. These were small boxes for nonresident students. Usually, items such as notes, memorandums, or leaflets were deposited in them.

The larger boxes were at the entrance to St. William's Hall. These were for residents, and they were larger than the other set because they were intended not only for notes and such but also for regular mail.

One further difference was that the residents' boxes could be locked, while the others were simply closed.

In both cases, the boxes were assigned in alphabetical order.

At precisely 8 P.M. a tall, somewhat heavyset man in cassock and clerical collar was examining the residents' boxes, obviously seeking one in particular. He located the one he wanted. He deposited an envelope through the slot. He looked up and down the hallway, but could see no one. He left.

At precisely 8:05 P.M., another lone figure went to the boxes. She wore a dark pants suit. She went directly to a box, unlocked it, removed the only article in the box—an envelope, which she inserted in the slot of the neighboring box. She closed and locked the original box. Then, empty-handed, she too left.

At 9:30 P.M., a knock sounded at Andrea Zawalich's door.

Andrea was expecting a caller. She hoped it was the right one. She opened the door. It was as she had planned. "Gretchen, what brings you here?"

Gretchen O'Keefe was obviously deeply embarrassed. Her

233

face was so flushed she might have been ill. "Andrea . . . I found this. . . ." She held out an envelope. "I found it in my mailbox. I'm so sorry. I just automatically thought it was for me. I . . . I opened it. I read almost all of it before it dawned on me that it couldn't be for me. So I checked the envelope. It was addressed to you.

"I don't know what to tell you. I couldn't think of anything else except to give it to you. I don't know if I should do anything more. I . . . I just don't know. . . ."

Andrea took the envelope, removed the letter, and began reading it. She had planned a variety of possible actions, depending on what Gretchen would do and how she would react. In any event, Gretchen would have had to have read the note.

Andrea had, in a way, commissioned the document, so she had some idea of what it would contain. Even so, she was shocked and repelled by all that Bill Page promised.

The fact that Gretchen had, mistakenly or not, read it made the next step easier. "Gretchen, this is *awful*."

"I know. I know. Can I just try to forget about it? I mean, I could just go back to my room. After all, it was meant for you."

"I don't know either, Gretchen. But there's something I think we . . . *you* ought to do. It was in your box and you read it. I think this comes under . . . you know . . ."

"No, I don't. I don't know. What?"

"Fraternal correction. You know how we're always told that sometimes things happen that are very bad but hidden in secrecy. Sometimes we have to bring them out so they can be treated. So that the appropriate action is taken by authority."

"I don't want to get involved in this, Andrea!" Gretchen was almost whining.

"That's the very thing they told us: that we wouldn't want to get involved. But that it was important—essential—that we do. We *are* our brother's keeper, Gretchen."

"Oh, damn! You really think so? I mean, this could hurt you too. . . . I mean, it was addressed to you. . . ."

"But I didn't write it. I'm not sure who did—but it looks an awful lot like Bill Page's writing. I think you ought to go right now. It's not too late. Bring it to the rector. Let Bishop McNiff decide what to do. After all, he's the one who was pushing us to use fraternal correction."

"Now?"

"Now!"

"Well, all right . . . if you really think so . . ."

"I really think so."

Bishop McNiff was preparing a talk on spirituality that he would deliver to the students. That was a regular feature of his routine.

He put his notes aside when Gretchen reluctantly explained her mission. She gave him the letter, then hurriedly left.

There are various forms of sexual activity that are condemned by church teaching. And Patrick McNiff agreed with each and every condemnation. He was outraged by the contents of the letter.

Immediately, he summoned the principals: Gretchen O'Keefe, Andrea Zawalich, and, by no means least, William Page.

McNiff interviewed each of them separately, then sent them to their rooms, where they were to remain—alone— even for meals, until tomorrow afternoon when this matter would be submitted to the faculty for resolution.

Gretchen, the innocent bystander dragged into a messy situation by sheer accident and bad luck, was miserable.

Andrea regretted that it had to come to this. But she was satisfied that in good conscience she had done the right thing. Page, in her view, was a cancer on the priesthood. He had to be abscised for the health of the whole body. Beyond that, she was evening the score for her friend Patty.

Bill Page was bewildered. Since he'd had no personal communication with either Andrea or Gretchen, he had to presume that he had somehow slipped the letter into the wrong box—though how he could've done so eluded him.

In any event, the three followed their incarceration rules to the letter. They were already on dangerous ground; no use pushing matters to the edge.

Of course this extraordinary situation involving three of

their fellow students was bound to have its effect on the others. Rumors flew.

At five in the afternoon—normally a predinner happy hour, the deprivation of which did nothing to better their humor—the entire full-time faculty, plus Father Koesler, assembled in the faculty lounge.

Bishop McNiff explained why he had not settled the matter on his own. There were so many shadowy sides to this affair and since two senior students were implicated he felt that a faculty decision was called for.

Then, one by one, those involved were called in to present their cases.

Consensus promptly exonerated Gretchen, who by this time could have used either a physician or a counselor or both to bring down her blood pressure and calm her nerves. She got neither.

Andrea, as she had planned, told the simple truth. She explained her reasoning and her justification completely. She was convinced her actions had been fitting and appropriate. And she was certain the faculty would be understanding and in agreement that she had done what needed to be done.

Bill Page, when summoned to McNiff's office the previous night, had been grateful he would have almost twenty-four hours to come up with a defense. However, as time passed, it became clear to Page that no exculpatory explanation would hold water. At best he would buy a little time, delay the inevitable.

His only possible escape would be to claim he hadn't written the note. He hadn't signed it. But he had written it. And any handwriting analyst worth her salt could testify that Bill Page was indeed the author of the infamous note.

After long thought, and even a little prayer—there are no atheists in the sex crime defendant's dock—he decided in effect to throw himself on the mercy of the faculty.

Thus, in his testimony he described Andrea as a seductress—an agent provocateur. She had started the whole affair. She had entrapped him with her promises of sexual favors. It was outrageous conduct for someone who was about to be awarded a diploma in Pastoral Ministry.

He was weak—but not evil. He begged the faculty to take into consideration his conduct throughout his career, delayed though it was, in the seminary. He asked for mercy.

He had been eloquent. And, if one were to overlook Andrea's very strong motive, much of his defense was accurate.

Andrea and Page were sent to their respective rooms under the same rule of isolation as before. They were assured they would learn the verdict as soon as it was rendered. Before this evening, if possible.

The doors to the faculty lounge were closed and locked. Those within were in conclave.

Bishop McNiff swore the faculty members to a secrecy that would prevent them from divulging the details of the deliberation to the extent of identifying a particular speaker with his or her opinion. They could reveal the total number of votes. But again, they were not to identify an individual with his or her vote.

McNiff then led them in a prayer to the Holy Spirit for enlightenment and guidance.

The future of two students—one young, one close to ordination—was at stake. The welfare and integrity of the seminary were on the line.

Finally, votes might be cast by each and every member of the faculty present, including the rector. Father Koesler was there only as an observer.

Koesler was not wild about being the permanent dummy in this bridge game. On the other hand, he thought that the debate and the voting would be instructive and interesting.

Early discussion centered on William Page and his apologia for his admittedly crude overture to Andrea.

"He confessed to being weak. What are we about here? Do we ordain only saints, or are we, all of us, sinners who need forgiveness?" So spoke Father Frank Grasso. In most formalistic settings such as the present, Grasso was the principal spokesperson for the conservative side.

"Being weak is one thing," Father Paul Burke, a progressive, said. "We're talking about conduct you probably wouldn't find even in one of those X-rated movies!"

"You've been to one? Some?" Grasso challenged.

"Don't be a blithering idiot, Frank," Burke shot back. "We've all read Page's letter. Any redeeming social value there?"

"Follow Page's argument," Father Laurence Duross, a traditionalist, said. "It was no more than a slip . . . a *lapsus linguae*. He has an unblemished record in this seminary. Doesn't that count for anything?"

"Is his record unblemished because his heart was pure all this time?" said Father Cliff Rogers, Burke's buddy. "Or has this basically blemished character been there all the while, and did it surface when invited to show itself?"

"Look at the record," Duross remonstrated. "He's been an exemplary student and seminarian."

"Meaning he follows every dictate of the magisterium as if it were God sending down the tablets?" Burke said.

"The magisterium is God's word and God's will," Grasso declared.

"Says who?" Burke snapped.

"Gentlemen, gentlemen . . ." McNiff called for everyone's attention. "Please, let us not get into a theological donnybrook. We're trying to deal with some very serious conduct on the part of two of our senior students. Shall we confine ourselves to the issues at hand?"

There was a brief pause, giving everyone an opportunity to refocus on what they were about.

"It comes down to this," Rogers said. "Supposing we have Page ordained. He is sent to a parish—"

"St. Waldo's, I'm told," Burke interrupted.

"It just so happens," Grasso retorted, "that no other ordinand asked for that assignment."

"So," Burke argued, "we're supposed to feel very sorry because poor Page is slated to serve the wealthiest parish in the diocese?"

"Gentlemen!" McNiff intervened. "Father Rogers has the floor."

"As I was saying," Rogers proceeded, "supposing that Page is sent to Waldo's or just about any other assignment. It is not beyond reason that one or more of the ladies of the parish might find him debonair, mature, eloquent, even attractive. Supposing one or another of those women indulges in a little innocent flirting . . . you do see where this goes, don't you?"

"Directly," Duross replied, "into the trash heap labeled hypothesis-speculation."

"Not exactly," Rogers corrected. "Remember what you read in that note, eminent colleagues. All that sickening sexual excess awaits the gentle flirt. Next, we will find Page being bounced around the diocese. Assigned to one parish after another. Leaving behind a mounting series of scandals."

"I think," said Duross, "that Father Rogers's imagination has run wild. To elicit that sort of response from Page, you'd need not a flirt but a provocateur. A Salomé. And you're not going to find such a woman in the Rosary Altar Society."

"I submit," Grasso said, "that we're concentrating on the wrong character in this little drama. Miss Zawalich orchestrated this entire gambit. If she hadn't dreamed up this scheme, nothing, absolutely nothing, would have happened."

"Exactly," Duross agreed. "She is what's termed a whistle-blower. What happens if we confer a degree on her? She goes to a parish and if the pastor doesn't suit her standards, she entraps the poor man. And one more parish desperately in need of a pastor has no one to turn to but Little Miss Mata Hari."

"What's so bad about a whistle-blower?" Burke demanded. "It takes courage to take on any establishment or power-mad leader and expose the evil!"

"Doesn't anyone see," Duross asked, "the resemblance between what we're debating now and one of the earliest stories in the Bible?"

"You don't mean—" Burke began.

"Of course I mean Adam and Eve. Paradise and the first sin. Adam would not have fallen if it had not been for Eve. It's the woman every time. *Cherchez la femme.*"

"Well! Really!" Loretta Doyle breathed fire. She was that rare combination of liturgist, conservative, and feminist.

Duross and many of the other traditionalists knew they had just lost a sympathetic ear.

The debate continued for more than an hour, neither faction moving appreciably in their respective positions.

For some, Page was the victim. Trapped by a conniving female. To this camp, Andrea was all of the seducing, manipulative women in history.

Or, Andrea was willing to risk a Church career she'd been pursuing for the past eight years so that the Church would not be compromised by a totally unacceptable candidate for orders. To this camp, Page was a clear and certain danger. A time bomb set and ready to go off.

The debate slackened as all sensed that they were going over the same ground again and again. A motion was made and seconded that Page be given a reprimand and forgiven for all else. That was defeated 19–11. McNiff did not vote.

A motion was made and seconded that Page be reprimanded, confined to campus until after the Easter holidays, and that his request for assignment to St. Waldo's be denied. The motion passed 17–13.

As to the matter of Andrea Zawalich:

A motion was made and seconded that her behavior in this matter be made a part of her permanent record and that she be placed on probation for a year after graduation. Anything of this nature in that period and she would be stripped of her academic degree. That motion was defeated 20–10.

The handwriting was on the wall: The majority wanted Andrea's head.

A motion was made and seconded that she be expelled and denied her degree. The motion passed 18–12.

The meeting was over. McNiff took on the unwanted task of informing the two principals of the faculty's verdict.

Father Koesler was disheartened by the entire affair. He barely knew either student. But this escapade bore the earmarks of adolescent behavior. Easier to forgive Andrea than Page, if only because the young woman was chronologically closer to adolescence.

But the faculty had debated and voted. As they say in Rome, *causa finita*.

25

WITH BISHOP MCNIFF'S message of the faculty vote, both the accused were freed from detention. Andrea, however, was told to pack and make arrangements to leave immediately.

As soon as McNiff left Andrea's room, Patty joined her. And the two had a wrenching cry. Some of that gloom lingered as Andrea began to pack.

"How are you going to leave?" Patty asked bleakly.

"My mom and dad are on the way. I've got my car, but I just don't feel up to driving right now. I'll go home with Mom, and Dad will take my car."

"You did it for me, didn't you?" Patty asked, after a short silence.

"Partly . . ." Andrea thought for a moment. "Yes, only partly. The sleazeball did give you such a rotten time. I wouldn't have had any idea of the horrible things that he would do to the Church if I hadn't seen what he did, and what he tried to do, to you."

Patty shook her head. "It's my fault. I can't help it; I feel I'm responsible for what's happened."

Andrea stopped packing and sat on the bed. "Drive that out of your mind, honey. *I* did it. I did it all on my own. And it was stupid."

"It wasn't!" Patty protested. "There was no other way. Face it: If you had told the faculty how unfit Bill Page is for the priesthood, they would never have believed you. Look at what actually happened: Page himself told the faculty how low he could stoop. And all they did was give him a slap on the wrist."

241

"I don't know about that." Andrea smiled weakly. "I think he'll really miss Waldo's."

"Get serious!"

"I am. Oh, I am."

"What are you going to do? Do you have any idea?"

"It's too soon." Andrea sighed. "You know . . . I had my career firmly in place . . . everything was set . . . I had a parish ready for me and I certainly was ready for that parish." Andrea stood and resumed her packing. "I threw the whole thing away. What a fool I was!"

"You were a fool for God."

"That's debatable."

"Is there anything I can do?"

"No." Andrea stopped and ran her fingers through Patty's hair. "There is one silver lining—and only one that I know of. After he lowered the boom on me, that good old Bishop McNiff went off the record. He said he understood what I'd done and why. He said he didn't think it was very bright, but he thought it was very brave."

"Well, that's consoling. He didn't have to tell you that."

"Patty, it was more than mere words. He said I was an excellent student. He told me to scout around the country. If I found a diocese and a seminary that I really liked, he would vouch for me and explain what had happened here."

Patty's face brightened. "That was terrific of him, wasn't it?"

"Yes, I think so. But right now, I'm already missing that lovely little parish I had all set up. I said I wouldn't go to them without a diploma. And I won't."

A student appeared in the doorway. "Andrea, your folks are here."

"Tell them I'll be down in a couple of minutes." She turned to Patty. "So long, friend. I hope our paths will cross in the future."

"We can pray for each other," Patty said.

"And we will. Now get out of here before we start crying again."

But it was too late. The tears were flowing as Patty, shoulders hunched, turned and left the room, followed by the sound of Andrea's barely muffled sobs.

As she made her way almost blindly down the corridor, Patty thought she heard her name called. Dabbing at her tearstained cheeks with a couple of disintegrating tissues, she turned to see Al Cody. "D . . . Did you call me?"

"Uh-huh." He hurried to catch up with her. Pulling herself together, Patty glared at him. "I'm going to warn you right off the bat, *Reverend Mr. Cody*"—she gave him his title in a voice oozing with sarcasm—"if you've come to gloat, I'll flatten you!" She turned to continue on her way.

"Oh no. No. Please, I swear I'm not gloating. I just heard about it . . . about Andrea and Bill. I don't know any of the details. But right off the top, I just wanted to tell you how sorry I am." He circled in front of her, forcing her to halt. "Andrea was just about your best friend, wasn't she?"

"Not 'just about'; she *is* my best friend."

"Do you know what all this is about?"

"Are you for real?" As far as Patty was concerned, Cody was completely out of character in showing pity for not just one but two women. "When are you going to tip the chair against the table so I can't sit with you?" Her voice was not loud, but it was intense. "When are you going to laugh at me and humiliate me when I do something stupid? When are you going to break up in glee over Andrea's expulsion?"

Cody hung his head. "I hurt you *that* much! I'm sorry. I really am. If you want, I won't bother you again, ever. And I couldn't blame you. But I'd like to be your friend. And I know that will take a lot of forgiving on your part."

They stood staring at each other for what seemed a long time.

"Why should Andrea have a corner on Christian behavior?" Patty murmured finally. "Okay. What the hell, I'll give it a try."

Al beamed. "Will you tell me, then? What happened, I mean?"

Gretchen O'Keefe so far had been the only source of information regarding the infamous note. She had read it. The only others who knew the contents were Andrea, Bill, and the faculty. All of whom were sworn to secrecy.

However, Gretchen knew only what had been written, not the premise on which the note was based. That, among all the students, was the question of the day: What was in the letter? And what had occasioned it?

"We can't stand here all day," Patty said. "Want to go to the snack room?"

Al treated to coffee. Patty somewhat hesitantly—she was still not sure of him—filled him in on what she knew.

Al thought Andrea foolish to risk everything just to prove a point. But he did not voice this opinion; this new-made friendship was far too fragile to put to the test this soon. Instead, he expressed sympathy for what had happened to her friend. The sympathy was genuine.

Patty was curious: What did he think of his buddy Bill Page?

Al hesitated. "I'm fully aware that Bill is horny. Sometimes it seems all he can think about. But I was sure he was keeping his fixation in check."

He refrained from mentioning the plans that Bill had for postordination sexual activity. Al tended to treat that as a confidence not to be shared with anyone else.

"But," he said, "if Andrea offered him all that she reportedly promised, the result was predictable. He couldn't resist something like that."

Patty tilted her head to one side and studied him. "Al, you are either the most forgiving person I've met in a long time. Or you are terrifically indecisive. Once I would have said indecisive; now, I'm not so sure."

"In the spirit of our new friendship, I've got to confess that I have always had a real problem making up my mind. I don't know what's the matter . . . but I'm working on it."

"Okay, but what made you go along with all those childish pranks with Bill and the guys? You must've known you were hurting me. . . ."

He reddened. "Down deep I knew we were wrong. It was

shameful. It was foolish and adolescent. But I couldn't decide to go against the tide. I can only tell you again I am truly sorry. I apologize."

"Accepted. Now let's see if we can keep this friendship alive."

"My sentiments exactly."

The doorway darkened as Bill Page entered the room.

"It's good to see you, buddy," Bill directed at Al. "You're the first friendly face I've seen in quite a while."

"Don't count on it being friendly," Patty said.

"I wasn't speaking to you." His tone was derisive.

Patty shot a glance at her tablemate, who appeared to have been struck dumb. She turned back to Page. "I'm speaking for Al."

"Al? Not Al!" Page shot a glance at the mute deacon. "What are you doing, buddy: giving aid and comfort to the enemy?"

"The enemy isn't all that clearly defined," Patty said. "Things have changed." She looked at Al, tilting her head as if pointing toward Page. "Tell him, Al."

Silence.

Page, seemingly unruffled, got a coffee from the machine and sat down heavily at their table. "Yeah, tell me, Al. Tell me about the changes."

Al looked helplessly at Patty. "We've all got to be under-standing at a time like this. Bill's been through a rough period too."

Patty's jaw dropped. "After what we—?" She was sputter-ingly angry and getting angrier. "You're right, Al. You've got a backbone like a rubber band. If this is all our friendship means, forget it!" She pushed away from the table with such vehemence that her cup overturned, spilling coffee all over the table. Heedless, she stormed from the room.

Bill sighed coolly, picked up some napkins, and began mopping up the puddle. "Crazy broad . . . never cleans up her messes."

Al looked puzzled. "Bill, how can you act like this after what you've been through?"

"After what I've been through? You've got a point there. I have been through a lot. I am very definitely going to miss St. Waldo's, and all we could have done for each other. That is a spectacular loss. So how come I feel at all chipper?" He tossed the soggy napkins in the wastebasket. "It could have been a lot worse. I could have been tossed out on my ear like that poor bitch Zawalich."

"How come you weren't?"

A snide smile. "Lots of reasons, Al; lots of reasons.

"For one thing, I long ago made friends with the winning group. In case you haven't noticed, this faculty is up to its ears in traditional clergy and lay members. As soon as I knew that, I knew what kind of student I would be: Hooray for the Pope! In effect, my good buddies, my fellow conservatives, cleared me. The only surprise," he said parenthetically, "was that the vote wasn't 27–3."

"But that, Al, is what saved my ass more than anything else.

"On top of which, it was a deacon versus an embryonic pastoral minister. All they had to do was fire her. If they had done that to me, there would've been the mess of laicizing me. Which would mean bringing the matter to Rome—something most of the guys didn't want to do.

"And, maybe one more thing: I was damn good at pleading my case! Put them all together, they spell something close to vindication.

"But I *am* going to miss Waldo's. Maybe after I do really well wherever they send me, there'll still be a Waldo's in my future."

"That's it?" Al demanded. "That's all there is to it?" He looked incredulous. "As far as I can total it up—my father being a lawyer—you've been convicted of gross indecency in language and in intent. And you attempted to seduce a woman—never mind that she initiated it; you drew the pictures. And, as a result of your adolescent behavior, a damn good student has been expelled. In addition, you have lost an appointment to a prestigious parish." Brow knitted in a combination of puzzlement and amazement, he stared at Page. "And you call all that your 'vindication'?"

Page, seemingly unruffled, downed the remainder of his coffee, then crushed the Styrofoam cup in his fist. "Now, wait just a minute, buddy-whose-father-is-a-lawyer. The Zawalich broad tried to prove one indisputable conclusion: that a man is capable of being seduced. If there's a question there, it's rhetorical. She not only initiated this mess, she was the one who seduced *me*. I just went along with it.

"At best, the affair was a mistake. At worst, in terms of her future in the Church, it was a fatal mistake.

"So don't go getting holier than thou with me."

"God knows I don't want to be holier than anybody," Al protested. "I guess I was just disgusted with your flippant attitude. You're passing this off as a joke. And I'm pretty certain that it's no joke to Andrea."

"Forget Andrea. For the last time, forget Andrea. She's history." He smiled salaciously. "Let's consider Patty."

"Patty?!"

"The trouble is, Al, I'm not sure about what I'm hearing. I promised that you wouldn't leave these walls a virgin. I never got down to specifics on that promise. But I can tell you now, my nominee for your carnal knowledge was none other than Pat Donnelly."

"What?"

"That's right: pretty Patty. She may have a mighty mouth, but she's also got a great bod. I'll readily admit that I've had my share of fantasies and then some about Ms. Donnelly. However, being of a generous nature, I was reserving her for you. In what might have been your one and only indulgence in sexual encounter, I thought you deserved the very best.

"Besides, getting you and Donnelly together was a challenge to my ability as a romantic matchmaker. In the past, my record for getting others together was equaled only by my finding a willing woman for myself."

"Bill, you're talking about being a pimp!"

"Why quibble over words? The point is, I'm as good to my friends as I am to myself.

"But to be honest, Al, you took me by surprise getting next to Donnelly all on your own."

"You thought . . . ?"

"Look at yourself. Look at her. When was the last time you were with her, just the two of you?"

"Well," Al rummaged around his memory, "never before, actually. But that doesn't mean . . ."

"What else could it mean? You were doing this all on your own. Al, I'm proud of you. Only . . . only, I fear I screwed things up for you. It was obvious the two of you were hitting it off. I should have got out of here the minute I saw you two together. At the very least, I should have acted like it was the two of you against me.

"Instead, I started up where I'd left off: being her adversary. And I included you in my camp. I'm sorry, buddy. But," he reassured, "I think I can make good. From now on, I won't be your buddy. I'll make it obvious that you and I have split. Then you can make your move. And, by the way, if you want to check it out, I can give you some pointers on how to make that move."

Obviously Page was excited. He had excited himself. Apparently he anticipated living vicariously through Cody. It would be as much an affair between Page and Donnelly, in Page's mind, as it would be between Cody and Donnelly in the flesh.

Page was ready—ready to initiate what in effect was Plan B.

It seemed to be Al Cody's turn to speak. But he said nothing. He just regarded Page incredulously.

"I don't believe you," Cody said at length. "You have just been disciplined for your misconduct. And you want me to travel down the same road you were on."

"I'm doing this for your own good, Al. I can't stand to see a pal of mine go through life without a decent and fulfilling sexual encounter. I'm only thinking of you."

I'm only thinking of you. Such a familiar phrase. Cody recalled almost immediately: It was a song from *Man of La Mancha.* A series of relatives and "friends" of Don Quixote confess to a priest that—while meddling with, manipulating, and ruining the Don's life—they are only thinking of him.

Cody had only a little coffee left in his cup. He swirled it. He seemed to study it. As if it were not coffee but tea, and not tea but tea leaves, and he was about to tell his own future.

He put the cup down and stared at Page, who, unaccountably, became somewhat dismayed.

"Maybe," Cody said, "maybe we don't have to pretend, Bill."

"Huh? What do you mean?"

"Maybe it's gone beyond pretend."

"What . . . ?"

"It's just getting a little clearer. Ever since you came to the seminary and joined our class I've grown increasingly dependent on you, Bill. I looked up to you . . . I don't know why.

"I went along with you in a lot of adolescent behavior. The way we made life difficult for all the non-M.Divs, especially the women—and most especially Patty Donnelly.

"All that I learned from my mother—respect for women and sensitivity toward minorities—all down the drain. Just because I wanted your approval. That's becoming very clear now.

"Bill, I don't share your values. If I'm going to be a priest, I've got to be a straight arrow. If I've never had sex before I'm ordained, it's not going to cripple me.

"But it would cripple me if you—no, to be fair, *we* were to collaborate in a seduction of Patty Donnelly. That would be something I'd regret for the rest of my life—" He looked almost stricken. "And to think I was going to do it!

"I was just going to go along with you like I have so many times. You'd prop a chair against a table to block one of 'the great unwashed' from being in our company. And then so would I. You'd freeze someone out of our conversation and I'd follow your lead.

"And now it's happened again.

"It came as a great shock to me—what happened between you and Andrea. I felt really bad for both of you. Of course,

Andrea got the worst of it, by far, so my sympathy was mostly for her.

"And because I was so sorry for Andrea, I also was sad for Patty. The two of them were closer than you and I. I don't know where they put Andrea. I tried to find her. But before I could find her, she was gone.

"So I went looking for Patty, and I found her. And, as I thought, she was devastated. I apologized for all the misery I had caused them—"

"You what?!" Page could not permit such an act to go unchallenged. "I suppose you included me in this hangdog apology. Well, I'll have none of it! What's done is done. There's no going back. I don't regret a thing. I don't take back a thing. And there's no apology going to come from me!"

Ordinarily so forceful a counterattack would cow the submissive Cody. This evening proved an exception. Cody not only maintained eye contact, he wore a slight smile. It was Page who blinked.

"No," Cody said, "I did not offer your apology. And, now that I think of it, it didn't even cross my mind. It was I who had contrition. I didn't care about us—you and me. I had treated both Andrea and Patty and all the others shabbily. I, who acted less the Christian, played the unfunny practical jokes; I had a lot to be sorry for. The apology was from me.

"I didn't even think of you when I delivered the apology. Isn't that marvelous: If I had thought of you, I wouldn't have expressed any sorrow. Because I knew you wouldn't.

"But you fixed things anyway, Bill. You came in here swinging away. And you gave me the thing that I do worst at—a choice. Was I going to side with you or with Patty?

"I chose you! I asked Patty to understand the pressure you'd been under. What pressure? It turns out this whole thing has been a big lark for you. The only bruise you got was losing St. Waldo's. Big deal! You'll be ordained. You'll get a juicy assignment. Your friends in administration and on this faculty will see to that.

"I chose you. And I lost Patty as a friend. A new friend.

And I have this very strong feeling that I'll never regain her friendship. All because of you.

"Well, Bill, I don't think we'll ever have to pretend we are no longer buddies. In very fact, we aren't."

He dropped his cup in the trash can and left the room.

"Just a minute! You can't do this! You don't cut me out of your life. I drop you! Like a hot potato!" But Page was aware that he was shouting against a blank wall. Cody was gone.

Page felt alone. Not the aloneness of this otherwise vacant room. Deeper than that.

He began counting up the friends he had among his fellow students. Even stretching the definition and/or description of friendship, he really had no one. Acquaintances? Quite a few. Enemies? More than anyone might expect. Friends? Al Cody.

Actually, Al was more a lackey, a gofer, a flunky. Now, even Al was gone—at least for a while.

Would he return? Would he come back?

Surely he would. Here's a guy who couldn't decide whether or not to cross a street. For the past eight years, Bill Page had been posing questions and providing answers for this kid who simply couldn't make up his mind.

It was like taking a life preserver away from a non-swimmer. Al Cody needed Bill Page. Al was going to experience this need very soon. Page knew it. He pictured Cody as he must be right now: trying to decide whether to return to the protection and direction provided by Bill Page—mentor and guardian.

It was just a matter of time. Everything would work out. Things always did for Bill Page.

26

IT WAS LATE afternoon on the day after "the incident," as it was being popularly termed. It happened to be St. Patrick's Day. The communal Mass had just been celebrated.

In ordinary circumstances, much would have been made of the popular saint's feast. But this was not an ordinary time.

It seemed that all anyone was interested in was "the incident" involving Andrea Zawalich and Bill Page: one expelled, the other confined to the campus; all over a sexual matter the essence of which eluded the students' best efforts at detection. But it was virtually all everyone was talking about.

Several of the priest faculty had concelebrated the Mass along with Father Koesler and Bishop McNiff. Now, in the faculty parlor, the priests, having divested and hung the ornate white vestments in the sacristy closets, were headed for what some called the "happy hour" and others termed "attitude adjustment time."

Father Koesler was about to join the parade when McNiff motioned him over. "Robert," the bishop intoned, "how would you like to keep a tired old man company?"

"I'd consider it. Where is the old coot?"

"Yer lookin' at him, Bobby."

"I refuse to acknowledge that designation for you . . . mainly because I've only got a year on you."

As the other priests took to the stairs that led to the faculty lounge, Koesler and McNiff repaired to the bishop's suite.

Koesler, having declined a drink, joined McNiff on the sofa, easily the most comfortable article of furniture in the room.

"Things certainly didn't used to be like this, tall, dark and tall. . . ."

"You mean students involved in scandals?"

"No. I was thinkin' of St. Patrick's Day in the good old days."

"Ah, yes," Koesler recalled. "The day off, no studies, no classes. A holiday afternoon. The annual college basketball game between the Irish and the gentiles."

"Funny how the Irish used to win those games year after year, even though they were taking on the whole rest of the school."

"Well, you know how they always say that on St. Patrick's Day there are just the Irish and those who want to be Irish. There were some strange Irish names on that court: Kowalski, Slominski, Krause. . . ."

"Sure'n their mothers were O'Brien and Murphy and Bannon. And will you ever forget the year some hooligans painted all the toilet seats green on St. Pat's Day."

"There was retaliation for that."

"I know what you're going to say."

"Of course . . ." Koesler would revive the memory anyway. "It was the next year, on the Feast of the Circumcision, when some of the boys painted the toilet seats red."

"In either case, some heads would've rolled if the faculty hadn't been in a forgiving mood."

"That's something else that's changed," Koesler noted.

"What's that?"

"The mood of the faculty."

"You're referring to yesterday?"

"Indeed."

"I must say," McNiff mused, "I was surprised. Especially at the penalty on the Zawalich girl."

"I can't help thinking that what she and Page did wasn't that far removed from some of the escapades we got involved in when we were seminarians."

McNiff looked shocked. "We didn't challenge any girl to sex games!"

"There weren't any girls in the seminary in those days," Koesler reminded.

"Still . . ."

"Plus you could make a pretty good case that this penalty was a double standard. Expulsion is certainly a lot more severe than a few weeks' grounding."

"True. And she in her final year! I did tell her that if she found another seminary, I'd be willing to recommend her."

"Good for you! But what happens if the faculty gets word of that? I mean, those faculty members who voted her out?"

"They're just going to have to like it or lump it." There was a touch of defiance in the bishop's voice.

Koesler appreciated this. It marked a return of the Pat McNiff of yore. As a seminarian and as a priest, he had been a feisty little fellow. Lately, he had mellowed. While some of the mellowing process was welcome, particularly in his role as a bishop, there were times in this present assignment that cages needed to be rattled. Koesler was pleased at his friend's show of spunk. "That's the way to talk, Pat. Damn the torpedoes, full speed ahead."

"Actually," McNiff reflected, "yesterday we saw the good news–bad news routine."

"Oh?"

"The bad news is what happened to the Zawalich girl. She was so well put together. Every time I looked at her, the word that came to mind was 'competent.' She had her life so organized."

"Yes," Koesler agreed. "Wasn't she the one who had a job all lined up?"

"Yeah. St. George's in Southfield. She was all set to be pastoral minister there. She had her staff selected and pretty well trained. Andrea would've hit that parish running. Funny how she had Bennie Manor wrapped around her finger."

"Manor?" A name Koesler had not heard in many years. "I hadn't gotten wind of that."

McNiff chuckled. "You remember Manor, don't you?"

"Sure. He was a few years behind us in the seminary. But the memory is cloudy. He didn't do very much. He was sort of just

'there.' He didn't go out for sports or entertainment. He didn't
even break many rules. I'll bet when the seminary faculty got
around to calling him for ordination, there was a collective
'Who?' "

"Yep, that was pretty much Bennie Manor." McNiff cuffed
the arm of the sofa with his hand. "And he's never made waves
in all these years. If we hadn't run low on priests, Bennie
probably would never have made pastor. But when they got
near the bottom of the barrel, they came up with Bennie.

"Far as I know," McNiff reflected, "he just marked time in
the parish until it came time to retire. I understand he had that
pretty well planned. Which only indicates that there was something he could do well."

"Let's see . . ." Koesler began a silent count. "He must be
damn close to retirement now. What was he—three or four
years behind us?"

"That's what she used—his pending retirement—to scare
him into giving her free rein to update practically everything in
the parish."

"No!"

"Yes!"

"You know what this means?" Koesler said. "It means that
behind that bland look he always wore, there was nothing
going on. What did she do, tell him they wouldn't let him retire
until he updated the parish functions?"

McNiff nodded appreciatively. "The way she had it laid out,
Bennie would say Mass on weekends and, after the scare put
on him, probably every weekday as well."

"That makes her . . . what?"

"Pretty much the pastor."

"How did we ever let a catch like her get away?"

"Our faculty took care of that."

"Oh, yeah. But you said that the faculty's vote brought good
and bad news. Well, we've seen the bad. What about the
good?"

"The good news, Bob, was the tabulation of the ballots."

"How's that?"

"The verdict in this case . . . the trial, if you want, was pretty much decided before we even gathered. About the only thing that surprised me on the bad side was her expulsion."

"And the good?"

"The number who voted for forgiveness and tolerance. Until very recently the votes on a matter like that would be 27 to 3—over and over again. That's how unevenly divided this faculty was.

"Those votes yesterday were a victory for what I was sent here to do. Oh"—he raised a hand as if in warning—"it's not over. They weren't voting on any of the 'absolutes' in Doctrine or Morals. Or how we react to the Pope's latest word. But it's a step."

"Congratulations."

"To you, too."

"C'mon. I've been here just a little while."

"I know that. But you've had an effect. You probably can't see it. Our three acknowledged progressives have been a bit more sure of themselves. And the conservatives have unbent a little. You're just too close to this thing to see the changes. And of course the changes haven't been all that dramatic. But they're real—and yesterday's vote was a solid indication."

"Well . . . if you say so." Koesler had difficulty accepting compliments from someone like McNiff with whom a joking relationship held sway. "So . . . what next?"

"In this institution?"

"Um-hmm."

"Not much . . ." McNiff thought aloud. "Things should quiet down. Easter's coming up in about three weeks. Then it's all downhill till graduation, matriculation, and ordination.

"Take my word for it. Things will settle down. It's going to be business as usual. And"—he grinned wryly—"we could use a little bit of that."

Father Koesler made his way slowly and thoughtfully back to his room. "Business as usual," McNiff had predicted. All well and good . . . but what, exactly, was "business as usual" nowadays?

Koesler shook his head.

At the heart of it all was the polarity of Catholic conservatives and liberals. Those of the committed sort. The two groups might just as well consist of nitro and glycerine. Mix them and . . . murder.

Thirty-some years ago such sharp divisions were unknown in the broader Catholic Church.

The "Faithful" were faithful. They received the sacraments regularly and fervently. Most would not even think of missing Sunday Mass.

Priests—the diocesan or secular sort—were either pastors or assistants (curates). Pastors had lived long enough to outmaneuver the actuarial tables. Now they planned on surviving long enough to enjoy their triumph. Assistants prayed for their pastors, that they might soon be in heaven—or at least in purgatory.

Bishops—who "had achieved the fullness of the priesthood"—really had it made. If nothing was too good for Father, in Ireland nothing was too good for the bishop at all, at all.

Things changed in the Church at about a quarter of a resolution each millennium.

Then came Vatican Council II—roughly analagous to the turning point between Before Christ and Anno Domini.

The Council ushered in the Age of the Laity. Armed with the Conciliar phrase "The People of God are the Church," they (the laity) launched an incursion into hitherto priestly territory.

Where once only the consecrated hands of deacon-on-up could touch the Communion wafer, now there were Extraordinary Ministers of the Eucharist.

Priests might struggle to retain their territory. Or they might retire. Meanwhile there occurred a fission that divided the conservative and the liberal wings of the Church.

These were not conservatives who harkened back to the Apostolic days immediately following Christ. These conservatives merely wanted things to be again as they were immediately before Vatican II. As it turned out, they were trying to put the toothpaste back in the tube.

Liberals were marching resolutely into the twenty-first century even though, at that time, the world was only a little bit more than halfway through the twentieth.

Bishops, members of one of the more exclusive worldwide clubs, began to circle their wagons. They were squeezed between the Pope and their priests.

Tending to be mostly conservative, bishops tried to carry forward the dictates of the Pope. Ordinarily, they could accomplish this through their priests. But the priests were disillusioned, their morale was scraping bottom, and they were grievously overworked.

In 1966, the average age of seminarians was twenty-five. In 1993 the average age was thirty-two. Seminaries were not churning out priests in anywhere close to the numbers thirty-some years before. Active priests were trying to survive even as they served.

From the hierarchical aerie, the Church hardly was The People of God. It was the same old triangle that had existed quite comfortably before the Council.

The People of God formed the foundation. They were given "the word" by, in many cases, a hard-pressed clergy. The clergy were given "the word" by, in many cases, a bewildered hierarchy. The hierarchy was given "the word" by a confident if insular Pope.

Mother Angelica with her network TV toy sat at one end. Theologian Hans Küng sat at the other.

"Business as usual . . ." Koesler stood irresolute in front of the unopened door to his room. How long had it been . . . how many years—*decades?*—since things had been "usual" in the Church? He thought back to his service as an altar boy, to his years in the seminary, to his days as a fervent young priest, to his time at the helm of the archdiocesan newspaper, to his terms as a pastor. Where, along the way, had things stopped being "usual"?

Vatican II, that's where. What was the name of the tune the British had played when they surrendered at Yorktown— "The World Turned Upside Down"? Yup, that was it. Well, they might as well have played it for the post–Vatican II Catholics; for so many of them, their world *had* turned upside down.

Koesler opened his door, entered his room, and sank into a chair, to ponder more recent events.

Patty Donnelly wanted to become a priest. Polls revealed that most Catholics could find no reason to deny her that vocation. But the Pope and his Curia taught that it never would happen. This teaching bordered on the infallible.

Her desire and his opposition were on a collision course. One fine day, perhaps sooner than most expected, today's priest shortage will become a famine.

Catholicism is—as, to a slightly lesser degree, are almost all Christian denominations—a sacramental religion. Priests and ministers are needed to confect and to deliver sacraments. What happens if Christianity runs out of priests and ministers?

What happens to infallibility and the ordinary teaching office of the Church if it is compelled to ordain women and married people?

Bishop McNiff is not all that concerned with the conservative or liberal camps. Probably because he is an amalgam of both. Very few others have accomplished this.

His full-time seminary faculty numbers thirty—of which three are liberals.

Bishop McNiff's goal is to re-create a seminary faculty that may be predominantly conservative, but is marked by tolerance, openness, and understanding.

Even that goal would not necessarily prove daunting. Except that today's liberals want everyone in the boat, while today's conservatives want all dissidents out of the boat. Sort of Happy Days Are Here Again versus My Church, Love It or Leave It.

Closer to home, it looked as if Old St. Joseph's parish was about to be torn asunder.

When Koesler bequeathed St. Joe's to Zachary Tully, the tacit understanding—at least on Koesler's part—was that things would stay pretty much in status quo. Apparently that understanding was not understood by Tully.

No sooner had Koesler been gently swept out of the rectory than—according to Bill Cody—Tully had introduced an African-American Folk Mass to the regular Sunday liturgy.

Koesler understood Bill Cody well enough to know that scheduling a Folk Mass on Cody's territory was like waving any number of red flags before an extremely angry bull.

Did Zack Tully realize the consequences of what he'd initiated? What purpose could he hope to accomplish? Why had he not introduced this change to the parish council? Why had he made it a fait accompli instead of a proposal? Why would he add a Mass to a schedule already less than filled? Why would he do this especially in light of the priest shortage? Why would he add this weekend Mass at practically the same time he rejected Koesler's offer of help?

By Koesler's reckoning, Bill Cody was not a wild-eyed traditionalist. He was not the sort to tie his conservatism to the beginnings of Christianity. Nor did he demand that everything Catholic return to pre–Vatican II.

This was evidenced by his obvious belief that little of Christianity had changed between A.D. 30 and 1999. Which meant that he had not made much of a study of his religion. The battle cry of this concept was, "As the Church has always taught . . ."—a claim which held that no Church teaching had changed in nearly 2,000 years.

On the other hand, after struggling against the first fruits of Vatican II and losing, Cody and most reasonable conservatives had staged a strategic retreat to a more stable position.

Tully's seemingly autocratic scheduling of an African-American Folk Mass at St. Joseph's parish had crossed the line Bill Cody had drawn in the sand. And Koesler was amazed that Tully seemed unaware of this. Or—in the more likely chance that he fully understood what he was about—that he had gone ahead regardless. Why?

Finally, there was Al Cody and Bill Page and the conservative-liberal battleground.

If everything Bill Cody had said about Page was true—and now, in retrospect, it seemed to be—it would be extremely probable that the deacon should not be in a seminary, let alone a short time from ordination. Even with a critical shortage of priests, the Church did not need a representative whose major, almost exclusive goal was nothing more than the security that Mother Church could provide.

Now, when he thought of Page, Koesler envisioned someone floating through life on a Church-supplied air cushion. About all that would bestir him would be the infrequent but periodic heterosexual Arabian Night.

And then there was Al Cody.

Koesler clearly remembered Al Cody as a teenager. Not that many young people were involved at St. Joe's. Of those few, Al was by far the most faithful, even attending daily Mass.

So outstanding was Al's presence at St. Joe's that Koesler certainly would have recruited him for the seminary had not the young man's father already done so. By the time Al finished high school, he was all but signed, sealed, and delivered to the seminary. Koesler remembered regretting—not for the first time—that the seminary had closed its high school due to a scarcity of students. Al would have thrived on the complete offering of high school, college, and theologate.

However, the better acquainted Koesler became with Al Cody the more misgivings the priest had.

For one thing, seldom had he encountered anyone as indecisive as Al. Inconsequential decisions such as whether to light the altar candles five minutes before Mass or two. Major decisions such as which elective course to sign up for in school.

Al was so young to be so uncertain about so many things. When had he begun vacillating over nearly everything?

Getting to know his father made it a little easier to understand the son. Bill Cody was nothing if not sure of himself. But he had not passed this attitude on to his son. Rather, the father was virtually the son's deciding force.

The next and inevitable question had to be: Whose determination was it that Albert should become a priest?

What he was going to do with his life, the choice of a vocation or career was, by all odds, the most far-reaching decision he would ever make. Was Al's priesthood going to be the vicarious vehicle for his father?

Koesler, reflecting on his own involvement—no matter how tenuous—in all this, was forced to conclude—again—that this was not what he had expected from the golden years of retirement.

27

IT IS ALMOST axiomatic that liturgy on the parochial level never matches the beauty, the meaningfulness, the dedication, the near perfection of that of the seminary. This is especially true during the week preceding Easter.

Of all the Detroit parishes that tried for the higher achievement, the one that came closest was St. George's in Southfield. That was an unspoken tribute to Andrea Zawalich and the people she had trained. Andrea herself was absent from the scene. Her nonpresence would dim the joy of Easter.

This final week of the Lenten season was indeed called Holy Week.

It began with Palm Sunday commemorating Jesus' triumphant entry into Jerusalem. Holy Thursday was the next of the special feasts. It was on Thursday that all priests, except those unable for good reason to attend, gathered in the Cathedral to bless the oils that would be used in specific sacraments throughout the year. That evening was a reenactment of the Last Supper.

Good Friday remembered Christ's death. Easter Sunday was His resurrection.

For Al Cody, Holy Thursday was his focal point.

For a number of reasons, it had come to be known as the priests' day. The prime reason was that at the Last Supper Jesus spoke the words, "This is my body" and "This is my blood" over the bread and wine. Then He told his twelve closest friends to do in His memory what He had done.

Thus, in theologies that recognize ordained ministers or

priests who re-create the Last Supper, Holy Thursday is a celebration of the priesthood.

In Catholic theology, while the bread and wine retain their appearance, the substance changes to the body and blood of Christ. This is the centerpiece of Catholicism, and its observance the highest function of its priests.

Al Cody set aside the Day of Priests as the time he would spend in prayer and total fasting. He had concluded that he could not take so permanent and demanding a step as ordination as long as there was the slightest waffling. By the end of Holy Thursday, with the help of God, he would know what his future held.

As a member of the seminary choir, he boarded the bus taking the group to the Cathedral. Bill Page was also in the choir. They greeted each other civilly and nothing more. Page still believed Cody would return to the fold and was amazed that it had not yet happened. They did not sit together as they certainly would have before the split.

The Holy Thursday liturgy, conducted by trained seminarians, proceeded impressively and smoothly. The choir was excellent. The goodly showing of laity thought they had found a small corner of heaven.

Al Cody listened carefully as the Cardinal archbishop led his priests through promises of faith and service. Next year at this time, he, Al Cody, would be among these priests, doing then what they were doing now.

Or not.

When the bus returned to the seminary, the students went straight to the refectory for lunch. Except for Al, who had skipped breakfast as well. He took only water, as he would through the day.

He went to the chapel, where he experienced a moment of panic. The day was half gone and no decision was in sight. Maybe what everyone said of him was true: He just couldn't make a decision.

Would he go through life like this? Indecisive to the end?

What could he bring to the priesthood? He knew how to refute most of the ancient heresies that had been all but forgotten by just about everyone. He knew his way around Canon Law. So did most of his classmates.

He had some good insights into Scripture.

He had learned Moral Theology from one of the faculty's strictest traditionalists. Those who believed the Church's seeming preoccupation with sexual mores to be somewhat voyeuristic found a champion of that preoccupation in the Moral prof.

While Al had learned Moral Theology on the rigid side, he couldn't imagine himself teaching the strict interpretation or holding penitents to its strict observance. Perhaps, in a negative sort of way, that was a good thing to bring to the priesthood: to not teach what he'd been taught.

These thoughts brought him to an important point: He was very good at understanding others, particularly in times and areas of disagreement. This spoke well of how he would handle the confessional. He knew he could be patient. And there was a lot to recommend in this virtue.

However, this was not getting him anywhere close to a decision. And it was midafternoon. Not much time left.

Well, why did the decision have to come down on Holy Thursday? Where was that carved in stone?

No, no. He had struck an agreement with God. Today! This was God he was dealing with . . . and one doesn't fool with God.

For the umpteenth time, he made the Stations of the Cross—fourteen "stands" or separate incidents marking events that happened to Jesus from the sentence of death to the body being taken from the cross.

These Stations had been a favorite prayer for Al many times. Now, when he badly needed enlightenment, the Stations gave him nothing.

It occurred to him that he'd been occupied in a game of balance. Putting things he was good at on one side of the scale, things he did poorly on the other. That wasn't going to get the job done. There was no way he could remember all the things that he did well or badly.

There had to be another way. There just had to.

Students began to file in for the late afternoon liturgy. The color scheme in the chapel, from the decorations to the floral arrangements to the altar linens, was white on white. The purity of the sacrifice.

It was so late in the day. He felt guilty. It wasn't a culpable fault. Still, he was not delivering on a promised agreement. Maybe his answer would come as he participated in this Mass.

The liturgy began and the celebrant intoned the Gloria—a hymn of praise to God. Some of the students rang bells of assorted shapes and sizes, while the organist played a triumphant refrain. Neither bells nor organ would sound again until the Gloria of the Easter vigil on Holy Saturday.

The liturgy moved forward with a sense of foreboding. This night, after the supper, Jesus was arrested and the nightmare began.

But first there was the ceremony of bathing the feet. The celebrant bathed the feet of twelve parishioners. Just as Jesus had washed the feet of the twelve Apostles, saying, "You call me master, and you do well to do so. But if I, your master, wash your feet, so must you do for each other."

Although Al Cody had witnessed this ceremony many times, for some reason it took on a new meaning today.

He could not recall ever having washed anyone's feet but his own. Not physically, that is. But figuratively . . . that was something else.

In order to please and win the approval of his mother and father he had figuratively washed their feet many times. He dated: girls his mother approved. He did not date: His father was structuring him into a celibate personality. He lived in a seminary and associated with males. His mother wanted him to be at home with mixed company. He roughed it in the woods during deer season. His dad wanted him to grow up to be a real man like the priests his dad admired. He stood up for the underdog: a value his mother instilled in him. He was leary of people of other colors and creeds: as was his father. He put away his guns for his mother: He took them out for his father. And on and on.

Figuratively, he was constantly washing the feet of his

mother and father. In the words of William S. Gilbert, he never thought of thinking for himself at all.

He was confused and indecisive. And the authors of his confusion were his parents. But especially his father. Left on his own, or under his mother's formation alone, Al doubted he ever would have entered a seminary.

So, in answer to what sort of priest he would be: his father's sort of priest.

Al felt excitement. He sensed that he was nearing a decision. The most important decision of his life.

Throughout his training, from parochial school to Catholic boys' high school to the seminary, he had learned things. Now that he was giving panoramic perspective to this body of knowledge, he knew that as a priest he would be eclectic.

Of course he believed in the core of Catholic doctrine. But once he was ordained, once he was dealing with a hurting humanity, he would be more selective. He would not bother already troubled souls with those rules and regulations that had nothing to do with Christ's law of love.

In just a couple of months he would be ordained. No longer would any of the faculty be looking over his shoulder. He had given them the answers their questions demanded. He would be free of all that.

Still there was hesitation, some radical wavering.

He sought the cause. This was one time when he would not—could not—be satisfied with a partial decision. He had made a bargain with God. He would spend this entire holy day in prayer. He was searching for a decision on his vocation that would be conclusive, absolute, final.

Instinctively, he knew there was more ground to cover.

All the while, the Holy Thursday liturgy continued.

It was Communion time. Al received the consecrated wafer and felt the bonding with the Lord that always came at this intimate moment.

The Mass was concluded. But there was no recessional procession. Most of the students and faculty remained in the chapel to savor the memory of that first Holy Thursday and its foreboding of doom.

The Apostles had just been "ordained." As their first priestly acts, one would betray Him, and all but John would abandon Him. The seminarians would keep Him company for as long as their eyes would remain open.

Al remembered Jesus in the Garden of Olives praying while His friends slumbered. "Father, if it is possible, let this cup pass from me. But not my will, but yours be done."

It came to Al quickly.

Not Al's will, but his father's.

After ordination, the faculty would be out of his hair and his mind. As long as he did nothing publicly bizarre, he should be able to be the sort of priest he wanted to be.

The faculty would not stand in his path. His father would.

Heretofore, Al had quite naturally imagined himself in a parochial setting where he and his parishioners would interact. That's not how it would be.

Why had he been so slow to see what his life as a priest would actually be? Between his parishioners and himself stood the omnipresent figure of William Cody. Bill Cody would live his lost priesthood through his son, Father Al Cody.

This changed everything.

In seconds, he went from a joyful solution to his dilemma to a despondent certainty that he was facing a brick wall which would not fall.

Was there any way he could get his father out of the picture?

None. Nothing but death. And he could not, under any circumstances, wish his father dead.

He spent much time testing the presumption that his father would never let him be what he felt he must be in the priesthood. Every theory tested failed. All doors were closed. No windows were opened.

As the self-sustained argument continued, it became more and more clear what he must do.

Yes, he wanted to be a priest. But not a puppet priest being pulled in directions in which he did not wish to go. And the puppeteer was not going to flag or go away.

Under these circumstances he could not be a priest. Eventually, the conclusion was inescapable.

He could not be a priest.

There was a certain sadness. The priesthood had been a lifetime goal. But, as it became clear through intense prayer, not *his* goal but his father's.

Nor could his decision be brushed aside with the words, "Not my will but thine be done." God's will was a far, far thing from Bill Cody's will.

As the turmoil within Al slowly subsided, it was replaced by a quiet sort of peace. It was an entirely new sensation. Al found it comforting.

Just to be sure, he played the script through once again. Again he arrived at the same conclusion.

He was convinced. It was inescapable.

He felt he could not hesitate another hour. He must go and see someone. He must tell his decision to someone. The first name that came to mind was Father Koesler. He would be sensitive and supportive. He would know what to do.

Repeated knocking on Father Koesler's door elicited no answer. Father Koesler must be out. Probably helping at some Holy Thursday parish liturgy.

The next best person with whom to consult had to be the rector. Bishop McNiff had been the principal celebrant of the seminary's liturgy. He must be here.

28

IT WAS A spent bishop, fatigued to the point of grayness, who opened the door to Al Cody. The liturgy had been unhurried and lengthy. It had sapped McNiff's seventy-one-year-old reserve, his physical and psychic stamina.

Al eyed the haggard bishop, frazzled in rumpled black pants and damp T-shirt. "You seem awfully tired. Maybe I should come back some other time. . . ."

McNiff wearily studied the young man. "Is it important, Al?"

"To me, yes. Very important."

"Then come in and make yourself comfortable. I'll just go in and change this shirt. Holy perspiration does not guarantee the fabled odor of sanctity." The bishop disappeared into his bedchamber, emerging a minute or two later in a fresh white T-shirt. "I hope you won't mind the informality."

"Oh no. Of course not. I know you're pooped. I appreciate your seeing me."

McNiff gamely lowered himself into his desk chair and gestured toward a facing seat. "Now, then: What's on your mind?"

The floodgates spread wide as Al Cody poured out his story. Beginning with his fresh decision to leave the seminary, he then retraced his path toward ordination and the role his father had played in this journey.

McNiff's impulse was to stop Al's recitation early on, but he restrained himself; he would hear the lad out.

When Al had finished, the bishop began with the obvious questions. Did Cody not realize that his call to holy orders was certain? That ordination was only weeks away? The effect this would have on his parents, his relatives and friends, the others in the seminary?

The bishop reminded Al that he had spent eight long years devoted solely and completely to training for nothing other than the priesthood. Did this not seem an extremely abrupt, ill-thought-out, hastily made decision? How could he wash away eight years of preparation with one day of no matter how intense prayer?

Al Cody was among those few whom McNiff desperately desired to recommend for ordination. His immediate reaction to this bombshell was to attempt to talk Al out of resigning—at least until the matter was more extensively examined.

Through it all, Al Cody remained unperturbed, relaxed, serene.

So much so that eventually he convinced a most resistant bishop that there would be no turning back from his decision. "Bishop, I truly am flattered that you have this faith in me. I am really impressed that you think I should be a priest. I know you have high standards. And I'm grateful that you think I've met them. I'm grateful you want me.

"But I cannot go on."

"You know, Al, once a very young Martin Luther found himself in the midst of a most violent storm. He feared he would die. He prayed that if he was spared he would become a priest. He was and he did. Whether that was bad or good for Christianity is not my point. Making a life-forming decision after one day of prayer may not lead to a justifiable conclusion."

"I understand, Bishop. But I believe—I truly believe—that this is the course I must take. I'm really convinced."

McNiff looked long and hard at the blotter on his desk, then locked on Al's eyes. "Very well." He sighed. "If that's your final word, it still will not be mine. I'm granting you a leave of absence for six months. At the end of that time, the leave can be renewed."

"And if I meet a woman I want to marry?"

"Do you have anyone in particular in mind?"

"No, no one. Just *if*."

"You'd have to go through laicization. You *are* a deacon."

"If this makes you satisfied, Bishop, I have no objection. It's kind of you, really. But I won't be changing my mind."

In his inner heart, McNiff knew that was so. Al Cody, as suited as he was for the priesthood, would never be ordained. The bishop nodded reluctantly.

Cody stood, then knelt. "I'd like your blessing before I go."

McNiff stepped around the desk and prayed a blessing over the young man. It was a heartfelt blessing.

They shook hands, and Al Cody left.

As he walked toward his room, Cody wondered whether it might be appropriate to see if Patty Donnelly had softened since she had thrown his offer of friendship back in his face.

That had been a charged moment when he had made his peace with Patty only to embitter her by offering an excuse for Bill Page's actions. In the space of mere minutes, he had lost the friendship of two people.

Losing a friendship was something Al Cody seldom, if ever, had done. But two in one fell swoop? Never.

The incident with Page and Donnelly was largely caused by Al's indecision—the failing that had plagued almost his entire life.

But, no more.

Jesus had given him strength through prayer.

Cody had three possible paths. He could see if Patty would talk—leading, he hoped, to friendship renewed. Or he could see if Bill Page was open to a resumption of their relationship. In either case someone had to break the ice; it might as well be he. The third option was to put all this on the back burner till tomorrow.

Tomorrow. He thought for a moment, then nodded to himself. That was it: He would stay in the seminary till Easter. Plenty of time to smoke the peace pipe. Yes, he would follow the third course. Realistically, he was too tired to pursue any détente without a good night's sleep.

It wasn't the liturgy that had drained Al, but the prayer and fasting. Even so, he would not try to scrounge up some food.

Rather, he would continue his fast—now a prayer of thanksgiving and triumph.

So, he continued on toward his room.

Suddenly, he stopped, panic clutching at his heart.

He had forgotten to touch a base. A vital base.

He turned, scooped up his cassock, freeing his young legs to stretch out, and ran full tilt along the corridor and down the steps. He reached the door and pounded on it furiously.

After several moments that seemed an eternity to Cody, the door was opened by an obviously shaken bishop. His entire body seemed to be experiencing a slight tremor, though he tried to affect a self-control that belied this appearance. "Oh, Al. What a coincidence. Come in."

McNiff stepped aside and Cody entered. He feared he knew the cause of the bishop's underlying emotion. By the time the two reached their chairs on either side of the desk, each was deeply troubled.

"Bishop, I forgot to mention that I would prefer notifying the others of my decision myself. I think it will work out better that way."

McNiff would not meet Cody's eyes. "It's a little late for that."

Cody's worst case scenario! "What do you mean, a little late?"

"Just after you left, I called your home. Your father answered."

"And . . . ?"

"I thought it wouldn't matter whether I talked to your mother or your father. I just wanted to break the news gently. I thought I could soften the blow . . . that if I told them of your decision, they'd have tonight to think it through. By tomorrow, they could've calmed down and could talk to you about it. I wouldn't have blamed them if they had been bewildered; in all my experience, I can't recall a single seminarian who resigned only weeks before ordination." McNiff bowed his head and shook it slowly. "I called them for their own good!"

"What happened?" Even as he asked, Al was sure he knew. Indeed, this was the reason he'd returned to the bishop's suite.

"The strangest thing." It seemed that McNiff was going to leave his explanation just there, well short of the mark.

"*What!?*" Al's impatience took over.

"He . . . your father accused me of expelling you! You know that's the last thing on my mind. I all but begged you to stick it out. When I realized he was trying to put the responsibility on my shoulders, I chose my words very carefully, and I insisted this was your decision.

"But I couldn't get a word in edgewise. He kept saying—well, shouting—that he knew the Cardinal was up to no good by making me rector of the seminary, that I was sent here to get rid of candidates who wouldn't go along with the modern Church." McNiff squinted as if trying to comprehend—or as if he were in pain. " 'All its excesses and heresies,' he said."

The bishop looked at Al almost apologetically. "I shouldn't involve you in this."

"I am involved." In this match between the mature, experienced rector and the youthful, inexperienced student, the younger man seemed strangely in command of the situation.

After a moment's reflection, McNiff nodded. "Yes, you are involved. But if only I hadn't made that call . . ."

"It might have happened anyway." Al tried to relieve the bishop. "Was that all he said? That you were responsible for this decision?"

"No." McNiff hesitated. He disliked being on the defensive. But he was. "Then came the threats. What he swore to do to me. Much of it was incoherent . . . and to be perfectly frank, I was so unnerved that I couldn't understand what he was shouting about. But this I know"—the words came slowly, but forcefully—"he was threatening my life!"

Al groaned.

"Do you . . . do you think he really meant it?" The bishop's question pleaded for a denial.

But Al dodged it. "Not long after you became rector, my dad gave me practically the same evaluation of your appointment. He made the same statement to Father Koesler recently. Of course at these times he didn't make any specific threats. But, now that I think of it, the threats have always been lurking."

"But," McNiff pressed the point, "was he serious, do you think?"

Al could not be certain. If he had to guess, he would say his father was, indeed, serious. But there was no need to further alarm the rector. Not unless it became necessary.

Al's mind was racing. He startled himself. Only hours ago he would have been hopelessly mired in indecision. Now he was clearheaded and in control.

His father was not one to issue idle threats. If he threatened McNiff's life, it wasn't a mere scare tactic. "You don't mind if I use your phone?" He didn't wait for a reply. By the time McNiff nodded, Al was halfway through dialing.

His mother recognized his voice immediately. "Al"—she sounded frightened—"what's going on? I was just going to call you."

"We're trying to piece it together."

"Al, why would Bishop McNiff fire you?"

"He didn't. That's part of the problem. I haven't got a lot of time, Mother. You can help by finding out something for me. And, please: Time is of the essence."

"What? What?" She caught the urgency in his voice.

"Is Dad home?"

"No. He left a little while ago."

"Did you see . . . did he take anything with him?"

"I don't know. I didn't actually see him leave."

"Mom, can you quick check the gun rack? See if any of them are missing?" Al had to risk the probability of unnerving the bishop still further, but this was no time for subtlety.

Within a couple of moments she was back. "I'm not sure, honey, but I think there's a rifle missing. The guns are dumped all over the floor. But I think he took one of the hunting rifles."

"Thanks, Mom. I've gotta go now."

"Is there anything I can do?"

"Pray, Mom, pray!"

Unless he was terribly mistaken, his father was headed for the seminary. He would come intending to kill the man who, he believed, had derailed the express carrying his son to the priesthood.

And, in his present condition, the bishop wasn't a lot of help.

Should he call the police? Probably. But Al had learned enough from TV cop shows and real-life police stories to know that the police can't act until a crime has been committed. And there wouldn't be a crime here until after his dad attempted to kill the bishop. And that, by anyone's gauge, would be too late.

Al thought intently. Who might comprehend the seriousness of this situation? Who might be able to cut through the red tape and do something about it?

Father Koesler. He knew Bill Cody's opinion of the rector *and* he knew his way around the police department and its procedures. "Where can I reach Father Koesler?"

McNiff knew where Koesler was, but, startled by the question, he hesitated. "He's . . . uh, helping with the liturgy at St. Joseph's. Why?"

Al ignored the question. He glanced through the Catholic directory and began dialing. Al was very much in command. Secretly, McNiff was grateful.

Al caught Koesler just as the priest was about to leave St. Joseph's rectory. Quickly but comprehensively Al explained what had happened. Father Koesler immediately grasped the danger. He knew that Cody's apartment contained an ample supply of killing weapons. And he had heard Cody's vow of action should anyone come between Al and the priesthood.

Koesler would borrow Father Tully's car with its mobile phone and leave for the seminary immediately. En route he would try to reach Lieutenant Tully, or, if that wasn't possible, one of the other officers he knew.

Before hanging up, Koesler warned Al not to attempt anything heroic, but to do nothing other than stay out of the way and pray.

29 LIEUTENANT ZOO TULLY was "on the street," meaning simply that he was on duty but away from headquarters. Because the officer who answered knew the priest, he had the call patched through to Tully.

Bishop McNiff's life was threatened; immediate action was called for. Fortunately, the lieutenant was cruising not far from the seminary. He trusted Koesler's perception of the seriousness of the situation and shoved the red tape aside.

Koesler gave the lieutenant the bishop's room number and its location. He also urged Tully to be on the lookout for Cody's son, a seminarian who had put himself in the middle of this thing.

The lieutenant called for backup, slapped the flasher to the roof, and, siren blaring, headed for the seminary.

Though Tully had been nearby when Koesler contacted him, Cody, with his head start, reached the seminary first.

The parking lot was unattended. Security began just inside the heavy Gothic door.

Bill Cody stormed through the entrance. His eyes were wild, his face reflected fury. Struck by Cody's demented expression, the guard, rather than staying in his protective cage, stepped out into the foyer and into Cody's path. Only then did he catch sight of the rifle.

The guard was unarmed and too elderly to be agile. Cody said nothing. He brought the rifle butt up with as much force as his right arm possessed, catching the guard just under the chin.

The blow broke several of the guard's teeth. But he would

not know that for a couple of hours as he dropped unconscious to the floor.

Without a glance at the fallen man, Cody headed for the bishop's suite.

As Tully rushed through the seminary door, his trained eye instantly took in all. He didn't stop to check on the guard's condition; that would have to take its turn. He was either dead or alive. If he was dead, there was no hurry to bury him.

One thing was clear. Somebody—undoubtedly Cody—had done this. Judging from the small pool of blood forming around the guard's head, the perp had been here only minutes ago.

And, following that, Koesler had been right: Cody was determined and dangerous.

On the surface, Tully appeared cool, but inside, adrenaline was sending shock waves through his body. His heart was pounding, his blood was pumping at fever pitch. Movie and TV cops did this sort of thing all the time. In real life, even in the busiest precincts such a chase was rare.

Tully drew his gun as he raced down the tiled corridor, hoping the directions Koesler had given him were correct. He had no time now to look out for Al Cody. Besides, Tully had no idea how the young man figured in this case. All that was on his mind, all his training, his years of experience, his discipline—all converged to keep him focused on one objective: reaching the bishop's suite as quickly as possible.

That, and being ready for anything.

Bill Cody arrived at the bishop's suite. Having made his threats, he'd half expected to find some sort of security or protective barrier here. Nothing.

A guard inside with the bishop perhaps?

But Cody was not concerned with any possible confrontation. To hell with confrontation! This was a time for action, for retribution.

He turned the knob and the door swung open.

There he was, not twenty feet away, seated at his desk.

Cody wasted not a second. He raised the rifle, aimed at the red zucchetto just above the back of the chair, and fired.

From the lower corridor, about halfway between the front door and the bishop's rooms, Lieutenant Tully heard the crack of the rifle. There was no way he could increase his speed. He was already at full throttle.

Leaving caution aside, he raced up the steps, turned the corner, and reached the open doorway. The odor of gunsmoke was strong. The rifle had been fired only inches from where he stood. Now with caution, he let his gun lead him around the doorway and into the room.

A rifle lay on the floor where it had been dropped, seemingly haphazardly. Farther into the room but this side of the large desk a chair lay on its side. Nearby, was a scene similar to those Tully had observed too many times.

A kneeling man clutched a younger man to his chest.

The older man? Very probably Bill Cody—the object of Tully's pursuit. Cody allegedly was intent on causing great bodily harm to or killing a bishop—Patrick McNiff.

Tully had seen the elder Cody during a Folk Mass at St. Joe's when Tully had been a reluctant member of the congregation and Cody had been one of three observers in the choir loft. That had been at a considerable distance. But this seemed to be the same man.

It was not the scene Tully had expected, especially when he'd heard the rifle shot. He expected to find Cody, certainly. But the victim Tully anticipated was a much older man. As he continued to inhale the crime scene, it seemed obvious there had been a tragic mistake.

The initial impression: The young man was William Cody's son. As the elder man rocked back and forth, he moaned repeatedly, "My son! My son! I didn't mean it to be you."

Tully stepped forward. He leaned down to check for signs of life, while not taking his eyes off the elder man, who offered no resistance as Tully felt the victim's neck for a pulse. He couldn't find any.

Tully stepped back. Cody Senior, still in a kneeling position, seemed to have turned to stone, his eyes glazed. Tully stood between Cody and the rifle, fixing the scene in his mind.

The victim was garbed in a black cassock with red buttons and matching piping. The ill-fitting cassock seemed too small for the victim; it gapped in spots where it was unbuttoned. A red skullcap lay nearby, a darker crimson staining its original shade.

Judging from the position of the blotter and the books on the work surface, the chair was on the wrong side of the desk.

Tully guessed that the younger Cody, masquerading as the bishop, had been sitting with his back to the door. He had gambled on his father's impulsiveness and had won—or lost. Instead of coming around the desk to confront the man he thought was the bishop, the perpetrator had fired upon entry.

But where was the bishop?

And where, as Tully impatiently tapped his foot on the carpeted floor, was his backup?

The latter question was answered as a commotion in the corridor grew louder, and police of various disciplines poured into the room.

Father and son were separated; the father, virtually in shock, led into an adjoining room.

Arriving next, almost simultaneously, were Bishop McNiff and Father Koesler. Each had questions, but first there was Al Cody. They both started toward the inert body, then Koesler looked to Tully, who nodded. "Just don't touch anything."

McNiff and Koesler knelt by Al. They prayed for the young man whose life had held such rich promise and who was now far beyond the pain and sorrow of his death.

As the two clergymen stood, Tully approached. "What happened here?"

After a brief moment during which each waited for the other to speak, McNiff proceeded to recount how Al had come to him with the decision—out of nowhere—to resign, though he had only a few weeks till ordination.

McNiff's voice was flat as he went on to tell how all his efforts to persuade Al to change his mind were for naught: Al would not be budged.

Then there was McNiff's well-intentioned call to the Codys and William's off-the-wall reaction to what he thought was McNiff's role in this. Then came the threats of murder.

From that moment on, McNiff related, Al simply took charge. It was the most amazing transformation the bishop had ever witnessed. Al all but physically steered the bishop to the chapel and told—ordered—him not to emerge from there until he was summoned by Al or someone else—anyone else except Bill Cody.

Apparently the young man had then put on the bishop's zucchetto and one of his cassocks, then offered his own back as bait for his father. It had worked. Too well. It had cost Al his life, and his father might just as well have lost his too.

Koesler filled in the missing pieces. Al's phone call telling of his father's intent and the rifle his dad must've taken with him.

At that point, Tully gestured toward the desk, where two pages from a yellow legal pad lay. "Apparently the victim was writing a note to the perpetrator. The message may be more clear to you two than it was to me."

"May we touch it?" Koesler asked.

Tully nodded. "The techs are done with it."

Koesler made room for McNiff alongside the center of the desk. But McNiff shook his head. "I can't, Bob. I'm afraid my eyes are watering. Read it out loud, would you?"

Koesler picked up the sheets. His problem was similar to McNiff's. But he resolved to fight his way through it.

Dear Dad,

If you are reading this, I am probably dead. If, somehow, I survive your coming here tonight, I will destroy this note. If I do not survive, this will be my farewell to you.

Koesler was amazed that Al's handwriting was so legible.

Dad, I think you misunderstood—or, let me be plain—I think you refused to understand that leaving the seminary was my choice, my initiative. Bishop McNiff had absolutely nothing to do with it. Neither did anyone else. It was my decision alone.

In fact, Bishop McNiff did everything in his power to talk me out of it. He even insisted on this being a leave of absence rather than a permanent break, so that I could return to the seminary and pick up from about where I left off.

You must know, Dad, that I did not come to this resolution lightly. I've spent hours and hours in intense prayer. I'm convinced, totally convinced, this is the right solution to my problem.

Now a word—if I've got time—about this charade.

I learned from Mother that you were on your way here and that you probably were armed. You planned to kill the man you thought was responsible for my leaving the seminary.

Bottom line (as you like to say, Dad): I didn't think I could stop you.

I've seen your determination. When you want something done, or you want to do something, if you really want it, you let nothing stand in your way. Nothing.

Why did I stand in for Bishop McNiff? Because you would have killed him. Nothing or no one, including me, could have stopped you. I took the bishop's place because I love you—and because you love me. You will be far more contrite, more repentant for killing me than you would be for killing anyone else in the world.

I don't know how much time I have. I intend to keep writing to the end.

One more thing: Please tell Father Koesler it was just the way he told me it would be. We were talking about making decisions and how a person can know that he's made the right decision.

Father told me that when you reach the right decision, you feel an abiding sense of peace.

That's the way it was, Dad. I've spent this whole day in prayer. Prayer about my vocation. When I finally decided that leaving the seminary was my final decision on the matter, a deep, deep peace came over me. It was right, and I knew it.

Then, tonight, when I learned that you were headed here to kill Bishop McNiff, I had just a couple of minutes to make up my mind. I decided to take his place. Once again there was this deep sense of peace. I knew it was right. I know it is right.

Tell Father Koesler—he'll understand—It is a far, far— Oh, Dad, you're here. I

A dull murmur from street traffic was the only sound in the room.

Father Koesler looked at the clock on the wall. It was after midnight. It was Good Friday.

Epilogue-Conclusion

KOESLER BURIED HIS head in his hands. It was foolish to try to relive the past. Raising his eyes heavenward, he mused aloud: "It is a far, far better thing that I do, than I have ever done—"

"It is a far, far better rest that I go to, than I have ever known," declaimed another voice.

Koesler almost jumped out of his skin. He whirled to see who was behind him. At first he knew only that someone else had joined him in the chapel. Then, as his eyes adjusted to the darkness just beyond the candles' illumination, he made out the elfin face of Bishop McNiff.

"You had trouble sleeping too," McNiff said. It was not a question.

Koesler took a deep breath and exhaled. "You scared me. I thought I was alone."

"I'm good at that. Once, long ago, I went over to lock the church late at night. But before I locked it, I knelt in the sanctuary to pray. I didn't know it, but the pastor sent a kid over to lock the church. Neither the pastor nor the kid knew I was there. By then my eyes were accustomed to the dark. The kid walked down the middle aisle with his arm extended in front of him so he wouldn't run into anything.

"To me it looked like he was going to shake hands with me. So I walked over and took his hand."

"Has he come down to earth yet?"

McNiff ignored the satirical question. "I've been tossing and turning for hours. I saw a flickering light in the chapel. I thought maybe it was a fire: Just what we needed!"

"I was trying to collect my thoughts for a eulogy."

"Anything come?"

"Just the Dickens quote and John Fifteen:thirteen."

"I must confess I'm familiar with the Dickens, but not the citations of John's Gospel. Terrible admission for a bishop, eh?"

"Oh, I don't know. You still remember the formula for absolution?"

"I think so."

"You're all right. For a bishop."

"What's the John text?"

"'There is no greater love than this: to lay down one's life for one's friends.'"

"There's a connection, isn't there?"

"I think so." Koesler straightened one of the candles. "That's what Al and I were developing when he came to see me about his homily."

"I remember that sermon. It went over well. We got a lot of good feedback on it."

"Well, it was almost as if Sydney Carton was following Christ's example, word for word. Carton gave his life for his friend. And that's what Al did." Pause. "For you."

"I'll never forget it!"

"Actually, I think Al had more than one objective."

"Oh?"

"Yeah. He was trying to save your life. Which he did. And, I think, he was trying to save his dad's soul."

"How's that?"

"We'll never know, of course; Al took this secret with him into eternity. But look at it this way: If Bill Cody had killed you, it's anybody's guess if he would ever have repented the sin. He wanted to kill you and he did—or so he thought. But with this mistaken identity, he will never cease being repentant over having killed his own son.

"Just a thought."

"Speculation. True. But worth the thought."

They sat silently, each lost in recollections of the events leading up to this moment.

*   *   *

"You know," Koesler said, "when I began this vigil I was trying to think through all the things that happened over these months that built to this conclusion. Things that, because they happened, Al Cody was killed."

"I would be at the top of that list," McNiff said sadly.

"You mean because you phoned the Codys?"

"Exactly."

"Did you ever do that before? When a kid either was kicked out or quit?"

"Couple of times. Not in every case by any means. But parents invest a lot when they send us their kids. Usually it's a considerable blow when the son goes home short of ordination. In the past, when I felt that the parents needed a buffer to accept the fact that their kid would not be ordained, I've broken the news to them.

"That's what happened Thursday night." McNiff studied the wrinkles in his soft hands. "I've never known anyone as involved in his son's vocation as Bill Cody was. I thought he'd fly off the handle if Al tried to tell him it was quits.

"So I phoned to let him know, as gently as possible, that as far as the seminary was concerned, Al satisfied everyone on the faculty. That his quitting was completely his own choice. And that I was leaving the door ajar almost permanently for his return whenever he wanted to come back.

"It just seemed the right thing to do.

"Cody's reaction, though, was totally unexpected. I wasn't even halfway—I didn't even get a chance to explain, before he just exploded. From that point on, I couldn't get a word in. I've never been so roundly cursed in my life."

Koesler had been gazing at the coffin as McNiff spoke. Now he turned toward the bishop and smiled. "It's true, Pat, that your call triggered this—" He gazed again at the coffin, then turned back to his friend. "But you couldn't have known that. Nobody could. You tried your best to help. It wasn't your fault that Bill Cody misread you. For all we know, if you hadn't phoned and Al had the next morning, Bill could have flipped then, pushed Al aside, and come after you anyway.

"Put it out of your mind, Pat."

"I'll try. But I wouldn't bet on my success."

"Actually," Koesler said, "the root of this problem was Bill Cody. He might just as well have taken over his son's personality. He devoured him. If he had let the kid develop for himself, none of this would've happened."

"I haven't been following the news lately. Where's Bill Cody now?"

Koesler shook his head. "I went to see him yesterday—no, wait: Yesterday was Sunday—Easter Sunday. I saw him Saturday. He's being held without bond in the Wayne County Jail, under a charge of murder in the first degree." Noting McNiff's quizzical expression, Koesler explained. "It's called 'transferred intent'; it's the same charge as if he had killed—uh, his intended victim." Koesler bit his lip as he shook his head. "He's shattered, demolished. His attorney plans a plea of temporary insanity."

"Think he has a chance?"

"I guess it depends on whether his lawyer can convince a jury that a man can become temporarily insane over his son's loss of vocation. I don't know. . . ."

McNiff rubbed his hands together. The only heat in the chapel came from the candles. Which hardly warmed anything. "Speaking of Bill Cody, there's something I've been meaning to ask you. . . ."

Koesler looked at McNiff inquiringly.

"It had to do with something that Lieutenant Tully said to me. He said when you called him, you mentioned Al Cody as someone to look out for and protect. It didn't hit me right away. But later I wondered why you'd say that. I was the only one in danger, no? Bill Cody was after me!"

"You're right, of course. But I remembered the talk we had over Al's sermon. The parts about the 'far, far better thing' and 'no greater love.' I thought, in that light, that Al might try to intervene and fulfill the promise of 'no greater love,' thus becoming a victim. I wish I'd thought of it sooner—then maybe all this wouldn't have happened."

They fell silent again.

"Now that I think of it," Koesler said, "there's another thing that contributed to this death."

"What's that?"

"If Bill Cody had only looked. Instead of looking, he just fired."

McNiff stroked the stubble on his face. "You're right. If Cody hadn't been so bound and determined on revenge, he might've wondered why I would sit in a chair with my back to the door.

"If only he had looked," McNiff concluded.

The two fell silent.

"What about the other players in this tragedy?" Koesler asked, after reflection. "Andrea Zawalich, for instance?"

"Andrea?" McNiff smiled for the first time. "In the few weeks since she was expelled, she's found several dioceses that are eager to have her. She picked Naples, Florida. The deal is the Naples diocese gives her full credit on her degree, and she's got a parish that is almost a carbon copy of St. George's up here. She's got one of those FBI pastors who'll give her free reign to run any programs she wants."

"And, I assume that since the pastor is Foreign Born Irish, he's probably elderly. She'll practically *be* the pastor."

McNiff feigned shock. "At our age, you shouldn't toss the word 'elderly' around."

"How about Patty Donnelly?"

"Donnelly? She'll finish up here in a few more weeks. Then she's going to join Andrea and really make that parish smoke. The only fly in the ointment is that Patty feels some responsibility for what happened to Al. She thinks that if she hadn't rejected his friendship . . ."

"That's nonsense," Koesler said. "I can see how she'd feel bad about what happened. But she had no part in Al's death. That was strictly between Al and his father."

"I know, I know. I think Andrea will be good for her. Andrea always impressed me as having both feet on the ground. They'll work it out."

McNiff looked at his watch. He had trouble seeing the

hands in the flickering light. "Wanna try for a couple hours of shut-eye?"

Koesler checked his watch. "Not enough time. As we've been talking, I've gotten the essence of the eulogy. Which is good, since I still feel a little queasy preaching in front of this faculty. They never have completely accepted me."

"Oh, you'd be surprised, Robert. You haven't been with them since the shooting. I tell you, something's happened to them. Oh, not all of them . . . but a significant number."

"Oh?"

"It's very definitely the impact of what Al did. It was that simple but sublime act of love. For many on the faculty the supremacy of love just cut right through the textbook theology. I think the evenhandedness, the tolerance we were looking for has finally materialized. It's the beginning of a new beginning. It even hit Bill Page, of all people!"

"Page? I wouldn't have counted on that."

"Nor I. But—and you wouldn't have guessed this in a million years—Page has requested, and been granted, a leave of absence."

"No!"

"Uh-huh. Al's sacrifice shook Page to his bootstraps. He's not so sure of himself now. I think it's a near miracle. For the longest time, I was afraid we were going to be forced to send a shameless sycophant out into the archdiocese. Now maybe Page will leave religious life alone. Or, just maybe, he'll come back a decent priest."

"That's almost unbelievable. And while we're talking about the incredible, who's responsible for this coffin? The Cody family is not hurting financially. But that coffin is about the least expensive possible."

McNiff nodded. "True. But Bill Cody is out of this scene. His wife handled everything. She's holding up like a trooper. Her decision was to keep everything as simple as it could be. She was deeply impressed with her son's greater love. With that in mind, she projected what Al would've chosen in leaving this world. It was the simplicity of that love. It was a return to ashes in a container that didn't flaunt wealth, but reflected love alone.

"That's what she said. I thought it was sort of beautiful. Just what Al had become at the end of his too-brief life."

Koesler was silent. He had his eulogy. From now until it was time to get ready for the funeral, he would sit there and ponder.

When fate confronted Al Cody with his greatest challenge, he met it with his greatest decision.

Now he could know that he had made the selfless choice.

Now he was at peace—the peace that passeth all understanding.

A Conversation with
William X. Kienzle

Q. *Bill, you're on record as saying that "writing is just not as good as the priesthood can be." Given your decision to leave the priesthood, could you elaborate on your statement?*

A. That's a good question in that it has no easy answer. I think I'm looking at the two lifestyles in terms of people—as in the song of the same name.

I need people, I confess. And I need the sense that I am at least trying to help them. I believe I can do this, in some measured degree, in the series of mystery novels that I am writing and that you are so graciously publishing.

Feedback tells me that some readers feel challenged to think again about their Christian, theistic, or, simply, moral approach to life. Some are entertained to the point of distraction. As was one reader, who wrote that while reading one of my books for several hours, he was temporarily freed from chronic severe back pain. And another reader so carefully followed my guidelines that he granted himself a declaration of nullity for a previous marriage.

So, writing can be "good," if most of the time remote and lonely.

Priests, on the contrary, can serve people directly. The better priests I've known live and die for their people—to whom priests can introduce a loving, forgiving, and compassionate God. There is a satisfaction in this service that, at its core, is indescribable.

So, you ask, if the priesthood was so attractive, why did I leave?

A question that could easily foster a lengthy essay. But I think I can capsulize an answer in two words: Church law.

I do not—I cannot—speak for all priests. But I found the God epitomized in these laws to be harsh, legalistic, and only reluctantly forgiving. The Code's God is the antithesis of the God whom Jesus presented to us as our Father.

Q. *We're told that your first Father Koesler novel,* The Rosary Murders, *had its origins in a challenge, the issuance of a dare. Is that true?*

A. More an offer than a challenge.

A Minneapolis entrepreneur, Bruce Lansky, was beginning a publishing career in the mid-1970s. He was interested, among other publishing pursuits, in mystery novels. Not completed novels, just the plots.

I didn't give that proposition a thought until many months later. I wasn't even much given to reading mysteries. But I was aware that a mystery featured murder, clues, and red herrings—i.e., a puzzle. I was also aware of the storied advice to would-be authors: Go with what you know.

What I knew best was Catholicism and the priests and nuns who populated that faith. How to put that experience into a murder mystery? A bunch of priests and nuns going around killing people? Not hardly!

What about someone killing priests and nuns?

That was it. I was off and running. Except that I couldn't think of anyone who could flesh out that plot better than I. So I wrote what became *The Rosary Murders*. And the twenty-two sequels.

Q. *We know that you weren't happy with the film adaptation of* The Rosary Murders. *Do you care to discuss that whole experience?*

A. I feel I stand in a long line of authors who are not enchanted by film adaptations of their works.

I was naive. Since the movie was filmed entirely in Detroit and a friend was the producer, I thought I might be welcomed on the set. It might have been nice meeting Donald Sutherland, Charles Durning, and the rest.

Realistically, I guess, the last person the movie people want around is a writer running about, shouting, "What are you doing to my baby?"

I've never seen the movie version. Although since friends have told me about it, frame by frame, I feel as if I have seen it.

My advice? If you accept the money, don't look back.

Q. *For your multitude of fans, the arrival of a new Father Koesler mystery has been an annual event for (soon to be) twenty-two years. How have you maintained this admirably consistent schedule? And with each passing year, is the consistency easier (or more difficult) to maintain?*

A. To a certain extent I am quite disciplined. For that I have to thank twelve years of seminary rules and regulations as well as twenty years of intense responsibility as a priest.

It seemed to me (and to my publishers) that a book a year was par for the course.

I truly believe that writing for commercial purposes is among the more difficult tasks one can undertake. But consistency is a prime commitment for a professional in any field.

I like to think the writing improves over time.

A few years back, my wife, Javan, and I team-taught a course on writing at St. Mary's College in Orchard Lake, Michigan. As is true of teaching, generally, I think I learned a lot from that.

Here I must acknowledge the work of Javan, who was for many years a copy editor in the features department of the *Detroit Free Press*. She is a dedicated reader and writer. I owe much to her collaboration.

Q. *Your novels are filled with vivid details about the Catholic Church's inner workings. We realize how you come by this authenticity. But on whom do you rely for your portraits of matters homicidal?*

A. The homicide squads of the Detroit Police Department. Detroit was once known as the Murder Capital of the country. Our homicide squads get a good workout.

I am particularly indebted to Sergeant Roy Awe (now retired) and Inspector Barbara Weide, both of the Homicide Division.

Once, when asking Roy how the police would react to a significant plot development, the sergeant said something to the effect that if the perpetrator did what I had him doing, ". . . we'd get him." I had to remind Roy that the police would never solve any of the mysteries. They would be a great help—but Father Koesler would always be the one to wrap things up.

In addition, I have been especially fortunate to have the assistance of Jim Grace, a detective with the Kalamazoo Police Department. Jim has been kind enough to vet the first twenty typescripts for any possible technical errors with regard to law enforcement. Several times, Jim has saved Father Koesler from error in such cases.

Q. *Books on Tape acquired the unabridged audio rights to your series. Have you listened to those tapes—and if so, what is your critical assessment?*

A. I've listened to some of the tapes and hope to hear them all.

I think I could listen to Edward Holland read the telephone book.

I am thrilled to be included in Books on Tape. And honored to be heard by drivers, the sight-impaired, and armchair detectives.

Q. *Papal infallibility is a hot (and hotly debated) topic. (In fact, one of your recent novels—*Call No Man Father—*addresses it.) What is your own overview on the issue of infallibility?*

A. In *Call No Man Father*, I tried to record fairly several facets of the notion of papal infallibility.

I tend to think of it as a sort of overkill.

The Catholic Church teaches. (And it is disputed whether that teaching should originate from the bottom—the laity, the People of God—or from the top—the Pope.)

The Church has developed what is called the Ordinary Magisterium, the ordinary teaching authority. With an occasional nod to episcopal conferences (regional bishops' groups), the Ordinary Magisterium belongs almost exclusively to the Pope. To the traditional minded, his encyclicals and pronouncements, almost everything the Pope does or says, are the body and soul of the Ordinary Magisterium.

With clout like that, I don't know why infallibility is seen as a necessary teaching tool.

I think it would be interesting if a Pope were to speak from the throne *(ex Cathedra)* and, using distinctively infallible language, declare infallibly that he was not infallible.

Then let the Church lawyers quibble about that for the next millennium.

Q. *Any favorite writers you want to mention—as pure pleasure reading or as actual inspirations for your own work?*

A. Pat Conroy, Donald Westlake, Loren Estleman, Ferrol Sams, and Matthew, Mark, Luke, and John.